LUNAR PARK

BRET
EASTON
ELLIS

LUNAR
PARK

ALFRED A. KNOPF · NEW YORK · 2005

THIS IS A BORZOI BOOK PUBLISHED BY ALFRED A. KNOPF

Copyright © 2005 by Bret Easton Ellis

All rights reserved. Published in the United States by Alfred A. Knopf, a division of Random House, Inc., New York, and in Canada by Random House of Canada Limited, Toronto.

www.aaknopf.com

Knopf, Borzoi Books, and the colophon are registered trademarks of Random House, Inc.

Grateful acknowledgment is made to Hal Leonard Corporation for permission to reprint "The Way We Were" from the motion picture *The Way We Were,* words by Alan and Marilyn Bergman, music by Marvin Hamlisch. Copyright © 1973 (Renewed 2001) Colgems-EMI Music Inc. All rights reserved. International copyright secured. Reprinted by permission of Hal Leonard Corporation.

Library of Congress Cataloging-in-Publication Data

Ellis, Bret Easton.
　Lunar Park / Bret Easton Ellis.— 1st American ed.
　　p.　cm.
　ISBN 0-375-41291-3
　1. Novelists—Fiction.　2. Suburban life—Fiction.　3. Married people—Fiction.　4. College teachers—Fiction.　5. Hallucinations and illusions—Fiction.　I. Title.

　PS3555.L5937L86 2005
　813'.54—dc22

2005040923

Manufactured in the United States of America
Published August 22, 2005
Reprinted One Time
Third Printing, August 2005

for

ROBERT MARTIN ELLIS

1941–1992

and

MICHAEL WADE KAPLAN

1974–2004

The occupational hazard of making a spectacle of yourself, over the long haul, is that at some point you buy a ticket too.

—THOMAS McGUANE, *Panama*

People who have made up their minds about a man do not like to have their opinions changed, to reverse their judgments on account of some new evidence or new arguments, and the man who tries to compel them to change their minds is at least wasting his time, and he may be asking for trouble.

—JOHN O'HARA

From the table of my memory
I'll wipe away all trivial fond records,
All saws of books, all forms, all pressures past
That youth and observation copied there.

—*Hamlet,* I: v. 98

LUNAR PARK

1. the beginnings

"You do an awfully good impression of yourself."

This is the first line of *Lunar Park* and in its brevity and simplicity it was supposed to be a return to form, an echo, of the opening line from my debut novel, *Less Than Zero*.

"People are afraid to merge on freeways in Los Angeles."

Since then the opening sentences of my novels—no matter how artfully composed—had become overly complicated and ornate, loaded down with a heavy, useless emphasis on minutiae.

My second novel, *The Rules of Attraction*, for example, began with this:

and it's a story that might bore you but you don't have to listen, she told me, because she always knew it was going to be like that, and it was, she thinks, her first year, or actually weekend, really a Friday, in September, at Camden, and this was three or four years ago, and she got so drunk that she ended up in bed, lost her virginity (late, she was eighteen) in Lorna Slavin's room, because she was a Freshman and had a roommate and Lorna was, she remembers, a Senior or Junior and usually sometimes at her boyfriend's place off-campus, to who she thought was a Sophomore Ceramics major but who was actually either some guy from N.Y.U., a film student, and up in New Hampshire just for The Dressed To Get Screwed party, or a townie.

The following is from my third novel, *American Psycho*.

ABANDON ALL HOPE YE WHO ENTER HERE is scrawled in blood red lettering on the side of the Chemical Bank near the corner of Eleventh and First and is in print large enough to be seen from the backseat of the cab as it lurches forward in the traffic leaving Wall Street and just as Timothy Price notices the words a bus pulls up, the advertisement for *Les Misérables* on its side blocking his view, but Price who is with Pierce & Pierce and twenty-six doesn't seem to care because he tells the driver he will give him five dollars to turn up the radio, "Be My Baby" on WYNN, and the driver, black, not American, does so.

This, from my fourth novel, *Glamorama*:

Specks—specks all over the third panel, see?—no, *that* one—the second one up from the floor and I wanted to point this out to someone yesterday but a photo shoot intervened and Yaki Nakamari or whatever the hell the designer's name is—a master craftsman *not*—mistook me for someone else so I couldn't register the complaint, but, gentlemen—and ladies—there they are: *specks*, annoying, tiny specks, and they *don't* look accidental but like they were somehow done by a machine—so I don't want a lot of description, just the story, streamlined, no frills, the lowdown: who, what, where, when and don't leave out why, though I'm getting the distinct impression by the looks on your sorry faces that *why* won't get answered—now, come on, goddamnit, what's the *story*?

(*The Informers* was a short story collection published between *American Psycho* and *Glamorama* and since much of it was written while I was still in college—before the publication of *Less Than Zero*—it was an example of the same stripped-down minimalism.)

As anyone who had closely followed the progression of my career could glimpse—and if fiction inadvertently reveals a writer's inner life—things were getting out of hand, resembling something that according to the *New York Times* had become "bizarrely complicated . . . bloated and trivial . . . hyped-up," and I didn't necessarily disagree. I wanted a return to that past simplicity. I was overwhelmed by my life, and those first sentences seemed reflections of what had gone wrong. It was time to get back to basics, and though I hoped that one lean sentence—"You do an awfully good impression of yourself"—would start the process, I also realized that it was going to require more than a string of words to clear away the clutter and damage that had amassed around me. But it would be the beginning.

When I was a student at Camden College in New Hampshire I took a novel-writing tutorial and produced during the winter of 1983 a manuscript that eventually became *Less Than Zero*. It detailed a wealthy, alienated, sexually ambiguous young man's Christmas break from an eastern college in Los Angeles—more specifically Beverly Hills—and all the parties he wandered through and all the drugs he consumed and all the girls and boys he had sex with and all the friends he passively watched drift into addiction, prostitution and vast apathy; days were spent speeding toward the beach club with beautiful blondes in gleaming convertibles while high on Nembutal; nights were lost in VIP rooms at trendy clubs and snorting cocaine at the window tables of Spago. It was an indictment not only of a way of life I was familiar with but also—I thought rather grandly—of the Reagan eighties and, more indirectly, of Western civilization in the present moment. My teacher was convinced as well, and after some casual edits and revisions (I had written it quickly in an eight-week crystal-meth binge on the floor of my bedroom in L.A.) he submitted it to his agent and publisher, who both agreed to take it on (the publisher somewhat reluctantly—one member of the editorial board arguing, "If there's an audience for a novel about coke-snorting, cock-sucking zombies, then by all means let's publish the damn thing"), and I watched with a mixture of fear and fascination—laced with excitement—its transformation from a student assignment into a glossy hardcover that became a huge best seller and zeitgeist touchstone, was translated into twenty-five languages and made into a big-budget Hollywood movie, all within the space of about sixteen months. And in the early fall of 1985, just four months after publication, three things happened simultaneously: I became independently wealthy, I became insanely famous, and, most important, I escaped my father.

My father made the bulk of his money from highly speculative real estate deals, most of them during the Reagan years, and the freedom this money bought made him increasingly unstable. But my father had always been a problem—careless, abusive, alcoholic, vain, angry, paranoid—and even after my parents divorced when I was a teenager (my mother's demand) his power and control continued to loom over the family (which also included two younger sisters) in ways that were all monetary (endless arguments between lawyers about alimony and child support). It was a mission of his, a crusade, to weaken us, to make us intensely aware of how we—not his behavior—were to blame for the fact that he was no longer wanted in our lives. He left the house in Sherman Oaks under protest and moved to Newport Beach and his rage continued to clash with our peaceful Southern California surroundings: the lazy days hanging by the pool beneath a relentlessly clear and sunny sky, the mindless wanderings through the Galleria, the endless driving with swaying palm trees guiding us toward our destinations, the easygoing conversations over a soundtrack of Fleetwood Mac and the Eagles—all the laid-back advantages of growing up in that time and place were considerably darkened by his invisible presence. This languid lifestyle, decadent and loose, never relaxed my father. He remained, always, locked in a kind of demented fury, no matter how mellow the surface circumstances of his life really were. And because of this the world was threatening to us in a vague and abstract way we couldn't work ourselves out of—the map had disappeared, the compass had been smashed, we were lost. My sisters and I discovered a dark side to life at an unusually early age. We learned from our father's behavior that the world lacked coherence, and that within this chaos people were doomed to failure, and these realizations clouded our every ambition. And so my father was the sole reason I fled to a college in New Hampshire rather than stay in L.A. with my girlfriend and enroll at USC like most of my classmates from the private school we attended in the San Fernando Valley suburbs ultimately did. That was my desperate plan. But it was too late. My father had blackened my perception of the world, and his sneering, sarcastic attitude toward everything had latched on to me. As much as I wanted to escape his influence, I couldn't. It had soaked into me, shaped me into the man I was becoming. Whatever optimism I might have held on to had been swept away by the very nature of his being. The uselessness in thinking that escaping him physically would make a difference was so pathetic that I spent that first year at Camden paralyzed by anxiety and depression. The thing I resented most about my father was that the pain he inflicted on me—verbal and physical—was the reason I became a writer. (Added fact: he also beat our dog.)

Since he had no faith in my talent as a writer my father demanded that I attend business school at USC (my grades were poor but he had connections), even though I wanted to enroll somewhere as geographically distant from him as possible—an art school, I kept stressing over his roar, that offered no business courses. I found none in Maine so I chose Camden, a small liberal arts college nestled in the bucolic hills of northeastern New Hampshire. My father, typically enraged, refused to pay the tuition. However, my grandfather—who at the time was being sued by his son over a money matter so circuitous and complicated that I'm still not sure how or why it began—footed the bill. I'm fairly certain the reason my grandfather paid the outrageously expensive tuition had to do with the fact that it would upset my father greatly, which it did. When I started attending Camden in the fall of 1982, my father and I stopped speaking, which for me was a relief. This mutual silence prevailed until *Less Than Zero* was published and became a success. His negative, disapproving attitude about me then metamorphosed, by the popularity of the novel, into a curiously glowing acceptance that intensified my loathing for him even more. My father created me, criticized me, destroyed me and, then, after I reinvented myself and lurched back into being, became a proud, boastful dad who attempted to reenter my life, all within what seemed to me a matter of days. Again I felt defeated, even though I had gained control through my newfound independence. Not accepting phone calls or requests to visit—refusing any and all contact with him—gave me no pleasure; it didn't vindicate anything. I had won the lottery yet still felt poor and needy. So I threw myself into the new life that was now offered, even though—being a savvy, jaded L.A. kid—I should have known better.

The novel was mistaken for autobiography (I had written three autobiographical novels—all unpublished—before *Less Than Zero*, so it was much more fiction-based and less a roman à clef than most first novels) and its sensational scenes (the snuff film, the gang rape of the twelve-year-old, the decomposing corpse in the alley, the murder at the drive-in) were taken from lurid rumors that whispered through the group I hung with in L.A. and not from anything experienced directly. But the press became extremely preoccupied with the book's "shocking" content and especially with its style: very brief scenes written in a kind of controlled, cinematic haiku. The book was short and an easy read (you could consume this "piece of black candy"—*New York Magazine*—in a couple of hours) and because of its large type (and no chapter lasting more than a page or two) it became known as "the novel for the MTV generation" (courtesy of

USA Today) and I found myself being labeled by just about everyone as the voice of this new generation. The fact that I was only twenty-one and there were no other voices yet seemed not to matter. I was a sexy story and no one was interested in pointing out the paucity of other leaders. Besides being profiled in every magazine and newspaper that existed, I was interviewed on the *Today* show (for a record twelve minutes), on *Good Morning America*, by Barbara Walters, by Oprah Winfrey; I appeared on Letterman. William F. Buckley and I had a very lively conversation on *Firing Line*. For an entire week I introduced videos on MTV. Back at Camden I was engaged (briefly) to four different girls who hadn't seemed particularly interested before the book was published. At the graduation party my father threw for me at The Carlyle the attendees included Madonna, Andy Warhol with Keith Haring and Jean-Michel Basquiat, Molly Ringwald, John McEnroe, Ronald Reagan Jr., John-John Kennedy, the entire cast of *St. Elmo's Fire*, various VJs and members of my massive fan club, which five Vassar seniors had started, with a film crew from 20/20 covering the event. Also attending was Jay McInerney, who had recently published a similar first novel, *Bright Lights, Big City*, about young people and drugs in New York, that made him an overnight sensation and my closest East Coast rival; one critic pointed out in one of the many articles comparing the two novels that if you substituted the word "chocolate" for "cocaine" both *Less Than Zero* and *Bright Lights, Big City* would be considered children's books, and because we were photographed together so often people began to mix the two of us up—to simplify things the New York press simply referred to us as the Toxic Twins. After graduating from Camden I moved to New York and bought a condo in the same building both Cher and Tom Cruise lived in, a block from Union Square Park. And as the real world continued to melt away I became a founding member of something called the literary Brat Pack.

The Brat Pack was essentially a media-made package: all fake flash and punk and menace. It consisted of a small, trendy group of successful writers and editors, all under thirty, who simply hung out together at night, either at Nell's or Tunnel or MK or Au Bar, and the New York as well as the national and international press became entranced. (Why? Well, according to *Le Monde*, "American fiction had never been this young and sexy.") An updating of the movie-star Rat Pack from the late 1950s, it consisted of me (Frank Sinatra), the editor who discovered me (Morgan Entrekin in the Dean Martin role), the editor who discovered Jay (Gary Fisketjon/Peter

Lawford), hepcat Random House editor Erroll McDonald (Sammy Davis Jr.) and McInerney (the group's Jerry Lewis). We even had our own Shirley MacLaine in the guise of Tama Janowitz, who had written a collection of short stories about cute, drug-addled hipsters trapped in Manhattan that stayed on the *New York Times* best seller list for what seemed like months. And we were in hyperdrive. Every door swung wide open. Everyone approached us with outstretched hands and flashing smiles. We did layouts in fashion magazines, the six of us lounging on couches in hip restaurants, wearing Armani suits and in suggestive poses. Rock stars who were admirers invited us backstage: Bono, Michael Stipe, Def Leppard, members of the E Street Band. It was always the A booth. It was always the front seat of the roller coaster. It was never "Let's *not* get the bottle of Cristal." It was never "Let's *not* have dinner at Le Bernardin," where our antics included food fights, hurling lobsters and hosing one another down with bottles of Dom Perignon until the unamused staff would ask us to vacate the premises. Since our editors were taking us out all the time on their limitless expense accounts, the publishing houses were actually paying for this debauchery. It was the beginning of a time when it was almost as if the novel itself didn't matter anymore—publishing a shiny booklike object was simply an excuse for parties and glamour and good-looking authors reading finely honed minimalism to students who would listen rapt with slack-jawed admiration, thinking, I could do that, I could be them. But of course if you weren't photogenic enough, the sad truth was you couldn't. And if you were not a supporter of the Brat Pack, you simply had to accept us anyway. We were everywhere. There was no escaping our visages staring out at you from the pages of magazines and TV talk shows and scotch ads and posters on the sides of buses, in the tabloid gossip columns, our blank expressions caught in the dead glare of the camera flash, a hand holding the cigarette a fan was lighting. We had invaded the world.

And I was on display. Everything I did was written about. The paparazzi followed me constantly. A spilled drink in Nell's suggested drunkenness in a Page Six item in the *New York Post*. Dining at Canal Bar with Judd Nelson and Robert Downey Jr., who costarred in the movie adaptation of *Less Than Zero*, suggested "bad behavior" (true, but *still*). An innocuous script meeting with Ally Sheedy over lunch at Palio was construed as a sexual relationship. But I had put myself out there—I hadn't hidden—so what did I expect? I was doing Ray-Ban ads at twenty-two. I was posing for the covers of English magazines on a tennis court, on a throne, on the deck of my condo in a purple robe. I threw lavish catered parties—sometimes complete with strippers—in my condo on a whim ("Because It's Thursday!" one invitation read). I crashed a borrowed Ferrari in Southampton and its owner just smiled (for some reason I was naked). I attended three fairly exclusive orgies. I did guest spots as myself on *Family Ties* and *The Facts of Life* and *Melrose Place* and *Beverly Hills 90210* and *Central Park West.* I dined at the White House in the summer of 1986, the guest of Jeb and George W. Bush, both of whom were fans. My life was an unfolding parade made all the more magical by the constant materialization of cocaine, and if you wanted to hang out with me you had to carry at least an eight ball. And soon I became very adept at giving off the impression that I was listening to you when in fact I was dreaming about myself: my career, all the money I had made, the way my fame had blossomed and defined me, how recklessly the world allowed me to behave. Whenever I revisited L.A. over the Christmas holidays I usually chalked up four or five moving violations in the cream-colored 450 SL my father had handed down to me, but I lived in a place where the cops could be bought off, a place where you could drive at night without headlights, a place where you could snort coke while getting blown by the B-list actress, a place that allowed the three-day smack binge with the upcoming supermodel in the four-star hotel. It was a world that was quickly becoming a place with no boundaries. It was Dilaudid at noon. It was not talking to anyone in my immediate family for five months.

The two main events during the next phase of my life were the hurried publication of a second novel, *The Rules of Attraction,* and my affair with the actress Jayne Dennis. *The Rules of Attraction* was written during my senior year at Camden and detailed the sex lives of a small group of wealthy, alienated, sexually ambiguous students at a small New England liberal arts college (so like Camden itself that this is what I called the fictional university) during the height of the Reagan eighties. We followed them as they wandered from orgiastic party to orgiastic party, from one stranger's bed to another, and the text catalogued all the drugs devoured, all the alcohol guzzled, how easily they drifted into abortions and vast apathy and skipping classes, and it was supposed to be an indictment of, well, really nothing, but at that point in my career I could have submitted the notes I had taken in my junior year Virginia Woolf course and would still have received the huge advance and copious amounts of publicity. The book was also a best seller, though not as successful as *Less Than Zero*, and the press became even more fascinated with me, and by the decadence portrayed in the book and how it seemed to mirror my public lifestyle as well as the decade we were all trapped in. The book cemented my authority as *the* spokesman for this generation, and my fame grew in direct proportion to the number of copies the book sold. It all kept coming: the cases of champagne consumed, the suits Armani sent over, the cocktails in first class, the charting on various power lists, the court seats at Lakers games, the shopping after hours at Barneys, the groupies, the paternity suits, the restraining orders against "determined fans," the first million, the second million, the third million. I was going to start my own line of furniture. I was going to have my own production company. And the spotlight's white glare kept intensifying, especially when I started dating Jayne Dennis.

Jayne Dennis was a young model who had seamlessly made the transition to serious actress and had been steadily gaining recognition for her roles in a number of A-list projects. Our paths had crossed at various celebrity functions, and she had always been extremely flirtatious—but since everyone was flirting with me at that point in my life, her interest barely registered until she arrived at a Christmas party I threw in 1988 and basically hurled herself at me (I was that irresistible). At the after-party at Nell's I found myself making out with her in one of the club's front booths and then whisked her back to my suite at The Carlyle (it took the caterers two days to decorate the condo and three days to clean it up—there were five hundred guests—so I moved into a hotel the week of that party), where we had sex all night and then I had a plane to catch the next morning to L.A. for the holidays. When I returned to New York we officially became a high-profile couple. We could be seen at an Elton John AIDS benefit concert at Madison Square Garden, we were photographed at a Hampton's polo match, we were interviewed by *Entertainment Tonight* on the red carpet at the Ziegfeld premiere of the new Eddie Murphy comedy, we sat in the front row at a Versace fashion show, paparazzi followed us to a friend's villa in Nice. Though Jayne had fallen in love with me and wanted to get married, I was simply too preoccupied with myself and felt the relationship, if it kept running its course, would be doomed by summer. Besides her neediness and self-loathing, there were other insurmountable obstacles: namely drugs and, to a lesser extent, massive alcohol consumption; there were other girls, there were other boys; there was always another party to get lost in. Jayne and I broke up amiably in May of 1989 and kept in touch in a sad/funny sort of way; there was a continuing wistfulness on her part and a high level of sexual interest on mine. But I needed my space. I needed to be alone. A woman wasn't going to interfere with my creativity (plus, Jayne didn't add anything to it). I had started a new novel that was beginning to demand most of my time.

W hat's left to say about *American Psycho* that hasn't already been said? And I feel no need to go into great detail about it here. For those who weren't in the room at the time, here's the CliffsNotes version: I wrote a novel about a young, wealthy, alienated Wall Street yuppie named Patrick Bateman who also happened to be a serial killer filled with vast apathy during the height of the Reagan eighties. The novel was pornographic and extremely violent, so much so that my publishers, Simon & Schuster, refused the book on grounds of taste, forfeiting a mid-six-figure advance. Sonny Mehta, the head of Knopf, snapped up the rights, and even before its publication the controversy and scandal the novel achieved was enormous. I did no press because it was pointless—my voice would have been drowned out by all the indignant wailing. The book was accused of introducing serial killer chic to the nation. It was reviewed in the *New York Times*, three months before publication, under the headline "Don't Buy This Book." It was the subject of a 10,000-word essay by Norman Mailer in *Vanity Fair* ("the first novel in years to take on deep, dark, Dostoyevskian themes—how one wishes this writer was without talent!"). It was the object of scornful editorials, there were debates on CNN, there was a feminist boycott by the National Organization of Women and the obligatory death threats (a tour was canceled because of them). PEN and the Authors Guild refused to come to my rescue. I was vilified even though the book sold millions of copies and raised the fame quotient so high that my name became as recognizable as most movie stars' or athletes'. I was taken seriously. I was a joke. I was avant-garde. I was a traditionalist. I was underrated. I was overrated. I was innocent. I was partly guilty. I had orchestrated the controversy. I was incapable of orchestrating anything. I was considered the most misogynist American writer in existence. I was a victim of the burgeoning culture of the politically correct. The debates raged on and on, and not even the Gulf War in the spring of 1991 could distract the public's fear and worry and fascination from Patrick Bateman and his twisted life. I made more money than I knew what to do with. It was the year of being hated.

What I didn't—and couldn't—tell anyone was that writing the book had been an extremely disturbing experience. That even though I had planned to base Patrick Bateman on my father, someone—*something*—else took over and caused this new character to be my only reference point during the three years it took to complete the novel. What I didn't tell anyone was that the book was written mostly at night when the spirit of this madman would visit, sometimes waking me from a deep, Xanax-induced sleep. When I realized, to my horror, what this character wanted from me, I kept resisting, but the novel forced itself to be written. I would often black out for hours at a time only to realize that another ten pages had been scrawled out. My point—and I'm not quite sure how else to put this—is that the book *wanted* to be written by someone else. It wrote itself, and didn't care how I felt about it. I would fearfully watch my hand as the pen swept across the yellow legal pads I did the first draft on. I was repulsed by this creation and wanted to take no credit for it—Patrick Bateman wanted the credit. And once the book was published, it almost seemed as if *he* was relieved and, more disgustingly, satisfied. He stopped appearing after midnight gleefully haunting my dreams, and I could finally relax and quit bracing myself for his nocturnal arrivals. But even years later I couldn't look at the book, let alone touch it or reread it—there was something, well, evil about it. My father never said anything to me about *American Psycho*. Though oddly enough, after reading half of it that spring, he sent my mother a copy of *Newsweek* with the cover that asked, over the angelic face of a baby, "Is Your Child Gay?" unaccompanied by any kind of note or explanation.

The death of my father occurred in August of 1992. At the time I was doing the Hamptons in a $20,000-a-month cottage on the beach in Wainscott, where I was trying to work through my writer's block while preparing for weekend guests (Ron Galotti, Campion Platt, Susan Minot, my Italian publisher, and McInerney), ordering the forty-dollar plum tart from the specialty bakery in East Hampton and picking up the two cases of Domaines Ott. I was trying to stay sober but I'd started opening bottles of chardonnay at ten in the morning, and if I'd drunk everything the night before, I would sit in the Porsche I'd leased for the summer in a Bridgehampton parking lot waiting for the liquor store to open, usually sharing a cigarette with Peter Maas, who was waiting there too. I had just broken up with a model over a bizarre argument while we were barbecuing mackerel—she complained about the drinking, the spacing out, the exhibitionism, the gay thing, my weight gain, the paranoia. But it was the summer of Jeffrey Dahmer, the infamous homosexual/cannibal/serial killer from Wisconsin, and I became positive that he had been under the influence of *American Psycho*, since his crimes were just as gruesome and horrific as Patrick Bateman's. And since there *had* been a serial killer in of all fucking places *Toronto*, for Christ's sake, who *had* read the book and based two of his murders on scenes from it, I made a number of frantic, drunken phone calls to my agent at ICM as well as to my publicists at Knopf to make sure this wasn't the case (it wasn't). And yes, it was true, I had gained forty pounds—I was so sunburned and fat that if you had drawn a face on a giant pink marshmallow and plopped it in front of a laptop, you could not have told the difference between the two of us. And, of course, being this out of shape, I was prone to skinny-dipping in the Atlantic just fifty yards from my $20,000-a-month cottage, and yeah, I had also developed a minor crush on a teenage guy who worked at Loaves and Fishes. So Trisha's leaving me was semiunderstandable. Calling me a "fucking lunatic" and speeding away in that leased Porsche was not.

And then the summer was interrupted by a phone call in the middle of the night. He was found naked by the twenty-two-year-old girlfriend on the bathroom floor of his empty house in Newport Beach. That was all we knew.

I had no idea what to do, who to call, how to cope. I collapsed into shock. Someone had to remove me from that cottage and get me back to California. There was eventually only one person who could do all this for me—or, more pointedly, would. So Jayne left the set of a movie in Pennsylvania she was costarring in with Keanu Reeves and made plane reservations on MGM Grand and dragged my shivering hulk out of the Hamptons and flew to L.A. with me—all within twenty hours of hearing about my father's death. And that night, at the house in Sherman Oaks that I grew up in, drunk and terrified, I brutally made love to her in my childhood room while we both wept. Jayne returned the next day to the set in Pennsylvania. Keanu sent me flowers.

My father had made me trustee of his estate, which was worthless, and he also owed millions in back taxes, so there was a protracted legal battle with the IRS (they could not understand how someone who had made $20 million in the last six years of his life had spent it all—but this was before we found out about the rented Learjet and all the bad art) that kept me in Los Angeles for several months, locked in an office in Century City with three lawyers and half a dozen accountants until all the financial matters were cleared up. In the end I was left with two Patek Philippe watches and a boxful of oversized Armani suits, as well as a monumental relief that he was gone. (My mother and sisters—nothing.) The autopsy revealed that he had suffered a massive stroke at 2:40 a.m., though the coroner was mystified by certain irregularities. No one wanted to pursue these irregularities and he was cremated immediately. His ashes were put into a bag—even though his (invalid) will stated that he wanted his children to spread them at sea off the coast of Cabo San Lucas, where he vacationed frequently— and we stored the ashes in a safe-deposit box in a Bank of America on Ventura Boulevard next to a dilapidated McDonald's. When I brought some of the Armani suits to a tailor to be altered (I had dropped all the weight I had gained that summer in a matter of weeks) I was revolted to discover that most of the inseams in the crotch of the trousers were stained with blood, which we later found out was the result of a botched penile implant he underwent in Minneapolis. My father, in his last years, due to the toxic mix of diabetes and alcoholism, had become impotent. I left the suits with the tailor and drove back to Sherman Oaks in tears, screaming while punching the roof of the Mercedes as I swerved recklessly through the canyons.

And when I returned to New York, I was told by Jayne that she was pregnant and that she intended to keep the child and that I was the father. I begged her to have an abortion. ("Change it! Fix it! Do something!" I screamed. "I can't be doing this! I'll be dead in two years! Don't look at me like I'm crazy!") Children had voices, they wanted to explain themselves, they wanted to tell you where everything was—and I could easily do without witnessing these special skills. I had already seen what I wanted and it did not involve children. Like all single men the first priority was my career. I had a fantasy bachelor's life and wanted to keep it. I raged at Jayne, confronted her with entrapment, insisted it wasn't mine. But she said she expected as much from me and had the child prematurely the following March at Cedars-Sinai, in L.A., where she was now living. I saw the child once during its first year—Jayne brought him over to the condo on 13th Street in a pathetic attempt at bonding when she was in town for the premiere of the movie she had made with Keanu Reeves the previous summer. She had named him Robert—Robby. Again I raged at her and insisted the child wasn't mine. She asked, "Then who the hell do you think the father is?" I immediately made a connection and pounced on it. "Keanu Reeves!" I shouted. (Keanu had been a friend of mine when he was initially cast in *Less Than Zero*, but he was replaced by Andrew McCarthy when the studio producing the movie—Twentieth Century–Fox—scored a hit in the spring of 1987 with *Mannequin*, a low-budget sleeper which starred McCarthy, and was produced, ironically, by the father of the girl the character Blair—the heroine of *Less Than Zero*—was based on; my world was that small.) I threatened to sue Jayne if she asked for child support. Since I refused to participate in any testing, she hired a lawyer. I hired a lawyer. Her lawyer argued that "the child bears a striking resemblance to Mr. Ellis," while my lawyer countered, reluctantly, at my urging, with "said child bears a striking resemblance to a certain Mr. Keanu Reeves!" (the exclamation point being my idea; blowing my relationship with Keanu because of this, not my idea). Tests I was legally obliged to undergo proved that I was the father, but I claimed that Jayne had misrepresented the facts when she said she was using contraception. "Ms. Dennis and Mr. Ellis were in a non-exclusive relationship," my lawyer argued. "Regardless of Mr. Ellis being the father, it is her choice to be a single mother." I learned in cases such as these that ejaculation was the legal point of no return. But one morning, after a particularly acrimonious phone call between my lawyer and Jayne's, Marty hung up the phone, stunned, and looked at me. Jayne had given up. She no longer expected any child support and promptly dropped her lawsuit. It was at that moment in my lawyer's office at One World Trade Center that I realized she had named the child after my father, but when I confronted her about it later that day, after we had tentatively forgiven each other, she swore it had never occurred to her. (Which I still do not believe, and which I am certain is the reason that the following events in *Lunar Park* happened—it was the catalyst.) What else? Her parents hated me. Even after it was proven that I was the father, Jayne's last name remained on the birth certificate. I started wearing Hawaiian shirts and smoking cigars. Jayne had another child five years later—a girl named Sarah—and again the relationship with the father did not work out. (I knew the guy vaguely—a famous music executive in L.A.; he was a nice guy.) In the end, Jayne seemed practical and maternal and stable. We amiably kept in touch. She was still in love with me. I moved on.

Jayne always demanded Robby's name not be connected with mine in any of the press I did and of course I agreed, but in August of 1994, when *Vanity Fair* assigned a profile to run when Knopf published *The Informers*, that collection of short stories I had written when still at Camden, the reporter suggested who Robby's father might be and in his first draft—

17

which ICM suspiciously got a peek at—cited a "reliable source" as saying that Bret Easton Ellis was in fact Robby's dad. I relayed this information to Jayne, who called my agent, Binky Urban, and the head of Knopf, Sonny Mehta, to demand that this "fact" be excised, and Graydon Carter—the editor of *Vanity Fair* and also a friend—agreed to cut it, much to the chagrin of the reporter who had "endured" a week with me in Richmond, Virginia, where I supposedly was hiding out at a friend's house. Actually, I was secretly attending the Canyon Ranch that had recently opened there to get in shape for the brief book tour I'd promised to do for Knopf to support *The Informers*. That information never made it into the article, either.

Very few people (close friends included) knew anything about this, my secret son, and—except for Jay McInerney and my editor, Gary Fisketjon, both of whom Robby met when Jayne and I attended the wedding of a mutual friend in Nashville—no one I was acquainted with had ever seen him, including my mother and my sisters. At that wedding in Nashville, Jayne informed me that Robby had been asking where his father was, why his dad wasn't living with them, why he never came to visit. Supposedly there were an increasing number of tearful outbursts and long silences; there was confusion and the demand of proof; there were anxieties, irrational fears, attachment disorders, tantrums at school. He wouldn't let people touch him. Yet at the wedding in Nashville he had instinctively reached for my hand—I was still a stranger, his mother's friend, nobody—to show me a lizard he thought he had seen behind a hedge outside the hotel where a large number of the wedding guests were staying. This was something I pretended didn't bother me, and I tried to refrain from mentioning him at the thousands of cocktail parties I attended during the following years. But at that moment in the evening when someone brought out the cocaine (which had admittedly become nightly by that point), fragments of this hidden life would tumble teasingly from my mouth. Though when I noticed the saddened, shocked expressions of people who sensed the yearning behind the mask, I would quickly shut up and offer my new mantra—"I'm kidding, I'm just kidding"—and then I would reintroduce whatever new girl I was dating to people she had known for years. The girl would look up from a mirror piled high with cocaine and stare at me wonderingly, shudder and then lean back down, causing another line to disappear through a tightly rolled twenty-dollar bill. The wedding—after Robby took my hand for the first time—was the beginning. This was the moment when the son suddenly became real to the father. It was also the first year I spent close to

$100,000 on drugs. Money that—what?—could have gone to Robby, I suppose. But Jayne was commanding $4 to $5 million per picture, and I was high all the time, so it stopped bothering me.

But a lot of people thought I was gay so they would soon forget that Bret Easton Ellis had mentioned—raving, coked-up, sucking back another Stoli—that he had fathered a child. The gay thing being the outcome of a drunken British interview I was doing to promote the BBC documentary about my life thus far at thirty-three, its title taken from *American Psycho's* last line: *This Is Not an Exit: The Bret Easton Ellis Story* (the fame, the excess, the falloff, the dysfunction, the heartbreak, the DUI, the shoplifting incident, the arrest in Washington Square Park, the comeback, walking tiredly through a gym in slow motion while Radiohead's "Creep" blasted over the soundtrack). Noting casually that I appeared "rather effete" in many of the clips, and instead of asking if I was on drugs, the reporter wondered if I was a homosexual. And I said, "Yeah, you bet I am—sure!" adding what I thought to be a jaunty and overtly sarcastic remark about coming out of the closet: "Thank God!" I shouted. "Someone has *finally* outed me!" I had told countless interviewers about sexually experimenting with men—and went into explicit detail about the collegiate threesomes I had at Camden in a *Rolling Stone* profile—but this time it struck a nerve. Paul Bogaards, my publicist at Knopf, actually called me a "potty-mouthed butt pirate" after reading the piece in the *Independent,* while relishing the storm of controversy this admission caused, not to mention the increased sales of my backlist. The creator of Patrick Bateman, author of *American Psycho,* the most misogynistic novel ever written, was actually—gasp!—a homosexual?!? And the gay thing sort of stuck. After that interview appeared I was even named one of the *Advocate's* 100 Most Interesting Gay People of the year, which drove my legitimately gay friends nuts and prompted confused, tearful phone calls from Jayne. But I was just being "rambunctious." I was just being a "prankster." I was just being "Bret." Over the years photos of me in a Jacuzzi at the Playboy Mansion (I was a regular when I was in L.A.) kept appearing in that magazine's "Hanging with Hef" page, so there was "consternation" about my sexuality. The *National Enquirer* said I was dating Julianna Margulies or Christy Turlington or Marina Rust. They said I was dating Candace Bushnell, Rupert Everett, Donna Tartt, Sherry Stringfield. Supposedly I was dating George Michael. I was even dating both Diane Von Furstenberg *and* Barry Diller. I wasn't straight, I wasn't gay, I wasn't bi, I didn't know what I was. But it was all my fault, and I enjoyed the fact that people were actually interested in who I was sleeping with. Did it matter? I was a mystery, an enigma, and that was what mattered—that's what sold books, that's what made me even more famous. Propaganda designated to enhance the already very chic image of author as handsome young playboy.

On heroin I thought everything I did was innocent and full of love and I had a yearning to bond with humanity and I was relaxed and serene and focused and I was frank and I was caring and I signed so many autographs and made so many new friends (who dwindled away, who didn't make it). At the time I discovered dope I also started the decade-long process (the nineties) of outlining, writing and promoting a 500-page novel called *Glamorama*, about an international terrorist ring using the fashion world as a cover. And the book promised—predictably—to make me a multi-millionaire again and even more famous. But I had to do a world tour. This is what I promised when I signed the contracts; this was what was required of me to become the multimillionaire again; this was what ICM insisted on so they could collect the commissions from the multimillionaire. But I was heavily into smack and the sixteen-month-long tour was considered by the publishing house to be a potentially "precarious" situation, since I was, according to Sonny Mehta, "kind of high all the time." But they relented. They needed me to do the tour to help recoup the massive advance they'd laid out. (I told them to send Jay McInerney in my place—no one could tell the difference, I argued, plus I was positive Jay would actually do it. Nobody at Knopf thought this was even vaguely feasible.) Besides, I wanted to be that multimillionaire again, so I promised them I was clean—and for a little while I was. An internist they sent me to was convinced I would need a new liver by the time I was forty if I wasn't careful, which helped. But not enough.

To make sure I stayed drug-free during the first leg of the *Glamorama* tour, Knopf hired a Jamaican bodyguard to keep an eye on me. Sometimes he was easy to elude; other times he was not. Like many esteemed (albeit sloppy) drug users, I usually had cocaine powder all over my jackets when I came out of bathroom stalls, dusting my lapels, dotting itself in chunks on the trousers of my new Cerruti suits so at times it was noticeable that I wasn't entirely clean yet, which eventually led to daily searches by Terence, who would find the packets of meth and coke and dope lodged in my Armani overcoats, which he then sent out for dry cleaning. And then there were the more serious side effects of doing drugs on a long, exhausting tour: the seizure in Raleigh and the life-threatening coma in St. Louis. Before long Terence just didn't care anymore ("Mon, if you wanna do de dope, do de dope," Terence tiredly told me as he fingered a dreadlock. "Terence don wanna know. Terence? He tired, mon.") and soon I was doing bumps every ten minutes during interviews in a hotel bar in Cincinnati while guzzling double cosmopolitans at two in the afternoon. I was smuggling propane torches and large quantities of crack onto Delta flights. I overdosed in a bathtub in Seattle (I had technically died for three minutes in the Sorrento). And that was when the real worry began settling in. If the increasing number of handlers in each city couldn't find me by lunch they were instructed by my publishers to get the house detective of whatever hotel I was staying at to unlock the door—and if the chain was up or I'd wedged a chair under the handle, they were instructed to "kick the fucker in"—to make sure I was still alive, and of course I was always still alive (literally, if not figuratively) but so wasted that PR reps would have to piggyback me from limousine to radio station to bookstore, where I would commence with my reading while sitting slumped in a chair, mumbling into a microphone, while a bookstore clerk nervously stood close by, ready to snap her fingers in front of my face if I zoned out (and sometimes during the signings they held my hand, guiding me to a recognizable signature when all I wanted to sign was an X). And if drugs were unavailable I became less committed to the cause. For example, since a dealer I knew in Denver had been—unbeknownst to me, before my arrival—stabbed to death in the head with a screwdriver I had to cancel an appearance at the Tattered Cover due to lack of dope. (I escaped the Brown Palace and was found on the front lawn of another dealer's condo, moaning, my shoes and wallet stolen, my pants around my ankles.) Without drugs I couldn't take showers because I was afraid of what might come out of the showerhead. Occasionally a book signing groupie who'd hinted she had drugs was dragged back to my hotel room and would attempt to revive me with dope and oral sex (which required a lot of patience on the groupie's part). "It only takes a week to come off heroin," one of these girls said hopefully while trying to gnaw her own arm off after she realized I had done all six bags of her smack. Without drugs I became convinced that a bookstore owner in Baltimore was in fact a mountain lion. If that was happening how could I endure the six-hour flight to Portland sober? My solution? Find more drugs. And so I kept scoring dope and continued to nod off during interviews in hotel bars. I passed out on planes, lying sprawled and unconscious in first class before being wheelchaired through airports with an airline attendant by my side to keep me from sliding out. "Food poisoning," the press was told by Paul Bogaards, now the head of publicity at Knopf. "He was poisoned by . . . um . . . y'know, food."

And the tour roared on.

I woke up in Milan. I woke up in Singapore. I woke up in Moscow. I woke up in Helsinki. I woke up in Cologne. I woke up in various cities along the eastern seaboard. I woke up cradling a bottle of tequila in a white limo with bullhorns attached to its front fender as it raced across Texas. "Why did Bret miss the reading?" Paul Bogaards was constantly asked by the press. After a pause Paul would answer with his now customary vagueness. "Um, fatigue . . ." A new tack: "Why did Bret postpone this whole leg of the tour?" Another long pause before "Um, allergies." Then a longer pause before the confused journalist tentatively mentioned, "But it's January, Mr. Bogaards." Finally, after another drawn-out pause on Bogaards's part, in a small voice: "Fatigue . . ." This was followed by yet another very long pause and then in barely a whisper: "Food poisoning." But people were making so much money (there was enough pornography and dismemberment to appease my fan base so the book was on just about every best seller list despite reviews that usually ended with the word "Yuck") that schedules were inevitably readjusted, because if they weren't my publisher would suffer huge financial losses. Everything about my career was now measured in economics, and giant bouquets of flowers had to be sent to my hotel suites in order to soothe my "insecurity rages." Every hotel on the *Glamorama* world tour was required to provide "ten votive candles, a box of chewable vitamin-C tablets, an assortment of Ricola throat lozenges, fresh gingerroot, three large bags of Cool Ranch Doritos, a chilled bottle of Cristal, and an unlisted outgoing-only phone line," and at all readings the lights above the podium had to be "orange-tinted" because this would bring out the darkness of my salon-induced tan. If these contractual demands weren't met the fine would be split between Knopf and myself. No one said being a Bret Easton Ellis fan was easy.

An actual "drug cop" was hired for the second U.S. tour; somehow during all of this the paperback had been published (I had been on the road that long). Terence had slipped out of the picture months ago and a fresh-faced young woman—"motivational helper" or "celebrity baby-sitter" or "sober companion," or whatever—was now on hand to basically make sure I didn't snort heroin before the readings. But of course she was hired to protect my publisher, not me. They didn't really care about the underlying reasons of my addiction (but then neither did I) and were only interested in the amount of book sales the tour was generating. I thought I was "fragile yet functioning," but according to memos the drug cop e-mailed to Knopf's publicity department from the road, I was most decidedly *not* functioning.

> E-mail memo #6: "15 miles southwest of Detroit writer was found hiding in back of stalled van on the median of a divided highway, picking at nonexistent scabs."
>
> E-mail memo #9: "Somehow writer has been teargassed at anti-globalization demonstration in Chicago."
>
> E-mail memo #13: "Berkeley; angry drug dealer was found choking writer due to 'lack of payment' in alley behind Barnes & Noble."
>
> E-mail memo #18: "Cleveland; writer slept until three p.m., missing all morning and lunch interviews; was then found 'pigging out on junk food' until compelled to 'throw up.' Also witnessed standing in front of hotel mirror sobbing 'I'm getting so old.' "
>
> E-mail memo #27: "Santa Fe; writer allegedly encouraged a Dober-man pinscher to perform cunnilingus on unconscious groupie and when said animal failed to show interest in said groupie writer punched said animal in head and was severely bitten."
>
> E-mail memo #34: "Miami Book Fair; writer locked himself in book-store bathroom repeatedly yelling at concerned employees to 'Go away!' When writer emerged an hour later he started to 'freak out' again. 'I have a snake on me!' writer screamed. 'It's biting me! It's IN MY MOUTH!' Writer was dragged to a waiting squad car while holding on to bewildered young yeshiva student attending the reading—whom writer continuously fondled and groped—until ambulance arrived. His eyes rolling back into his head, writer's last words—shouted—before being driven off were quote 'I am keep-ing the Jew-boy' unquote."

Paul Bogaards would respond with his own e-mails, such as: "I don't care if you have to stick a broom up writer's ass to get him upright and onstage—Just Do It." I felt as if I had been hijacked. The tour seemed so long and monstrously unfair. I kept fainting from the endless pressure of it all. Well-butrin helped me cope, along with my refusal to admit anything was wrong.

My handler was now calling the tour "a legitimately traumatic experience." When I countered with "It's an escapade!" she snapped back, "You need to hit rock bottom." But it's a difficult thing to hit rock bottom when you are making close to $3 million a year.

The reviews of my readings did not vary: "Rambling, unfocused and self-obsessed, Ellis buried the night under the weight of so much gibberish that all his appearance offered was the experience of seeing a celebrity author unravel" was not an atypical critical response. Because of the Internet, word raced through cyberspace of my "bedraggled" and "unintentionally humorous" signings, and this made people buy books. It put asses in all those folding chairs at the readings the publisher had set up, which ended up being massive affairs because I was radiating the numb, burned-out cool so popular during that particular moment in the culture. But the desire to erase myself was too great—it was winning at a game in which there were no winners. I had become so malnourished that in the middle of a reading in Philadelphia (where I had thrown the book aside and started ranting about my father) a front tooth came loose.

I was exhausted by the nonstop barrage of press (and my duplicity and the truths I hid) and after the premiere of the movie version of *American Psycho*—which is what the sixteen-month *Glamorama* world tour was heading for, what it was culminating toward—I realized that if I wanted to live again (i.e., not die) I had to flee New York. I was that burned out. A weeklong coke and heroin binge began in the limo during the drive to the premiere at the Sony Theater on Broadway and 68th and continued into the long night of parties that started at the Cerruti store on Madison (they had supplied the movie's fashions), moved downtown to Pop, then danced itself to Spa and then dragged itself into my condo on 13th Street, where the cast members and their various agents and PR reps and DJs and other notable members of young Hollywood boogied until the building's superintendent arrived the following morning and demanded I kick everyone out due to the intolerable noise level, even though, high and reeking of vodka and base, I tried bribing him with a roll of hundreds. After all that, I lay alone in bed for the next seven days, watching porn DVDs with the sound off and snorting maybe forty bags of heroin, a blue plastic bucket that I vomited into continually by my side, and telling myself that the lack of respect from the critical community was what hurt so much and why I had to drug myself away from the pain. I just lay back and kept waiting for the tawdry end of the incendiary career.

. . .

The following week there was a useless stint at the Exodus Clinic in Marina del Ray (where I was diagnosed with something called "acquired situational narcissism"). It didn't help. Only the speedballs and cocaine and the blotters of acid stamped with Bart Simpson and Pikachu meant anything to me, were the only things that made me *feel* something. Cocaine was destroying the lining of my nose and I honestly thought a good solution was to switch solely to basing, but the two quarts of vodka I was drinking daily made even that goal seem hazy and unattainable. I also realized I had written only one thing in the last two years: a horrible short story involving space aliens, a fast food restaurant and a talking bisexual scarecrow, even though I had promised ICM the first draft of my memoir. Since, according to Binky, we were turning down authorized biography requests at least twice a month, more than a dozen publishers had made inquiries about the memoir. I had talked brazenly about it during the *Glamorama* tour, where it was most prominently detailed in the (incoherent) *Rolling Stone* interview I did in the 1998 year-end double issue. I had even given it a title without having written a single usable sentence: *Where I Went I Would Not Go Back.* It was to deal primarily with the transforming events of my childhood and adolescence, ending with my junior year at Camden, a month before *Less Than Zero* was published. But even when I simply *thought* about the memoir it wouldn't go anywhere (I could never be as honest about myself in a piece of nonfiction as I could in any of my novels) and so I gave up. (There is, however, an unauthorized biography Bloomsbury is publishing next year by a writer named Jaime Clarke that I will vehemently protest the publication of—its title: *Ellis Island.*) And the drugs continued.

There was also the money problem—I didn't have any. I had blown it all. On what? Drugs. Parties that cost $50,000. Drugs. Girls who wanted to be taken to Italy, Paris, London, St. Barts. Drugs. A Prada wardrobe. A new Porsche. Drugs. Rehab treatment that wasn't covered by health insurance. The movie money from polishing jobs that had, at one point, showered down on me started drying up when the drug rumors became too detailed to ignore and after I sent back several screenplays with none of the requested changes made and just my random notes scrawled in the margins: "Not so good" and "I think this rather excellent" and "Let's beef it up" and the ubiquitous "I hated my father." The spark that had once animated me had majorly fizzled out. What was I doing hanging out with gang-bangers and diamond smugglers? What was I doing buying kilos? My apartment reeked of marijuana and freebase. One afternoon I woke up and realized I didn't know how anything worked anymore. Which button turned the espresso machine on? Who was paying my mortgage? Where did the stars come from? After a while you learn that everything stops.

It was time to minimize damage. It was time to renew contacts. It was time to expect more from myself.

I had lost the hustle, the nerve, the *shit* it took to keep myself standing in the spotlight. My desire to be part of the Scene shrank—I was exhausted by it all. My life—my *name*—had been rendered a repetitive, unfunny punch line and I was sick of eating it. Celebrity was a life lived in code—it was a place where you constantly had to decipher what people wanted from you, and where the terrain was slippery and a world where ultimately you always made the wrong choice. What made everything less and less bearable was that I had to keep quiet about this because I knew no one else who could sympathize (maybe Jay McInerney, but he was still so lost inside it all that he never would have understood) and once I grasped that I was totally alone, I realized, only then, that I was in serious trouble. My wistful attitude about fame and drugs—the delight I took in feeling sorry for myself—had turned into a hard sadness, and the future no longer looked even remotely plausible. Just one thing seemed to be racing toward me: a blackness, a grave, the end. And so during that terrible year there were the inevitable 12-step programs, the six different treatment centers, the endless second chances, the fourth intervention, the unavoidable backsliding, the multiple relapses, the failed recoveries, the sudden escape to Las Vegas, the tumble into the abyss and, finally, the flameout.

I ultimately called Jayne. She listened. She made an offer. She held out a hand. I was so shocked that I broke into tears. What I was being given—I understood immediately—was extremely rare: a second chance with some-one. I was briefly reluctant at first, but there was one factor overriding everything: no one else wanted me.

And because of this I instantly rebounded. I got clean in May, signed a huge contract for a new novel with a reluctant Knopf and an insistent ICM in June and then moved into Jayne's newly built mansion in July. We married later that month in a private ceremony at City Hall with only Marta, her assistant, as a witness. But Jayne Dennis was a well-known actress and "somehow" the news leaked. Immediately the *National Enquirer* ran an article on Jayne's "spectacularly bad luck in love" and listed all of her ill-fated relationships (when had she dated Matthew McConaughey? Billy Bob Thornton? Russell Crowe? Who in the hell was Q-Tip?) before asking its readers, "Why is Jayne Dennis with a man who let her down so cruelly?" Comparisons were made to Anjelica Huston and Jack Nicholson, to Jerry Hall and Mick Jagger. A clinical psychologist hypothesized that famous women were no different from nonfamous women when it came to bad choices in relationships. "You can be beautiful and successful and still be attracted to a loser," the clinical psychologist was quoted as saying, adding that "beautiful women are often geek magnets." The article went on about my "crude insensitivity" and "refusal to disavow the comments made about Keanu Reeves's role" in all of this. One anonymous source offered, "The novelty of dating a skunk must be arousing—she must really crave a challenge." A "close friend" of Jayne's was quoted as saying, "Marrying Bret Easton Ellis was one of the leading dumb choices of the new century."

Damage control. We sat for a *Talk* magazine profile (titled "Cad or Catch?") in which Jayne defended me and I repented. The article detailed the years I'd spent mired in drugs and alcohol, though I said I was now reformed. "Vicious false things have been said about Bret," Jayne offered. When prodded by Jayne I "indignantly" added, "Yeah, I'm bitter about them as well." Jayne went on to lament: "This business can be so hard on relationships that I've lost a lot of self-confidence" and "I think nice guys— whatever that means—were so intimidated by me that the men I dated weren't usually very caring." The writer noted the "sidelong glance" Jayne gave me. The writer noted my "grim countenance" and did not seem to believe me when I said, "I always try to be in the moment when I'm with my kids—I'm really devoting my life to fatherhood." (The journalist failed to notice how darkly amused I was by everything at this point in my newly sober life: a crestfallen expression, the smear of blood on a hand, the heart that had stopped beating, the cruelty of children.) This writer had his own pop-psychology take on matters: "Famous women are known for sabotaging themselves because they don't feel they deserve what they have" and "It takes character to resist a cad, and celebrities definitely do not have stronger than average character." The writer also asked me questions along the lines of "Some reviewers have doubts about your sincerity—how do you respond?" and "Why did you pass out at the Golden Globe Awards last year?" But Jayne kept coming through with sound bites like "Bret is my source of strength," to which an unnamed friend responded, "That's a joke. Let's face it, the reason Jayne married Bret Ellis is all about low self-esteem. She deserves better than a professional frat boy, okay? Ellis is a complete hoser." Another unnamed friend was quoted as saying, "Bret wouldn't even escort her to prenatal care appointments! We're talking about a guy who smoked Thai sticks in taxicabs." Jayne admitted that being attracted to "bad boys" had been an addiction and that their "unpredictability" gave her a rush. "Hey, I'm an interesting date," I'm somehow quoted as saying. Another anonymous source: "I think she's with Bret because Jayne's a fixer-upper—she has convinced herself that a good guy's in there." Another nameless source disagreed and put it more succinctly: "He's. A. Dick." My own conclusion was "Jayne makes my life complete—I'm a grateful guy." The article ended—shockingly, I thought—with: "Good luck, Jayne."

B y this time, Jayne had moved out of Los Angeles and into the anonymous suburbia of the Northeast, close enough to New York for meetings and business but at the same time safely distant from what she saw as the increasing horror of urban life. The attack on the World Trade Center and the Pentagon was the initial motivation, and Jayne briefly considered some exotically remote place deep in the Southwest or the vastness of the heartland, but her goal eventually simplified itself into moving at least two hours away from any large city, since that's where suicide bombers were blowing themselves up in crowded Burger Kings and Starbuckses and Wal-Marts and in subways at rush hour. Miles of major cities had been cordoned off behind barbed wire, and morning newspapers ran aerial photographs of bombed-out buildings on the front page, showing piles of tangled bodies in the shadow of the crane lifting slabs of scorched concrete. More and more often there were "no survivors." Bulletproof vests were on sale everywhere, because scores of snipers had suddenly appeared; the military police stationed on every corner offered no solace, and surveillance cameras proved useless. There were so many faceless enemies—from within the country and abroad—that no one was certain who we were fighting or why. Cities had become mournful places, where everyday life was suddenly interrupted by jagged mounds of steel and glass and stone, and grief on an unimaginable scale was rising up over them, reinforced by the stained, tattered photocopies of the missing posted everywhere, which were not only a constant reminder of what had been lost but also a warning of what was coming next, and in the endless CNN montages of people wandering around in a slow-motion daze, some wrapped in American flags, while the soundtrack was Bruce Springsteen softly singing "We Shall Overcome." There were too many fearful moments when the living envied the dead, and people started moving away to the country, the suburbs, anywhere. Cities were no place to raise a family, or, more pointedly according to Jayne, start one. So many people had lost their capacity for love.

Jayne wanted to raise gifted, disciplined children, driven to succeed, but she was fearful of just about everything: the threat of pedophiles, bacteria, SUVs (we owned one), guns, pornography and rap music, refined sugar, ultraviolet rays, terrorists, ourselves. I took anger management sessions and went over "past wounds" with a therapist after a brief and heated exchange concerning Robby popped up in an otherwise innocuous conversation between the two of us. (It was all about what he wanted. It was all about what he needed. Everything I desired was overridden, and I had to accept this. I had to rise up to it.) I spent that summer trying to get to know this worried, sad, alert boy who gave evasive answers to questions I felt demanded clarity and precision, and also Sarah, who was now six and basically just kept informing me of how bored she was by everything. Since camp had been canceled, Jayne and I organized activities to push them out of their stupor: the karate class, the oboe lesson, the phonics tapes, the smart toys, the trip to the wax museum, the aquarium we visited. The summer was saying no to Robby (who considered himself a "professional" video game player) because he wanted to fly to Seoul for the World Cyber Games. The summer was getting acquainted with the wide array of meds the kids were on (stimulants, mood stabilizers, the antidepressant Lexapro, the Adderall for attention-deficit/hyperactivity disorder and various other anticonvulsants and antipsychotics that had been prescribed). The summer was building a fort. It was decorating cookies. It was a silver robot I purchased for Robby, to which he responded, "I'm too old, Bret." It was the astronomy CD-ROM he wanted instead. It was the summer of the trampoline I bought and the minor injury Robby sustained while attempting a stunt. We went for walks through a forest. We took nature hikes. I couldn't believe I actually toured both a farm and a chocolate factory, and also petted a giraffe (who later was killed by lightning after a freak summer storm) at the local zoo. I became reacquainted with Snuffleupagus. The summer was colors and shapes and counting with Sarah, who could say

"*Hola,*" and there was always the blue dog and the friendly dragon and the puppet shows where the animals interacted suggestively with one another, and I would read *The Poky Little Puppy* to her on CD-ROM, which made the book seem cold and barren, the illustrations staring out at us from the empty glow of the computer screen. It all seemed vaguely unreal to me. I was thrust into the role of husband and father—of protector—and my doubts were mountainous. But I was moving with a higher purpose. I was involuntarily striving toward something. I took a more commanding tone with the children when they were acting surly or indifferent or spoiled, which seemed to relieve Jayne. (But Jayne also requested that I stay "focused," and so I easily secured a position as a creative writing teacher at the local college—even if the group of students met only once a week for three hours.) I found myself changing and had no choice but to feel that this conversion validated me. I no longer craved action. The tightness of city life vanished—the suburbs were fragmented and rambling; there was no more flipping through the devil's dictionary (Zagat's) to find a decent restaurant, and the bidding war for reservations disappeared. Who cared about the VIP booth anymore, or mugging for paparazzi on the red carpet at movie premieres? I was relaxed in the suburbs. Everything was different: the rhythm of the days, your social status, suspicions about people. It was a refuge for the less competitive; it was the minor leagues. You simply didn't have to pay as much attention to things. The precise pose was no longer required. I had expected to be bored, and to be angered by that boredom, but it never materialized. Passing by someone pruning a shrub did not spark the powder keg of regret I expected. I had canceled my subscription to *I Want That!* and for a while I was okay. One day late in August I drove by a simple field dotted with poplars and I suddenly held my breath. I felt a tear on my face. I was happy, I realized with amazement.

But by the end of that summer everything I had learned started to disappear. The "problems" that developed within the house over the next two months actually began late in October and hit crisis point in November. Everything collapsed in a time frame made up of twelve days.

I've recounted the "incidents" in sequential order. *Lunar Park* follows these events in a fairly straightforward manner, and though this is, ostensibly, a true story, no research was involved in the writing of this book. For example, I did not consult the autopsy reports concerning the murders that occurred during this period—because, in my own way, I had committed them. I was responsible, and I knew what had happened to the victims without referring to a coroner. There are also people who dispute the horror of the events that took place that autumn on Elsinore Lane, and when the book was vetted by the legal team at Knopf, my ex-wife was among those who protested, as did, oddly enough, my mother, who was not present during those frightful weeks. The files that the FBI kept on me—beginning in November of 1990, during the prepublication controversy surrounding *American Psycho*, and maintained ever since—would have clarified things, but they have not been released and I'm barred from quoting them. And the few "witnesses" who could corroborate these events have disappeared. For example, Robert Miller, the paranormal investigator I hired, simply vanished, and the Web site where I first contacted him no longer exists. My psychiatrist at the time, Dr. Janet Kim, offered the suggestion that I was "not myself" during this period, and has hinted that "perhaps" drugs and alcohol were "key factors" in what was a "delusional state." Names have been changed, and I'm semivague about the setting itself because it doesn't matter; it's a place like any other. Retelling this story has taught me that *Lunar Park* could have happened anywhere. These events were inevitable, and would have occurred no matter where I was at that particular moment in my life.

The title *Lunar Park* is not intended as a take on Luna Park (as it mistakenly appeared on the initial Knopf contracts). The title means something only to my son. These are the last two words of this book, and by then, I hope they will be self-explanatory to the reader as well.

Regardless of how horrible the events described here might seem, there's one thing you must remember as you hold this book in your hands: all of it really happened, every word is true.

The thing that haunted me the most? Since no one knew what was happening in that house, no one was scared for us.

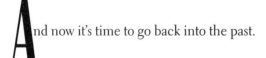

And now it's time to go back into the past.

2. the party

Y ou do an awfully good impression of yourself."

Jayne said this after she looked me over with a confused expression and asked pointedly what I was going as to the Halloween party we were throwing that night, and I told her I'd decided to go simply as "me." I was wearing faded jeans, sandals, an oversized white T-shirt with a giant marijuana flower emblazoned on it and a miniature straw sombrero. We were in a bedroom the size of a large apartment when we shared this exchange, and I tried to clarify things by raising my arms up and turning slowly around to give her a chance to check out the full-on Bret.

"I've decided against wearing masks," I said proudly. "I want to be real, honey. This is what's known as the Official Face." As I continued to turn I noticed Victor, the golden retriever, staring at me, curled in a corner. The dog kept staring and then yawned.

"So you're going as—what? A Mexican pot activist?" she asked, too tired to glare anymore. "What should I tell the kids about that lovely shirt you're wearing?"

"I'll explain to the kids if they ask that—"

"I'll just say it's a gardenia," she sighed.

"Just tell them Bret's just really into the Halloween spirit this year," I suggested, turning around again, arms still raised. "Tell them I'm going as a hunk." I made a playful grab at Jayne, but she moved away too quickly.

"That's really great, Bret—I'm so proud of you," she said unenthusiastically as she walked out of the room. The dog glanced at me worriedly, then heaved itself up and followed Jayne. It did not like to be left alone in any room that I was in. The dog had been a mess ever since I'd arrived in July. And since Jayne had been obsessing over a book called *If Only They Could Speak* (which I thought was an exposé on young Hollywood but was actually an investigation of zoo animals) she had taken the dog through hydrotherapy and acupuncture and to a massage therapist ("Hey, why not get it a personal trainer?" I muttered at one point) and finally it visited a canine behaviorist who prescribed Cloinicalm, which was basically puppy Prozac, but since the drug caused "compulsive licking" a kind of canine Paxil had been prescribed instead (the same medication Sarah was on, which we all thought was extremely distressful). But it still did not like to be left alone in any room that I was in.

The party was my idea. I had been "a good boy" for four months and thought something celebratory was deserved. But since lavish Halloween parties had been a part of my past (the past that Jayne wanted to deny and erase) we fought about this "bash" (my word; Jayne used the term "bacchanal") amiably, even playfully, until—surprise—she gave in. I credited this to the distraction of the upcoming reshoots for a movie she thought she had finished in April but that the studio wanted to tweak after audience testing proved clarifications were needed to simplify a totally ludicrous big-budget thriller that was impossible to follow. I had seen a rough cut in New York the month before and was secretly appalled but in the limo ride back to the Mercer I raved about the thing until Jayne, seething and staring straight ahead, said, "Shut your mouth now, please." In the limo that night I realized Jayne was essentially a simple, private person, a woman who had lucked into a career that seemed fast and baffling to her and that this worry about the reshoots was at the heart of why she relented and allowed me to throw the party on the evening of the thirtieth (trick-or-treating would take up the following night). The invitations had been e-mailed to a smattering of my friends (Jay, who was in town on his book tour; David Duchovny; a few cast members from last season's *Survivor*; my Hollywood agent, Bill Block; Kate Betts, who was here covering something for the *New York Times* Style section; and students from my writing workshop) and also, unfortunately, to a couple of Jayne's acquaintances (mostly parents of Robby's and Sarah's friends, whom she couldn't stand either but had invited in a moment of passive aggression; I kept my mouth shut). Jayne's second way of protesting the party: no costume, just black Tuleh slacks and a white Gucci blouse. "Nothing accessorized with straw and no apple bobbing" were further demands, and when I complained during the planning stages that

Jayne was lacking in Halloween spirit, her concession was to hire an expensive catering company from town. The kids were forewarned that this would be an adult party; they'd be allowed to mingle for the first hour and then it was up to bed since it was a Thursday and hence a school night. In one last-ditch effort Jayne suggested it should be a school night for me as well, that maybe my time would be better spent working instead of throwing a party. But Jayne never understood that the Party had *been* my workplace. It was my open market, my battleground, it was where friends were made, lovers were met, deals were struck. Parties seemed frivolous and random and formless but in fact were intricately patterned, highly choreographed events. In the world in which I came of age the Party was the surface on which daily life took place. When I tried explaining this in earnest, Jayne just stared at me as if I had suddenly become retarded.

I removed the sombrero and looked at myself in the multitude of mirrors in Jayne's bathroom (we each had our own), checking my hair from various angles. I'd had it colored the day before to cover the gray on the sides but was afraid I was slowly losing it, like my father had, even though Joelle, my hairdresser, kept stressing that hair loss was represented by the mother's side of the family. For some reason, "the golden autumnal night" was a phrase that kept repeating itself in my mind as I looked at my hair, and I liked it so much that I decided to incorporate it into my new novel once I sat down the next day to go over the outline. Behind me was a walk-in steam shower with multiple showerheads and a huge tub made from Italian marble that I stared at admiringly whenever I was in Jayne's bathroom; its extravagance touched something in me, defined in some way who I was now, what I had become even as it was also evolving into a symbol of my precariousness in this world. Hair inspection completed, I left the bathroom and ran my hands across the Frette sheets that hugged our massive bed before turning off the lights.

As I made my way down the grand, curving staircase the cell phone in my back pocket rang. After glancing at my Tank watch I checked the incoming number. It was Kentucky Pete, my dealer, and when I answered the phone he said he was en route.

Note to reader: Yes, I was no longer technically clean. I had mildly relapsed. It hadn't taken long. A student party on campus during the third week of September, to be somewhat exact. A geek from the graduate program offered me a line—and then another—in a dingy dormitory bathroom, and then I guzzled twenty beers tapped from a keg while students huddled around me as I regaled them with stories about my former successes. Jayne was hardly oblivious but there were certain waves of information she could not bring herself to ride. If her faith in me had been vaguely faltering since the beginning of October—a sense that taking me back was turning into a mistake—it had not yet hit a crisis point. Though I could tell she was fearful, it was contained and hadn't bloomed out of control. I felt I had time to redeem myself. But not on Halloween.

Because everything was set. The house had been redecorated by the catering company to resemble a huge haunted castle complete with cobwebs dripping everywhere and plastic skeletons and oversized vampire bats dangling from the ceilings and purple lights dousing each wall and a strobe in the foyer. A friend, the artist Tom Sachs, had designed the shipping crate that sat in the middle of the living room and shook and growled at anyone who came near it. From speakers placed outside came the sounds of chains clanking along with various authentic groans and the laughter of the dead. Ghosts made from white crepe paper were floating in the trees and intricately carved jack-o'-lanterns, burning brightly, dotted the stone path leading up to the house. And though this was most decidedly an adult party there was nothing too frightening going down at 307 Elsinore Lane—just something playful and innocent to amuse the guests. As a precaution against crashers we had hired two security guards (one made up as Frankenstein, the other wearing a Dick Cheney mask) and stationed them at the front door behind a velvet rope, each equipped with a blood-spattered guest list and a walkie-talkie. The party would be camcorded by one of my students.

I walked by the kitchen, where Jayne was conferring about canapés with women from the catering company who were dressed suggestively as sexy witches or very alluring cats. Behind them, through the sliding glass doors leading to the backyard, dry ice was being poured into the bubbling Jacuzzi, where the underwater light had been replaced by a dark red bulb for an eerie, cauldronlike effect. And beyond that the crowning touch: the entire nine acres that led from the backyard to a dark bank of trees had been transformed into a giant mock cemetery with crooked gravestones scattered throughout the field, and propped up against the nearest headstone was a plastic ghoul gnawing on a rubber femur.

In the living room a DJ was setting up an elaborate sound system in front of the Andy Warhol silk screen of me holding a pen, and after I introduced myself we went over the song list: "Funeral for a Friend/Love Lies Bleeding," "The Ghost in You," "Thriller," "Witchy Woman," "Evil Woman," "Rhiannon," "Sympathy for the Devil," "Werewolves of London," "Spooky Girlfriend," "The Monster Mash," etc., etc. The DJ assured me there were enough "scary" songs to last the duration of the party. Across the room was a full bar presided over by a werewolf who was preparing the evening's specialty drink: a mandarin-flavored margarita punch, with floating lime rinds shaped like tiny green spiders, which would be served from a huge skull-shaped bowl (I would be holding a nonalcoholic beer can filled with that mandarin-flavored margarita punch). I noticed a row of severed hands lining the bar.

The kids were upstairs. Robby and a friend were locked in a Play-Station 2 frenzy (the zombies with Howitzers, the charging minotaur, the deadly extraterrestrials, the forces of hell, the games that commanded "Let me eat you") while Marta watched over Sarah, who was gazing at her hundredth viewing of *Chico, the Misunderstood Coyote.* Since they were taken care of for the night, it was time to do something about the dog. I noticed Victor sniffing disinterestedly at one of the dozens of stuffed black cats the decorators had placed around the house, and I called for Jayne to put the dog in the garage. Victor and I had a staring contest for two minutes until Jayne came out of the kitchen and simply said his name without looking at me. He loped over to her, grinning, wagging his tail, and as she led him away, the dog turned its head and glared at me. I let it go. The dog had its world—its reasons—and I had mine.

My cell phone rang again. Kentucky Pete was outside and having trouble getting past Frankenstein, who then buzzed me on the intercom and said that someone—not on the list and dressed as the corpse of Slim Pickens—was waiting impatiently by the velvet ropes. Walking toward the front door I told Pete, "Hang on, I'll be right there, dude," and then offered a drawn-out, ghoulish chuckle.

Kentucky Pete was a resilient dinosaur from the seventies that one of my students had hooked me up with. Overweight, with long gray hair and snakeskin boots and a tattoo of an unthreatening scorpion (it was smiling and held a Corona in its pincer) on a forearm covered with sores from the repeated use of nonsterile needles, he was the total opposite of the drug runners I had scored from in Manhattan: trim, sober, good-looking young guys who wore three-button Paul Smith suits and wanted an "in" to the movie business. To make up for his lack of sleekness Kentucky Pete had a more varied selection—he sold everything from lime green Super Vicodin caplets to two-milligram Xanax sent in from Europe to crack dipped in PCP to joints sprayed with embalming fluid to pretty pure coke, which was all I really wanted from him tonight (along with a couple of the two-milligram Xanax to get to sleep, of course). I told Jayne that he was one of my students when she caught him here the first week of October, lounging with me in the media room while we were watching a DVD of *American Psycho*. When she dragged me into the kitchen and just stared in disbelief, I stressed, "Graduate student, honey. *Graduate* student." (When Jayne and I dated in the eighties she basically had an ice cream habit—sometimes she'd indulge, but more often than not she wouldn't.) Not wanting Jayne to see him here tonight, I needed to take care of business fast—even though the house was now doused in so much deep purple light she could easily mistake him for someone in costume. If Jayne ran into him I would just tell her that he was a student dressed as "the grizzled prospector."

I let Kentucky Pete in and, after hesitantly granting him a margarita, quickly led him to my office, where I locked the door and pulled out my wallet. He was in a hurry anyway; he needed to get to the college by eight to sell a large amount of dope to an affluent group of juniors. When he asked if I had a pipe he could borrow, I opened my safe. He downed the punch and heaved a huge, satisfied sigh, humming along to the Zombies singing "Time of the Season."

(What's your name? Who's your daddy? Is he rich? Is he rich like me?)

"What's in there?" he asked, craning his neck, and then, "Dig the sombrero."

"This is where I keep my cash and guns." I reached into the safe and gave him a crystal pipe that under no circumstances did I want returned after its use. I needed two eight balls of the pure stuff and a couple of the heavily cut grams for drunken guests who were going to bum off me and be too wasted to notice the difference. After the transaction was finalized and a discount given in exchange for the pipe, I pocketed the tightly wrapped multicolored packages and led Kentucky Pete outside, walking him across the pumpkin-scattered lawn as he admiringly stared back at the elaborately decorated house.

"Whoa—this place has been turned into one spooky shack, man," he murmured appreciatively.

"It's a spooky world, dude," I said hurriedly, checking my watch.

"Ghoulish, man, ghoulish."

"The spirits will be moaning tonight, my man," I said, maneuvering him toward the motorcycle parked lopsidedly at the curb. "I know all about the darkness, dude. I am primed to party and ready for anything."

Even though it was the end of October an Indian summer had lingered and I shivered at the incongruity of this decidedly nonautumnal weather while Kentucky Pete explained the origins of the holiday: Halloween was based on the Celtic day of Samhain—this was the last day of their calendar and the one time of the year when the dead came back and "grabbed you, dude." And if you went out you had to wear a costume that made you look like one of the dead so they'd be fooled and leave you alone. I kept nodding and saying, "The dead, yeah, the dead." We could hear "Time of the Season" playing from inside the house.

"Adios, amigo," he said, revving up.

"Always a pleasure," I said, patting him on the back. Then, wiping my hands on my jeans, I scurried up to the house and locked myself in my office, where I snorted two massive lines, and exhaling with relief I rushed to the bar with my empty nonalcoholic beer can and had the werewolf fill it with punch. I was now ready for the night to begin.

The guests started arriving. Costumes were fairly predictable: vampires, a leper, Jack the Ripper, a monstrous-looking clown, two ax murderers, someone who seemed to be just hiding under a large white sheet, a bedraggled mummy, a few devil worshippers, and there were a number of fashion models and a plague-ridden peasant, and, as expected, all of my students were zombies. Someone I didn't recognize came as Patrick Bateman, which I didn't find funny and had a problem with; watching this tall, handsome guy in the bloodstained (and dated) Armani suit lurk around the corners of the party, inspecting the guests as if they were prey, freaked me out and somewhat diminished my high, but another trip to the office reclaimed it. Cliques began forming. I was forced into meeting a few of the parents of Robby's and Sarah's friends, discussing another national tragedy before the conversation turned to topics about as interesting as last week's weather: the daughter who didn't get into the desired preschool, unfair soccer leagues, and a book club someone had just started—and when I suggested that they begin with one of my books I was met with what could only be described as "uneasy laughter." Jayne was hiding her anger exquisitely by playing the charming hostess while I waited impatiently for Mr. McInerney, who was giving a reading in town and had called earlier asking for our address again. Sometime during all this Jayne insisted I strap the guitar I kept in my office (a leftover souvenir from my Camden days when I was in bands and thought I was going to be the next Paul Westerberg) over my shoulder to hide the marijuana leaf, after she noticed the concerned looks from a few of the parents, and so I was soon spinning around the party greeting guests while strumming the guitar—which was also a clever way of disarming my students from wanting to talk about their stories (always one of my least favorite topics of conversation—and tonight I did not want to be asked, "Mr. Ellis, have you read 'What I Was Thinking When I Gave Him Head' yet?"). And I didn't really focus on anything in particular until Aimee Light appeared.

Aimee Light was in the graduate department at the college and, though not a student of mine, was doing her thesis on my work, despite the consternation of her advisor, who had tried unsuccessfully to talk her out of it. We met at that same party I relapsed at. She was enamored of me but coolly, objectively, and this distance made her far more alluring than the usual round of sycophants I was accustomed to. I played my own role distractedly, which I could tell subtly frustrated her. Yes, it was back to the youthful game playing I experienced as a college student and I felt younger because of it. Aimee Light was lithe and agile and had the perfect body of a big-breasted, small-boned teenager even though she was nearing twenty-four. Blond hair with hard blue eyes and a steely attitude—she was exactly my type and I had been trying to get her into bed for about a month now, but so far had managed only a few makeout sessions in my office at school and one in her off-campus apartment. She kept pretending that her purpose was obscure. As with so many things in my life she just appeared from nowhere.

She was standing with a friend by the bar and chatting up the were-wolf while the Eagles' "One of These Nights" blasted out and I started to dance across the room toward her. Seeing my approach she quickly whispered something to her companion—a girlish gesture that betrayed her innocence—just as I appeared directly in front of her, flushed and beaming in the purple light, lip-synching the song, gyrating my hips, strumming the guitar. It was a risk inviting her, but she took a bigger risk by actually showing up. I winked at her discreetly.

After Aimee introduced us—"This is Melissa—she's a harridan," and pretty hot as well—I looked around the packed living room and saw Jayne taking David Duchovny outside to show him the fake graveyard.

"Was that wink your idea of an icebreaker?" Aimee asked.

"Wanna play Pass the Pumpkin?" I asked back.

"I like the shirt," she said, lifting the guitar up.

"I like the whole package," I said, looking her over. "What are you going as?"

"Sylvia Plath's divorce attorney."

I took her hand and asked the harridan, "Will you excuse us?"

"Bret—" Aimee warned, but her grip on my hand didn't loosen.

"Hey, we need to talk about your thesis."

She turned back to her friend and made a pleading face.

Still dancing to the Eagles I dragged her through the maze of the party until we reached a bathroom that I made sure was empty before dancing us both inside and locking the door. It was so hushed in there that we might have been the only two people in the house. She leaned against a wall— casual, sly, not really there. I took a long pull from my beer can and then spit out a small lime green spider.

"I thought you weren't going to come," I said accusingly.

"Well, neither did I . . ." She paused. "But, sigh, I wanted to see you."

I took out a gram and asked, "Wanna bump?"

She stared at me, amused, her arms folded across her chest. "Bret, I don't think that's a good idea."

"What are these reluctance issues you have?" I asked, annoyed. "Where do they come from—that uptight little town in Connecticut you escaped?" I busied myself with the gram and poured a small pile onto the counter by the sink. "I'm just offering you a line. How difficult a decision is that?" Then, in a bachelor's voice: "Who's your hot friend?"

She ignored my tactic. "It's not the line."

"Well, good, then I'll do yours."

"It's your wife."

"My wife? Hey, I've only been married three months. Give me a break. We're still testing the waters—"

"Your wife is here plus you're a little blotto." She reached for a black and orange hand towel and wiped my forehead.

"When has that ever stopped us?" I asked "sadly."

"From *what*?" she asked with mock outrage, but then smiled lasciviously.

I hunched over the sink and Hoovered up both lines with a straw and then immediately turned around and pressed into her, the guitar dividing us. When I kissed her mouth, it opened with no resistance and we fell against a wall. I swung the guitar over my shoulder and kept pushing up against her, an erection pulsing in my jeans, while she kept pretending to push me away, but not really. Somewhere during all of this my sombrero fell off.

"You're so hot I can't keep my hands off you," I panted. "Have you ever played doctor?"

She laughed and broke away. "Look, this isn't gonna happen here," and then, studying my head, "Did you do something to your hair?"

I kissed her on the mouth again. And she responded even more urgently this time. We were suddenly interrupted by my ringing cell phone. I ignored it. We kept kissing but I already felt the pangs of disappointment—there was no chance anything more was going to happen in this bathroom tonight—and the phone kept vibrating in my back pocket until I had to answer it.

Aimee finally pushed me away. "Okay—that's enough."

"For now," I said in my sexiest voice, though it came out sounding merely ominous. My arm still around her, I held the phone to my ear with my free hand.

"Yo?" I said, checking the incoming number.

"It's me." It was Jay but I could barely hear him.

"Where are you?" I whined. "Jesus, Jay, you are one lost bastard."

"What do you mean, where am I?" he asked.

"You sound like you're at some kind of party." I paused. "Don't tell me that many people showed up at your goddamn reading."

"Well, open the door and you'll see where I am" was his reply.

"Open which door?"

"The one you're behind, moron."

"Oh." I turned to Aimee. "It's the Jayster."

"Why don't you just let me out first," Aimee suggested, hurrying toward the mirror to make sure everything was in place.

But I opened the door, high and not caring, and Jay stood there, his hair fashionably tousled, wearing black slacks and an orange Helmut Lang button-down.

"Ah, I thought I'd find you in a bathroom." And then Jay turned his gaze on Aimee and said, after looking her over appreciatively, "It's where he can usually be located."

"I have a weak bladder." I shrugged and bent down to retrieve my sombrero.

"And you also have"—Jay reached over and touched my nose as I stood up—"what I am and am not hoping is baby powder above your upper lip."

I leaned toward the bathroom mirror and wiped off the residue of coke, then placed the straw hat back onto my head at what I thought was a raffish angle.

"So creative yet so destructive, I know, I know," Jay said, causing Aimee to crack up.

"Jay McInerney, Aimee Light." I leaned closer to the mirror and checked my nose again.

"I'm a big fan—" Aimee started.

"Hey, watch it." I scowled. "Aimee's a student at the college and she's doing her thesis on *me*."

"So that explains . . . this?" Jay said, gesturing at the scene in the bathroom.

Aimee looked away nervously and said, "Nice to meet you, but I've gotta go."

"Want a bump?" I asked Jay, blocking Aimee's exit.

"Look, I've really gotta go," Aimee said more insistently and squeezed past me, and then I took one last look in the mirror and followed, closing the bathroom door behind us. The three of us, outside in the hall, were suddenly approached by a very tall and sexy cat holding a tray of nachos. I slung the guitar back across my chest, almost hitting her with the neck but she ducked in time. Stevie Wonder's "Superstition" was now pumping through the house.

"Meow," Jay said, and took a chip dripping with cheese.

"I'll see you tomorrow," Aimee muttered.

I nodded, watching as she moved back to where her friend was still chatting up the werewolf. "Hey," I called out. "Enjoy the rest of your evening." And I continued to stare until it became apparent she was not going to look back.

Knocking me out of my reverie, Jay gestured at the cat with the nachos. "I take it the thought of food is the furthest thing from your mind?"

"Want a bump?" I whispered into his ear involuntarily.

"Even though you're sounding like a parrot, there is really no other reason to be here." He looked around the darkened living room as a man dressed as Anna Nicole Smith pushed past us to use the bathroom. "But is there someplace more private?"

"Follow me," I said, and when I noticed him taking another nacho I snapped, "And stop flirting with the help."

But we were trapped. Jay and I were huddled on the periphery of the party, and I was strategizing how to get to my office without Jayne seeing us; back inside, she was introducing David Duchovny to the Allens, our neighbors and truly tiresome bores, and my plans had become increasingly urgent since I desperately needed another line—the garage, I suddenly realized, the *garage*—when I felt someone tugging at my guitar. I looked down: it was Sarah. "Daddy?" she said, her face a frown of concern. She was wearing a little T-shirt with the word BABE on it.

"And who is this?" Jay asked sweetly, kneeling beside her.

"Daddy," Sarah said again, ignoring him.

"She calls you 'Daddy'?" Jay asked, sounding worried.

"We're working on it," I said. "Honey, what is it?"

I noticed Marta on the outskirts of the living room, craning her neck.

"Daddy, Terby's mad," Sarah said, pouting.

Terby was the bird doll I had bought Sarah in August for her birthday. It was a monstrous-looking but very popular toy that she'd wanted badly yet the thing was so misconceived and grotesque—black and crimson feathers, bulging eyes, a sharp yellow beak with which it continuously gurgled—that both Jayne and I balked at buying her one until Sarah's pleas drowned out all reasoning. Since the awful thing was sold out everywhere I'd resorted to using Kentucky Pete—who was very adept at obtaining contraband—to secure one that according to him had been smuggled in from Mexico.

"Terby's mad," Sarah whined again.

"Well, calm him down," I said, glancing around. "Bring him up some nachos. Maybe he's hungry."

"Terby says it's too loud and Terby's mad." Her arms were crossed in a parody of an upset child.

"Okay, baby, we'll take care of it." I stood on my tiptoes and waved at Marta, then pointed down and mouthed, *She's here.* Relieved, Marta started pushing toward us through the mass of bodies.

And suddenly Sarah was surrounded. Adorable children, I'd begun to notice, had that effect on people. Put them in a room full of adults and they were always the star attraction. Girls from my workshop and some of the cat-woman caterers were now leaning in and asking her questions in baby-doll voices, and Sarah soon seemed to forget all about Terby as I slowly pulled McInerney away. The cute little BABE basked in everybody's atten-tion even as "Don't Fear the Reaper" roared through the house—an unset-tling moment, but also my chance to escape.

As I led Jay down a long hallway toward the door that opened into the garage, he said, "You took care of that so well."

"Jay, she's six years old and thinks her bird doll's alive," I said, exasper-ated. "Now, do you want me to stand there and deal with that, or do you want to shut up and do a line with me?"

"You really don't know how to do this, do you?"

"Do what? Throw a kick-ass party?"

"No. Be married. Be the dad."

"Well, being married's okay—but the dad thing's a little tougher," I said. " 'Daddy, can I have some juice?' 'How about some water, honey?' 'Daddy?' 'Yes?' 'Can I have some juice?' 'How about some water instead, honey?' 'Daddy, can I have some juice?' 'Okay, honey, you want some juice?' 'No, it's okay, I'll just have some water.' It's like some fucking Beckett play that we're rehearsing constantly."

Jay just stared at me, grim-faced.

"Hey, but I bought a book," I said flippantly. *Fatherhood for Dummies,* and it is helping immensely. If only *my* father—"

"Okay, I can see what sort of evening this is turning into."

"Hey, how was the reading?" I asked, switching gears.

"I like your little town" was his noncommittal answer, and I realized that the reading had probably been a bust. Not high, I would have wanted to pursue this, but wasted I did not.

I opened the door and ushered Jay into the garage and then peered back down the hallway to see if we'd been followed. I closed and locked the door and flicked on the fluorescent lights. The four-car garage contained my Porsche, Jayne's Range Rover and a motorcycle I'd just purchased with unexpected Swedish royalties. And, I just noticed, a miserable golden retriever that lay waiting for us in the corner, curled up against Robby's bike. But Jay aroused so little interest that Victor barely looked up.

"Ignore that dog," I told him.

"Ah yes, your intimacy problems with animals. I forgot."

"Hey, I dated Patty O'Brien for three months." And then: "Ready for a little *acción*?"

"Indeed." Jay rubbed his hands together eagerly.

"I have brought us some very pure Bolivian Marching Powder," I said, rummaging through my pockets.

"Ooh—the Devil's Dandruff."

I quickly located the stash and handed Jay a packet. He opened it, inspected the coke and then put it down on the hood of the Porsche and started rolling a twenty into a tight green straw.

After I did two huge bumps from my own gram I wanted to show off my new bike.

"Hey, Jayster—check it out. The Yamaha Y2F-RI. A hundred and fifty-two horsepower. Top speed: a hairsbreadth under a hundred and seventy miles per hour," I purred.

"How much?"

"Only ten grand."

"Well spent. What happened to the Ducati?"

"Had to sell it. Jayne thought it was giving Robby bad ideas. And my argument that the kid doesn't care about anything proved totally useless."

"Like father, like—"

"Start panting with eagerness and just do the fucking coke."

Jay did a bump and then paused, grimacing. A moment passed.

"What's the matter?" I asked.

"Actually, this baking powder is cut with *way* too much laxative."

"Oops, wrong stuff." I took the heavily cut junk from Jay, refolded the packet and handed him a proper gram.

"Where's your guy, your dealer?" he asked, still grimacing, licking his lips.

"Um, back at the college. Why?" I asked. "And please don't take a dump in our garage."

"So your refund for that shit is unlikely?" he asked, opening the fresh packet. "Suck-ah!"

"That crap's for wastoids who can't tell the difference—I just gave you the real stuff."

"You're so cheap," he muttered. He did two bumps and flung his head back and then smiled slowly and said, "Now, that's much better."

"Anything for a bud."

"So, really, how is married life?" he asked, lighting a Marlboro and easing into coke chat. "The wife, the kids, the posh suburbs?"

"Yeah, the tragedy's complete, huh?" I laughed hollowly.

"No, really." Jay seemed mildly interested.

"Marriage is great," I said, opening my own packet again. "Unlimited sex. Laughs. Oh yeah, and continuous companionship. I think I've got this down to a science."

"And the ubiquitous student in the bathroom?"

"Just part of the package here at Casa Ellis." I did another bump and then bummed a cigarette.

"No, seriously—who is she?" he asked, lighting it. "I hear today's college women are 'prodigious.' "

"Prodigious? Is that really what you heard?"

"Well, I read it in a magazine. It was something I wanted to believe."

"The Jayster. Always a dreamer."

"I am so relieved. I knew the whole suburban scene was a great idea for you. By the way," he said, gesturing at a plastic skeleton hanging from a rafter, "is this how the house normally looks?"

"Yeah, Jayne loves it."

He paused. "And you're still sleeping on the couch?"

"It's a guest bedroom and it's just a phase—but, wait, how did you know?"

He just inhaled on his cigarette, debating whether to tell me something.

"Jay?" I asked. "Why do you think I'm sleeping in the guest bedroom?"

"Helen told me that Jayne said something about you having bad dreams."

Relieved to have an out, I said, "I'm not having any dreams at all."

Jay's expression led me to believe that this was not all he'd been told.

"Look, we're in couples counseling," I admitted. "It helps."

Jay took this in. "You're in couples counseling." He considered this as I nodded. "After three months of marriage? That does not bode well, my friend."

"Hey, earth to Jayster! We've known each other for almost twelve years, man. It's not like we met last July and just decided to elope." I paused. "And how in the hell did you know I'm sleeping in the guest room?"

"Um, Bretster, Jayne called up Helen." He stopped, did another bump. "Just thought I'd warn you."

"Oh, Jesus, why would Jayne call up your wife?" I tried to toss off this question casually but shuddered with coke-induced paranoia instead.

"She's worried that you're using again, and I guess"—Jay made a gesture—"she's wrong . . . right?"

"Haven't we outgrown all this tired irony? Weren't we supposed to give up acting twenty-two forever?"

"Well, you're wearing a marijuana T-shirt at your own Halloween party, where you just were making out with a coed in the bathroom, so the answer to that, my friend, is a definite nope."

Suddenly the dog had enough and started barking for us to vacate the garage.

"On that note," I said. "We're heading back to the party."

We reentered the labyrinth and weaving through the darkness I felt twitchy. The rooms seemed even more crowded than before, and outside people were swimming in the pool. Realizing that a lot of kids from the college had crashed I started worrying about what Jayne was making of all this. The hallways were so jammed that Jay and I had to walk through the kitchen to get to the living room for drinks and just then Joe Walsh's familiar opening riffs to "Life's Been Good" blasted me into a manic moment of air jamming. Jay looked suitably amused. The sweet aroma of pot began announcing itself in the living room. My heartbeat had doubled because of the cocaine, and I had acquired a new crystalline focus and wanted everyone to be friends. That's when I noticed Robby wandering around in a Kid Rock T-shirt and baggy jeans so I grabbed him roughly by the neck and pulled him toward us. "I bet it took a lot outta you, huh? Coming down all them stairs?" Robby shrugged, and I introduced him to Jay and then handed them both margaritas, which Robby took so reluctantly that I had to playfully smack him around, urging him to drink it. Robby and Jay started having the kind of inane conversations eleven-year-olds have with people approaching fifty. Robby had taken his usual stance when talking to an adult: You mean nothing to me. I noticed he was gripping a baseball designed to look like the moon.

And then more tugging on my guitar: Sarah again.

I rolled my eyes and muttered a curse under my breath. I looked down and sighed: she was wearing tiny white hot pants.

"These are the kids," I told Jay, gesturing at Robby and Sarah. "Her look is glam, and pink is very in on six-year-olds this season. Robby's wearing white hip-hop and is now officially a tween."

"A tween?" Jay asked, then leaned toward me and whispered, "Wait, that's not like a gay thing, is it?"

"No, it's a tween," I explained. "You know, someone who isn't a child or a teenager."

"Jesus," Jay muttered. "They've thought of everything, haven't they?"

Our conversation had not deterred Sarah.

"Daddy?"

"Yes, sweetie? Why aren't you up in bed? Where's Marta?"

"Terby's still mad."

"Well, who's Terby mad at?"

"Terby scratched me." She held out her arm, and I squinted in the purple darkness but couldn't see anything. This was exasperating.

"Robby—take your sister back upstairs. You know she needs her usual twelve hours and it's getting late. It is now officially bedtime."

"Then can I come back down?" he asked.

"No, you cannot," I said, noticing that half his margarita was gone. "Where's your friend?"

"Ashton took a Zyprexa and then fell asleep," Robby said blankly.

"Well, I suggest you take one too, buddy, because tomorrow's a school day."

"It's just Halloween. Nothing's going on."

"Hey, I said it's bedtime, buster. Jeez, kids demand so much attention."

"Daddy!" Sarah shouted again.

"Honey—you've got to get in bed."

"But Terby's *flying*."

"Okay, well, you've got to put him to bed too."

Robby rolled his eyes anxiously and kept sipping from the margarita. Something got stuck in his teeth and he pulled a green spider out of his mouth and studied it as if it meant something.

"Terby's angry," Sarah whined, pulling on my guitar until I knelt down at her level.

"I know, honey," I said soothingly. "Terby sounds like he's a big mess."

"He's on the ceiling."

"Let's get Mommy. She'll get him down."

"But he's on the *ceiling*."

"Then I'll get a broom and knock Terby off the ceiling. Jesus, where's Marta?"

"It tried to bite me."

"Maybe it wants you to brush your teeth and get into bed."

Suddenly Jayne was behind me and above me, talking to Jay, but I couldn't hear their conversation because of the music. They both looked down at me with accusatory expressions, and when I motioned to her she excused herself from Jay and, as I stood up, Sarah still clutching my hand, gave me a withering look. I suddenly realized I was waving a cigarette around and sweating profusely. The room was so packed with people that we were practically crushed together.

"Are you okay?" she said, but it was a statement, not a question.

"Sure, honey, why wouldn't I be okay?" I sniffed loudly. "This is one rockin' party. But your daughter—"

"You're very talkative and sniffly." She was glaring. "And you're sweating."

Sarah tugged on my arm again.

"That's because I'm having fun."

"And look, all around us, half the college showed up and is already inebriated to the point of unconsciousness."

"Honey, you've got to deal with your daughter—her doll's freaking out on her."

"People are complaining that the music's too loud," Jayne said.

"Only your friends, *chica*." I paused. "Plus I can hear you perfectly fine."

"*Chica*? Did you just call me *chica*?"

"Look, if you don't want to be sociable and can't be tremendously cool about how to throw a party . . ." I found myself absently fondling a bowl of candy corn.

"There are students in our pool, Bret."

"I know," I said. "What? They're swimming."

"Jesus, Jay's wasted and so are you."

"Jay does calisthenics," I said indignantly. "He doesn't get wasted."

"What about you, Bret?" she asked. "Do you get wasted?"

"Look, being America's greatest writer under forty is a lot to live up to. It's so hard."

She gave me a scathing look. "I marvel at your courage."

"Will you deal with your daughter, please?"

"Why don't you deal with her?" she said. "She's holding *your* hand."

"But who's going to greet the mystery guests and—"

Jayne walked away midsentence and started talking to someone dressed as Zorro, who was in real life a runner-up on last season's *Survivor*.

I dragged Sarah over to Jayne and said, "Listen—will you take Sarah back up to bed?" I asked, no joke.

"You do it," she said without looking at me.

A moment later, after noticing I was still there, she added, "Get lost."

But Sarah wouldn't go back to her room—she was too frightened, so Marta escorted her to ours. The cocaine was flowing through me as the Ramones were singing, "I don't want to be buried in a pet sematary/I don't wanna live my life again" and when I staggered through a mob of dancing students and saw the Patrick Bateman guy was still here, there was suddenly the sense that the party was verging out of control. Something in me dropped and exploded—a moment of pure, almost visceral despair—and I needed another line. I looked back into the crowd. Jay had drifted over to the celebrities—my wife and David Duchovny—and Robby had disappeared. So I walked up the curving staircase to the second floor to check out Sarah's room—using my investigation of the alleged Terby incident as an excuse to do more blow.

It was so quiet up there that you could barely hear the party downstairs; that's how large the house was. It was also freezing, and I shivered uncontrollably as I moved down the darkened hallway. I walked by Robby's room—his friend was zonked out in the huge king-sized bed, the Steven Spielberg movie 1941 (which had been on a lot lately) glowing from the wide-screen TV, the only light in my son's room. I continued my walk down the hall and stopped at a huge expanse of window that looked out over the backyard: people were swimming in the heated pool and sprawled on chaise longues. A group of students had congregated in the mock graveyard, sharing a joint, and another group was crawling around each other through the headstones. And above the headstones I noticed the moon and a lunar light fanning over the field and there was actually a mist rolling in from the woods and drifting toward the house. I wanted suddenly to do another massive line and join the students when something behind me flickered, then dimmed—it was a wall sconce, wrought-iron and gold-rimmed, one of many that lined the hallway walls about six feet up from the floor. Tonight, though, they'd all been switched off.

But when I walked toward a sconce it lit up briefly and then dimmed as I passed by. This happened at the second sconce I passed, and then at the third. Each time I neared one it began glowing and then as I passed the sconce it dimmed again, as if they were moving with me, lighting my way down the darkened hallway. I started giggling at what I thought was a brief hallucination, but since it kept happening with each sconce I approached my hope that this was a drug-induced vision no longer made any sense. So I concluded it had something to do with how complicated the electrical situation had become due to the party—all the purple lights and extension cables causing problems throughout the house. That was what I told myself as I made my way toward the darkness of Sarah's room.

The first thing I noticed was that her window was open, the curtains billowing in the hot night wind. I turned on the lights and moved through the faux French country–style room and looked out the window. The guitar was blocking me from getting a decent vantage point so I took it off and laid it gently on the cowhide carpeting that covered the floor. Below me, I could see the bouncers talking to two girls who were trying to crash the party, all four of them laughing and gesturing intimately at one another and I realized the girls had already been inside and were now just flirting with the guys guarding the door. I also noticed the number of cars crowding Elsinore Lane and then, moving among them, a tall figure dressed in a suit. I breathed in and stuck my head farther out the window to get a better look. The figure briefly turned as if he knew he was being watched, and I glimpsed the face of the guy who came to the party dressed as Patrick Bateman. I shuddered with relief that he was leaving—again, another reminder to boost myself up. (He was just a prank, I told myself; he was just the unexpected detail that materializes at every party, I told myself.) When I shut the window and turned around, whatever whimsy the room once held—cool, girly, Crayola-inspired—had inexplicably vanished.

The only real damage I initially noticed was that a small bookshelf had been overturned. I knelt down and pushed it back up against the wall and haphazardly piled books and toys into its shelves when I remembered something Sarah said and slowly looked up at the ceiling. There were marks directly above her bed. I couldn't be sure at first but as I neared them I noticed that these marks looked like scratches—as if something had been crawling along the length of the ceiling, hooking its claws into it. I began fumbling for the packet of coke in my jeans when I glanced at the bed. And that was the moment I saw the pillow. Something had torn the pillow open, clawing it in two (yes, that was the word that sprang to mind: *clawing*) and scattering feathers all over the comforter. The pillow looked as if it had been, well, attacked, since the pillowcase was shredded, as if something had lunged at it continually, and when I touched the pillow, hesitantly, I recoiled, because the pillow was also wet. At that point—when my index finger came away *slimed*—I immediately wiped my hand on my jeans and decided to head downstairs and lock myself in the office for the duration of the night. I was going to let Jayne and Marta deal with this. My first thought was that Jayne's troubled daughter had caused this damage herself, and I would leave the pillow as evidence.

But as I turned to leave the room, there it was: the Terby. It was sitting innocently by the door. I had not remembered seeing it when I first entered the room and it just sat there, waiting, covered with its black and crimson feathers, its bulging yellow doll eyes and its sharp glistening beak. I realized, somewhat sickeningly, that I would have to pass the thing in order to get out of the room. Stepping forward, I neared it cautiously, as if it were alive, when suddenly it moved. It started wobbling on its claws toward me.

I gasped and backed away.

I was freaked out but only momentarily, since I realized someone had just left the thing on. So I composed myself and moved toward it again. Its movements were so clumsy and mechanical that I giggled at myself for having become so frightened. The gurgling noises it was now making sounded prerecorded and filled with static — nothing like the abnormal bird sounds I had expected.

I sighed. I needed to take a Xanax and I would go down to my office, maybe finish what was left of one of the grams, drink another margarita and mellow out alone. That was the plan. I was flooded with relief and I continued laughing at myself — at how the combination of the coke and the doll had struck something awful in me, and that awful feeling dissipated entirely as I leaned down and picked up the doll. I turned it over and saw that the red light on the back of its neck was blinking, meaning that the thing had been activated. I flipped a small switch beneath the light and turned the Terby off. There was a whirring noise and the doll went limp. As I laid the doll down on Sarah's bed next to the mutilated pillow I realized the thing was actually warm and something was pumping beneath its feathers. An unnerving silence had filled the room, even though the party was dancing below me. I suddenly needed to get out of there.

And as I turned away from Sarah's room something sang out in a clear, high-pitched voice that turned into a guttural squawking — it was coming from the bed — and an adrenaline rush surged through me, out of me, enveloping the cavernous bedroom. I didn't look back as I raced down the hallway, the sconces flickering on and off as I rushed past them, and as I tumbled down the curving staircase heading toward the sanctity of my office, I realized that for me the party had ended.

3. morning

woke up in the guest bedroom with no idea of how I'd gotten there, but I didn't panic—I took this in stride—because the guest bedroom was something that had been happening with a regularity I hadn't found alarming yet. Victor was barking from somewhere inside the house, and the clock on the nightstand said 7:15. I groaned and pushed my face deep into a pillow (it was damp; I had been crying in my sleep again) but then sat up quickly, with the realization that I needed to prove something this morning: that I was responsible, that I wasn't an addict, that I was clean. But I couldn't rouse myself because the hangover was intense and accompanied by its usual horniness: a painfully hard erection was sticking out of my boxers, which I stared at futilely, doing nothing with it. Finally I was gazing at myself in the mirror of the guest bathroom. I had the dehydrated and haggard face of a man ten years older, and my eyes were so red that you couldn't see the irises. I guzzled water from the tap, then decided to make myself halfway presentable by pulling off the T-shirt with the marijuana leaf on it and then putting it back on inside out. Since I couldn't find my jeans I tore the top sheet off the bed and draped myself in it. I walked out of the room a ghost.

Trudging toward the kitchen, I passed the housekeeper, Rosa, vacuuming the living room and I followed large footprints that seemed to have been stamped in ash onto the beige carpeting, which this morning seemed shaggier and darker than normal. As the ghost padded through the living room it stopped when it noticed the odd formation of the furniture. The sectional couch, the Le Corbusier chairs and the Eames tables had been rearranged for the party, yet this new setup now seemed weirdly familiar to me. I wanted to figure out why, but the sound of the vacuum merging with Victor's barking forced the ghost to move quickly toward the kitchen.

The house had been referred to as a McMansion in the *Talk* article: nine thousand square feet and situated in a fast-growing and wealthy suburb, and 307 Elsinore Lane wasn't even the grandest in the community—it merely reflected the routine affluence of the neighborhood. It was, according to a spread in *Elle Decor*, "minimalist global eclectic with an emphasis on Spanish revival" but with "elements of midcentury French chateau and a touch of sixties Palm Springs modernism" (imagine that if you can; it was not a design concept everyone grasped). The interior was done in soothing shades of sandcastle and white corn, lily and bleached flour. Stately and lavish, slick and sparsely furnished, the house had four high-ceilinged bedrooms and a master suite that occupied half of the second story and included a fireplace, a wet bar, a refrigerator, two 165-square-foot walk-in closets and window shades that disappeared into pockets in the ceiling, and each of the two adjoining bathrooms had a giant sunken tub. There was a fully equipped gym where I sometimes exercised halfheartedly and where Jayne's personal trainer, Klaus, helped sculpt her flawless body—and there was a sprawling media room with a plasma TV that had a screen the size of a small wall and surround sound and hundreds of DVDs shelved alphabetically on either side of it, as well as a red felt antique pool table. And the house flowed: large, carefully designed empty spaces merged seamlessly into one another to give the illusion that the house was far grander than it actually was.

The ghost floated toward the kitchen, or "family headquarters," that really was a marvel—all stainless steel and countertops made from Brazilian concrete, a Thermador range, a Sub-Zero refrigerator, two dishwashers, two stoves with noiseless fans, two sinks, a wine cooler, a drawer freezer and an entire wall of sliding glass that overlooked an Olympic-sized swimming pool (without guard rails since Sarah and Robby were already expert swimmers) and a Jacuzzi and a vast, intensely green and lush lawn, which was bordered by a huge and carefully maintained garden blooming with flowers I didn't know the names of, and beyond all that was the clearing and then the woods. The ghost saw no party detritus cluttering the house. It was immaculate. Confused but impressed, the ghost stared at a vase of fresh tulips sitting in the center of the kitchen table.

Marta was already up, fiddling with a Gaggia espresso maker as the chic, hungover ghost wrapped in the Frette sheet hovered around the kitchen, placing his burning forehead against the wine-cooling cabinet for one brief moment (the ghost noticed bitterly that it was empty) before falling into a chair at the giant round table on the far side of the room. Marta was a purposefully unattractive woman in her midthirties whom Jayne had befriended while shooting a movie in L.A. She was loyal and discreet and handled all of Jayne's business effortlessly—just one of the thousands of women from that town so attracted to celebrity and so devoted to its demands that she followed Jayne across the country to these cold and unknown suburbs. Before Jayne she had worked for Penny Marshall, Meg Ryan and, briefly, Julia Roberts, and she had the eerie ability to intuit whatever need or request the celebrity might have at any moment. Plus the kids seemed responsive to her, which took a lot of pressure off their mother. Jayne's trust in her was what gave Marta drive and ambition; it was what flattered her and gave her sustenance. This was as close as she was ever going to get to being famous herself, and Marta took the job seriously. But she seemed sad to me, since growing up in that world I had encountered hundreds of Martas—women (and men) so enslaved to the cause of celebrity that their own world was annihilated. She had a small apartment—that Jayne paid for—in town. (I didn't know where Rosa lived, only that her quiet Salvadorian father would pick her up from Elsinore Lane at eight in the evening and bring her back the next morning at dawn.)

The ghost needed coffee.

And suddenly Marta was setting an Hermès Chaine d'Ancre china cup filled with steamy, milky espresso in front of him, and the ghost mumbled his thanks as she went over to the Waring juice extractor and started squeezing oranges. Strung out, the ghost stared at the copper pans hanging from a rack above the island in the middle of the kitchen, morosely sipping his coffee as his eyes shifted to the *Daily Variety* already sitting on top of a pile that included the *New York Times*, the Calendar section from the *Los Angeles Times* and the *Hollywood Reporter*. Hearing voices from upstairs, I breathed in deeply as I reached for our local paper, preparing myself, because I was still—even without a hangover—having trouble adjusting to the schedules everyone inhabiting this house maintained. So after Marta left the kitchen to get Sarah (who was practicing a second language on flash cards) I roused myself and poured a large glass of freshly squeezed OJ and dosed it with a half-empty bottle of Ketel One left over from the party and neatly hidden among all the olive oil at the end of the counter. It was a small miracle no one had gotten rid of it. I sipped the cocktail carefully and returned to the table.

The newspapers kept stroking my fear. New surveys provided awful statistics on just about everything. Evidence suggested that we were not doing well. Researchers gloomily agreed. Environmental psychologists were interviewed. Damage had "unwittingly" been done. There were "feared lapses." There were "misconceptions" about potential. Situations had "deteriorated." Cruelty was on the rise and there was nothing anyone could do about it. The populace was confounded, yet didn't care. Unpublished studies hinted that we were all paying a price. Scientists peered into data and concluded that we should all be very worried. No one knew what normal behavior was anymore, and some argued that this was a form of virtue. And no one argued back. No one challenged anything. Anxiety was soaking up most people's days. Everyone had become preoccupied with horror. Madness was fluttering everywhere. There was fifty years of research supporting this data. There were diagrams illustrating all of these problems — circles and hexagons and squares, different sections colored in lime or lilac or gray. Most troubling were the fleeting signs that nothing could transform any of this into something positive. You couldn't help being both afraid and fascinated. Reading these articles made you feel that the survival of mankind didn't seem very important in the long run. We were doomed. We deserved it. I was so tired. (What worried Jayne besides the upcoming reshoots? The kids were mimicking our facial expressions, which for the last month had consisted of hassled grimaces.)

And so many children were missing that it bordered on an epidemic. About a dozen boys had disappeared since I arrived in July — only boys. Their photos were flashed on the Internet and updates were posted on special Web sites devoted to them, their solemn faces staring out at you, their shadows following you everywhere. I read about another missing Boy Scout — the third in the last year. This boy, too, was Robby's age, and his witless, angelic face now graced the front page of the newspaper. But none of these children had been found. No bodies discovered in the ravine or in the concrete drainpipe; no remains in the dry creek bed or in the suspicious duffel bag tossed off the turnpike; nothing lying naked and defiled in the woods. These boys had vanished without a trace, and there were no hints that any of them was ever coming back. Investigators were on "frantic searches." Parents of the missing boys were urged to appear on CNN and humanize their child in case the abductors were watching. Except for increasing ratings, these news conferences accomplished nothing beyond serving as a reminder of "the incidental malice of the universe" (courtesy of *Time*). This publicity was supposed to mobilize volunteers but people were giving up hope—so many boys were missing, people had simply become alienated and longed for a lesser horror to take this one's place. There were candlelight vigils where families linked hands and lowered their heads, grief-stricken and praying, though to me they more often resembled participants in a séance. Various organizations proposed plaques to memorialize the lost. Students at Buckley (the private school Robby and Sarah attended) were encouraged to e-mail condolences to the bereaved parents. We were supposed to rehearse our children on the usual tired litany: don't talk to strangers, ignore the well-dressed soft-spoken man looking for help to find his puppy; "Yell and Tell" and "Rehearse a Route" and "Avoid the Clown." Distrust everybody was the message. Everywhere people heard the sound of children weeping. Silly Putty was used in school classes for squeezing out tension. We were advised to always keep recent photographs of our children on hand.

And now the missing Boy Scout inevitably provoked the flicker of worry I experienced every morning before Robby and Sarah went off to school, especially if the hangover was bad or I'd had too much coffee. This wide-awake nightmare lasted no more than thirty seconds, a rapid montage that nonetheless required a Klonopin: a rampage at the school, "I'm so scared" being whispered over the cell phone, what sounds like firecrackers popping off in the background, the ricocheting bullet that hurls the second-grader to the floor, the random firing in the library, the blood sprayed over an unfinished exam, the red pools of it forming on the linoleum, the desk spattered with viscera, a wounded teacher ushering dazed children out of the cafeteria, the custodian shot in the back, the girl murmuring "I think I've been hit" before she faints, the CNN vans arriving, the stuttering sheriff at the emergency press conference, the bulletins flashing on TV screens, the "concerned" anchorman offering updates, the helicopters hovering, the final moments when the gunman places the Magnum in his mouth, the overcrowded hospital emergency rooms and the gymnasiums transformed into makeshift morgues, the yellow crime tape ribboned around an entire playground—and then, in the aftermath: the .22 rifle missing from the stepfather's cabinet, the journal recounting the boy's rejection and despair, a boy who took the teasing hard, the boy who had nothing to lose, the Elavil that didn't take hold or the bipolar disorder not detected, the book on witchcraft found beneath the bed, the X carved into his chest and the attempted suicide the month before, the broken hand from punching a wall, the nights lying in bed counting to a thousand, the pet rabbit found later that afternoon hanged from a hook in a small closet—and, finally, the closing images of the endless coverage: the flag at half-staff, the memorial services, the hundreds of bouquets and candles and toys that filled the steps leading up to the school, the bloody hand of a victim on the cover of *Newsweek*, the questions asked, the simple shrugs, the civil suits filed, the copycats, the reasons you quit praying. Still, the worst news comes out of your own child's mouth: "But he was normal, Dad—he was just like me."

Though I hadn't realized it, Jayne had walked into the kitchen without saying anything to the sniffling blob wrapped in the sheet hunched over the table. She was standing over the stove waiting for a pot of water to boil (she was making oatmeal for the kids), her back to me. I tried to translate her body language and failed. I zoned out again on the countertop specifically designed for the placement of olive oil bottles. Victor soon shuffled in. The dog stared at me. *You bore me,* it was thinking. *Go ahead—make my day,* it was thinking.

"Why does that very rude golden retriever bark all night long?" I asked, glaring back at the dog.

"Maybe because he got freaked out by the sight of your nineteen-year-old students screwing in our garage," Jayne said immediately, without turning around. "Maybe because Jay McInerney was skinny-dipping in our pool."

"That doesn't sound like . . . the Jayster," I said tentatively.

"Someone had to haul him out after you disappeared," she said. "With a net."

"Who's Annette?" I realized something. "Oh, what net?" I asked flippantly. "We don't own a net." Worried pause. "Do we?"

"I looked around but you were already passed out in the guest room." She said this with the fake nonchalance she had been developing since I moved into the house.

I sighed. "I did not 'pass out,' Jayne. I was exhausted."

"Why, Bret? Why were you so exhausted?" she asked, her voice now clenched.

I sipped my drink. "Well, that dog's been doing its big barking routine and begging for attention the entire week. You know, honey, this happened to coincide with me starting my novel and so it's extremely distracting and suspicious."

"Yes, I know, Victor doesn't want you to write another book," Jayne said, turning the stove off and moving toward the sink. "I'm so with you on that one."

"I never see that dog frolic," I muttered. "He's been depressed ever since I moved in and I never see him frolic."

"Well, when you kicked him the other night—"

"Hey, he was trying to eat a stick of butter," I exclaimed, sitting up. "He was going after that loaf of cornbread on the counter."

"Why are we talking about the dog?" she snapped, finally facing me.

After a contained silence I sipped my juice again and cleared my throat. "So, you wanna read me my rights?" I sighed.

"Why bother?" she said tightly, turning away. "You're still in a coma."

"I suppose we'll be discussing this in couples counseling."

She said nothing.

I decided to change the topic, hoping for a softer reaction. "So who was the guy who came as Patrick Bateman last night?" I asked. "The guy in the Armani suit with all the fake blood on it?"

"I have no idea. A student of yours? One of your legions of fans? Why do you care?"

"I . . . didn't recognize him," I murmured. "I thought—"

"You thought what? That I knew him?"

"Never mind." I shut up and thought about things for a moment or two. "And did you ever figure out what happened in Sarah's room?" I asked gently. "Because, Jayne, I think maybe she did it." I paused for emphasis. "But she told me her doll did it—that bird thing, you know, the Terby I bought last summer—and, y'know, that's pretty worrisome. And by the way, where was Marta when this so-called attack happened? I think that's pretty—"

Jayne whirled toward me. "Why are you avoiding the fact that maybe one of your drunk, fucked-up students did it?"

"My students had better things to do last night than ransack our daughter's—"

"Yeah, like fuck in our shower—I have no idea who they were—and snort coke off the countertop in the kitchen." She was still glaring at me, hands on her hips.

A long pause in which I built to an outraged "People were in the kitchen last night?!?"

"Yeah. People were doing drugs in the kitchen, Bret." She recited this line in her hip-wary mode.

"Honey, look, drugs may have been done, but I'm sure they were consumed quietly and with discretion." I paused helplessly.

"And I know you were doing them too." Something caught in her throat, the sarcasm evaporated and she turned away from me again. She bowed her head. I noticed one hand was curled tightly into a fist. I could hear the erratic breathing that comes before tears.

"You mean I used to be doing them," I said softly. "That sentence should be in the past tense." I paused. "I'm up, aren't I?"

"Barely," she muttered. "You're a wreck."

"Look." I made a useless gesture. "I'm sipping juice and scanning the papers."

She suddenly composed herself. "Oh, forget it, forget it, forget it."

"And why are you calling up Jay's wife and asking—"

"I wouldn't have to call Helen if you weren't using again," she said in a loud, anguished voice. She stopped and took a series of deep breaths to calm herself down. "I can't do this now. Let's just forget it."

"That sounds reasonable," I murmured gently, turning back to the papers. I attempted a long gulp from my glass but juice sloshed over the rim so I gave up and put it down on the table with a shaking hand.

Outraged by my casual tone, Jayne whirled around again. "It is illegal, Bret. Just because it was consumed in our house—"

"A private residence!" I shouted back.

"—doesn't make it any more legal."

"Well, it isn't technically legal, but . . ."

She waited for me to finish the sentence. I chose not to.

"I didn't do drugs last night, Jayne."

"That's a lie." She broke down. "You're lying to me, and I don't know what to do about it."

With great effort the ghost stood up and shuffled over to her. The ghost wrapped itself around her, and she let him. She was shaking, and between sobs was the trembling intake of uneven breaths.

"How about you believe me . . . and . . ."—I turned her around so we were facing each other and I stared at her pleadingly, my eyes sad and wistful—"just love me?"

There was a new silence in the kitchen. I glanced over at the dog as Jayne collapsed into me, hugging so tightly that I started to wheeze. Victor was staring at me. *You bore me*, it was thinking. *You are a jerk*, it was thinking. I glared until he lost interest, licked a paw and then turned away. He couldn't stand the sight of me, and he knew that I knew it. And he liked that

I knew. That's what drove me crazy: the dog knew that *I* knew it hated me and *liked* it. When I looked back at Jayne, she was staring at me so hopefully that her expression almost bordered on madness and I wanted to let go first.

But then Jayne gently pushed me away and simply said, "We're having dinner at the Allens' on Sunday. I couldn't get out of it."

"That sounds like . . ." I gulped. "Fun. Really fun."

After she left to get Robby my stomach erupted, and leaving my cocktail on the table I hurriedly ran into the closest bathroom and sat down on the toilet just as an explosive torrent of diarrhea hit the water. Gasping, I reached for the latest issue of *Wallpaper* and flipped through it while my stomach kept emptying itself. I stared at another sunken tub and then out the small bay window as Elsinore Lane began waking up, and I saw the boy who spent the night walk from our house—the pumpkins still dotting the path—to the house next to ours and realized it was Ashton Allen; he was momentarily so close to the window that I could read his T-shirt—KEEP STARING, I MIGHT DO A TRICK—and then a sparrow landed on the sill and I turned away. The bathroom was soon enveloped in an odor particular to the remnants of a drunken night—the smell of excrement and alcohol commingled in a rancid stench that forced me out of the room almost as quickly as I had rushed in.

When I hobbled back into the kitchen, Jayne was pouring hot water into ceramic bowls and Robby was standing at the table drinking from my glass, grimacing. "Mom, this orange juice tastes funny. Is there any Tropicana left?"

"Robby, hon, I don't want you drinking Tropicana," Jayne said. "Marta squeezed some fresh juice for you. It's by the sink."

"This *is* fresh juice," he muttered.

I stood in the doorway until Robby put the glass down and moved over to the juicer. (Nonfresh juice was largely prohibited because it caused cavities and obesity.) As I made my way to the table Robby turned around and saw me and did the subtlest double take before casually moving over to his backpack, which he was in the process of rearranging. Robby still didn't seem used to my presence, but I wasn't used to his either. We were both scared and wary of each other, and I was the one who needed to make a connection, to mend us, but his reluctance—as loud and insistent as an anthem—seemed impossible to overcome. There was no way of winning him over. I had failed him utterly—his downward gaze whenever I entered a room reminded me of this. And yet I still resented the fact that he—not myself—lacked the courage to make that first move.

"Hey, kid," I said, sitting down at the table and chugging the rest of the screwdriver. It went down sourly, and I shut my eyes until the alcohol's warmth began coursing through my system, causing my eyelids to flutter open. Robby mumbled a response. It was enough. School lasted from 8:15 until 3:15, and various after-school programs often pushed their return to 5:15, so there was usually nine hours of peace. But then I realized tonight was trick-or-treating and that I had to be at the college by noon (a counseling day, but mostly an excuse to see Aimee Light) and then I had an appointment with my shrink, Dr. Kim, and somewhere during this ordeal a lot of Xanax was going to have to be ingested and a nap taken. The housekeeper walked in and said something to Jayne in Spanish. They had a little conversation I couldn't possibly follow until Rosa nodded intensely and moved out of the kitchen.

Since it was Halloween and a free-dress day at school Robby was wearing a WHAT? ME WORRY? T-shirt and oversized cargo pants—his clothes were always too big, too baggy, and everything had a label on it. A pair of Rollerblades were slung over his shoulder, and he let Jayne know that he'd just downloaded something from a *Buffy the Vampire Slayer* Web site and he was wondering how to fit a soccer ball into a new Targus RakGear Kickflip backpack, which weighed an "acceptable" twenty-five pounds (the Nike BioKNX had caused "spinal aching" according to his physician). He was holding a magazine, *GamePro*, to read on the car ride to school, and was anxious about an oral quiz on the formation of waterfalls. As I flipped through the papers Robby complained about noises last night, after the party was over. But he was unsure where they were coming from—the attic, or maybe on the roof, but also definitely on the sides of the house. There were scratching sounds at his door, he said, and when he woke up this morning, his furniture had been rearranged, and he found three or four deep grooves on the bottom of his door (which he insisted he didn't make), and when he touched the doorknob it was wet. "Someone slimed it," he said, shuddering.

I looked up from the paper and saw Jayne glaring at me while she asked, "What do you mean, hon?"

But, as usual when Robby was asked for specifics, he drooped and went silent.

I reanimated myself and tried to think of a question to ask him that would not require any elaboration, but then Sarah and Marta wandered in. Sarah was wearing a frilly T-shirt with the word *lingerie* in spangly silver letters. And then Victor bounded up to her, relieved and wiggling with happiness, before moving to the glass wall and staring intently into the backyard while barking like mad, causing my head to explode.

"Sit, Victor! Heel. Heel!" I demanded. "Jeez, can't somebody get that dog to mellow out?" I turned back to the papers but Sarah was leaning into me with the Christmas list she'd already made, a Pokémon stadium leading a long computerized column. I reminded her it was October (this didn't register) and then started going down the list with her until I looked to Jayne for help, but she was on her cell phone and bagging the kids' lunches (the sugar-free graham crackers, the bottles of Diet Snapple) while saying things like "No—the kids are booked solid."

Sarah kept explaining to me what each item on the list meant to her until I casually interrupted. "How's everything with Terby, honey?" I asked. (Had I really been so afraid of it last night? Everything seemed different now in the light of morning: bright, clean, sane.)

"Terby's okay" is all she said, but it worked: she forgot about the Christmas list and moved over to finger paintings she'd made yesterday for show-and-tell and carefully started sliding them into a manila envelope. Robby was checking his palm pilot while swaggering around the kitchen—his way of acting tough.

I suddenly noticed a paperback of *Lord of the Flies* in the mass of school gear on the table and picked it up. Opening the cover I was shocked to find Sarah's name handwritten on the first page. "Wait a minute," I said. "I can't believe they're letting first-graders read this."

Everyone—except Sarah—glanced at me.

"I don't even understand this book *now*. Jeez, why don't they just assign her *Moby Dick*? This is absurd. This is *crazy*!" I was waving the book at Jayne when I noticed Sarah staring at me with a confused expression. I bent toward her and said, in a calm, soothing, rational tone, "Honey, you don't need to read this."

Sarah glanced fearfully at her mother. "It's on our reading list," she said quietly.

Exasperated, I asked Robby to show me his curriculum.

"My what?" he asked, standing rigidly still.

"Your schedule, dummy."

Robby tentatively rummaged through his backpack and pulled out a crumpled computerized list: Art History, Algebra 1, Science, Basic Probability, Phys Ed, Statistics, Nonfiction Literature, Social Studies and Conversational Spanish. I stared at the list dully until he sat down at the table and I handed it back to him. "This is insane," I muttered. "It's outrageous. Where are we sending them?"

Robby suddenly concentrated on his bowl of muesli—having pushed aside the oatmeal Marta had placed in front of him—and reached for a carton of soy milk. Jayne kept forgetting that Robby couldn't stand oatmeal, but it was something I always remembered since I couldn't stand oatmeal either.

He finally shrugged. "It's okay."

"The school counselor said that getting a child into an Ivy League school starts in first grade," Jayne said casually, as if not to alarm the children, who I assumed weren't listening anyway.

"Actually earlier," Marta reminded her.

"She's hyping you, baby," I sighed. "Don't play dat game, sistah."

Robby suddenly giggled, much to my gratification.

Jayne scowled. "Don't use fake rap talk around the kids. I hate it."

"And I hated that counselor," I said. "You know why? Because she was feeding off your anxiety, baby."

"Let's not have this conversation now," Jayne said, washing her hands in the sink, her neck muscles taut. "Are we almost ready, kids?"

I was still dumbfounded by Robby's schedule and I wanted to say something consoling to him but he had finished the muesli and was reloading his backpack. He studied a computer game, Quake III, as if he didn't know what to do with it, then pulled out his cell phone to make sure it was charged.

"Hey, buddy, what are you doing taking a cell phone to school?"

He looked nervously over at Jayne, who was now drying her hands with a paper towel. "All the kids have them," she said simply.

"It's abnormal for eleven-year-olds to have cell phones, Jayne," I said, hitting what I hoped was the right tone of indignation.

"You. Are. Wearing. A. Sheet," Jayne said—this was her response.

Robby seemed lost, as if he didn't know what to do.

Finally, thankfully, Sarah broke the silence.

"Mommy, I brushed my teeth," she offered.

"But don't you brush after eating, honey?" Jayne asked, pointing out something to Marta in her datebook concerning the trip to Toronto next week for the reshoots. "I think you should brush your teeth after breakfast."

"I brushed my teeth," Sarah said again, and when that got no response from Jayne she turned to me. "Bret, I know the alphabet."

"Well, you should by now," I said encouragingly but also confused about why a girl so proud of having learned the alphabet should be reading *Lord of the Flies*.

"I know the alphabet," she stated proudly. "A B C D E F—"

"Honey, Bret has a big headache. I'm gonna take your word on this one."

"—G H I J K L M N—"

"You can identify the sounds letters make. Sweetie, that's really excellent. Jayne?"

"—O P Q R S T U V—"

"Jayne, would you please give her a sugar-free doughnut or something?" I touched my head to indicate *migraine approaching*. "Really."

"And I know what a rhombus is!" Sarah shouted gleefully.

"Fabulous."

"And a hexagon!"

"Okay, but take pity on me just now, munchkin."

"And a trapezoid!"

"Honey, Daddy's grouchy and sleepy and about to throw up so couldn't you keep it down a little?"

She immediately turned to Jayne. "Mommy, I'm keeping a journal," she announced. "And Terby's helping me with it."

"Maybe Bret can get a little help from Terby with his writing," Jayne offered caustically, without looking up from the notes she was going over with Marta.

"Baby, my novel is so happening right now I can hardly believe it myself," I droned, flipping through *USA Today*'s Sports section.

"But Terby's sad," Sarah said, pouting.

"Why? I thought he was doing okay," I said, partially disinterested. "Is he having a bad fur day?"

"He says you don't like him," Sarah said, twisting in her chair. "He says you never play with him."

"The thing is lying. I play with him constantly. While you're at school. In fact, Terby beat me at backgammon on Tuesday. Don't believe a thing Terby—"

"Bret," Jayne snapped. "Stop it."

"Mommy?" Sarah asked. "Does Daddy have a cold?"

"Honey, your daddy's contaminated right now," Jayne said, placing a bowl of oatmeal topped with raspberries in front of Sarah.

"And Mommy's all bitched up," I muttered.

Jayne either didn't hear me or pretended to ignore that one. "And we'll all be late if we don't hurry."

And then I zoned out on everything surrounding me until I heard Jayne say, "You'll have to ask your dad."

When I snapped out of it, Robby was looking at me anxiously.

"Forget it," he mumbled.

"No, come on," I said. "Ask me what?"

His face was so troubled that I wished I knew the question myself and could simply answer it without Robby having to ask it.

Dreading this, he asked, "Can we get *The Matrix* DVD?"

Quickly, I thought this through. He braced himself for my answer.

"But we already have it on video," I said slowly as if answering a trick question.

"Yeah, but the DVD has extras and—"

"Of what? Keanu—"

"Bret," Jayne said loudly, interrupting her discussion of Sarah's ballet schedule with Marta, then turned on Robby. "Why are you wearing that T-shirt?" she suddenly asked him.

"What's wrong with it?" I interjected, trying to save myself.

"We can't wear costumes to school, remember?" Robby darkly muttered. "Remember?" he asked accusingly.

He was referring to the e-mail sent out to parents about Halloween this year. Even though there would be parties in the afternoon, the school was warning against costumes, preferring that the kids come as "themselves." The school originally had okayed "appropriate" costumes while actively discouraging anything inappropriate (nothing "violent" or "scary" or "with weapons"), but predictably, the children, even on all their meds, started to freak out en masse, so costumes were simply banned (exhausted parents pleaded for a compromise—"Nominally frightening?"—which was rejected). This disappointed Robby gravely, so while Jayne was inspecting glasses that had just been in the dishwasher, I tried to console my son. In a fatherly way I assured him that going without a costume was probably in everyone's best interest, offering as a cautionary tale my own seventh grade Halloween when I'd gone to school as the Bloody Vampire and wasn't allowed to march in the annual parade for the elementary students because I had slathered so much Fun Blood on my mouth and chin and cheeks that it was certain to frighten them, according to the principal. This had been so deeply embarrassing—a pivotal moment, really—that it was the last time I ever wore a costume. It was that shameful. The memory of sitting alone on a bench while my classmates marched in front of the delighted elementary students still burned. I suddenly expected Robby to find me far more interesting than he previously had.

An awkward silence filled the kitchen. People had been listening to my story. Jayne was holding a cracked margarita glass and staring at me strangely. I slowly noticed that everyone else—Sarah, Marta, Robby, even Victor—was also staring at me strangely.

Robby, looking completely confused, finally spoke, quietly and with as much dignity as he could muster. "Who said I wanted to go as . . . the Bloody Vampire?" He paused. "I wanted to go as Eminem, Bret."

"Just because your father was a total freak at your age doesn't mean you are, honey," Jayne said.

"The Bloody Vampire?" Robby stared at me, aghast.

I looked helplessly at Jayne, whose face now suddenly relaxed. She studied me for a longish moment, trying to figure something out.

"Yeah?" I asked her, as I slowly handed Robby a fifty-dollar bill.

"I just realized something I wanted to ask you," Jayne said.

"What is it?"

The dog became interested in my answer. It gave me a quick sideways glance.

"Have you ever had to empty a dishwasher? I'm just curious."

"Um, Jayne . . ." The dishwasher line sounded like another in a long series of loaded insinuations. The strange guilt I felt—the sense of having done something wrong—never left me in that house. I tried to appear quiet and thoughtful, instead of my only other option: fainting in pain and defeat.

"Well?" She was still waiting for an answer.

"No, but I am seeing Dr. Kim today."

I imagined relief filling the kitchen in a great oceanic wave. I wanted badly for breakfast to end—I closed my eyes and wished it—and for everyone in the house to slip quietly away. And then they did.

4. the novel

I had started the outline for *Teenage Pussy* over the summer and a lot had been accomplished despite the hours playing Tetris on my Gateway and constantly checking e-mails and rearranging the endless shelves of foreign editions that lined the walls of my office. Today's interference: I needed to come up with a quote for a banal and harmless book written by an acquaintance of mine in New York, yet another mediocre, polite novel (*The Millipede's Lament*) that was bound to get a spate of respectful reviews and then be totally forgotten. The quote I ultimately devised was glib and evasive, a string of words so nonspecific that they could have applied to just about anything: "I don't think I've probably come upon a work so resolutely about itself in years." And then I turned to a short story by one of my students from the writing class and quickly went through it. In the margins I wrote question marks, I circled words, I underlined sentences, I corrected grammar. I felt I made some balanced decisions.

Before resuming work on *Teenage Pussy* I went through my e-mails. There were only two. One was from Buckley: something about a parent/teacher night next week, with a pointed P.S. from the principal noting that Jayne and I had failed to make the one in early September. And then I sighed when I saw where the other e-mail came from (the Sherman Oaks branch of the Bank of America) and when it was sent (2:40 a.m.). I sighed again and clicked on it, and as usual was faced with a blank screen. I'd been receiving these e-mails since the beginning of October, unaccompanied by any explanation or demand. I had called the bank several times since I had an account at that branch (where my father's ashes were still stored in a safe-deposit box) but the bank had no record of these sent e-mails and patiently explained that no one could possibly be working at that hour (i.e., the middle of the night). Frustrated, I let it go. And the e-mails kept coming, with a frequency that I simply became used to. But today I scrolled through my filing cabinet until I found the first one. October 3 at 2:40 a.m. The date seemed familiar, as did the time, but I couldn't figure out why. Annoyed at my inability to piece this together, I clicked off AOL and eagerly went to the *Teenage Pussy* file.

The original title of *Teenage Pussy* had been *Holy Shit!* but Knopf (who'd shelled out close to a million dollars for the North American rights alone) assured me that *Teenage Pussy* was the more commercial title. (*Outrageous Mike* was considered briefly but finally deemed "noncontroversial.") Knopf was going to call it a "pornographic thriller" in their catalogue, which excited me immensely, and told me privately that Alfred and Blanche Knopf would be rolling over in their graves when the thing was published. Since I realized I was creating an entirely new genre, my bout of writer's block had vanished and I was working on the book daily, even though it was still only in the outline stage. The book was the story of Michael Graves and this young, hip Manhattan bachelor's erotic life—a "guy who loves to give love and loves to get loved back" is what I promised my publishers—and I had envisioned a narrative that was elegantly hardcore and interspersed with jaunty bouts of my trademark laconic humor. It was going to contain at least a hundred sex scenes ("I mean, Jesus, why not?" I guffawed to my editor over lunch in the bar at Patroon while he idly checked his blood sugar) and you could read the novel as either a satire on "the new sexual obnoxiousness" or as the simple story of an average guy who enjoys defiling women with his lust. I was going to turn people on *and* make them think and laugh. That was the combo. Scatological humor intended and achieved. That was the plan. It seemed like a good one.

Teenage Pussy would contain endless episodes of girls storming out of rooms in high-rise condos and the transcripts of cell phone conversations fraught with tension and camera crews following the main characters around as well as six or seven overdoses (attempts on the girls' part to win our lothario's attention). There would be thousands of cosmopolitans ordered and characters camcording each other having anal sex and real-life porn stars making guest appearances. It was going to make *Sodomania* look like *A Bug's Life*. Chapters were titled "The Facial," "The Silicone Queen," "The Porta-John," "The Intrepid Threesome," "Her Boobage," "The Cliterati," "The Getaway," "Hairy Pinkish Tacos," "Am I Too Big for You?," "You Know, I Really Don't Want a Girlfriend Right Now," "Look, I Have to

Catch an Early Flight, Okay?," "Hey—Did You Get a Chance to Pick Up My Dry Cleaning?," "I Am Probably Going to Be Quite Distant Now" and "Do You Mind If I Just Jack Off?"

Our hero, who calls himself the Sexpert, dates only models and carries around a large bag filled with various lubricants, ben-wa balls, vibrating clitoral stimulators and about a dozen strings of anal beads. Every girl he meets he makes wet with excitement. He has the cute habit of licking their faces in public and fingering them beneath tables at Balthazar while drugging their gimlets with OxyContin. He fucks one girl so hard that he breaks her pelvic bone. He fucks a semifamous TV actress in the greenroom minutes before she's supposed to appear on *Live with Regis and Kelly*. He flashes his biceps and shows off his washboard abs ("Michael didn't have a six-pack—he had a twenty-four-pack; a *case!*") to anyone who might look. Women keep pleading with him to be more open and emotional, and they indignantly throw out lines like "I am not a slut!" and "You never want to talk about *anything!*" and "We should have gotten a room!" and "That was rude!" and "No—I will not have sex with that homeless man while you watch!" as well as my two favorites: "You tricked me!" and "I'm calling the police!" His usual answers: "Swallowing *is* about communication, baby" and "Okay, I'm sorry, but can I still come on your face?" A lot of his bad behavior is excused because in many respects Mike is an innocent, though it's far more likely that forgiveness is always extended because he makes every girl he fucks multiorgasmic. But many women become so upset by his behavior that they have to be tranquilized before returning to their "lesbian pasts," and then there's the scandal involving videos Mike had made while having sex with various older married women that "suspiciously" started surfacing on the Internet. "What? You're gonna fuck your way through life?" one of these older women (the wife of a wealthy industrialist) shouts at him. He stares at her as if she's a ditz, then forces a gas mask onto her head. He also invents a variety of cocktails, including the Bareback, the Crotchless Pantie, the Raging Boner, the Weenus, the Double Penetration, the Shag Man and the Jizzbag.

His most recent conquest is—hence the title—a particularly vapid sixteen-year-old who thinks you can get pregnant from oral sex and contract AIDS from drinking a Snapple. She also talks to birds and has a pet squirrel ·named Corky, as well as a problem with silverware; at restaurants, when a waiter recites the specials, she always has to interrupt by asking oh so slowly: "Do you have to use a fork to eat that?" But Mike finds her innocence alluring and soon initiates her into his world, a place where he makes her wear flimsy clothes (transparent lace thongs are high on his list) and has her say, "Throw me a bone" before they have sex and "Who's my daddy?" once he's penetrated her. He applies cocaine to her clitoris. He forces her to read Milan Kundera paperbacks and makes her watch *Jeopardy!* They fly to L.A. for an orgy at the Chateau Marmont and buy sex toys at the Hustler Boutique on Sunset Boulevard and pile them into the trunk of his rented black Cadillac Escalade SUV while she giggles "amply." He even charms her father—who had threatened to personally kick our hero's nicely shaped ass if he didn't stop dating his underage daughter. In a very tender moment, Mike buys her a fake ID. "She doesn't mean to be that stupid," he always apologizes to his aggravated friends, other bachelors living in the same lost world as Mike's. One night he gets her so high on mushrooms that she is unable to locate her own vagina.

But beyond all this riotousness is the tragic ex-girlfriend who has done so much cocaine, her face has caved in on itself ("You damn Russian whore!" Mike screams at her in despair) and there are rooms filled with dead flowers and Mike loses almost all of his trust fund at the Hard Rock Casino in Las Vegas and then attends yet another orgy (this one in Williamsburg—Brooklyn, not colonial) that descends into "utter depravity" and the novel ends sadly with an abortion and a tense Valentine's Day dinner at Nello (a powerful scene). "How could you do that to me?" is the novel's last line. The book was all about the hard sell (the million-dollar advance guaranteed that) but it was also going to be poignant and quietly devastating and put every other book written by my generation to shame. I would still be enjoying huge success and notoriety while my better-behaved peers were languishing on "Where Are They Now?" Web sites.

Today I was going through a list of all the sex "injuries" Mike was going to endure: rug burn on knees, back clawed until bleeding, intense muscle cramps, ruptured testicles, testicular hickies, broken blood vessels, bruises due to excessive suction, a penile fracture ("There was a loud pop, then excruciating pain, but Tandra wrapped crushed ice in a Ralph Lauren towel and drove Mike to the ER") and, finally, just general dehydration.

The phone rang—my line lit up—and I screened the call while staring into the computer. It was Binky, my agent. I picked up immediately.

"How's my favorite author?"

"Oh, I bet you say that to all your authors. In fact, I know you do."

"Actually, I do, but please don't tell any of them."

"I promise. But it means something to hear you say it nevertheless."

"In fact, one of my favorite authors called me today."

"And who might that have been?"

"It was Jay." Binky paused. "He said you had quite the blowout last night."

"A kick-ass party indeed." I also paused, realizing something. "And don't believe anything Jay tells you."

"Indeed," she said ominously. "By the way, did you get that big royalty check for *American Psycho* from the Brits? I had it transferred to your New York account."

"Yes, I got the statement. Excellent." I did my Monty Burns.

"How's Jayne? How are the kids?" She paused, then said blankly, "I can't believe I just asked you that. I've known you for over fifteen years and never thought I would ask you a question like that."

"I am now a committed father and husband," I said proudly.

"Yes," Binky murmured hesitantly. "Yes."

I snapped her out of disbelief. "And I'm teaching."

"Unbelievable."

"It's just one day a week at the college but the kids love me. Legend has it that more students tried to enroll in my writing class than for any other visiting writer who ever taught there. Or so I'm told."

"How many students do you have?"

"Well, I only wanted three, but the administration said that wasn't an acceptable number." I breathed in. "So I have fifteen of the little bastards."

"And how's the book going?" Binky asked.

"Oh—so much for pleasantries?"

"Those were pleasantries?"

"I'm almost done with the outline and the book is moving along right on schedule." I needed a cigarette and started looking through my drawers to find a pack. "I am no longer sweating the small stuff, Binky."

"Well, would you have time for a detour?"

"But this is Knopf's lead title for next fall, which means I need to finish it by January, no?"

"Well, Bret, you were the one who said you could write this thing in six months," she said. "No one believed it but that due date is in your contract and the Germans running your publishing house are displeased by extensions."

"You're sounding coy, Binky," I said, giving up on the cigarette. "You're sounding very coy. And I like it."

"And you sound like your allergies are acting up," Binky said flatly. "I have a feeling we didn't take our Claritin today. And I *don't* like it."

"My allergies are acting up like mad," I protested, and then thought it through. "And don't believe anything Jay tells you."

"Seriously, Bret—allergies?"

"Do not mock my allergies. My nose is stuffed up and I am exceedingly wheezy. Because of . . . them." I paused, knowing this wasn't very convincing. "Hey—I actually do yoga and have a Pilates trainer. How's that for rehabilitation?"

She let it go with a sigh. "Have you ever heard of Harrison Ford?"

"The very famous and once popular actor?"

"He liked the polish you did on *Much to My Chagrin* and wants to talk to you about writing something. You'd have to go out there and meet with him and his people in the next couple of weeks. Just for a day or two." She sighed again. "I'm not sure if it's such a great idea at this point. I'm just relaying the information."

"And you did it so well." I paused. "But why can't they come here? I live in a perfectly nice town." A longer pause. "Hello? Hello?"

"You'd have to go out just for a day or two."

"What's this thing about?"

"Something about Cambodia or Cuba. It's all very vague."

"And I suppose they want me—the writer—to figure it out, huh?" I asked indignantly. "Jesus."

"I'm just relaying the info, Bret."

"As long as Keanu Reeves is not costarring I would be more than delighted to take a meeting with Harrison." Then I remembered certain stories I'd heard. "But isn't he supposed to be this giant blowhard?"

"That's why I think it would be a perfect match."

"Um, Binky, what does that mean?"

"Listen, I've gotta run. It's the day from hell." In the background I heard an assistant calling out. "I'll tell them you're interested, and you can start figuring out the dates you can be in L.A."

"Well, thank you very much for the call. I love our mock formality."

"Oh, by the way . . ."

"Yeah?"

"Happy Halloween."

And as we hung up I suddenly realized what had been bothering me about the e-mails that were coming from the Bank of America in Sherman

Oaks. October 3. That was my father's birthday. And that segued into another realization. 2:40 a.m. That was when, according to the coroner, he had died. I pondered this for about a minute—it was a disturbing connection. But I was hungover and exhausted and I needed to be on campus in thirty minutes so maybe it was just a coincidence and maybe I was giving it more significance than it deserved. When I got up to leave the office, I noted one more thing: the furniture had been rearranged. My desk was now facing the wall instead of the window, where the couch had been repositioned instead. A lamp had been moved to a different corner. Again, at that moment, I blamed it on the party, as I did everything else that day.

5. the college

P art of the town we lived in seemed dreamed up and fractured and
modern: tilted buildings spaced widely apart, with facades that resembled cascading ribbons, and concrete slabs fluttering over one another,
and electronic signs wrapped around the buildings, and there were
gigantic liquid-crystal display screens, and zip strips quoting stock prices
and delivering the day's headlines, and neon decorated the courthouse, and
a Jumbotron TV was perched above the Bloomingdale's that took up
four blocks of downtown. But beyond this district the town also boasted a
2000-acre nature preserve and horse farms and two golf courses, and there
were more children's bookstores than there were Barnes & Nobles. My
route to the college ran past numerous playgrounds and a baseball field,
and on Main Street (where I stopped to buy a Starbucks latte) there were a
variety of gourmet food stores, a first-class cheese shop, a row of patisseries, a
friendly pharmacist who filled my Klonopin and Xanax prescriptions, an
understated cineplex and a family-run hardware store, and all the surrounding streets were lined with magnolia and dogwood and cherry trees. At a
stoplight festooned with fresh flowers I watched a chipmunk climb a telephone pole while I sipped my nonfat latte. The latte revived me to the point
where my hangover seemed like something that had happened last week.
And I was suddenly, inexplicably content as I drove through the town's
shady streets. I passed a potato field. I passed horses grazing outside a barn.
At the campus gates, the security guard tipped his hat to me as I raised my
latte, acknowledging him.

The first time I spotted the cream-colored 450 SL was on that warm,
clear Halloween afternoon. It sat at the curb just outside the faculty parking
lot and I smiled as I passed it in recognition of the fact that it was the same

make and color of the car my father had driven in the late seventies, a car I'd inherited when I turned sixteen. This one was a convertible as well, and the intriguing coincidence brought a brief rush of memories—a freeway, sun glinting off the hood, staring out the windshield at the twisting roads of Mulholland while the Go-Gos blared from the stereo, the top down and palm trees swaying above me. I made nothing of it at the time: there were plenty of rich kids at the college, and a car like that wasn't necessarily out of place. So the memories vanished once I parked in my designated space, lifted the stack of paperbacks of my short story collection, *The Informers*, off the passenger seat and headed toward my office, which was in a small and charming red barn that overlooked the campus—the building was, in fact, called the Barn. Still smiling to myself, I realized that my sole reason for being here today was that my office was the only place Aimee Light would meet me now—under the auspices of a student-teacher counseling session, even though she wasn't my student, I wasn't her teacher and no counseling was planned. (We had attempted a single tryst at her off-campus apartment, but there was an obnoxious cat inhabiting it that I was deeply allergic to.)

On the steps of a library sheathed in metal and glass, hungover students were catching rays. Walking across the quad I stopped to help tap a keg (and sneak a beer) in front of a new art installation. Soccer players in DKNY sportswear loped across the quad's green field, and except for a few Goths sitting beneath the overhang of Commons (where I dropped off the stack of *The Informers*, placing it on the "Free with Student ID" table) everyone looked as if they'd stepped out of an Abercrombie and Fitch catalogue. It all resembled something extremely enticing, and again I was taken back into the past, to my years at Camden. In fact the whole campus—the vibe, the placement of the dorms, the design of the main buildings—reminded me of Camden, even though this was just another small and expensive liberal arts college in the middle of nowhere.

"Yo, Mr. Ellis, great party last night—what's going down?" someone called out. It was a jock from my writing class who had a modicum of talent.

"Yo, I'm down, I'm very down, Jesse," I called back good-naturedly and then added, as an afterthought, "Rock on."

Students kept calling out as I walked up to the Barn, thanking me for the party none of them had been invited to but that they all had apparently attended nonetheless. And so my professorial smile was followed by their gratified laughter. There was also the nervous-looking Jewish student (David Abromowitz) I nodded to as I passed and who, I must confess, I was a little into. The compliments about the rad party kept rolling in, and I returned friendly waves to students I'd never even seen before.

On the door of my office was a note from a student I never heard of canceling an appointment I didn't recall having made, apologizing for her "outburst" in last Wednesday's class. I tried hard to remember the student and what the outburst had been about but couldn't come up with anything, because the class was a sleepwalk—so laid-back and comfortable and informal that even the suggestion of an outburst was worrisome. In class I always tried to sound lighthearted and encouraging, but since I was so famous and probably closer to their age than any other teacher (though I was completely autonomous from the rest of the faculty and really didn't know for sure) my students looked at me in awe. While critiquing their stories I tried to ignore their expressions of fear and alarm.

I sat down at my desk and immediately flipped open my laptop and started making up a dream to feed Dr. Kim, the diminutive Korean shrink my wife found through our couples counselor, Dr. Faheida. Dr. Kim, a strict Freudian and a big believer in how the unconscious expressed itself in dream imagery, wanted me to bring in a new dream every week so we could interpret it, but because her accent was so thick that half the time I had no idea what she was saying, and the added fact that I was no longer having dreams, these sessions were almost unbearable. But Jayne insisted on (and was paying for) them, so it was easier to endure these hours than face the hassles of not showing up. (Besides, this charade was my only means of keeping the Klonopin and Xanax prescriptions up to date—and without them I was a goner.) Meanwhile Dr. Kim was catching on—becoming more suspicious with each new made-up dream—but my assignment was to bring in one today, so while waiting for Aimee Light to arrive (and hopefully undress) I dutifully concentrated on what kind of dream would be burbling in my unconscious at this point. Glancing at my watch I saw this had to be quick. I had to make up the dream, type it up, and print it out, and then—after somehow having sex with Aimee Light—dash over to Dr. Kim's office by three. Today: water, plane crash, being chased by . . . a lively badger (remember: animals were not my friends); I was naked on the plane, the lively badger was . . . also on the plane, and maybe its name was . . . Jayne.

When I looked up a student had appeared in the doorway and was staring at me sheepishly. There was nothing unusual about him at first glance: tall, handsome in a generic way, a lean face, slightly chiseled, thick reddish brown hair very tightly cropped, a backpack slung over his shoulders. He was wearing jeans and an antique olive green Armani sweater with the designer's emblem—an eagle—on it (antique because it was a sweater I had once owned when I was a college student). He was holding a Starbucks cup and seemed more alert than the squinty-eyed slackers that populated the campus. And though I couldn't place him I knew I'd seen him before, and so I was intrigued. Plus he was holding a copy of my first novel, *Less Than Zero*, which made me stand up and say, "Hello."

The boy seemed almost shocked that I'd acknowledged him and was suddenly incapable of saying anything until I quickly spoke again.

"That's a wonderful novel you're hold—"

"Oh, yeah, hi, hope I'm not bothering you."

"No, not at all. Come in, come in."

He looked away and blushed deeply, then shuffled into the office and carefully sat down in the chair across the desk from me.

"Well, I'm a big fan, Mr. Ellis."

"Isn't there a law against formality at this place?" I said with an expression of mock distaste, hoping to relax him since he was sitting so rigidly in the chair. "Call me Bret." I paused. "And have we met before?"

"Um, I'm Clayton and I'm a freshman here and I don't think so," the boy said. "I just wanted to know if you could sign this for me." His hands trembled slightly as he held up the book.

"Of course. I'd be happy to." I studied him as he handed me the book, which was in pristine condition. I opened it to the copyright page and saw it was a first edition, which made the book I was holding an extremely rare and valuable copy.

"I have class in a couple of minutes, so . . ." He gestured at himself.

"Oh, of course. I won't keep you long." I set the book down and searched my desk for a pen. "So, Clayton . . . I assume all your friends call you Clay."

He stared at me and then—understanding what I was getting at—grinned and said, "Yeah." He waved a hand at the book. "Like Clay in the novel."

"That's the connection I made," I said, opening a drawer. "Is there another?" I found a pen and then looked up. He was staring at me questioningly. "That's the right one. You were correct," I assured him, but then I couldn't help it: "You look very familiar."

He just shrugged.

"Well, what are you majoring in?" I asked.

"I want to be a writer." It seemed hard for him to admit this.

"Did you apply to my writing course?"

"I'm a freshman. It's only open to juniors and seniors."

"Well, I could have pulled a few strings," I said delicately.

"Based on what?" he asked, a snap in his voice.

I realized that I was flirting with him and suddenly looked back at the book and the pen in my hand, embarrassed for myself.

"I'm not really any good," he offered, sitting up, noting the sudden, subtle shift in the room's vibe.

"Well, neither are any of my other students so you'd fit right in." I laughed dryly. He did not.

"My parents . . ." Again, he hesitated. "Well, my dad, actually . . . he wanted me to go to business school and so . . ."

"Ah yes, the age-old dilemma."

Clayton purposefully checked his watch—another gesture that indicated he needed to go. "You can just sign my name—I mean, your name." He stood up.

"Are you working on anything?" I asked gently as I signed my name with an uncharacteristic flourish on the title page.

"Well, I have part of a novel done."

I handed him back the book. "Well, if you're interested in showing me anything . . ." I left the offer hanging there, waiting for him to accept.

At that point I realized where I'd seen Clayton before.

He was at the Halloween party last night.

He was dressed as Patrick Bateman.

I had seen him when I was looking out Sarah's window as he disappeared into the darkness of Elsinore Lane.

I breathed in, something caught in me and I shivered.

He was putting the book in his backpack when I asked, "So, you weren't at the party my wife and I threw last night?"

He stiffened and said, "No. No, I wasn't."

This was answered so genuinely that I couldn't register if he was lying or not. Plus, if he'd crashed the party, why admit to it now?

"Really? I thought I saw you there." I couldn't help but keep pressing.

"Um, no, wasn't me." He just stood in front of my desk, waiting.

I realized I needed to say something that would get him moving.

"Well, it was nice meeting you, Clayton."

"Yes, you too."

I held out a hand. He abruptly shook it and looked away, mumbling his thanks as I heard footsteps coming down the hall.

Clayton heard the footsteps too and, without saying anything else, turned to leave my office.

But Aimee Light bumped into him in the doorway and they glanced at each other briefly before Clayton rushed away.

"Who was that?" Aimee asked casually, swaying in.

I walked over to the door, still slightly dazed from the encounter, and watched as Clayton disappeared down an empty corridor. I stood there trying to figure out why he had lied about being at the party last night. Well, he was shy. Well, he hadn't been invited. Well, he wanted to come. Whatever.

Aimee spoke again. "Was that a student of yours?"

"Yeah, yeah," I said, closing the door. "A very interesting young man whose allotted seven minutes had just expired."

Aimee was leaning against my desk, facing me, and wearing an alluring summer dress, and she knew exactly what the response to an alluring summer dress at the end of October would be—a carnal promise. I immediately walked up to her and she pushed herself up until she was sitting on the desk and then spread her legs and I walked between them as she wrapped them around my waist, straddling me as I stood looking down at her. This was all extremely encouraging.

"A sycophant?" she asked demurely.

"No—then he would have received an allotted ten minutes."

We kissed.

"So democratic," she sighed.

"Hey, it's part of my teacher's oath." Kissing her, I kept tasting lip gloss, which took me back to high school and the girls I'd dated when flavored lip gloss was the rage and I was making out on a chaise longue next to a black-bottomed pool in Encino and I was tan and wearing a puka shell necklace and Foreigner's "Feels Like the First Time" was playing and her name was Blair and the delicious, slightly fruity odor of bubble gum was drifting into the office now and I was lost until I realized Aimee had pulled back and was staring up at me. My hand was at the nape of her neck.

"I just saw Alvin," she said.

I sighed. Alvin Mendolsohn was her thesis instructor. I had never met him.

"And what did Alvin say?"

She sighed too. " 'Why are you wasting your time on this?' "

"Why does your advisor hate me so much?"

"I have my speculations."

"Would you care to share them with me?" I was gently running a finger-tip up and down her forearm. I lightly stroked her wrist.

"He thinks you're part of the problem."

"Jesus, what an asshole." I kissed her again, my hands' innate sense of direction leading them to her breasts.

She nudged the hands away. "How's the house—not too wrecked, I hope," she asked, as I pressed my erection against her thigh, which she tensed. I was becoming more insistent and about to push away the laptop and lay her down on the desk when she asked, "Does Jayne know about us?"

I moved away from her slightly, but she grinned and kept me in position with her legs.

"Why do you ask?" I said. "Why are you asking this *now*?"

"She was looking at me strangely last night."

I moved in again, kissing her neck and then her inner arm—she now had goose bumps. "It was just the lighting. Forget about it."

Aimee leaned away from me again. "I got the definite impression that she was studying me."

I sighed and stood up straight. "Are we ever going to do it, or what?"

"Oh, God—"

"Because I, for one, do not think I'm too young."

She laughed loudly, throwing her head back. "No, it's not that."

"And you're becoming very quickly the biggest cocktease I've ever met in my life and it's not funny, Aimee." I grabbed her hand and moved it toward my crotch. "You wanna feel how not funny it is?"

"I shouldn't be involved with you for any number of reasons," she said, sitting up. But I wouldn't budge from my position. She kept sighing. "Look, number one is you're married—"

"For only three months!" I wailed.

"Bret—"

I moved in again, burying my face in her neck. "Married guys live longer."

"There's no research that indicates being married is a good idea."

I moved down to my knees until I was staring between her parted thighs. I placed a hand beneath her dress, feeling the navel ring in the middle of her soft, tanned stomach. My hand glided across her lower abdomen and down around her hip bones. The little slope at the base of her spine, right above her ass—I rubbed that indentation delicately, massaging it with very gentle, circular motions, and then my hands moved to the spot where her ass cheeks met her thighs. My hands started moving toward her panties and the uncharted territory that lay beneath them. She tried to close her thighs but I gripped them tightly, holding them open. Straining, I managed to say, "I read a study in a magazine somewhere." She struggled to close her thighs. My teeth were clenched. "Something connecting coital frequency to life span." I finally let go, panting.

"That is such bullshit," she said, laughing.

"Look, I'm trying to trigger a sexual response in you, so why aren't you convulsing with pleasure?"

She relaxed as I stood up, and we kissed again. I became lost in her once more. "God, what are you wearing?" I murmured. "That smell, it takes me back."

"To where?"

I was licking her mouth. "Just, like, back. The past. I'm reexperiencing my whole adolescence."

"Just with this lip gloss?"

"Yeah," I sighed. "It's like those little tangerines in Proust."

"You mean madeleines."

"Yeah, like those little tangerines."

"How . . . did you get this job?"

"Shapely legs." I was feeling her stomach again, pulling gently on the ring piercing her navel. "Can I get one of those too? We can have matching navel rings. Wouldn't that be cool?"

"Yeah, it would really set off those abs of yours."

"Are you talking about my six-pack?"

"I think I'm talking about your, um, *keg*."

"You're very sexy, baby, but I'm equally hot."

And then, as usual, it stopped. This time it was mutual. She had places to go, and I had to print out a dream and head over to Dr. Kim's.

While we were getting ready to leave the office, Aimee said something.

"That boy who was in here earlier . . ."

"Yeah. Do you know him?"

She paused. "No, but he looked familiar."

"Yeah, I thought so too. Did you see him at the party last night?" I asked, while the printer started cranking out my assignment.

"I'm not sure, but he reminded me of someone."

"Yeah, he went as Patrick Bateman. He was the guy in the Armani suit. Very creepy."

"Um, Bret, I have news for you: you were so wasted I don't think you could have recognized anybody by the time that party hit full force."

I shrugged, slipped the dream into my jacket and picked up a few stories students had left in the bin by my door. It was quiet. Aimee was thinking about something else while she lit a cigarette.

"Yeah? What is it?" I asked. "I'm gonna be late."

"It's weird you said Patrick Bateman," she said.

"Why?"

"Because I thought he looked a little like Christian Bale."

We were both silent for a long time, because Christian Bale was the actor who had played Patrick Bateman in the film version of *American Psycho*.

"But he also looked like you," Aimee said. "Give or take twenty years."

I started shivering again.

Back in the parking lot, the cream-colored 450 SL was no longer there. I noticed.

6. the shrinks

S ince I was late I drove instead of walking over to the building housing the practices of Dr. Kim and our couples counselor, Dr. Faheida. Unfolding my dream I raced into the lobby and bumped into a woman exiting the elevator. I was staring at my dream, feeling like a child about to be tested, when she stepped aside and said, "Hello, Bret." I looked up and stared into the woman's face: gaunt, midforties, vaguely Spanish, dark wispy hair, a crooked smile. Holding an armful of folders and books, she stood there patiently as I squinted at her, assessing who she was.

It took a moment before I realized.

"Ah, Dr. Fajita. How are you?" I said, relieved.

She paused slightly. "It's Dr. Fe-hay-da."

"Dr. Fe-hay-da," I mimicked. "Yes, and how are you?"

"I'm fine. Will I be seeing you and your wife next week?"

"Yes, and this time we'll both be there," I promised.

"That's good. See you then." She slowly shuffled off as I hopped into the elevator.

The couples counseling had started due to the lack of sex in our marriage. This was, admittedly, my problem, and the guilt I felt led me to follow Jayne to Dr. Faheida. Even when I first arrived in July we were having sex only once a week, though Jayne kept trying to initiate it more regularly. But she was being turned down so often that she soon quit trying. And I couldn't figure out where this lack of interest on my part was coming from. Jayne— whom I was once so highly attracted to that she'd complained about the frequency of sex—resembled something new to me now, something other than the hot girlfriend. She was the wife, the mother, my savior. But how did that begin to constitute a celibate relationship? ("Ah yes, how indeed?"

the dark voice in the back of my mind whispered frequently.) I simply blamed it on whatever convenient lie I came up with when we were lying in the massive bed in the darkened bedroom, the door locked, the curtains drawn, my softened penis lying immobile against my thigh: exhaustion, stress, the novel, the natural ebb and flow of desire, the antidepressants I was on; I even hinted about sexual scars from my childhood. She kept checking her resentment. I held in my shame but not enough to make her feel guiltless about questioning my manhood, to the point where she felt bad about forcing the issue. She kept asking if I still found her attractive — which I did, I kept assuring her. I was proud to have Jayne Dennis as my wife. Millions of men found her image magnetically sexual. She was a young and popular movie star. Yet, mysteriously, sex had become mundane and increasingly rare between us. I no longer had the hard-on for her that I once did, and tried to soothe her with vague generalities I'd picked up on Oprah. "Is sex more important than our kids or our careers, Jayne?" I asked one night. "I think we have it pretty good." She sighed in the darkness. "Just because the sex isn't here now doesn't mean you aren't," I said gently (that was the first night I slept in the guest room). And so in counseling with our "marriage educator," theories were tossed around. Maybe it was the deterioration of my testosterone levels. But I was tested and the levels were normal. I started taking daily herbal supplements. We opted out on Viagra since I had a mitral valve prolapse — a slight heart condition that the drug could agitate. Other options included Levitra and Cialis — *But I'm not impotent!* I wanted to scream. However I *was* "value neutral." I couldn't grasp "shared commitment." I was the master of "negative communication." I had helped create an "unstable union." I needed to develop "collaborative alliances." I only offered "counterproposals." I was accused of "cutting deals." (Jayne was the one intent on "separation avoidance," even though she admitted to having a problem with "self-differentiation.") We were told to get a babysitter, leave provocative notes for each other, pretend we were still dating, check into a hotel, plan for intimacy, schedule intercourse. But by the end of September our sexual relationship was in major gridlock, and that was when I realized why. The thing that was causing it now had a name: Aimee Light. According to Jayne, the "most amazingly sad aspect" of our marriage was that she still loved me.

I breathed in deeply and walked into Dr. Kim's office. Her door was open and she was scanning the *New York Review of Books* while waiting for me. She looked up — her small, brown, inquiring face creased with a tight smile.

"I'm sorry I'm late," I said, closing the door behind me, flopping into the armchair across from her. That the office was serenely anonymous always helped me relax before we began the sessions, but today she jumped right in, and her increasing worry about my "abuse problems" was soon dominating the conversation. This probably due to the Kleenex I kept reaching for and the bloody ropes of snot I kept blowing from my sore and damaged nose. Then she wanted to talk about Robby and if I was still resentful of him, and next it lurched to Jayne and exactly what I was aiming for with her, and soon my patience expired and I had to interrupt what now resembled an interrogation. She balanced a legal pad on her lap and furiously kept writing notes.

"Look, I'm only here because I promised my wife I would try and get help and so I'm here and trying to get help and I don't need another lecture about how I'm wasting everybody's time, 'kay?" I reached for another Kleenex and blew my nose. The tissue came away red and glistening.

"So why are you here, Mr. Ellis?"

"Well, I have anxiety and these, y'know, anxiety disorders."

"About what?"

"Um . . . plane crashes . . . the terrorists . . ." I paused and then added genuinely, "Those missing boys."

She sat up. "Mr. Ellis, I much more concerned about cirrhosis of liver than plane crash for you." She sighed and marked something down, then immediately segued into: "So, any fresh dreams?"

"Yes, a major one," I said, trying to hide my reluctance as I handed her the printed-out sheet.

Dr. Kim looked over the words typed hastily earlier this afternoon and got to a particular sentence where she blanched and then stared at me from where she was sitting. I was casually admiring a small cactus on a shelf, humming mindlessly to myself as I waited.

"This dream seems very, very fake to me, Mr. Ellis." She glared at me suspiciously. "I think you make this dream up."

"How dare you!" I sat up indignantly—a posture I realized that I adopted quite often in her office.

"You expect me to believe this dream?" She glanced back at the page. "Large-mouthed bass chase you into pond where you escape onto floating airplane and then are flying business class—a plane that has your father's name on side of it?"

"This is my unconscious, Dr. Kim." I shrugged. "These just may be legitimate concerns." I sighed and gave up.

"You have not told your wife that you are using drugs again," she said.

"No." I sighed once more and looked away. "But she knows. She knows."

"And are you still sleeping on the couch?"

"It's the *guest room*! I'm in the fucking *guest room*! You can't sleep on our fucking couch."

"Mr. Ellis, you do not need to shout."

"Look." I sighed. "It's been really hard fitting into this whole world, and all these pressures about being the man of the house or whatever you wanna call it are getting to me, as well as the fact that, yeah, I'm using again—but only a little—and drinking again—but only a little—and yeah, okay, Jayne and I aren't having sex and I've been flirting with this girl at the college and I think another student's pretending to be a character from one of my novels and Jayne's little girl is, I think, really messed up and she thinks that her doll's alive and attacking her plus she keeps calling me 'Daddy' and Harrison Ford wants me to write this script for him and I'm getting these weird e-mails from L.A. that have something to do with my father, I think, and all those missing boys are scaring the hell out of me and it's all causing enormous conflicts within my psyche." I paused, mid-rant. "Oh, and our golden retriever hates my guts." I let out a huge sigh. "So, I've got a lot on my plate—chill out." And then I reached for the page she was holding and said, "Give me that."

She kept a firm grip, glaring at me. I kept pulling. She wouldn't let go. Our eyes locked. I finally sat back, panting.

She waited patiently. "Mr. Ellis, the main reason you are here is to find ways to get to know your son. That is essential. That is necessary. That you connect with your son."

There was nothing to say except "I'm getting a grip on that situation."

"I don't think you are."

"Why not?"

"Because you haven't mentioned him once since you've been here."

7. robby's room

Marta was in the kitchen making dinner, stir-frying vegetables in an aluminum wok, while the kids were upstairs getting dressed for trick-or-treating. It was dark out now but on the drive from Dr. Kim's back to the house I noticed parents were already walking their costumed children through the town's neighborhoods as dusk approached, which I took as a sinister reminder of the missing boys and which moved me to stop at a liquor store and buy a bottle of Groth Sauvignon Blanc and a magnum of Ketel One, and once I was safely ensconced in my office I poured half the wine into an oversized coffee cup and hid both bottles beneath my desk (my furniture was still rearranged). I wandered around the house with nothing to do. Passing the bowl of mini Nutri-Grain bars on a table by the front door, I went outside. Someone had already lit the jack-o'-lanterns. Victor was lying on the lawn. When he gave me a cursory look I gave one back and then picked up a Frisbee and threw it at the dog. It landed near where he was lying. He glanced at it contemptuously, then lifted his head and looked over at me as if I were a fool before nudging the orange disc away with his snout.

Back in the house I moved through the living room and noticed that the furniture had been placed back in its original position. Yet I still felt like I was viewing the room from an unfamiliar angle. The carpet looked darker, shaggier, the pale beige now morphing into something that bordered on teal or green—and the morning's vacuuming still hadn't cleaned up the footprints that were embedded in it. I kicked lightly at one of them—it was large and ash-colored—and was trying to smooth out the carpeting with the toe of my loafer when from upstairs I suddenly heard Jayne shout, "You're *not* going as Eminem!" and a door slammed. I took a Klonopin, finished my wine, poured myself the rest of the bottle and carefully walked upstairs to Robby's room to see if he was okay.

As I approached his door I saw the scratches he had mentioned that morning. They were clustered near the bottom of the door, and though they weren't the deep grooves I had anticipated, the paint *had* been clawed off and I thought it was probably just Victor trying to gain entry. No one from the party had been upstairs, but then I flashed on Sarah's torn pillow and fleetingly thought that maybe Robby had made the scratches himself— a hostile gesture, something to garner attention, whatever—until I realized that this didn't seem like something Robby would ever do; he was far too passive and enervated to pull off a stunt like that. And then I flashed back on the Terby and the ripped pillow again. The kids were unreliable—their meds were proof of that. Plus Robby had recently switched antidepressants. Luvox had now been added for the anxiety attacks that had plagued him since he was six, and which had increased in intensity since I arrived—and who really knew what the side effects were? His physician had assured us that except for mild gastrointestinal problems there weren't any, but that's what they always say, and anyway, without the drugs Robby couldn't sit still. Without the meds he wouldn't have been able to visit the planetarium. Without the Ritalin he couldn't have cruised the mall earlier in the week for a costume. I almost tripped over a skateboard as I entered his room, but the TV's volume was so high that Robby, who was sitting on the bed, didn't notice.

Robby's room had a space-age theme: planet and comet and moon decals were pasted all over the walls suggesting that you were now floating within a night black sky somewhere deep in space. The carpet revealed itself to be a Martian landscape, impressively detailed with canyons and fissures and craters. Spheres made of glass beads dangled from a glittering, savage-looking asteroid that hung from the ceiling above a king-sized art deco bed fitted with a stylish comforter. Along with the ubiquitous Beastie Boys and Limp Bizkit posters were those of various moons: Jupiter's Io and Saturn's Titan and the massive rifts of Uranus's Miranda. The room also contained a minifridge, brightly colored lamps, a leather sofa and a stereo, and one entire wall was a stark black-and-white photo mural of a deserted skate park. Video game cartridges were scattered across the floor in front of the wide-screen TV, now hooked up to PlayStation 2 amid a pile of *Simpsons* and *South Park* DVDs. There was a stack of new Tommy Hilfiger shirts on his bed. Japanese action figures lined the bookshelves, which contained mostly wrestling magazines and the entire Harry Potter series, and above the shelves was a large bronze painting of the zodiac. The remains of a Starbucks iced chai sat next to a giant translucent moon that glowed from the computer—Robby's screensaver.

Robby was staring at *Nintendo Power Monthly* while slipping on a pair of Puma socks and then he was tying his Nikes. The TV was turned to the WB channel and as I stood in the doorway I watched a raunchy cartoon zap into one of the many commercials pitched toward the kids—one in a series of ads that I hated. A scruffy, gorgeous youth, hands on his skinny-boy hips, stared defiantly into the camera and made the following statements in a blank voice, subtitled beneath him in a blood red scroll: "Why haven't you become a millionaire yet?" followed by "There is not more to life than money" followed by "You *do* need to own an island" followed by "You should never sleep because there are no second chances" followed by "It *is* important to be slick and evocative" followed by "Come with us and make a bundle" followed by "If you aren't rich you deserve to be humiliated." And then the commercial ended. That was it. I'd seen this ad numerous times and had yet to figure out what it meant or even what product it was trying to sell.

Robby's shoulders were slumped and the Hilfiger sweater tied around his waist fell to the floor as he stood up and stretched. There was a young adult book on his pillow called *What Once Had Been Earth.* My son was eleven and had a Prada wallet and a Stussy camouflage eye patch and a Lacoste sweatband clung to his wrist and he had wanted to start an astronomy club but due to lack of interest among his peers it never materialized and his favorite songs had the word *flying* in the title, and all of this saddened me. He sprayed Hugo Boss cologne on the back of his hand and didn't smell it. He still hadn't noticed that I was standing in the doorway.

"So, Mom wouldn't let you go as the rap star, huh?" I said.

He whirled around and gasped. And then he regained his composure.

"No," he said sullenly. He looked shameful, handcuffed.

Something in me broke. I swallowed another mouthful of wine and walked into the room.

"Well, you need platinum blond hair and a wife to beat, and since you don't have either . . ." I had no idea what my point was; all I wanted to do was make him feel better, but every time I tried, it just seemed to add to his general confusion.

"Yeah, but Sarah's going as Posh Spice," he grumbled as I turned down the volume on the television.

"Well, your mom has a problem with the whole rap thing . . ." I drifted off, then caught myself. "So what are you gonna go as?"

"Um, nothing. Nothing, I guess." A pause. "Maybe an astronaut."

"Just an astronaut?" I asked. "Can't you think up something a little more . . . entertaining? Mom said that's what you were last year."

He said nothing.

I just shuffled amiably around the vast room and pretended to be interested in a variety of things.

"Is there something wrong?" I heard him ask worriedly. "Did I do something wrong?"

"No, no, no, Robby," I said. "Of course not. I was just admiring your room."

"But, um, why?"

"You're very . . . lucky."

"I am?"

I hated the way he asked that. "Yeah, I mean, you should be grateful for all the things you have," I said. "You're a fortunate kid."

Wearily, slumped over, his arms at his sides, he looked around the room, unimpressed. "They're just things, Bret."

"I mean all I ever wanted was a TV and a lock on my door." I made a superficial gesture with my hand. "All I wanted to do was play with Legos."

I stared at the mobile of planets hanging in the middle of the room—the universe floating below the star-studded ceiling. The satellites in orbit, the rockets and astronauts, the spaceships and moon rocks and Mars and the fiery meteorite heading toward Earth and the concerns about extraterrestrial sightings and the need to establish colonies throughout the solar system. It all seemed horribly useless to me because the sky was always black in space and there was no sound on the moon and it was another world where you would always be lost. But I knew that Robby would argue that far beneath its freezing craters and treacherous sand-blown surfaces lay a warm and yielding heart. It took only two and a half seconds for a laser to flash from Earth to the moon and back again, as Robby had told me at that wedding in Nashville so many years ago.

"Yeah, I guess an astronaut," he said.

"Okay, that's cool," I said. "I think that's a cool costume."

I finally noticed the helmet on the bed and the accompanying orange NASA suit hanging on a hook in the closet. "I'll see you downstairs, bud."

Robby kept staring at me until I left the room and closed the door behind me. I flinched when I heard it lock. A sconce flickered as I walked past it.

8. halloween

It was sweltering—the warmest October 31 on record—but having grown up in Los Angeles I was used to this weather, even though Jayne and the kids were sweating by the time we reached the end of the block. Robby had already taken off his helmet, his hair matted wet, and hooked up with Ashton Allen, who dissed the idea of going as a famous baseball player once the gay rumors surfaced, and whose parents, Mitchell and Nadine, now joined us along with their younger daughter, Zoe, who was trick-or-treating with Sarah and their guardian for the evening, Marta. (Zoe was Hermione Granger and, yes, Sarah was Posh Spice, complete with a T-shirt that read MY BOYFRIEND THINKS I'M STUDYING.) The two boys would wait on the sidewalk and then inspect their sisters' treats before deciding to hit that particular house or not. I was drunk.

As we walked through the neighborhood I idly recognized the costumes from various video games (boys dressed as Shadow Phoenix Ninja and Mortal Kombat Scorpion) and movies (Anakin Skywalkers with Jedi hair braids wielding light sabers) while Harry Potters roamed Elsinore Lane everywhere you looked—wearing Quidditch robes, and they held broomsticks and magic wands, and there were green lightning bolt scars on their foreheads that glowed in the darkness as they chatted up a number of bloated ogres that I recognized as Shreks. There were no ballerinas or witches or hobos or ghosts—none of the simple homemade costumes from my childhood—and I was getting old and when I saw Nadine take a swig from the bottle of Fiji water she was carrying I suddenly craved another drink badly. Sarah kept running ahead of everyone, gyrating, while Zoe and Marta tried to keep up, and the four parents kept calling out to their children to stay in sight. There was collective murmuring about why there were

so many cars this year—a long, slow-moving stream of them—with costumed kids meekly piling out and running up to the houses and then clam-
bering back into the parade of SUVs that filled the lane. A quiet hesitancy
hovered over everything. It was another reminder of the missing boys, and
Nadine noted that there were more flashlights than usual and happier-
looking jack-o'-lanterns (this was supposed to be an upbeat Halloween). I
tried to listen attentively as a zombie pedaled past me on a bike, glaring.
Jayne held a digital camera that sometimes she used but mostly didn't. We
ran into Mark and Sheila Huntington, an attractive duo made up of hard
edges, as well as Adam and Mimi Gardner—both couples neighbors of ours
as well as invitees to the Allens' dinner on Sunday. As we watched our children move from house to house I noticed how apprehensive everyone
seemed, and how lame our attempts at masking it were. People murmured
about taking the kids over to North Hill this year, even though none of the
missing boys came from our general vicinity. And I noticed how quiet it
was, as if no one wanted to attract any unwanted attention from the stranger
lurking in the shadows. Someone walked up to Jayne and asked for her
autograph.

I couldn't concentrate on the conversation the various couples were having (the cat that meditated, the healthy multitasking) because I had the
feeling that we were being followed—or, more accurately, that I was. I tried
blaming it on the lack of sleep, the bottle of wine, the halfhearted realizations in Dr. Kim's office, my failure to find the jeans from the night before
with the leftover coke in them, the sexual frustration, the boy who had lied
to me in my office that afternoon.

But I saw the car again.

The cream-colored 450 SL was gliding down Elsinore Lane and came to
a stop at Bedford Street. I just stared helplessly as it sat there, idling, and I
tried distracting myself by figuring out when I could go to Los Angeles next
week. The eight adults, now walking in pairs along the sidewalk, were moving toward it. Suddenly—and in retrospect I don't know why—I asked
Jayne for the digital camera. While commiserating with Mitchell about the
new In-N-Out Burger that was opening on Main Street, she handed it to
me. I looked through it and aimed it at the Mercedes. The light from the
lampposts was ridiculously bright and washed out everything, making it
hard to focus. I couldn't understand why the car no longer seemed innocent, and why it was beginning—after just two sightings—to *mean* something; something dark, a reminder of something black. As I walked closer,

zooming in on its trunk and then the rear window, it seemed as if the car itself sensed my interest and—as if *it* made the decision and not the driver—turned off Elsinore and disappeared down Bedford. I was in a haze. I felt haunted, and then there was a hot wind and the barely audible hum of what sounded like electrical equipment, and I was shivering. My heartbeat accelerated, and then, inexplicably, I felt sorrow. The moon was giant that night, hanging low in the black sky, and orange-tinted, and people kept commenting on how close to the earth it seemed.

Jayne was explaining to the fascinated parents why she had to go to Toronto next week when I suddenly had to excuse myself. I simply said I was tired. The pavement was wobbling beneath me and my skin was alive with perspiration. Jayne was about to say something when she saw Sarah attempt a cartwheel and yelled out for her to be careful. I said goodbye to everybody, assured the Allens that we were looking forward to Sunday night and then handed Jayne the camera. I knew that leaving was not a smart play but I had no choice but to go with it. I noted her ambivalence and dissatisfaction and headed back toward the house, which was dark, except for the jack-o'-lanterns, whose faces were already caving in. I could still feel Robby's relief when I stumbled away.

In my office I poured myself a large glass of vodka and wandered outside onto the deck overlooking the lit pool and the backyard and the wide expanse of field leading to the woods. The trees looked black and twisted beneath the orange light of the moon. I sipped the vodka. I wondered: Were the strange lights flickering in the low gray sky that people had reported seeing back in June somehow connected to the disappearance of the boys, which began around the same time? The other explanations I came up with made me hope so.

Something passed over me and then flew away.

Suddenly Victor rushed out of the house and was standing near me, barking and panting. He was facing in the direction of the woods.

"Shut up," I said tiredly. "Just shut up."

He looked at me worriedly and then sat down with a whimper.

I tried to relax, feeling the hot wind on my skin, but my eyes were drawn to something lying next to the Jacuzzi, which I also noted was bubbling— someone had turned on the jets—and steam was rising off the heated water. I set my drink on the barbecue and moved hesitantly across the deck until I was standing over a pair of swimming trunks. I assumed the trunks were something left over from the party but when I picked them up they were soaked, as if someone had just climbed out of the Jacuzzi and removed them. And then I noted the patterns on the shorts: large, abstract red flowers. Hawaii suddenly was flying through my mind and it landed at the Mauna Kea Hotel, the resort my family stayed at when I was a kid. Are these mine? I asked myself silently, because I had once owned a pair (as did my father), yet almost immediately knew that the answer was no. I calmly wrung out the trunks and draped them over the deck banister to dry. I sipped my drink and then took a deep swallow. I breathed in and looked back into the woods.

The night was drenched with darkness and the darkness really was dazzling. And the sound of the wind seemed amplified, and I noticed that Victor was standing up again and staring out into the woods, the hot wind ruffling his golden coat. I just kept staring into the blackness of the woods, drawn toward the darkness as I always had been. And the wind rushed up against me and the wind felt . . .

. . . feral . . .

There was no other word for it. The wind felt feral.

"Hello darkness my old friend . . ." The lyric drifted into my thoughts and I felt as if a boundary were being erased. I closed my eyes. I suddenly realized how alone I was. (*But this is how you travel*, the wind whispered back, *this is how you've always lived.*) I opened my eyes when a moth landed on my arm. It looked as if the entire world were dying and turning black. The darkness was eclipsing everything.

And then Victor started barking—much more insistently this time, shaking as he stared out at the woods, and his barking was soon interspersed with growls. And, just as suddenly, he stopped.

He stood still. He had heard something.

He kept looking into the woods.

And then he leapt off the deck and ran toward them, barking again.

"Victor," I called out.

I could see his shadow loping along the field as if he was chasing something and he was still barking, but when he entered the woods the barking stopped.

I sipped my drink and decided to wait for him to come back.

I looked at the bathing suit. I thought about the Mercedes cruising down Elsinore Lane. How long had it been following us? Who had been in the Jacuzzi?

And then I thought I saw Victor. A shape, low and hunched over, had emerged from the woods but I couldn't make out what it was. It was the size of Victor, perhaps larger, but its movements were spiderlike as it lurched grotesquely sideways, clumsily darting in and out of the trees at the edge of the woods.

"Victor!" I called again.

The thing stopped moving for a moment. And then its dark shape scuttled sideways and picked up speed and it began shambling back into the woods. I realized, sickeningly, that it looked as if it was hunting something.

"Victor!"

I heard what sounded like squeals of despair coming from the dog but they stopped abruptly and there was only silence.

I waited.

Squinting, I could make out Victor's bulk as he slowly walked back across the field and I couldn't help feeling weak with relief when the dog—now eerily calm—moved past me and into the kitchen. But then something forced me to understand that I was not alone out here.

Can you feel me? it asked.

"Go away," I whispered. I was too fucked up to deal with this. "Go away . . ."

It was time you learned something, I could hear it moaning.

I was not alone.

And whatever was out there knew who I was.

Something was moving in the woods again.

The swings on the swing set began rattling in a sulfurous rush of hot winds and then, almost immediately, they stopped swinging.

I could hear the soft, snapping sounds of something approaching. And it was moving eagerly. It wanted to be noticed. It wanted to be seen and felt. It wanted to whisper my name. It wanted to deceive me. But it wasn't making itself visible yet. And as I kept peering into the darkness, I saw another figure hurrying across the field, grasping what looked like a pitchfork. I stood immobilized on the deck. My teeth had started chattering. The wind gusted again. And then there was the sound of locusts swarming. I started shaking. I'm scared, I suddenly thought. When it sensed how frightened I was, there was a strange odor in the air.

Get inside, I told myself. Get inside the house now.

But when I looked back at the house I knew it couldn't protect me from what was out there. Whatever it was could get in.

And then I saw the headstone. It was off to the side at the edge of our yard, and it sat at a crooked angle, jutting up from the weeds that blanketed the field, and my momentary annoyance that the decorators hadn't carted it off turned to dread as I found myself unable to stop moving toward it. The ground beneath the headstone was burst apart—as if something buried there had clawed its way out. Over the roar of the wind I could hear an oddly distinct flapping sound. As I moved toward the headstone I felt convinced that something had actually crawled out of that fake grave. Something huge and black was passing over the house—it was flying—and then it spun around in midair and it was suddenly beneath me and the wind kept howling and there was briefly the snarl of animals fighting in the woods and then the thing began circling above me as I knelt in front of the headstone next to the hole in the ground. There was something written on it. I started brushing the fake moss and cobwebs aside. The headstone was streaked with dried blood.

And scrawled on it in red letters was

ROBERT MARTIN ELLIS 1941–1992

The wind knocked me off-balance and I fell backwards.

The field was damp and spongy and as I tried to stand up I slipped on a large wet patch of dirt. But when I put a hand down to steady myself it wasn't wetness I felt but something viscous and slimy that smelled dank and I kept trying to stand up because something was getting closer to me. The wind slammed the kitchen doors shut. Whatever was approaching me was hungry. It was pitiful. It was awesome. It needed something I didn't want to give. I shouted out as I finally lifted myself up and lunged toward the house. Whatever was behind me kept shambling forward, its arms outstretched and grasping.

Once inside, I ran into the guest room and locked myself in it.

I waited desperately for Jayne and the kids to get home.

When they returned I made sure all the doors to the house were locked and that the various alarms were set. I pretended to be interested in Sarah's candy. Jayne ignored me. Robby barely looked my way before climbing the stairs to his room.

Back in the guest room, drinking from the magnum of vodka, I kept thinking one thing, just two words.

He's back.

9. outside

I woke up in the guest room to the sound of a leaf blower, and when I peered out the window (the gardener's flatbed truck in the driveway a reminder that it was Saturday) I felt momentarily okay about things until I realized I was fully clothed (not a good sign) and had no recollection of how I fell asleep last night (ditto), which morphed into a spasm of anxiety. I immediately swung my legs off the bed, knocking over the bottle of vodka I had bought the previous night—but it was empty (another bad sign). Yet the Ketel One suggested that my fear was the result of a hangover and nothing else—I was safe, I was alive, I was okay. I had a mixed response, however, to the jumbo Slurpee cup I kept hidden under the bed and which now sat on the nightstand half-filled with urine, meaning I had been too intoxicated to make it to the guest bathroom a few feet away from the guest bed in the middle of the night but not so intoxicated that I was unable to direct the stream carefully into the cup and not onto the beige carpet, so it came down to: okay, peed into jumbo Slurpee cup and not on rug—plus or minus? I walked quickly to the guest room door and made sure I'd locked it before passing out. And the usual morning anxiety dissipated slightly when I realized I had in fact locked the door, which meant that Jayne wouldn't have been able to check on me (passed out, reeking of vodka, a cup filled with my urine by the side of the bed). But the anxiety returned when I realized that she probably hadn't even tried.

I carried the cup carefully toward the kitchen (forgetting to pour out its contents in the guest bathroom), again noticing the darkened carpet beneath my feet as I passed through the living room—the beige now bor-

dering on a faint green, and shaggier (first reaction: the carpet is *growing*).
Rosa was vacuuming, running the Hoover over one spot in particular. I gin-
gerly walked closer, until I saw the footprints stamped in ash and thought,
Why didn't she clean those *yesterday*? When Rosa looked up she turned the
vacuum off and waited for me to say something, but I was noticing that the
furniture still had not been put back the way it was, and my hangover and
confusion (because this room now seemed inescapably familiar to me)
made saying anything superfluous.

Finally, Rosa gestured at the carpeting. "I think the party cause this, Mr.
Ellis."

I stared down at the ashy footprints embedded there. "How can the party
cause the carpet to change its color?"

"I hear there was many people." She paused. "Maybe they spill their
drink?"

I slowly turned to face her. "What do you think we were serving them?
Green dye?"

Rosa stared at me, humbled. A pause that seemed to last a decade ensued. I tried to offset the harshness of my tone by making a casual gesture.
Without thinking I raised the Slurpee cup to my lips and then, just as casually, stopped myself.

"Miss Dennis—she outside" was all Rosa said, then looked away from
me and turned the Hoover on again as I moved toward the kitchen.

On the table were the morning papers, and there was another headline
about yet another missing boy, this one named Maer Cohen. I glanced at
his photo quickly (twelve, nondescriptly Semitic) and noticed that he'd disappeared from Midland, which was only a fifteen-minute drive down the
interstate from where we lived. My response was to turn the paper over.
"Not today, can't deal with that today," I said aloud as I moved to the sink
and discreetly poured out the contents of the Slurpee cup and rinsed it. And
when I leaned against the counter, my hands picked up the vibrations of
the whisper-quiet Miele dishwasher concealed behind the cherrywood panels. The vibration was soothing, but soon the sound of the leaf blower moving around the side of the house and into the backyard caused me to look
up and out the wall of glass.

And then I remembered the headstone.

Craning my neck, I cautiously scanned the field.

I hesitated before accepting that it was no longer there.

And the epic darkness of last night flowed back to me.

But I walked outside onto the deck and it was a clear, beautiful day, still unseasonably warm, and everything seemed so less menacing in the light, almost as if the things I'd seen last night (and the fear I had felt) never existed. Victor lay in a heap in front of me, undisturbed by the roar of the leaf blower, and when I opened the kitchen door his tail started thudding expectantly against the deck but it stopped in midair when he realized who it was and then the tail lowered itself slowly until it curled between his hind legs. The dog flared its nostrils and let out a wet and heavy sigh. I searched my jeans for a Xanax and popped two and something briefly lifted off me, but then I saw the pool man (yes, this was definitely a Saturday) fishing what looked like a dead crow out of the Jacuzzi. (On Sunday night at the Allens' I would find out that another crow had been nailed to the trunk of a large pine tree in front of the Larsons' house and another crow had been "broken in half" and stuffed into the Moores' mailbox; there was also one found mangled—"chewed on" is the phrase Mark Huntington will use—in the back of Nicholas Moore's Grand Cherokee, and yet another crow was dangling from a massive spiderweb that spanned the two oaks in the O'Connors' front yard.) As I moved closer toward the Jacuzzi, I noticed that what differentiated this particular crow from any I had ever seen was its abnormally long and pointed beak. The pool man and I stood there studying the bird, both of us speechless, until he asked, "Do you guys have a cat?" The smell of smoke was in the air, and the sun was still climbing the sky. Sarah had left her Terby lying by the pool, and in the morning light it resembled something black and dead.

I looked over at the field again to make sure that the headstone was gone.

I stared at the empty field and out to where the ground rose slightly just before the woods began and remembered how Jayne called the field a "meadow," making it seem far more innocent than I now felt it was. The sound of the leaf blower kept getting closer, and I motioned to the gardener—a young white kid I'd never spoken to before. He turned the blower off and walked over, squinting in the harsh sunlight. I told the gardener there was something I wanted to show him and gestured toward the field. As we walked across the yard I asked if he had seen or heard anything strange lately. I noticed how deliberately I was walking while waiting for his answer, our feet crunching over the dead leaves.

"Strange?" he asked. "Well, Ms. Dennis was complaining that something was eating her plants and flowers. A couple of dead mice, a squirrel or two—pretty torn up. That's about it." The gardener shrugged. His tone suggested that none of this was unusual.

"It was probably our dog," I said brusquely. "That thing on the deck. He has a cruel, prankish streak in him."

The gardener didn't know what to say after that. Just a pause in which he smiled but the smile faded when he saw I wasn't joking.

"Well, dogs don't usually eat the kind of flowers Ms. Dennis has."

We were now on the periphery of the yard.

"You don't know this dog," I said. "You have no idea what he's capable of."

"Is that . . . right?" I heard the gardener murmur.

"I found something strange last night in the field."

We stepped over a low concrete divider and were now standing where the headstone had been and someone had dug a hole (my most hopeful scenario). I pointed at the wide, black, wet patch I'd slipped in, and which now led from where the headstone had stood and stretched toward our yard, where it abruptly ended at the divider. The gardener laid down the leaf blower and, taking his cap off, wiped the sweat from his forehead. The black trail was glistening in the midmorning sun—there was a white veneer of crust overlaying it but the trail wasn't entirely dry yet.

"What is it?" he asked, and I caught an expression usually associated with dead things.

"Well, that's what I want to know."

"It looks like, um, mud."

"That's not mud. It's slime."

"It's what?"

"Slime. That's *slime*." I realized I had now said that word three times.

The gardener grimaced slightly. Kneeling down, he murmured a few noncommittal suggestions that I couldn't hear. I looked back at the pool man, who was dumping the crow into a white plastic bucket. A warm wind was rippling the water in the pool, and high white clouds moved swiftly across the sky, blocking the sun and darkening the spot where we were standing. This field is a graveyard, I suddenly told myself. The ground beneath us was jammed with dead bodies, and one of them had escaped. That's what caused the trail. That's what dragged itself toward our house. The sound of kids playing somewhere in the neighborhood—their cries of surprise and disappointment associated with something *living*—momentarily comforted me, and the Xanax had increased my blood flow to the point that I could inhale and exhale without my chest aching.

"I slipped in that last night," I finally said, and then added, before I could stop myself, "What made it?"

"What *made* it?" he asked. "Well, it *is* a slime trail of some kind." The gardener paused. "I'd say a snail, a slug, or a whole hell of a lotta them made it but damn . . . this is really too big for a . . . slug." He paused again. "Plus we haven't had any snail problems here."

I stood there, staring down at the gardener. "Too big for a slug, huh?" I sighed. "Well, that really sums it up nicely. This is encouraging."

The gardener stood up, still staring at the trail, perplexed. "And it *smells* funny—"

"Can you just get rid of it?" I asked, cutting him off.

"This is really weird . . ." he muttered, *but so are you* his expression told me. "Maybe it's that dog you've got such a problem with." He shrugged lamely, aiming for levity.

"I wouldn't put it past him," I said. "He's capable of anything. He's got quite the attitude."

We both turned and looked at Victor innocently lying on his side, oblivious. He slowly raised his head and, after a beat, yawned at us. It looked as if he were going to yawn a second time, but instead his head lolled forward and rested itself lazily on the deck, his tongue flopping out of his mouth.

"He's, um . . . bipolar," I told the gardener.

"Yeah, he looks like a problem . . . I guess," the gardener murmured.

I didn't say anything.

"I'll hose it down and . . . we'll just hope it doesn't come back."

(*But it will,* I heard the woods whispering.)

That was the extent of the conversation. It wasn't going to proceed anywhere else so I left the gardener and as I started walking back across the yard I could hear voices from the side of the house that faced the Allens'. I moved toward them.

When I came around the corner, Jayne was standing with our contractor, Omar (there had been lengthy discussions recently about adding a skylight in the foyer), and they both had the same stance: hands on hips, faces tilted upward toward the second floor. Jayne noticed me and actually smiled, which I took as an invitation to smile back and join them. Walking over I also looked up. Surrounding the large windows of the master bedroom, and above the French doors that framed the media room situated below it, were huge patches where the lily white paint was peeling off the side of the house, revealing a pink stucco underneath. Omar was holding an iced coffee from Starbucks, Persols pushed up on his forehead, totally confused. At first glance it looked as if the house was peeling randomly, as if someone had blindly scraped at the wall in a rushed and curving motion (could that have been what Robby heard in the middle of the night?), but the longer you stared at the swirling patches they began to seem patterned and deliberate, as if there was a message hidden in them, some code being spelled out. The wall was telling us (me) something. I know this wall, I thought to myself. I had seen it before. The wall was a page waiting to be read. At our feet were flakes of paint so finely ground that they resembled piles of flour.

"This shouldn't be happening," Omar said.

"Could it be kids? A Halloween prank?" I was asking. "Could it have happened the night of the party?" I paused and then, trying to gain favor with Jayne, added, "I bet Jay did it."

"No," Jayne said. "This started happening at the beginning of the summer and it's just been accelerating."

Omar touched the side of the house (I shuddered) and then brushed his palms off on his khakis. "Well, it looks like . . . claw marks," he said.

"Is that some kind of tool?" I asked. "What's a clawmark?"

"No—like something's clawing at it." And then Omar stopped. "But I don't know how anybody—whatever it was—got up there."

"Well, who lived here before?" I asked. "Maybe it's just naturally peeling." And then I reminded them of the heavy rains from late August and early September.

Jayne and Omar both glanced at me.

"What? I mean, why was this painted over?" I asked, shrugging. "That's . . . a nice color."

"The house is new, Bret," Jayne sighed. "There was no other paint."

"Plus that wasn't the base color," Omar added.

"Well, maybe the paint's oxidizing, y'know, the enamel, um, underneath?"

Frowning, Omar grew quickly tired of me and pulled out a cell phone.

Jayne took one more look at the wall and then turned my way. She seemed inordinately cheerful this morning, and when she looked at my face she smiled again. Her hair was pulled back in a ponytail and I reached out to touch it—a gesture that only widened the smile.

"I don't know why you're smiling, baby. There's a dead crow in our Jacuzzi."

"It must've happened after you got out of it last night."

"I didn't take a Jacuzzi last night, babe."

"Well, there was a wet pair of shorts on the railing by the deck."

"Yeah, I saw them but they aren't mine," I said. "Maybe Jay stopped by."

Jayne's forehead creased. "Are you sure they're not yours?"

"Yeah, I'm sure, and hey—did somebody from the decorating company come by this morning?"

"Yeah, they forgot a gravestone." She paused briefly. "And a skeleton and a few bats."

"That always happens on Saturdays, doesn't it?" I grinned and then, trying to keep everything on a light note, I asked the following in a manner as casual as possible: "Did you know that someone wrote my father's name on that headstone?"

"What are you talking about?" she asked.

"When I came back last night—wait, you're not mad at me because I got tired and had to skip out on trick-or-treating . . . are you?"

She sighed. "Look, it's the first of the month. Let's forget everything that's been happening and let's try to start over. How's that? Let's just start over. New beginnings."

The hangover vanished. The fear was gone. This could all work out, I thought.

"I love your recovery time," I said.

"Yeah, fast to get pissed, faster to forgive."

"That's what I love and admire about you."

She flinched. "What—that I'm a total enabler?"

Behind her, Omar was on his cell, pacing and gesturing at the wall, which I couldn't help looking up at again. How *could* something get up there? I wondered. *What if it could fly?* came back in response.

"What about the gravestone?" Jayne was asking. "Bret—hello?"

I made the effort and focused away from the wall and back on Jayne. "Yeah, when I came home last night I noticed it was left over from the party and when I went down to take a look at it I saw that somebody had written my dad's name on it . . . and they also knew his birth date and, um, the year he died."

Jayne's expression darkened. "Well, it wasn't there this morning."

"How do you know?"

"Because I took the guys out there when they removed it." She paused. "And there was nothing on it."

"Do . . . you think it rained last night?" I cocked my head.

"Do . . . you think you had too much to drink last night?" She also cocked her head, mimicking me.

"I'm not drinking, Jayne—" I stopped myself.

We studied each other for a long time. She won. I settled. I rose up to it.

"Okay," I said. "New beginnings."

I placed my hands on her shoulders, which caused her to smile ruefully at me.

"Hey—what's going on today?" I asked. "Where are the kids?"

"Sarah's upstairs doing homework and Robby's at soccer practice and when he returns you shall be taking them to the movies at the mall," she said in her "theatrical" voice.

"And of course you'll be accompanying us."

"Unfortunately, I will be with my trainer for most of the day at his small and lovely gymnasium downtown rehearsing for the reshoots. So, alas, you're on your own." She paused. "Think you can handle it?"

"Ah yes," I said. "You need to learn how to be flung around the top of a skyscraper at midnight. I forgot."

I swallowed hard. There was a slight tremor and then I accepted the reality of my Saturday. I involuntarily glanced at the side of the house Omar was pacing beneath and the paint was the color of salmon and it was touching something in me, taking me back somewhere. Jayne spoke again.

"Yeah, sure, the mall . . ." I murmured reassuringly.

"I'm going to ask you something and don't get mad." The smile was no longer there.

"Honey, I'm always furious so you can't make me mad."

"Have you had anything to drink today?"

An intake of breath on my part. This lack of trust was a horrible realization. It was such a pure and concerned question that I could not possibly be offended by it.

"No," I said in a small voice. "I just got up."

"You promise?" she asked.

My eyes started tearing. I felt awful. I hugged her. She let me and then gently broke away.

"I promise."

"Because you're driving the kids to the mall and, well . . ." The implication was strong enough that she didn't need to finish the sentence. She saw my reaction and tried to ask in a playful way, "Can I make sure?"

I decided to be playful too. "This is a very easy test to pass." I exhaled and then kissed her. Against me she felt soft and small.

The smile returned as I pulled back, yet she still seemed worried (would that ever leave?) when she asked, "And nothing else?"

"Honey, look, I wouldn't put *myself* behind the wheel of a car under the influence, let alone our kids, okay?"

Her face softened and for the first time this morning she smiled genuinely, without forcing it, without any affectation. It was spontaneous and unrehearsed.

This moved me to ask, "What? What is it?"

"You said something."

"What did I say?"

"You said 'our.' "

had scanned the papers to see what was playing at the Fortinbras Mall sixteen-plex and chose something that wouldn't confuse Sarah or annoy Robby (a movie about a handsome teenage alien's disregard for authority and his subsequent reformation), and since I suspected there was no way Robby would have agreed to this excursion unless he'd been cajoled into it by Jayne (I didn't even want to imagine that scene — her pleading versus his furtive begging) I anticipated that he wouldn't come without a fight, so I was surprised by how calm and placid Robby was (after a shower and a change of clothes) as he shuffled out the front door and walked with his head bowed down to the Range Rover, where Sarah sat in the front seat, trying to open a Backstreet Boys CD (which I eventually helped her with and slipped into the disc player), and where I was staring out the windshield thinking about my novel. When Robby climbed into the back seat I asked how soccer practice had gone, but he was too busy untangling the headphones to the Discman in his lap. So I asked again and all I got back from him was "It's soccer practice, Bret. What do you mean, how did it go?" This was not the way I wanted to spend my Saturday — *Teenage Pussy* was waiting for me — but I owed Jayne this outing (and besides, Saturdays weren't mine anymore). The guilt that had been building since I moved into the house in July was announcing itself more clearly and it was coming down to: I was the one responsible for Robby's misery, yet Jayne was the one trying to cut the distance between me and him. She was the one on her knees pleading, and this reminded me again of why I was with her.

"Seat belts on?" I asked cheerfully as I pulled out of the driveway.

"Mommy doesn't let me sit in the front seat," Sarah said. She was wearing a Liberty-print shirt with a Peter Pan collar and cotton velvet bootcut pants and a pure angora poncho. ("Are all six-year-olds dressing like Cher?" I asked Marta when she delivered Sarah to my office. Marta just shrugged and said, "I think she looks cute.") Sarah was holding a tiny Hello Kitty purse that was filled with Halloween candy. She took a small canister and started popping Skittles into her mouth and throwing her head back as if they were prescription pills while kicking her legs up and down to the beat of the boy band. ,

"Why are you eating your candy that way, honey?"

"Because this is how Mommy does it when she's in the bathroom."

"Robby, will you take that candy away from your sister?"

"She's not my real sister," I heard from the back seat.

"Well, I'm not her real father," I said. "But that has nothing to do with what I just asked you."

I looked in the rearview mirror. Robby was glaring at me through his orange-tinted wraparounds, one eyebrow raised, while tugging uncomfortably at his crewneck merino sweater, which I was certain Jayne had forced him to wear.

"I can see that you're very cold and withdrawn today," I said.

"I need my allowance upped" was his response.

"I think if you were friendlier that wouldn't be a problem."

"What's that supposed to mean?"

"Doesn't your mom handle your allowance?"

A huge sigh emanated from him.

"Mommy doesn't let me sit in the front seat," Sarah said again.

"Well, Daddy thinks it's okay. Plus you look quite comfortable. And will you please stop eating the Skittles that way?"

We suddenly passed a three-story mock-colonial monstrosity on Voltemand Drive when Sarah sat up and pointed at the house and cried out, "That's where Ashleigh's birthday was!"

The mention of that party in September caused a surge of panic, and I gripped the steering wheel tightly.

I had taken Sarah to Ashleigh Wagner's birthday party as a favor to Jayne, and there was a sixty-foot stegosaurus balloon and a traveling animal show and an arch made up of Beanie Babies framing the entrance and a machine spewing a continuous stream of bubbles around the backyard. Two weeks prior to the actual event there had been a "rehearsal" party in order to gauge which kids "worked" and which did not, who caused trouble and who seemed serene, who had the worst learning disability and who had heard of Mozart, who responded best to the face painting and who had the coolest SCO (special comfort object), and somehow Sarah had passed (though I suspected that being the daughter of Jayne Dennis was what got her the invite). The Wagners were serving the lingering parents Valrhona hot chocolate that had been made without milk (other things excised that day: wheat, gluten, dairy, corn syrup) and when they offered me a cup I stayed and chatted. I was being a dad and at the point at which I vowed that nothing would ever change that (plus the Klonopin was good at reinforcing patience) and I appeared hopefully normal even though I was appalled by what I was witnessing. The whole thing seemed harmless—just another gratuitously whimsical upscale birthday party—until I started noticing that all the kids were on meds (Zoloft, Luvox, Celexa, Paxil) that caused them to move lethargically and speak in affectless monotones. And some bit their fingernails until they bled and a pediatrician was on hand "just in case." The six-year-old daughter of an IBM executive was wearing a tube top and platform shoes. Someone handed me a pet guinea pig while I watched the kids interact—a jealous tantrum over a parachute, a relay race, kicking a soccer ball through a glowing disc, the mild reprimands, the minimal vomiting, Sarah chewing on a shrimp tail (*"Une crevette!"* she squealed; yes, the Wagners were serving poached prawns)—and I just cradled the guinea pig until a caterer took it away from me when he noticed it writhing in my hands. And that's when it hit: the desire to flee Elsinore Lane and Midland County. I started craving cocaine so badly, it took all my willpower not to ask the Wagners for a drink and so I left after promising to pick Sarah up at the allotted time. During those two hours I almost drove back to Manhattan but then calmed down enough that my desperate plan became a gentle afterthought, and when I picked up Sarah she was holding a goody bag filled with a Raffi CD and nothing edible and after telling me she'd learned her four least favorite words she announced, "Grandpa talked to me."

I turned to look at her as she innocently nibbled a prawn. "Who did, honey?"

"Grandpa."

"Grandpa Dennis?" I asked.

"No. The other grandpa."

I knew that Mark Strauss (Sarah's father) had lost both parents before he met Jayne and that's when the anxiety hit. "What other grandpa?" I asked carefully.

"He came up to me at the party and said he was my grandpa."

"But honey, that grandpa's dead," I said in a soothing tone.

"But Grandpa isn't dead, Daddy," she said happily, kicking the seat.

It was silent in the car—except for the Backstreet Boys—as that day came rushing back and I forced myself to forget about it while I cruised onto the interstate.

"Daddy, why don't you work?" Sarah now asked. She was making satisfied smacking sounds after swallowing each Skittle.

"Well, I do work, honey."

"Why don't you go to an office?"

"Because I work at home."

"Why?"

"Because I'm a stay-at-home dad," I answered calmly. "Hey, where are we? A cocktail party?"

"Why?"

"Please don't do this now, honey, okay?"

"Why do you stay at home?"

"Well, I work at the college too."

"Daddy?"

"Yes, honey?"

"What's a college?"

"A place I go to teach singularly untalented slackers how to write prose."

"When do you go?"

"On Wednesdays."

"But is that work?"

"Work puts people in bad moods, honey. You don't really want to work. In fact you should avoid work."

"You don't work and you're in a bad mood."

Robby had said this. Tensing up, I glanced at him in the rearview mirror. He was staring out the window, his chin in his hand.

"How do you know I'm in a bad mood?" I asked.

He didn't say anything. I realized the answer to that question required an elaboration that Robby wasn't capable of. I also realized: Let's not go there.

"I think I come off as a pretty happy guy," I said.

A long, horrible pause.

"I'm very lucky," I added.

Sarah considered this. "Why are you lucky, Daddy?"

"Well, you guys are very lucky too. You lead very lucky lives. In fact you're even luckier than your dad."

"Why, Daddy?"

"Well, Daddy has a very hard life. Daddy would like snack time. Daddy would like to take a nap. Daddy would like to go to the playground."

I could see in the rearview mirror that Robby had clamped his hands over his ears.

We were passing a waterslide that had closed for the season when Sarah shouted, "I want to go on the waterslide!"

"Why?" It was my turn to ask.

"Because I wanna slide down it!"

"Why?"

"Because it's fun," she said with less enthusiasm, confused at being on this side of the questioning.

"Why?"

"Because . . . I like it?"

"Why do you—"

"Will you stop asking her why?" Robby said fervently, pleading.

I quickly glanced in the rearview mirror at Robby, who looked stricken.

I averted my gaze to where the Backstreet Boys CD was spinning. "I don't know why you kids listen to this crap," I mumbled. "I should buy you some CDs. Make you listen to something decent. Springsteen, Elvis Costello, The Clash . . ."

"Who in the hell is Elvis Costello?"

We had pulled off the interstate and were heading toward the mall on Ophelia Boulevard when Robby asked this and when I slowed down for a stop sign I saw Aimee Light's BMW pull out of the Whole Foods parking lot on the other side of the road.

And I could see that someone was in the passenger seat. And that it was a man.

Robby's comment about Elvis Costello, the stop sign, spotting Aimee's car, realizing that she was driving with a *man*—all this happened within the space of a few seconds, almost simultaneously.

I immediately made a U-turn and started trailing them.

Sarah was lip-synching to the Backstreet Boys when suddenly she whirled around in her seat. "Daddy, where are we going?"

"We're going to the mall, honey."

"But this isn't the way to the mall."

"Just sit back and appreciate your father's driving skills."

"But Daddy, where are we going?"

"I'm just curious about something, honey."

She was driving. She was laughing. I was directly behind them and she was laughing. And then she reached over and touched the side of his face.

At the next light (three blocks in which I heard nothing but her laughter and saw only the back of a white BMW) she kissed him.

I immediately had to resist the urge to press down on the horn.

I wanted to pull over next to them. I wanted to see who the guy — my rival — was.

But the boulevard was crowded and I couldn't pull next to her in either lane. I don't remember if the kids were saying anything to me (I had blocked them out) as I reached for my cell phone and dialed her number (I had planned to do this at the mall anyway while the kids were watching the movie) and — even in this panicked, jealous state — I experienced the pang of guilt I always felt dialing Aimee Light's number because I had it memorized yet had trouble remembering the number of the house in which I lived.

I watched very carefully as both she and the guy (I caught a glimpse of his profile but not enough to see a face) looked at the control panel in the same instant.

I waited. Aimee picked up the cell and checked the incoming number.

And then she placed the phone back down.

Her voice: "It's Aimee, please leave a message, thanks."

I clicked off. I was sweating. I turned on the air conditioning.

"She didn't pick up," I said out loud.

"Who, Daddy?" Sarah asked. "Who didn't pick up?"

The light turned green. The BMW drove away. As it did, the guy turned in his seat and looked back at the Range Rover, but the sun was reflecting off the rear window and I couldn't make out any of his features. My anxiety restrained me from following them. I didn't even want to know where they were going. Plus what would the kids tell Jayne? *Mommy, Daddy followed somebody and when he called her she didn't pick up.* A car blaring its horn was my reminder to start moving again. I made another U-turn and drove toward the mall, where I circled the miles of asphalt that surrounded it until Robby leaned over and said, pointing, "There's a space right there, Bret. Just park the car." I did.

We went straight to the multiplex. I was too distracted by the guy in the passenger seat to proceed with this day leisurely. Could it have been Alvin Mendolsohn, her thesis instructor? No, this guy was younger, her age, a student maybe. I flashed on the profile and the blurred face but came up with nothing. I purchased the tickets for *Some Call Him Rebel* and was so out of it that when the kids asked for candy and popcorn and Cokes I numbly bought them whatever they wanted even though Jayne had warned me not to. I let them choose their seats in the cavernous auditorium, which was oddly empty for a Saturday matinee and I feared that I'd chosen an unpopular movie but Robby—who was a movie nut—didn't complain. Again, I thought of all the bartering Jayne had gone through to get him here and realized that he probably would have sat through *Shoah*. Sarah sat between Robby and me and was drinking her soda too quickly and when I warned her not to Robby rolled his eyes and sighed while opening a box of Junior Mints and soon both of them were concentrating on the action storming across the screen. About twenty minutes into the movie when I could stand it no longer I leaned over and told Robby to watch his sister while I went to make a phone call, and I hesitated because I remembered the name of the most recent missing boy: Maer Cohen. Robby nodded intently without looking at me and I realized that no one was going to take him anywhere (*unless he let them*, came an unbidden thought). I paced the lobby of the multiplex while dialing Aimee's number again and this time I left a message: "Hey, Aimee, it's Bret. Um, I saw you about forty minutes ago coming out of Whole Foods and it looked like you were, um, having fun . . ." I laughed weakly. "Well, that's it. Call me on my cell." I clicked off. When I went back to the auditorium the screen was a blur. It was hopeless. I couldn't concentrate on anything except the fact that I kept thinking I had been in that car with Aimee Light. I thought the guy in the passenger seat was myself. When I focused: fleets of black hovercraft anchored in space.

After the movie I just went through the motions: soft-serve frozen yogurt in the food court, a game of laser tag in the arcade, and Sarah wanted to go to Abercrombie and Fitch, where I flipped through a catalogue, clutching my cell phone and willing it to ring and the kids tried on clothes until Robby told me he wanted to stop by Mail Boxes Etc. I remember asking him why but don't remember his answer (this would prove to be a key mistake on my part). Sarah and I followed him to the other side of the mall. Sarah was numbering her steps and telling me that she wanted lots of neon and a curtain made of beads in her room. Outside Mail Boxes Etc., Robby ran into a group of his disaffected clique, who were exiting the same upscale post office that Robby was (coincidentally) heading into and where he was forced to introduce me.

"This is Bret," he said.

"I'm his father," I offered the group of boys.

"Yeah, he's my dad," Robby said tonelessly.

Robby's face was suddenly flushed. He nodded even though his expression suggested that he didn't have the slightest idea of what that exchange signified. That this was the first time he had called me Dad. When I realized he was not going to introduce the boys (there were four of them) individually, I sat down with Sarah on a nearby bench and watched them interact. A discussion ensued about the school's banning of dodgeball and then they compared notes on Halloween. The boys glared at one another as they talked yet everything was said with a marked lack of enthusiasm, and they made vain, halfhearted threats at one another. All of them had headphones dangling around their necks and cargo pants from Banana Republic and they all wore the same orange-tinted wraparound sunglasses that Robby was wearing. When one of the boys glanced over at me as if I were contagious I finally understood that I was The Distraction—the reason this conversation was not going to last much longer. Once they realized I was observing them, the one I instinctively loathed the most gave me a look that said "Who the fuck are you?" and I overheard the term "dickweed"—though in relation to whom I wasn't sure. The hard smooth faces barely touched by acne, the fashionable crew cuts, the hands jittery because of the meds, their uncertainty with one another—it all led to one thing for me: I did not trust any of them. And then, without warning, the group of boys broke up. Whatever interest they had in each other evaporated so rapidly that it seemed not to have existed at all. Robby trudged toward us under the glare of the mall light and it suddenly bothered me that so little of his life revolved around poetry or romance. Everything was grounded in the dull and anxious day-to-day. Everything was a performance. But what bothered me more—the thing that actually was the reason I became riveted by the boys—was that I'd heard one of them—as I turned away to guide Sarah to that nearby bench—say the name Maer Cohen. When I heard that name uttered I quickly glanced back as two of the boys made a hushing motion to the boy who'd spoken the name. Once they saw the startled expression on my face they perfected their poses. Poses they maintained despite the fact that Maer Cohen was one of them, was their age, was a boy who had lived only minutes from this mall, but now had vanished. And the thing that made me squirm with unease on that bench was the fact that not one of the five boys, including my son, had seemed frightened. None of them seemed scared. What bothered me most was how they had to dampen their enthusiasm—their glee—in front of the adult.

And then: an adrenaline rush interrupted by a question from Sarah.

"Daddy?" she asked.

"Yes?"

"Do you help people?"

But I wasn't answering her anymore because I realized who was in the passenger seat of Aimee Light's BMW.

It was the boy who had come to my office wanting me to sign a book.

It was the boy who came to a Halloween party dressed as Patrick Bateman.

The same boy that Aimee Light claimed she had never seen before.

It was Clayton.

"Daddy . . . do you help people?" Sarah asked again.

11. detective

Everything was suddenly a mirage. I drove Robby and Sarah home while replaying the first time I met Aimee Light: a girl staring at me blankly from across a campus party, the cocaine I'd snorted in the dingy bathroom giving me a burly, reckless confidence, the ensuing conversation about her thesis during which I realized I could probably control her even though she was throwing off the opposite vibe—I located it in the yawn after she told me its title ("Destination Nowhere"), and it was in the studied indifference, the (ho-hum) calculated laughter, her "boredom": all just defense mechanisms—but I was patient, and was so adept at pretending to be interested in women I simply wanted to sleep with that I had perfected my own performance: the devil grin, the deep and persuasive nodding, the off-the-cuff comments about other girlfriends and my famous wife. Ultimately, everything was an act. We were on a stage. The cup of beer she sipped from was a prop, and the subsequent foam cresting her upper lip caused my eyes, as if rehearsed, to hone in on her mouth, and when she realized I was gazing at her she swayed toward—and complimented—a sculpture made of wire hanging in a corner of Booth House. Male undergrads were slithering around her, merely outlines in the darkness, and her face was streaked orange by the glow of a lava lamp, and an hour later I had followed her around the entire room without realizing it and she was now smiling the whole time, even when I walked away since it was late and I was a family man who had to get home and it was wrenching and I had already lost my faith. But I regained it when I looked back and saw that her face was creased with a frown. Had she known Clayton then? Had Clayton stopped by my office knowing she'd be there? Had—

"Daddy, the light's green again," I heard Sarah whimper, and I shot forward.

As if guided by radar I drove to Ira's Spirits and parked in front. I told Robby to watch his sister but he had his Discman on, tuning out the world, his future flattened by my presence, and I mumbled something to Sarah and closed the door before she could say anything and rushed into the liquor store and purchased a bottle of Ketel One. Barely a minute passed before I was back in the Range Rover—the transaction occurred with that much urgency.

At Elsinore: Jayne wouldn't be home for an hour, Marta was conferring with Rosa about dinner, Robby ambled upstairs ostensibly to study for a test, Sarah went to the media room to play Pinobee, a video game about a flight-challenged and oddly charmless bumblebee whose expression of disgust always managed to fill me with alarm. I went to my office and locked the door, and filled a large coffee mug with vodka (I didn't need a mixer anymore, I didn't even need ice) and drank half of it before trying Aimee Light again on her cell. Waiting for an answer I sat at the desk and went over e-mails left unchecked from yesterday. One from Jay, one from Binky informing me that Harrison Ford's people were delighted by my interest and had inquired when I could get out to L.A., and there was an odd one from Gary Fisketjon, my editor at Knopf, who wrote that a detective saying he was from the Midland County Sheriff's Department had called his office asking how they could get in touch with me, and Gary hoped it was all right if he gave them my number. Before the fear began creeping in again I found another e-mail that arrived last night from the Bank of America in Sherman Oaks. Its arrival time: 2:40 a.m.

I scrolled down the blank page until Aimee's phone stopped ringing and her message played out. I clicked off the cell after the beep when I noticed that the light on my answering machine was blinking. I reached over and pressed Play.

"Mr. Ellis, this is Detective Donald Kimball. I'm with the Midland County Sheriff's Department and I'd like to talk to you about something that's, well, rather urgent . . . and so we should probably talk as soon as you can." Pause, static. "If you want we can meet here, in Midland, though considering what I want to talk to you about I think it might be best if I dropped by your place." He left a cell phone number. "Again, please call me as soon as you can."

I finished the mug of vodka and poured myself another.

When I called Kimball back he didn't want to discuss whatever "this" was over the phone, and I didn't want to discuss it in Midland, so I gave him our address. Kimball said he could be at the house in thirty minutes, but

Kimball showed up fifteen minutes after we hung up, a discrepancy which forced me to realize vaguely, uneasily, that this was probably more important than I'd first thought. I was hoping for a welcome distraction from fretting about Aimee. But what Kimball presented me with was not the respite I was hoping for. I was drunk when he arrived. I was sober by the time he left.

There was nothing much to notice about Donald Kimball—my age, vaguely handsome (*I'd do him*, I thought drunkenly, and then: *Do . . . what?*), dressed casually in jeans and a Nike sweatshirt, cropped blond hair, Wayfarer sunglasses he whipped off as soon as I opened the front door—and except for the nondescript sedan parked behind him at the curb he could have passed for any one of the handsome, affluent suburban dads who resided in the neighborhood. What singled him out was that he held a copy of *American Psycho*. It was frayed and yellowed and ominously dotted with Post-its. We shook hands and I ushered him into the house and after offering him a drink (which he declined) led him to my office while I kept glancing at the copy of the book. When I asked if he wanted it signed, Kimball paused grimly, thanked me and said that he did not.

I sat in my swivel chair and took little sips from the coffee mug. Kimball sat across from me on a sleek, modern Italian couch that should have been on the other side of the room but now had been moved beneath the movie poster for *Less Than Zero*. My office had been rearranged yet again. While Kimball began talking I drank the vodka and tried to understand why I was at a standstill about the room and the placement of the furniture within it.

"If you'd like to check in with the sheriff's department, please feel free to do so," Kimball was saying.

I started paying attention. "About . . . what?"

Kimball paused. "About my being here, Mr. Ellis."

"Well, I'm assuming my publishing house made sure everything was in order, no?" I asked. "I mean, my editor didn't seem to think anything was unusual." I stopped. "I mean, if you are who you're saying then I'm prone to believe you." I stopped again. "I'm a very trusting person." Another pause. "Unless, um, you're a deranged fan and you're after my wife." Pause. "You aren't . . . are you?"

Kimball smiled tightly. "No, no, nothing like that. We knew your wife lived in town but we weren't sure if you were here or in New York, and your publishing house simply gave us your business number and so, well, here we are." His expression became one of casual concern. "Do you get a lot of that—crazy fans and stalkers and all that?"

At that moment I instantly trusted him. "Nothing too unusual," I said, searching my desk for the pack of cigarettes that was never there. "Just the typical restraining order, y'know, nothing too scary. Just the average life of the . . . um, average celebrity couple."

Yes, this came out of my mouth. Yes, Kimball smiled awkwardly.

He breathed in and leaned forward, still holding the book, studying me. I took another sip from the coffee mug and saw him open a brown notepad he was holding along with my book.

"So, a detective is in my office with a copy of *American Psycho*," I rambled. "I hope you liked it, since I had something very special to say with that book." I tried to conceal a belch and failed.

"Well, I am a fan, Mr. Ellis, but that's not exactly why I'm here."

"So what's up, then?" Another small sip.

He looked down at the opened notebook resting on his lap. It seemed as if he was reluctant to proceed, as if Kimball was still making up his mind about how much he should reveal in order to gain my compliance. But his demeanor suddenly changed and he cleared his throat. "What I'm about to present you with will probably be upsetting, which is why I thought we should talk privately."

I immediately reached into my pocket and popped a Xanax.

Kimball waited politely.

After a moment of throat clearing, I eked out: "I'm ready."

Kimball now had his game face on. "Recently—very recently—my colleagues and I became convinced that a theory about a case Midland County has been investigating for the last four months was in fact no longer a theory and—"

I flashed on something and interrupted him. "Wait, this isn't about the missing children, is it?"

"No," Kimball said carefully. "It's not about the missing boys. Both cases did begin around the same time, at or near the beginning of summer, but we don't believe they're connected."

I did not feel the need to tell Kimball that the beginning of summer was when I first arrived in this town. "What's going on?" I asked.

Kimball cleared his throat. He skimmed a page in his notebook and then turned it over to inspect the next page. "A Mr. Robert Rabin was killed on June first on Commonwealth Avenue at approximately nine-thirty in the evening. He'd taken his dog out for a walk and was attacked on the street, and stabbed randomly in his upper body area and his throat was cut—"

"Jesus Christ."

"There was no motive for the crime. It was not a robbery. Mr. Rabin had no enemies as far as we could ascertain. It was just a random killing. He was—we thought—simply at the wrong place at the wrong time." He paused. "But there was something strange about the crime besides the viciousness of the attack and its apparent lack of motive." Kimball paused again. "The dog he was walking was also killed."

Another pause filled the office. "That's . . . also terrible," I finally said, guessing.

The length of Kimball's next pause was painting the room with a distinct and palatable anxiety.

"It was a Shar-Pei," he said.

I paused, taking this in. "That's . . . even worse?" I asked meekly, and automatically took another sip of vodka.

"Well, it's a very rare breed of dog and even rarer in this neck of the woods."

"I . . . see." I suddenly realized I had not hidden the vodka bottle. It was out in the open, sitting on my desk, half-empty and with its top off. Kimball glanced at it briefly before looking down at a page in his notebook. Sitting across from him I could make out a chart, lists, numbers, a graph.

"In the Vintage edition of *American Psycho*," he said, "on pages one sixty-four through one sixty-six a man is murdered in much the same way that Robert Rabin was."

A pause in which I was supposed to locate something and make a connection.

Kimball continued. "The man in your book was also walking a dog."

We both breathed in, knowing what was coming next.

"It was a Shar-Pei."

"Wait a minute," I automatically said, wanting to stop the fear that kept increasing as Kimball neared the information he wanted to impart.

"Yes?"

I stared at him blankly.

When he realized I had nothing further to say he looked back at his notes. "A transient—named Albert Lawrence—was blinded last December, six months before the Rabin murder. The case remained unsolved but there were certain elements that kept bothering me." Pause. "There were certain similarities that I couldn't quite put my finger on at first."

The atmosphere in the room had flown past anxiety and was now officially entering into dread. The vodka was not going to work anymore and I tried to set the mug back on my desk without trembling. I didn't want to hear anything else but I couldn't help asking, "Why?"

"Mr. Lawrence had been inebriated at the time of the attack. In fact he was passed out in an alley off Sutton Street in Coleman."

Coleman. A small town about thirty miles from Midland.

"Mr. Lawrence's account was considered somewhat unreliable due to the amount of alcohol he'd consumed, and we had very little to go on in the way of an accurate physical description of his assailant." Kimball turned a page. "He said the man who attacked him was wearing a suit and carrying a briefcase but he couldn't recall any physical characteristics as to the man's face, his height, weight, hair color, etcetera." Kimball continued studying his notes before looking up at me. "There had been a couple of articles about the case in the local press but considering what was happening in Coleman at that time—the bomb scares and all the attention those were receiving—the attack on Mr. Lawrence didn't really register, even though there were some murmurings that the attack had been racially motivated."

"Racially motivated?" And bomb scares? In Coleman? Where had I been last December? Either drugged out or in rehab was all I could come up with.

"According to Mr. Lawrence, his assailant apparently used a racial epithet before leaving the scene."

Kimball kept pausing, which I was now grateful for since it was helping me put myself back together after each new byte of information was handed out.

"So, this Mr. Lawrence . . . was black?"

After another pause, Kimball nodded. "He also had a dog. A small mutt that the assailant also attacked." He glanced down at his notebook again. "The assailant broke the dog's two front legs."

I did not want it to, but the point of Kimball's visit was becoming clearer to me.

"Mr. Lawrence also had a history of mental illness and had been institutionalized various times, and since Midland County doesn't have a large black community, the theory that this crime was racially motivated didn't really play out. And the case remains unsolved." Kimball paused. "But, again, there was something about it that kept bothering me. It seemed like I had read about this case before. And"—Kimball opened the copy of my book that sat in his lap—"on pages one thirty-one and one thirty-two in *American Psycho*—"

"A black homeless man was blinded." I murmured this to myself.

Kimball nodded. "And he had a dog that Patrick Bateman broke the legs of." He glanced again at his notebook and continued. "In July, a Sandy Wu, a delivery boy for a Chinese restaurant in Brigham, was murdered. Like Mr. Rabin, his throat was slashed."

I sat up. "Did . . . he have a dog?"

Kimball shifted uncomfortably and frowned, giving off the vibe that he did not think we were on the same track. But that wasn't true. I just wanted to prolong the inevitable.

"Um, no, he did not have a dog, but there was a detail that again took me back to *American Psycho*." Kimball pulled something from the notebook and reached forward to give it to me: a receipt from a restaurant called Ming's, encased tightly in a plastic slip. The receipt was wrinkled and—now I swallowed—spattered lightly with brown flecks. On the other side, scrawled in ink, were the words *I'm gonna get you too . . . bitch*.

Kimball paused after I handed the slip back to him.

"This particular order was being delivered to the Rubinstein family."

Kimball waited for my reaction, which wasn't forthcoming.

"On pages one eighty and one eighty-one a delivery boy is killed in the same manner as Mr. Wu and, as in the book, the assailant wrote the identical message that Patrick Bateman does on the back of the receipt."

I closed my eyes and then tried to open them when I heard Kimball sighing.

"We—well, actually just me at that point—backtracked to another unsolved case involving a Victoria Bell, an elderly woman who lived on Outer Circle Drive." Kimball paused. "She was decapitated."

I knew the name. A bolt of clarity shot through me when I realized where Kimball was going with this.

"There is a Victoria Bell in *American Psycho*—"

"Wait a minute, wait a minute, wait a minute—"

"—but this one was found in a motel off Route Fifty just outside Coleman about a year ago. She'd been stripped and placed in a bathtub and covered with lime."

"Wait—she was covered with *limes*?" I exclaimed, recoiling.

"No, *lime*. It's a dissolvent, Mr. Ellis."

I closed my eyes again. I did not want to go back to that book. It had been about my father (his rage, his obsession with status, his loneliness), whom I had transformed into a fictional serial killer, and I was not about to put myself through that experience again—of revisiting either Robert Ellis or

Patrick Bateman. I had moved past the casual carnage that was so prevalent in the books I'd conceived in my twenties, past the severed heads and the soup made of blood and the woman vaginally penetrated with her own rib. Exploring that kind of violence had been "interesting" and "exciting" and it was all "metaphorical" anyway—at least to me at that moment in my life, when I was young and pissed off and had not yet grasped my own mortality, a time when physical pain and real suffering held no meaning for me. I was "transgressive" and the book was really about "style" and there was no point now in reliving the crimes of Patrick Bateman and the horror they'd inspired. Sitting in my office in front of Kimball, I realized that at various times I had fantasized about this exact moment. This was the moment that detractors of the book had warned me about: if anything happened to anyone as a result of the publication of this novel, Bret Easton Ellis was to blame. Gloria Steinem had reiterated this over and over to Larry King in the winter of 1991 and that's why the National Organization for Women had boycotted the book. (In a small world filled with black ironies, Ms. Steinem eventually married David Bale, the father of the actor who played Patrick Bateman in the movie.) I thought the idea was laughable—that there was no one as insane and vicious as this fictional character out there in the real world. Besides, Patrick Bateman was a notoriously unreliable narrator, and if you actually read the book you could come away doubting that these crimes had even occurred. There were large hints that they existed only in Bateman's mind. The murders and torture were in fact fantasies fueled by his rage and fury about how life in America was structured and how this had—no matter the size of his wealth—trapped him. The fantasies were an escape. This was the book's thesis. It was about society and manners and mores, and not about cutting up women. How could anyone who read the book not see this? Yet because of the severity of the outcry over the novel the fear that maybe it wasn't such a laughable idea was never far away; always lurking was the worry about what might happen if the book fell into the wrong hands. Who knew, then, what it could inspire? And after the killings in Toronto it was no longer lurking—it was real, it existed, and it tortured me. But that had been more than ten years ago and a decade had passed without anything remotely similar happening. The book had made me wealthy and famous but I never wanted to touch it again. Now it all came rushing back, and I found myself in Patrick Bateman's shoes: I felt like an unreliable narrator, even though I knew I wasn't. Yet then I thought: Well, had he?

Kimball had articles printed off the Internet that he was now leafing through and wanting to share with me, as I sat disconsolately in my office, staring out the window at the lawn sloping toward the street and the detective's car parked there. Two boys raced by, teetering on skateboards. A crow landed on the lawn and picked disinterestedly at an autumn leaf. It was followed by another larger crow. The lawn instantly reminded me of the carpet in the living room.

Kimball could tell I was trying to distract myself, that I was trying to wish it all away, and gently said, "Mr. Ellis, you do understand where I'm going—"

"Am I a suspect?" I asked suddenly.

Kimball seemed surprised. "No, you're not."

There was a tiny moment of relief that fled in an instant.

"How do you know I'm not?"

"The night of June first you were in a rehab clinic. And on the night Sandy Wu was murdered you were giving a lecture at the college on . . ." Kimball glanced at his notes—"on the legacy of the Brat Pack in American literature."

I swallowed hard and collected myself again. "So this is obviously not a series of coincidences."

"We—that is, myself and the Midland Sheriff's Office—believe that whoever's committing these crimes is actually following the book and replicating them."

"Let me get this straight." I swallowed again. "You're telling me that Patrick Bateman is alive and well and killing people in Midland County?"

"No, someone out there is copycatting the murders from the book. And in order. It's not random. It's actually fairly careful and very well planned, to the point where the assailant has even gone so far as to locate people— victims—with similar names or similar, if not exact, occupations."

I was freezing. Nausea started sliding through me.

"You have got to be kidding me. This is a joke, right?"

"It's no longer a theory, Mr. Ellis" was all Kimball would say, as if he was warning someone.

"Do you have any leads?"

Again, Kimball sighed. "The big obstacle in terms of our investigation is that the crime scenes themselves—even with the fairly formidable amount of planning and time the killer spent at each one—are, well, they're"—and now he shrugged—"immaculate."

"What does that mean? What does that mean when you say 'immaculate'?"

"Well, basically forensics is baffled." Kimball checked his notes, though I knew he didn't need to. "No fingerprints, no hair, no fibers, nothing."

Like a ghost. That was the first thing I thought. *Like a ghost.*

Kimball repositioned himself on the couch, and then looking at me directly asked, "Have you received any strange mail lately? Any kind of correspondence from a fan that would lead you to suspect that maybe something isn't quite right?"

"Wait—why? You think this person might contact me? Do you think he's after me?" I was unable to contain my panic and immediately felt ashamed.

"No, no. Please, Mr. Ellis, calm down. That doesn't seem to be where this person is heading," Kimball said, failing to reassure me. "However, if you feel someone has contacted you in a way that's inappropriate or a violation of some kind, please tell me now."

"You're fairly sure whoever this is is *not* heading toward me?"

"That's correct."

"Well, I mean, then who is he heading for . . . next?"

Kimball looked at his notebook, even though again I was positive he didn't need to. It was a calculated and empty gesture and I resented him for it.

"The next victim in the book is Paul Owen."

"And?"

Kimball paused. "There's a Paul Owen in Clear Lake."

"Clear Lake is only fifteen miles from here," I murmured.

"Mr. Owen is now under heavy surveillance and police protection. And what we're hoping is that if anyone suspicious shows up, we'll be able to apprehend him." Pause. "This is also why these connections between the crimes haven't been leaked to the press. At this point that would only compromise the investigation . . . And of course we hope you won't say anything either."

"Why do you think this person isn't gonna come after me or my family?" I asked again. By now I was rocking back and forth in the swivel chair.

"Well, the author of the book isn't in the book," Kimball said, offering a pointlessly reassuring smile that failed utterly. "I mean, Bret Ellis is not a character in the book, and so far the assailant is only interested in finding people with similar identities or names of fictional characters." Pause. "You're not a fictional character, are you, Mr. Ellis?" Kimball knew this smile hadn't reassured me and he did not attempt it again. "Look, I can see why you're becoming so upset, but we really feel that at this point you're not in any danger. Still, if you'd rest easier we could offer you police protection that would be extremely unobtrusive. If you want to talk this over with Ms. Dennis—"

"No, I don't want my wife to know about this, yet. No. I'm not discussing this with my wife. There's no need to freak her out. Um, but I will let you know as soon as possible about your protection services and all that"—I had gotten up, and my knees were shaking—"and I really don't feel well so . . . um, I'm sorry, I really don't feel well." The room was now filled with despair, torrents of it. I knew even then, half-drunk on vodka, sobering up at a rapid pace, that Kimball would not be able to rescue anyone and that more crime scenes would be darkened with blood. Fear kept bolting me upright. I suddenly realized that I was straining not to defecate. I had to grip the desk for support. Kimball stood uneasily beside me. I was of no use at that point.

A card was handed out with various phone numbers on it. I was instructed to call if anything "suspicious" or "abnormal" (those two words uttered so soothingly that they could have existed in a nursery rhyme) came up, but I couldn't hear anything. I blindly walked Kimball out to his car while mumbling my thanks. And at that moment Jayne pulled into the driveway in the Porsche. When she saw me with Kimball she sat in the car and watched, pretending to be on her cell phone. Once Kimball drove away she bounded out of the car, smiling, and walked over to me, still beaming from the new beginnings we had promised each other that morning. She asked me who Kimball was and when I told her he was a student she believed me and took my hand and guided me back into our house. I didn't tell Jayne the truth about Kimball because I didn't want to scare her, and because I thought that if I did I would be asked to leave, and so I kept silent, adding something else to the list of all the things I had already hidden from her.

The rest of the evening was a daze. During dinner, while sitting at the table, the kids conceded that they'd had a good time at the mall and regaled Jayne with various scenes from the movie we saw, and then there was a long discussion about Victor (who didn't want to sleep in the house anymore but whose panicked barking outside at night made this demand impossible to meet). The only thing that had any impact—the one thing that broke through my fog—was when Sarah brought the Terby over to me, though I don't remember where I was at the time. Was I slouched in the armchair in front of the plasma TV? Or had it been during dinner, sitting with my family while zoning out on a plate scattered with zucchini and mushrooms, and where I was trying to smile and stay interested in the moment, concentrating on the flow of information being passed around? (I tried to appear casual by humming to myself, but this was maddening and I stopped just as casually when I saw Robby scowl.) All I know is that I was somewhere in that house when Sarah brought the horrible Terby over and asked me why its claws were encrusted with what looked like dried crimson paint and if I could help her wash off those claws in the kitchen sink. ("They're dirty, Daddy," Sarah explained, while I nodded dumbly. Yes, I remember that exchange. And I also remembered how bad the thing had smelled.) There was a football game on TV that I would have watched any other night but when I shut myself in the office and dialed Aimee Light's number again, Jayne opened the door and suddenly guided me upstairs, and she was murmuring things to me as she led me back into the master bedroom and past the flickering sconces, and I could tell by her velvet smile that she was expecting something, a promise of some kind. I felt the same tug but couldn't follow through—it was too late. I was supposed to see my reflection in her and simply couldn't. I had taken an Ambien and finished the rest of the Ketel One and after easing myself into bed I was soon sleeping soundly, freed from having to deal with my wife's desires, the scratching at the side of the house, the furniture that was rearranging itself downstairs and the darkening carpet it rested on, and as the four of us slept a madman I had created roamed the county while a cloud bank settled over the town and the moon somewhere above it was causing the sky to glow. *He's back.* I had whispered those two words to myself that dark night spent shivering in the guest room, replaying what I'd seen out in the desolate field behind our house. I had involuntarily been thinking of my father and not Patrick Bateman.

But I had been wrong. Because now they were both back.

12. the dinner party

I woke up in the master bedroom for what seemed like the first morning in weeks, stretching pleasurably in the empty bed, refreshed by the Ambien from last night, and in the kitchen Jayne was preparing brunch, and I took a leisurely shower before getting dressed to join the family. I stared at my reflection in the mirror before heading downstairs—no bags under the eyes, my skin was clear—and realized, shockingly, that I was actually hungry and looking forward to eating something. Sunday brunch was the one meal of the week with no dietary restrictions: sesame seed bagels and cream cheese, bacon omelets and sausage, and Krispy Kreme doughnuts and French toast for Robby (who again mumbled about the scratching sounds outside his door last night) and hot chocolate and pancakes for Sarah (who seemed withdrawn and tired, probably due to the new cocktail of meds that had been prescribed last month and were now finally kicking in), but because of the reshoots Jayne had only a banana soy milk smoothie and tried to downplay her anxiety about leaving for Toronto next week. For once, I was the one member of the family doing okay on that Sunday. I was mellow and content, even after leafing through the papers, which were filled with follow-ups on the Maer Cohen disappearance, as well as lengthy recaps of the (now) thirteen boys who had vanished in the last five months. Their photos took up an entire page in the County section of the local paper, along with physical descriptions, the dates they disappeared, and the places they were last seen. (Tom Salter rowing a canoe on Morningside Lake; Cleary Miller and Josh Wolitzer outside the post office on Elroy Avenue; the last image of Edward Burgess was of him walking serenely through the Midland airport, caught on film by the security cameras.) It was a year-book page for the missing, and I simply put the paper aside. Once Robby and Sarah went upstairs Jayne and I traded thoughts on how to get out of the Allens' dinner that night, but it was too late. It was easier to just suffer through it than to blow them off, so I planned my day accordingly until seven o'clock, at which time we'd leave.

I spent the rest of the morning putting the furniture in the living room back in its original position but realized while doing this that I *liked* how the furniture had been rearranged—and felt a weird pang of nostalgia as I pushed the couches and tables and chairs around. And the carpet—though still discolored—was spotless: the footprints stamped in ash were no longer evident, and even though the wide expanse of beige Berber bordering on green shag was bothersome, the room was no longer open to interpretation. I then went outside to the field and checked on the blackened wet patch; to my relief, it had almost dried up, and the hole was beginning to refill itself, and as I looked out over the acres of field leading out to the dark bank of woods, taking in deep breaths of the fresh autumn air, I briefly felt that maybe Jayne was right, that this *was* a meadow and not a place where the dead reside. Next I went upstairs to look at the scratches on Robby's door, and when I knelt down and ran my hand over the grooves I'd seen on Halloween I could detect no change. Again: relief. I felt now as if the bad news Kimball had brought yesterday was being balanced out. The afternoon was long and quiet and uneventful. I watched football games, and Aimee Light still hadn't called me back.

At six o'clock Jayne dressed me in a pair of black Paul Smith slacks and a gray Gucci turtleneck and Prada loafers—chic yet conservative and imminently presentable. While she took the next hour to pull herself together I went downstairs to greet Wendy, the girl who was going to watch over the kids tonight since Marta had Sundays off. Wendy was a not unattractive student from the college, whose parents Jayne knew and who also came highly recommended by all the mothers in the neighborhood. Jayne had initially resisted calling Wendy since we were only going next door for a few hours and could simply bring the kids with us, but Mitchell Allen mentioned something about Ashton's ear infection and subtly vetoed our plan. And considering what Kimball had told me yesterday, I was grateful to have someone in the house to look after the kids. While waiting for Jayne I downloaded onto the computer the pictures she'd taken on Halloween: Robby and Ashton, both sullen and sweaty, already too old for the holiday; Sarah looking like a child prostitute. An image of the cream-colored 450 SL initially caught my interest, but it no longer seemed fixed with meaning—it was simply someone's car and nothing more. I realized this after uselessly trying to enlarge the photo and locate the license plate, but it had been washed out in the glare of the street lamps and, as with everything else that Sunday, didn't seem to matter much. I skipped any shots that I was in, but the photos that bothered me most weren't the ones of me looking frightened and blitzed but those of Mitchell Allen and Jayne posing in front of the Larsons' house on Bridge Street, Mitchell's arm wrapped protectively around Jayne's waist, his lips raised in a mock leer. That seemed far more worrisome than the small and innocent car I'd briefly become so afraid of on Halloween night and now no longer was.

I had actually gone to Camden with Mitchell Allen but barely knew him there, even though the school was a tiny and incestuous place. What had surprised me to discover was not so much that Mitchell Allen was now living next door to Jayne, but rather that he was married and had fathered two children: Ashton, who because of their close proximity was Robby's default best friend, and Zoe, who was a year younger than Sarah. Given what little I knew about Mitchell at Camden I had assumed he was bisexual if not, in fact, totally gay. But back then, before AIDS hit, everyone was basically screwing everybody else during that brief, sexually freewheeling historical moment. After we graduated and the eighties passed, it was not unusual for the "lesbians" I'd known during that era to have married and become parents, and the same held true for many of the Camden men whose sexual identities remained hazy and blurred during their four years in New Hampshire. It was considered cool at Camden to be bisexual—or at least to be *perceived* as bisexual—and the student body not only was inordinately tolerant of its own sweeping pansexuality but actively encouraged it. Most guys shrugged off the occasional one-night stand with another male and some even wore it as a badge; Camden girls thought it was hot, and the Camden boys considered you mysterious and dangerous, so it opened doors and increased your desirability level and made you feel, within the context of everything, that you were more of an artist, which was really what we all strove for—to let our peers know that there were no boundaries, that everything was acceptable, that transgression was legitimate. And after getting over my initial surprise (because my only memories of Mitchell were composed of rumors that he'd initiated a lengthy affair with Paul Denton, another classmate of ours) I recalled a girl named Candice whom he hooked up with during his last couple of terms, before he began graduate school at Columbia, where he met Nadine on the steps of Low Library, a replica of the ditsy, hot blonde Mitchell had dated as an undergrad. When we were first reacquainted this summer at a neighborhood barbecue in Horatio Park he pretended to mistake me for Jay McInerney, a lame joke that Mitch was so enamored of that he repeated it three more times to other couples he introduced me to, but since these weren't readers they failed to "get it," causing Mitchell to realize that he didn't have an audience. Neither one of us was particularly interested in getting to know each other better or to reminisce about Camden and our respective raunchy pasts, even for the sake of our sons (the improbable best friends). For his part, Mitchell was simply too enthralled by Jayne to make any attempt at male bonding. We were older now and living in a different world, and Mitchell let Jayne's presence reduce him to that peculiar desperation frequently seen in men who fall into close contact with a movie star. The cool, uncaring facade Mitchell played out in Camden—the exquisite vagueness, the stab at bohemia, the Christmas in Nicaragua, the Buzzcocks T-shirt, the punch he spiked with MDA, the screwing around and the moving away—all of that had been zapped out of him. This was due, of course, in part to age, but this erasure was also connected to his immersion in suburbia (plenty of men my age in Manhattan still retained some semblance of their youthful edge). The handsome and edgy sexual adventurer was replaced by a dorky guy nearing forty with a slavish devotion to my wife. Nadine noticed this too and kept a tight rein on Mitchell whenever school activities or the occasional dinner party brought the four of us together, and I didn't really care; I had my own proclivities, and I knew that Jayne was so not interested. It was the inevitable outcome of being early-middle-aged and bored and having a beautiful wife. But when Nadine flirted shamelessly with me—that was when the tiredness and the cliché of suburbia would dampen whatever enthusiasm I had for my new life as a man trying to form himself into the responsible adult he probably would never become.

After we said goodbye to the kids (Robby was flopped in front of the giant plasma screen watching 1941 and barely acknowledged us, while Sarah sat with Wendy on the other side of the room, going over the CliffsNotes for *Lord of the Flies*) Jayne and I stepped out onto Elsinore Lane and on the brief walk to the Allens' she patiently reminded me who everyone was and what they did since I always seemed to forget, which in this circle was considered bad form. Mitchell was, of all things, a member of the investment banking community, while Mark Huntington was a golf course developer and Adam Gardner was yet another semimobster whose supposed career in waste management was clouded with fuzz—just a group of regular dads, living in the soft dreamlight of wealth we had all created, joined by our generically beautiful wives in trying to secure our perfect children's ascension in the world. A slight wind caused leaves to scratch along the pavement as Jayne and I walked from our house to the Allens'. Jayne held my hand and leaned into me. I moved away slightly so she couldn't feel the bulge of the cell phone in my pocket.

Mitchell opened the door and hugged Jayne tightly before remembering to shake the hand I was holding out in midair. We were the last couple to arrive, and Mitchell ushered us in quickly since Zoe and Ashton were about to perform the yoga poses they had learned the previous week for the adults. In the living room we nodded at Adam and Mimi Gardner and at Mark and Sheila Huntington, all of us standing in that vast space while Zoe pretended to be a tree for something like five minutes and her brother demonstrated his impressive breathing exercises in a downward dog stretch. (Ashton looked as if he'd been crying—his eyes red, his face flushed and swollen—and he obediently went through his routine as if forced, though at the time I blamed his apparent misery on the ear infection.) They both did the "sideways plank" and then they curled up into a "rock pose." This was all capped off by Zoe and Ashton's balancing beanbag pillows on their heads until the adults applauded. "How cute," I murmured to a delighted Nadine Allen, who I hadn't realized was standing beside me and whose hand was resting on my lower back. She smiled generously at me (a Klonopin rictus) and then reached out for Ashton, who abruptly turned away and stalked out of the room. Nadine's face flickered with worry—but only for a second—and then became the smiling mask of a hostess again. It was a significant moment. I was already stricken and exhausted.

The Allens' house was an almost exact replica of our place—palatial and minimalist and immaculate. There was even the same chandelier in the high-ceilinged foyer and the same curving staircase connecting the two floors, and Mitchell started taking drink orders once the kids had gone to their rooms and Jayne glanced at me when I asked for a vodka on the rocks and I returned the glance jokingly when she demurred and decided on a glass of white wine I knew she really didn't want, and we settled into cocktail chatter with a Burt Bacharach CD playing in the background—a knowing, kitschy touch presented with an ironic formality, operating not only as a dig at our parents' tastes, a way of commenting on how bourgeois and middlebrow they were, but also as something comforting; it was supposed to take us back to the safety of our childhoods, and I suppose that for some it worked like a balm, as did a menu that updated the meals our mothers had served: chicken Kiev (but with a Jamaican touch—I could not imagine what that would taste like) and au gratin potatoes (but made with manchego cheese) and that seventies stalwart sangria, which like so many artifacts from that era had made a comeback.

When we sat down to eat I took inventory of the people in the room, and the remnants of my good mood evaporated when I realized how very little I had in common with them—the career dads, the responsible and diligent moms—and I was soon filled with dread and loneliness. I locked in on the smug feeling of superiority that married couples gave off and that permeated the air—the shared assumptions, the sweet and contented apathy, it all lingered everywhere—despite the absence in the room of anyone single at which to aim this. I concluded with an aching finality that the could-happen possibilities were gone, that doing whatever you wanted whenever you wanted was over. The future didn't exist anymore. Everything was in the past and would stay there. And I assumed—since I was the most recent addition to this group and had not yet let myself be fully initiated into its rituals and habits—that I was the loner, the outsider, the one whose solitude seemed endless. My wonderment at how I had arrived in this world still hadn't deserted me. Everything was formal and constricted. The polite conversation that carried over from cocktails into dinner was so stifling that it carried a certain ruthlessness, so I honed in on the women, carefully weighing Mimi versus Sheila versus Nadine, all of whom I found attractive (though Jayne outshone them all). Mitchell was leaning into my wife and Nadine kept pouring me sangria that I was positive had no alcohol in it, and everywhere I glimpsed the withholding of a once casual promiscuity and it made me feel old. I briefly imagined all of us involved in an orgy (not a disagreeable fantasy considering how well put together the women were) until I heard that Mimi Gardner owned a Pomeranian named Basket.

And then talk turned to Buckley, which was really the only reason the four couples were sitting at the round table below the dimmed lights in the austere and barren dining room in the Allen home—all of our kids attended the school. We were reminded that it was parent/teacher night tomorrow, and would we be there? Oh yes, Jayne and I assured the table, we would. (I shuddered at what the consequences would have been if I had said, "Under no circumstances are we attending the Buckley parent/teacher thing.") The conversation leaned toward the shallow endowment, the deep denial, the value distinctions, the grand connections, that large donation, the right circumstances—big and personal topics that demanded specifics and examples but there was just enough anonymity hovering over them to make everyone feel comfortable. I had never been to a dinner party where all talk revolved around children and since I was basically the new dad I couldn't grasp the emotional undertow and anxiety pulsing below the casual chatter—and there was something off about the obsession with their children that bordered on the fanatical. It wasn't that they weren't concerned about their kids, but they wanted something back, they wanted a return on their investment—this need was almost religious. It was exhausting to listen to and it was all so corrupt because it wasn't making for happier children. What happened to just wanting your kids to be content and cool? What happened to telling them the world sucks? What happened to getting slapped around a little? These parents were scientists and were no longer raising their kids instinctually—everyone had read a book or watched a video or skimmed the Net to figure out what to do. I actually heard the word "portal" used as a metaphor for "nursery school" (courtesy of Sheila Huntington) and there were five-year-olds with bodyguards (Adam Gardner's daughter). There were kids experiencing dizzy spells due to the pressure of elementary school and who were in alternative therapies, and there were ten-year-old boys with eating disorders caused by unrealistic body images. There were waiting lists filled with the names of nine-year-olds for acupuncture sessions with Dr. Wolper. I found out that one of the children in Robby's class had drunk a small bottle of Clorox. And then it was: cutting the pasta from the school lunch program, and the nutritionist who catered the bar mitzvah, and the Pilates class for two-year-olds, the sixth-grader who needed the sports bra, the little boy who tugged at his mother in the upscale supermarket and asked, "Does this have carbs in it?" A conversation began about the connection between wheezing and dairy products. After that: a bogus debate about echinacea. The concussions, the snakebite, the neck brace, the need for bulletproof classroom windows—it all kept coming, things that to me seemed futuristic and pointless and hollow. But Jayne was nodding in agreement and listening thoughtfully and making helpful comments and I suddenly realized that the more famous Jayne became—and the more people expected from her—the more she seemed like a politician. When Nadine gripped my arm and asked me what my feelings were about a topic I hadn't been following I offered vague generalities about the despair in book publishing. When this didn't get any kind of reaction from the table, I understood then that what I wanted was to be accepted. So why wasn't I volunteering at computer classes? Why wasn't I coaching the tennis team? Nadine saved me by mentioning the hopeful rumor that one of the missing boys had been spotted on Cape Cod, before excusing herself from the table to check on Ashton again—which she did, by my count, seven times during that dinner. I started reaching for the sangria with a frequency that caused Jayne to move the pitcher away from me after I had filled my glass to its rim. "But what will happen when my drink needs replenishing?" I asked in a robot's voice and everyone laughed, though I wasn't aware I had made a joke. I kept glancing over at Mitchell, who was staring at Jayne with his dull carnal gaze while she uselessly explained something to him, his only response a constant panting. It took three hours for dinner to complete itself.

The women cleared the table and went into the kitchen to prepare dessert while the men sauntered outside to the pool area to smoke cigars, but Mark Huntington had brought four prerolled joints, and before I realized what was happening we started lighting up. I wasn't a pot fan but I was surprised at and grateful for its arrival: it was going to take forever to get through the rest of the evening—the sorbet with fresh fruit and the lingering goodbyes and the dreary promises of another dinner—and without getting stoned, falling into bed seemed impossibly distant. After the first toke I collapsed onto one of the chaise longues that were set in some particular and artful arrangement around the large yard, which unlike ours sat off to the side of the house instead of the back, and the night was dark and warm and the light from the pool shadowed the men's features in a ghostly phosphorous blue. From where I was slumped on the chaise I was facing the side of our house, and while taking deep drags off the joint I squinted my eyes and studied it. I could see through the French doors into the media room, where Robby was still lying on the floor in front of the TV and Sarah was still sitting on Wendy's lap as the babysitter read her the story about those stranded boys on that lost island, and above them was the darkened master bedroom. And surrounding everything was the great peeling wall. Yesterday morning, up close, the patches on the wall hadn't seemed as large as they looked from this angle. The entire wall was now almost entirely covered with pink stucco, with only small patches of the original lily white paint remaining. A new wall had been uncovered—it had *taken over*—and this was alarming enough to spread a chill through me (because it was a warning of some kind, right?) and after I was handed another joint and took a heavy toke, I hazily thought, *How . . . strange . . .* and then my thoughts drifted away to Aimee Light and I felt a faint pang of lust followed by disappointment, the usual combo. The silhouettes of the women could be seen in the kitchen and their voices, distant and muffled, were a gentle backdrop to the men's conversation. The men were trim with flat stomachs, their hair expensively colored, their faces smooth and unlined, so none of us looked our age, which I supposed, while yawning on the chaise, was a good thing. We were all a little detached and had a tendency to snicker, and I really didn't know any of them—everyone was still a brief first impression. I was looking at a weather vane on the Allens' roof when Mitchell asked me with an actual aura of concern and not the overlay of malice I had braced myself for, "So what brought you out to this part of the world, Bret?" I was drowsy and scanning the dark field behind our neighbors' house.

I aimed for the right note of detachment, and snickered. "Well, she read too many magazine articles about how children raised in fatherless homes are more likely to become adolescent delinquents. And voilà. Here I am." I sighed and had another toke. An enormous cloud was billowing across the moon. There were no stars.

A chorus of grim chuckles were followed by even more snickering. And then it was back to the children.

"So he's taking methylphenidate"—Adam pronounced it effortlessly— "even though it really hasn't been approved for kids under six," and then he went on about Hanson's and Kane's attention-deficit/hyperactivity disorder, which naturally led the conversation to the 7.5 milligrams of Ritalin administered three times a day, and the pediatrician who discouraged having a television set in the kid's bedroom, and *Monsters, Inc.*—so old school—and Mark Huntington had hired an essay writer for his son, who'd pleaded with him that he didn't need one. And then the talk turned to the missing boys, a lunatic, a recent bombing in New Orleans, another pile of corpses, a group of tourists machine-gunned outside the Bellagio in Vegas. The marijuana—which was pretty strong—had turned our speech into thick parodies of drug talk.

"Have you ever tried the deaf-daddy routine?"

I wasn't asked this, but I sat up, intrigued, and said, "No, what is it?"

"When he starts whining just pretend you don't understand what he's saying." This was Mitchell.

"What happens?"

"He gets so annoyed he simply gives up."

"How many hours did you spend on Google to get that info, Mitch?"

"It sounds excruciating," Adam sighed. "Why not just give him what he wants?"

"I've tried that. It does not work, my friend."

"Why not?" someone asked, even though we all knew the answer.

"Because they always want more" was Mark Huntington's response.

"Hell," Mitchell said with a shrug, inhaling, "they're my kids."

"We play hide-and-get-lost," Adam Gardner said after a long silence. He was also sprawled on a chaise, his arms crossed, staring up at the starless sky.

"How do you play that?"

"Kane is 'it' and has to count to a hundred and seventy."

"And then?"

"I drive over to the Loew's Multiplex and catch a matinee."

"Does he care?" Adam was asked. "I mean—that he can't find you?"

Gardner shrugged. "Probably not. Just goes and sits in front of the computer. Stares into that damn thing all day long." Gardner pondered something. "Eventually he finds me."

"It's a whole different world," Huntington murmured. "They've developed an entirely new set of skills that sets us way apart."

"They know how to handle visual information." Gardner shrugged. "Big fucking deal. I, for one, am not impressed."

"They have no idea how to put things in context," Huntington again murmured, spacing out as he took another hit off a fresh joint. We still had two going now and everyone was toasted.

"They're fragment junkies."

"But they're more technologically advanced than us." Mitchell said this, but I couldn't tell from his flat and detached tone if he was arguing with Mark.

"It's called disruptive technology."

I could suddenly hear Victor barking from our yard.

"Mimi doesn't want Hanson playing Doom anymore."

"Why not?" someone asked.

"She says it's a game the U.S. military uses to train soldiers." A deep sigh.

The only thing separating our property from the Allens' was a low row of hedges, yet the houses were spaced so widely apart that any complaints about a lack of privacy were irrelevant. I could still see the children in the media room but my gaze traveled upward, and the lights in the master bedroom were now on. I double-checked, but Wendy was still sitting in the chair, holding Sarah.

Again I thought, *How . . . strange . . .* but this time the thought was laced with a low-level panic.

I was sure the lights in the master bedroom hadn't been on before. Or had I just noticed this? I couldn't remember.

I refocused on the house, glancing first at the media room, but then a shadow behind the window in the master bedroom caught my attention.

Just as suddenly, it was gone.

"Look, I'm not exactly a strict disciplinarian," one of the fathers intoned, "but I make sure he takes responsibility for his mistakes."

I shifted restlessly on the chaise, still peering at the second floor.

There was no movement. The lights were still on but there were no more shadows.

I relaxed slightly and was about to rejoin the conversation when a silhouette darted past the window. And then it reappeared, just a shadow, crouched down as if it didn't want to be seen.

I couldn't make out who it was, but it had the shape of a man, and it was wearing what looked like a suit.

And then it disappeared again.

Involuntarily, I looked back at Robby and the babysitter and Sarah.

But maybe it wasn't a man, I automatically thought. Maybe it was Jayne.

Confused, I sat up and craned my neck to look behind me into the Allens' kitchen, where Nadine and Sheila were filling bowls with raspberries and Jayne was standing at the counter pointing out something in a magazine to Mimi Gardner, both of them laughing.

I slowly reached for the cell phone in the pocket of my slacks and I hit speed dial.

I saw the exact moment that Wendy's head bobbed up from the book she was reading to Sarah, and she carried her to the cordless phone hanging near the pool table. Wendy waited for whoever it was to leave a message.

The silhouette appeared again. It was now framed by the window and simply standing there.

It had stopped moving when it heard the phone ringing.

"Wendy, it's Mr. Ellis, pick up," I said into the machine.

Wendy immediately lifted the receiver to her ear, balancing Sarah in her arm.

"Hello?" she asked.

The silhouette was staring into the Allens' yard.

"Wendy, do you have a friend over?" I asked as carefully as possible.

I swung a leg — it was tingling — off the chaise and looked back down into the media room, at the three of them there, oblivious to whoever was upstairs.

"No," Wendy said, looking around. "No one's here but us."

I now stood up and was moving unsteadily toward the house, the ground wobbling beneath me. "Wendy, just get the kids out of there, okay?" I said calmly.

The silhouette continued to stand in front of the window, backlit, featureless.

I ignored the inquiries from the men behind me as to where I was going and walked along the side of the Allens' house and unlatched a gate, and then I was on the sidewalk, where I still had a view of the second-story window through the newly planted elms that lined Elsinore Lane.

As I got closer to the house I suddenly noticed the cream-colored 450 SL parked out front at the curb.

And that's when I saw the license plate.

"Mr. Ellis, what do you mean?" Wendy was asking me. "Get the kids out of the house? What's wrong?"

At that instant, as if it had been listening, the silhouette turned from the window and disappeared.

I froze, unable to speak, then moved up the stone path toward the front door.

"Wendy, I'm outside the front door," I said calmly. "Get the kids outside, now. Do it now."

Victor kept barking from somewhere out back, and then the barks turned to howls.

I started knocking on the door rapidly until it became pounding.

Wendy opened the door, startled, still holding Sarah, who smiled when she saw me. Robby was standing behind them, apprehensive and pale.

"Mr. Ellis, no one's in the house but us —"

I pushed her aside and walked into the office, where I opened the safe in a matter of seconds and grabbed the small handgun, a .38 caliber, I kept there, and then, breathing heavily and dizzy from all the grass, tucked the gun into the waistband of my slacks so as not to frighten the kids. I began moving toward the staircase.

But I stopped as I passed the living room.

The furniture had been rearranged again.

Footsteps stamped in ash crisscrossed the entire space.

"Mr. Ellis, you're scaring me."

I turned around. "Just get the kids outside. It's okay. I just want to check something."

Saying that made me feel stronger, as if I was in control of a situation I probably wasn't. Fear had been transformed into lucidity and calmness, which in retrospect I realize came from smoking Mark Huntington's grass. Otherwise I wouldn't have acted so recklessly, or even thought about confronting whatever it was in the master bedroom. What I felt walking up those stairs was, I had been expecting this. It was all part of a narrative. Adrenaline was smoothly pumping through me yet I wasn't moving quickly. My steps were slow and deliberate. I kept gripping the railing, letting it assist in my ascension. I felt so neutral I might as well have been in a trance.

At the top of the stairs I turned. It was dark in the hall leading to the master bedroom, and it was silent. But my eyes soon adjusted, and the corridor took on a purplish tint. The strength it took to walk through that hall came solely from a rising panic.

"Hello?" I called out into the darkness, my voice vibrating hoarsely. "Hello?"

I kept saying this as I moved down the hall toward the door at the end of it.

A sconce flickered and then dimmed as I passed it.

Another one followed suit.

And then I heard something. A shuffling sound. It came from behind the door of the master bedroom.

And from where I was standing in the middle of the darkened hallway, I saw, in the gap below the door, the band of light go black.

And then I heard giggling.

I moaned. The giggling continued from behind the door.

But it was giggling disconnected from humor.

The sconces had stopped flickering, and the only light in the hallway was the moon flooding through the large window that looked over the backyard. I could see Victor sitting on his haunches, staring intently at the house, as if he was standing watch (*But against what?*), and behind the dog was the field, which in the moonglow resembled a flat silver sheet.

The giggling turned into a high-pitched squeal.

I blindly made my way toward the master bedroom; I couldn't see any-thing. I was letting the wall I was leaning against guide me toward it. I was only a couple steps away when I heard the door opening.

"Hello? Who is it? Hello?" My voice was toneless. I reached under my shirt for the gun.

The squealing had stopped.

In the darkness the door opened and something rushed out.

It was padding toward me but I couldn't see anything.

"Hey!" I yelled, then it leapt into the air and flew by me.

I spun around, flailing at it.

And then the door to Robby's room slammed shut.

I was now holding the gun by my side and felt my way in the darkness, once again relying on the wall, until I was at Robby's door.

"Mr. Ellis?" I heard Wendy call. "What's going on? You're frightening the kids."

"Call the police," I shouted, making sure the thing in Robby's room could hear me. "Call 911 now, Wendy. Just do it!"

"Dad?" This was Robby.

"It's okay, Robby, everything is okay. Just get outside." I tried to keep my voice from wavering.

I breathed in and slowly opened Robby's door.

The room was completely dark except for the screen-saver moon glowing from the computer. The window looking onto Elsinore Lane was open.

I thought I sensed movement in the room and about four steps inside I heard something breathing raggedly.

"Who are you?" I shouted. Fear was crawling through me. I had no idea what to do. "I have a fucking gun," I shouted uselessly. (*That you don't know how to use*, I could imagine the thing chuckle, mocking me.)

I backed up and ran my free hand up and down the wall until I found the light switch.

And that was when something bit me on the palm of the hand that was reaching for the light switch. There was a hissing noise, then a stinging sen-sation in my hand.

I shouted involuntarily and flicked on the lights.

Holding the gun in my outstretched hand, I swept it across the room.

The only thing that moved was the Terby, which had landed on the floor and lurched forward before tilting over onto its side, its strange eyes fixed on me.

It was lying next to a small dead mouse that had been gutted.

But there was nothing else in the room. And I almost broke down with relief.

I swallowed hard and slowly moved to the open window.

When I heard the screeching of tires I ran toward it.

Outside on Elsinore Lane, the cream-colored 450 SL disappeared around the corner onto Bedford Street.

I stumbled down the staircase and out the front door, where Wendy and Robby and Sarah were now standing, dumbstruck. Wendy reached down and picked Sarah up and held her tightly, a protective gesture.

"Did you see that car?" I was panting and suddenly realized I was going to be sick. I turned away from them and leaned over and vomited onto the lawn. Sarah started crying. I vomited again—this time more violently—in spasms. I wiped my mouth with the back of the hand holding the gun, trying to regain my composure.

"Did you see anybody get into that car?" I asked again. I was still panting.

Robby stared at me with disgust and walked back into the house.

"You're crazy!" he shouted before I heard him furiously burst into tears.

"I hate you!" he screamed, his voice filled with such sureness and certainty.

"What car?" Wendy asked, her eyes wide with not fear but an awful incredulity.

"The Mercedes. That car that just drove down the lane." I was pointing at an empty street.

"Mr. Ellis—that car just happened to be driving by. What is going on?"

"No, no, no. Didn't you see the person get into that car and drive off?"

Wendy was staring at something behind me. I whirled around.

Jayne was walking slowly toward us, her arms crossed, her face grim.

"Yes, what is going on, Bret?" she asked quietly, nearing me.

I mistook the expression on her face for compassion but then saw that she was furious.

"Wendy, could you take Sarah to her room?" I walked up to the baby-sitter, who backed away as I reached out a hand toward Sarah, who turned her head from me, crying so hard she was drooling.

Jayne brushed past me and whispered something to her daughter and then to Wendy, who nodded and carried Sarah back into the house. Still panting, I wiped the spittle from my mouth as Jayne walked to where I was standing, limp with exhaustion. She was staring at the gun and then back at me.

"Bret, what happened?" she asked quietly. Her arms were still crossed.

"I was sitting in the Allens' yard talking with the guys and looking up at the house and I saw someone in our room." I kept trying to control my breathing but failed.

"What were you guys doing out there?" She asked this in the tone of a professional who already knew the answer.

"We were just hanging, we were just—" I gestured at something invisible. "We were just hanging out."

"But you were smoking pot, right?"

"Well, yeah, but that wasn't my idea . . ." I stopped. "Jayne, there was something—a man, I think—in our room and he was looking for something, and then I came over here and went upstairs to check but he pushed past me and ran into Robby's room and—"

"Look at yourself." She cut me off.

"What?"

"Look at yourself. Your eyes are completely red, you're drunk, you reek of grass and you freaked out the kids." Her voice was low and rushed. "Jesus Christ, I don't know what to do anymore. I really don't know what to do anymore."

Our voices were contained because we were standing on the front lawn, out in the open. I involuntarily scanned the neighborhood again. And then, wracked with frustration, I said, "Wait a minute, if you're telling me the grass caused me to hallucinate that thing upstairs—"

"What thing was upstairs, Bret?"

"Oh, fuck this. I'm calling the police." I reached for the cell.

"No. You're not."

"Why not, Jayne? There was something in our house that should not have been there." I kept gesturing. I thought I was going to be sick again.

"You're not calling the police." Jayne said this with a calm finality. She tried to reach for the gun but I pulled away from her.

"Why shouldn't I call the police?"

"Because I am not having the cops coming over here to see you in this pathetic condition and scaring the kids even more than they already are."

"Hey, wait a minute," I said, teeth clenched. "I'm scared, Jayne. I'm scared, okay?"

"No, you're wasted, Bret. You are wasted. Now, give me the gun."

I grabbed her arm and she let me pull her toward the house, where I pushed the front door open. She was standing behind me when I pointed into the living room and the rearranged furniture. And then I pointed at the footprints, in some kind of sickly triumph. I waited for her to react. She didn't.

"I arranged that furniture this morning, Jayne. This was not how it was when we left tonight."

"It wasn't?"

"No, Jayne, and don't take that fucking condescending tone with me," I said, scowling. "Someone rearranged it while we were gone. Someone was in this house and rearranged this furniture and left *those*." I pointed at the footprints stamped in ash and realized I was jabbering and soaked with sweat.

"Bret, I want you to give me that gun."

I looked down. My hand was a white-knuckled fist clenched around the .38.

I breathed in and glanced at the palm of my other hand. The small puncture wound appeared to be healing itself already.

She calmly took the gun away and resumed talking in a hushed tone, as if to a child. "The furniture was rearranged for the party—"

"No, no, no—I rearranged it this morning, Jayne."

"—and those footprints and the discoloration are also from the party, and I've already called a cleaning service—"

"Goddamnit, Jayne—I did not hallucinate this," I said scornfully, bewildered by her refusal to believe me. "There was a car out front, and there was someone upstairs and—"

"Where is this person now, Bret?"

"He left. He got in the car and left."

"How?"

"What do you mean?"

"You said you went upstairs and saw this person and then he ran outside and got into a car?"

"Well, yeah, but I couldn't see him because it was too dark and—"

"He must have run past the kids and Wendy then," Jayne said. "They must have seen him as he ran right by them to get into this car, right?"

"Well . . . no. No . . . I mean, I think he jumped from Robby's window . . ."

Jayne's face collapsed into disgust. She walked away from me and went into the office and put the gun back in the safe, locking it. I followed her silently, glancing around for any evidence that someone had been in the house and that this vision was not caused by too much sangria and marijuana and the general bad vibes that were now slouching toward me relentlessly. Jayne started moving up the staircase. I followed her because I didn't know what else to do.

The sconces in the hallway were lit, bathing the corridor with its usual cold glow.

Robby's door was closed, and when Jayne tried to open it she realized it was locked.

"Robby?" Jayne called. "Honey?"

"Mom—I'm fine. Go away" was what we heard from behind the door.

"Robby, let me in. I want to ask you something," I said, trying to push the door open.

But he never opened the door. There was no answer. I didn't ask again because I couldn't bear what his reaction might be. Plus the Terby was in there, and the dead mouse, and the open window.

Jayne was sighing as she went into Sarah's room, where Wendy had put her into bed. Beneath a lavender comforter, Sarah was holding that awful doll and her face was radiant with tears. I consoled myself with the lame fact that eventually the tears would stop, but how could I have asked her at that point how that thing had gotten from Robby's room into her arms during this time frame?

"Mommy!" Sarah exclaimed, her voice trembling with dread and relief.

"I'm here," Jayne answered hollowly. "I'm here, honey."

I was about to follow Jayne into the room but she closed the door on me.

I stood there. That she didn't believe anything I told her, and that she was moving away from me because of it, made that night even more frightening and intolerable. I tried in vain to downplay the fear, but I couldn't. Frantic, I just stood outside Sarah's door and tried to decipher the soothing whispers from inside and then I heard a noise from elsewhere in the house and I thought I'd be sick again, but when I walked downstairs it was only Victor scratching at the kitchen door, wanting to be let in, and then changing his mind. I kept peering out the windows, looking for the car, but the lane was quiet tonight, as it always was, and no one was out. What could I tell Jayne or Robby and Sarah that would make them believe me? Everything I wanted to tell them I witnessed would just serve as the potential catalyst for pushing me out of the house. Everything I had seen would never be believed by any of them. And suddenly, on that night, I knew that I needed to be in that house. I needed to be a participant. I needed to be grounded in the life of the family that lived there. More than anyone else in the world I needed to be there. Because on that night I came to believe that

I was the only one who could save my family. I convinced myself of this hard fact on that warm night in November. What caused this realization had less to do with the phantom shadows I saw pacing the master bedroom while I sat stoned in the Allens' yard, or the thing that rushed past me in the darkness of the hallway, or the Terby with the dead mouse, than with a detail I could never share with Jayne (with anyone) because it would be the last straw. It would be my exit ticket. The license plate numbers on the cream-colored 450 SL that had sat in front of our house only minutes earlier were the same exact ones on the cream-colored 450 SL my deceased father had driven more than twenty years ago.

13. parent/teacher night

I convinced myself I hadn't seen anything. I had done this many times before (when my father struck me, when I first broke up with Jayne, when I overdosed in Seattle, every moment I thought about reaching for my son) and I was adept at erasing reality. As a writer, it was easy for me to dream up the more viable scenario than the one that had actually played itself out. And so I replaced the roughly ten minutes of footage—which began in the Allens' backyard and ended with me holding a gun in my son's room as a car from my past disappeared onto Bedford Street—with something else. Maybe my mind had started shifting while listening to the grating voices at the Allens' dining table. Maybe the marijuana had created those manifestations I had supposedly witnessed. Did I believe what had happened last night? Did it make any difference if I did? Especially since no one else believed me and there was no proof? As a writer you slant all evidence in favor of the conclusions you want to produce and you rarely tilt in favor of the truth. But since on the morning of November third the truth was irrelevant—since the truth had already been disqualified—I was free to envision another movie. And since I was good at making up things and detailing them meticulously, giving them the necessary spin and shine, I began realizing a new film with different scenes and a happier ending that didn't leave me shivering in the guest room, alone and afraid. But this is what a writer does: his life is a maelstrom of lying. Embellishment is his focal point. This is what we do to please others. This is what we do in order to flee ourselves. A writer's physical life is basically one of stasis, and to combat this constraint, an opposite world and another self have to be constructed daily. The problem I encountered that morning was that I needed to compose the peaceful alternative to the terror of last night, yet the half world of the writer's life encourages drama and pain, and defeat is good for art: if it was day we made it night, if it was love we made it hate, serenity became chaos, kindness became viciousness, God became the devil, a daughter became a whore. I had been inordinately rewarded for participating in this process, and lying often leaked from my writing life—an enclosed sphere of consciousness, a place suspended outside of time, where the untruths flowed onto the whiteness of a blank screen—into the part of me that was tactile and alive. But, admittedly, on that third day of November, I was at a point at which I believed the two had merged and I could not tell one from the other.

Or so I told myself. Because I knew better. I knew what had happened last night.

Last night was the reality.

Yet in order to move on I needed to rationalize the things I had seen to prove to myself that I wasn't losing my mind. It took an immense amount of concentration and balance to pivot back and forth between the illusory and what you knew without a doubt was true and real, and you had to hope that you wouldn't unravel somewhere on that trail that connected the two. So I told myself things on November third. I needed to do this because another day was waiting for me, and if I was going to get through it with any semblance of sanity I would have to deny last night. Cut the following from the work-in-progress: The character I had created, a monster, had escaped from a novel. Convince yourself that he had not been in the house last night. (The cream-colored Mercedes was trickier because of the California plates.) Pretend that the Terby hadn't bitten you (despite the presence of a small scab on my palm) and that the detective who had stopped by on Saturday was full of ominous and confused bullshit. Invent a new chapter heading, "The Night That Never Happened." Tell yourself it was all a dream. Last night I dreamt that by the light of the pool I saw the Terby tottering by the chrysanthemum bush, delicately feeding on an orange flower. Last night I dreamt this image when I roamed the house in my sleep, checking the locks on every door and window. I dreamt that the doll had somehow escaped from Sarah's arms and made its way into the backyard. Last night I dreamt that the sounds I'd heard in the hallway coming from behind the door of the master bedroom were those of a child weeping. Last night I dreamt that another squirrel lay gutted on the deck, its intestines pulled from its stomach, its head missing. Last night I dreamt I hadn't been at that wedding in Nashville where I first saw Robby, and where he took my hand in his and whispered *sshhh* because there was something he wanted to show me underneath the hedges in a hotel garden. And I dreamt the gentle slope of the lawn we moved across and our shadows tracking along the grass below us, and I dreamt that Robby's forward motion was carrying me with him, just as I had dreamt the same hand of my father's when I had guided him toward a bank of palm trees in Hawaii to show him the same lizard Robby had tried to show me and which didn't exist in Nashville either. Because of this dreaming, the equilibrium required to get through the day returned. Because of this erasure the day was so much easier. I was gliding through it—partly because I was exhausted from lack of sleep (that night I hadn't gotten closer than an uncomfortable doze) and the Xanax I kept popping, and partly because the writer had convinced me that everything was normal even though I knew the day's surface tranquility was something brief, the respite from a nearing and total darkness.

My original plan that Monday was to keep out of sight until Jayne and I left for Buckley at seven that night. But there was no need to hide since the kids were at school and Jayne was training at the gymnasium in town for the reshoots. Once the house was empty (except for Rosa vacuuming the footprints that did not exist) I needed to occupy myself, so I inspected things.

First, I casually looked through the newspapers to see if there was any more information about the missing boys.

There was not.

I also looked for anything pertaining to what Donald Kimball had told me.

There was not.

When I entered the master bedroom I found nothing (but what was I looking for? what clues does a phantom leave?), and as I stood by the window I opened the venetian blinds and stared into the Allens' yard and, for a brief moment, thought I saw myself lying on that chaise longue, looking back up at myself. It was only a flash, but suddenly I was that silhouette from last night, the shadow that I had dreamt. (In the same flash I had suddenly become that boy sitting next to Aimee Light in her BMW.) I moved around the room, replicating the shadow's movements, wondering what it had been looking for. Nothing seemed to be missing from my closet or drawers, and there were no visible footprints on the carpet (though in my dreams they were in the living room and they were now in my office as well). I finally moved toward Robby's door and, yet again, hesitated before stepping in. The scratches were still in the bottom right-hand corner and they needed to be painted over and

(*I hate you.* How many times had I said that to my father? Never. How many times had I wanted to? Thousands.)

the mouse was gone, I told myself, because I had dreamt it, and the room didn't contain a single detail or clue or reminder of what I had dreamt in there last night. Boxes half-filled with old clothes for the Salvation Army sat in front of Robby's closet. The moon continued pulsing on the screen saver.

In my office, I couldn't concentrate on my novel so I reread the scene in *American Psycho* where Paul Owen is murdered and again was appalled by the details of the crime—the newspapers covering the floor, the raincoat worn by Patrick Bateman to protect his suit, the blade of the ax splitting Paul's head open, the spraying of blood and the hissing sounds a skull makes coming apart. The thing that scared me the most: What if there was no rage in this person haunting Midland County? What if he just serenely planned his crimes and carried them out methodically, his emotional level akin to pushing a shopping cart through a supermarket while crossing items off a list? There was no rationale for these crimes other than that whoever was committing them liked it.

I did try Aimee Light again. Again she didn't pick up. Again I didn't leave a message. I didn't know what to say anymore, since I had now dreamt seeing her pull out of the Whole Foods parking lot and onto Ophelia Boulevard with Clayton by her side. That—at this point in the dream—had not happened on Saturday afternoon.

I did not see Robby when he came home from school, and he did not sit down to dinner with the family, preferring to eat alone in his bedroom while ostensibly starting his homework. Sarah, sitting with Jayne and me, seemed unaffected by the events of last night, and during the meal I figured out why: she was part of the dream.

I dressed in a suit for parent/teacher night. I looked responsible. I was a concerned adult who yearned for news about his child's academic progress. The following is the dialogue I wrote for the bedroom scene that night, but which Jayne refused to play and rewrote.

"What should I wear?" I asked.

After a long pause. "I think a smile should be enough."

"So I can go as the naked grinning idiot?"

Muttered, barely audible: "All you have to do is nod and smile for ten minutes in front of a few teachers and meet the principal. Can you handle that without freaking? Or pulling out a gun?"

Apologetically: "I'll try."

"Stop smirking."

Jayne conferred with Marta about what time we would be returning home.

Jayne did not seem to realize how seriously I was taking things.

We took the Range Rover and drove to the school in silence except when Jayne told me that we were seeing Dr. Faheida tomorrow night. I refrained from asking why we weren't going at our usual time on Wednesday, because in the dream it no longer mattered.

At Buckley, security guards were everywhere. They stood at the gates, inspecting cars with flashlights while checking names on their lists. At the valet parking, more security guards—some armed—insisted on seeing photo IDs. The entire student body of Buckley, from nursery school through twelfth grade, amounted only to six hundred students (each class held about forty kids) and tonight just the parents of the elementary children were invited, and it seemed as if they had all turned out. The campus was mobbed with neatly dressed young couples, and Jayne received the requisite stares. By the Starbucks cart that had been set up outside the library, we ran into Adam and Mimi Gardner, and once it became apparent that they were ignoring me and no one was going to mention last night, I realized that they were part of my dream as well.

The school was sleek and industrial, with large steel doors that loomed above you wherever you turned, and the entire campus was surrounded by an immense amount of foliage. Trees canopied the school—it was hidden in a forest. Within these woods were a series of block structures—rows of anonymous bungalows dotted with small slotlike windows which comprised the bulk of the classrooms. The architecture was so minimalist that it possessed an unnerving glamour. And it was all based on control, yet it wasn't claustrophobic, even with all the elms and shrubs that enclosed the school's grounds. It was comforting, even playful. It was an undeniably chic little school. The gymnasium was a soaring space where we sat on concrete bleachers and listened to the principal make a compact but contrived speech about efficiency and organization, about the linking of mind and spirit, about safety and challenge, about our children's yearning for a greater sense of the unknown. The following lecture was given by a behavioral pediatrician who had made numerous TV appearances, a silver-haired, soft-spoken Canadian who at one point suggested a Bring Your Stuffed Animal to School Day. And after the desultory applause we went to brief meetings with the teachers. We were shown samples of Robby's artwork (all moonscapes) and we were told what was positive (not a lot) and what needed improvement (I zoned out). The teacher who worked with Sarah on language skills and word recognition and counting and primary numbers explained that Buckley tended to students' emotional needs as well as their educational needs and after observing that children are not immune to stress she suggested that we enroll both Sarah and Robby in a confidence-building seminar and we were handed a pamphlet filled with photos of garishly dressed puppets and tips on such relaxation techniques as how to master bubble-blowing ("steady breaths will produce a nice stream") and a reading list of books about positive thinking, texts to help children find "the quiet on the inside." When Jayne began protesting charmingly, we were told, "Ms. Dennis, children are often stressed not because they weren't invited to the right birthday party or were threatened by a bully, but, well, because their parents are stressed too." Jayne began protesting again, this time less charmingly, and was interrupted with "How well a parent copes with stress is indicative of how well a child will deal with it." We didn't know what to say to that, so the teacher added, "Did you know that eight and a half percent of all children under the age of ten tried to kill themselves last year?" which rendered me silent for the rest of the meetings. I overheard another teacher tell a concerned couple, "That could be the reason that your child may end up developing interpersonal difficulties," and the couple was shown a drawing of a platypus their son had made and was told that an average platypus should look "less deranged." At one point Jayne muttered softly, "I practice yoga," and we read a disturbing essay Sarah had written called "I Wished I Was a Pigeon," which reduced Jayne to tears, and I just stared mutely at the drawings of the Terby—there were dozens of them—swooping down on a house that resembled ours, angry and in full attack mode. Parents were handed complimentary "stress baskets," which included, among other items, a book called A Weed Can Be Transformed into a Flower. These meetings had wounded me sufficiently. I needed a drink more badly than I ever had. The dream was cracked and I needed it to keep streaming. There was no recourse except to smile darkly at everyone.

Finally, at the reception in the library, after four glasses of a sour chardonnay, I had to excuse myself from the proceedings.

Outside, I nodded at the armed security guard patrolling the stone walkway leading to the library and asked if he had a cigarette. He just said no and that smoking wasn't allowed on school grounds. I tried to make a joke but the security guard didn't smile when he stepped away from me and into the darkness. The average platypus, I thought, wandering off. The average platypus.

The library was three stories tall and framed one side of a large open courtyard. The windows of the building were translucent panels emitting a soft white light that filtered out into the darkness. From where I stood I could see the shadows of parents milling around, their murmurings from inside the building a distant soundtrack, and behind them were the long rows of bookshelves carving through the space. In the courtyard was a bronze statue of the Buckley Griffin, the school's half-eagle, half-lion mascot, and it rose up out of the courtyard, twelve feet tall, its wings outstretched, about to leap off its platform and into flight. I went down the steps to check out the griffin and to find some privacy, but when I reached into my jacket for the cell phone (calling Aimee Light had always been part of my plan for the evening) I realized I wasn't alone.

There was a figure encased in shadow, slumped on a bench. As I moved closer it said my name and I saw that it was Nadine Allen. I hesitated when I realized who it was. I looked around to make sure the word "Bret" was directed at me, hoping uselessly that it was not—but then she said the name again in a wearying monotone and I sighed and just kept nearing her.

Without saying anything I sat next to Nadine on the small bench jutting out of a tall granite wall. We were below ground level, I idly noticed, looking up at the library, ignoring Nadine. But movement caused me to glance at her. She was lifting a plastic cup half-filled with white wine to her lips and leaning lazily against the granite wall, and I was relieved that she was drunk, because that would keep the dream safely projected onto the wide screen, where it played as an alternative to what I was actually seeing.

In the courtyard, a small waterfall splashed lazily into a man-made pond, in which I briefly glimpsed the orange flashes of koi. Trees swayed overhead and coarse, thick vines were draped along the granite walls that surrounded us, lit up yellow and green by the colored bulbs of ground lamps. Nadine pulled her jacket tightly closed, even though it was warm out (though rain clouds had begun to obscure the moon), and she finished her wine and then, without saying anything, leaned into me, and I let her. She was a pretty woman, youthful for her age, and I watched as she lightly touched the highlights weaved throughout her hair. And when she still didn't say anything I turned my gaze on the bronze statue of the griffin. Nadine's silence finally succeeded in unnerving me, and so I prepared an innocuous conversation (oh, weren't they all?) about the dinner she served last night when suddenly she said something. I didn't quite catch it and I asked her to repeat the words she had just spoken. Her head lolled against my shoulder, and she giggled.

"They're going to Neverland."

I paused and adjusted my shoulder, causing Nadine to sit up sluggishly. I turned to look at her face. Her eyes were half closed and she was seriously buzzed. I was going to give the rest of the conversation sixty seconds and then quietly vacate the courtyard.

"Who . . . is going to Neverland?" I asked.

"The boys," she whispered. "They're going to Neverland."

I cleared my throat. "What boys?"

"The missing boys," Nadine said. "All of them."

I took this in. She was waiting for me to reply. I tried to make a connection.

"You think . . . Michael Jackson has something to do with all this?"

Nadine giggled again and leaned into me, but I felt nothing sexual because the mention of the missing boys began enveloping everything around us.

"No . . . not Michael Jackson, silly." And then she suddenly stopped giggling. She made a flying motion with her hands, mimicking a large, inebriated bird. She lurched forward and started swaying. "Neverland . . . like in *Peter Pan*. That's where the boys are." Mimicking the bird had taken a lot of effort and she leaned back against the wall without focusing on me. Her face—lost and heavily made up and the almond eyes wooden tonight—was lit half green by a ground lamp.

"Your . . . point, Nadine?" I asked cautiously.

"The point?" She sobered up too quickly. The tone became harsh. Maybe I looked frightened, which was what spurred her on. "You want to know what the 'point' is, Bret?"

I sighed and leaned against the wall. "No. Not really. No, Nadine. I don't."

"Why not?" She seemed activated by my admission, and the indignation in her voice seemed based not on drunkenness but on fear. "The point,

Bret, the point is"—and now she breathed in and made a muffled, sullen sound—"the point is that no one is taking them anywhere."

I nodded thoughtfully, as if mulling this over, and then said, "Sorry, but that just really doesn't resonate, Nadine."

"The point . . ."—she was now openly scornful—"the point is that you need to know this . . ." She reached down next to the granite bench and I was shocked to see her pick up a near-empty bottle of wine. Nadine had actually stolen a bottle of the Stonecreek Chardonnay from the reception and was nursing it in the dark courtyard of her children's school. She carefully poured what was left of it into her plastic cup. I might have laughed if it hadn't been for my growing concern that the vines were coiling around us. Suddenly, I was afraid. I was losing the signal of the dream. And I realized that Nadine's behavior was motivated not by alcohol but by a specific anxiety that was spiraling out of control. "The point is"—she took a sip and pursed her lips—"that none of them are ever coming back."

"Nadine, I think we need to find Mitchell, okay?" was all I could say.

"Mitchell, Bret, is standing next to your wife while Principal Cameron takes advantage of a photo op." The way Nadine said this opened something up while failing to clarify anything—all it did was add confusion. Suddenly, in the phrasing of the sentence, and the way she had pushed down on certain words, all of our relationships were rearranged. The dream was slipping away.

Nadine sipped her wine and kept staring at something invisible in the darkness. The vines rustled around us. I kept trying to avoid her face and then made an attempt to stand up. Nadine had been quiet for so long that I didn't think she would notice, but her hand shot out once I made my move and she gripped my forearm, pulling me back to her. She was staring at me now—her eyes bleeding with fear—and I had to turn away. That dream I had constructed so carefully was melting. I had to leave Nadine before it vanished totally, before it was consumed by someone else's madness. It was becoming Nadine's dream now, but the urgency in which she was relaying it to me had the horrible texture of truth. As I sat back down she said in a rushed whisper, "I think they're leaving us."

I didn't say anything. I swallowed hard and went cold.

"Ashton collects information about the boys." Nadine was still gripping my forearm and she was staring at me and she kept nodding. "Yes. There's a file on his computer, and he didn't know I found it. He collects information about the boys"—she breathed in and swallowed rapidly—"and he trades it with his friends . . ."

"This is really none of my business, Nadine."

"But it is, Bret. It's very much your business."

"Why is it my business, Nadine?"

I suddenly hated her for what she was confessing to me and again I wanted to walk away, but I couldn't. She lowered her voice and glanced around the courtyard to see if there was anything in the darkness listening to us, almost as if there was a risk associated in confessing this to me.

"Because Robby is one of the boys he's trading this information with."

I paused for breath. Everything started wasting away at that point.

"What are you talking about, Nadine?" I tried pulling my arm from her grasp.

"You don't understand, Bret"—she was almost panting—"there are hundreds of pages devoted to those boys that Ashton has downloaded."

I could feel her trembling as I tore my arm free and turned away.

"He e-mails them, Bret." Nadine said this so loudly that it echoed in the empty courtyard.

"He e-mails who?" I couldn't stop myself. I had to ask.

"He's sending e-mails to those boys."

I stopped pulling away and then, forced by fear, slowly turned to face her.

"He knew . . . some of the boys who disappeared?" I asked.

Nadine stared at me. I felt that if she said yes, everything would collapse.

"No," she said. "He didn't know any of them."

I sighed. "Nadine . . ." I started wearily.

"But he e-mailed them after they disappeared," Nadine whispered. "That's what I couldn't understand. He e-mailed them *after* they disappeared."

It took me a long time to ask, "How do you know this?"

"I found one the other day." She was sitting up, ignoring the wine, composing herself; suddenly she realized that she had a partner in this conversation. "It was in a code of some kind, and he forwarded it to Robby." She was trying to explain this by gesturing with her hands. "One message he sent to Cleary Miller, and another to Eddie Burgess, and when I checked the dates they were sent after they disappeared, Bret. It was after—do you understand?" She was panting again. "I found them in the filing cabinet of Ashton's AOL account but I had no idea what it meant or why he would do this, and when I confronted him he just yelled at me about invading his privacy . . . and now, the last time I looked, the files and the e-mails weren't there anymore . . ." And just when it seemed her lucidity had returned,

Nadine broke down. She began sobbing. I was vaguely aware that she was clutching my wrist. I remembered last night and Ashton's tear-streaked face and how Nadine kept excusing herself to check up on him. How many others had been the target of her paranoia? How many others were lured by this crazed theory of Nadine's? She kept wanting to guide me to a point that she was not capable of making.

I tried to calm her by playing along. "So Ashton was writing to the boys in Neverland, right?"

"That's right." She choked back another sob. "The Lost Boys." Her eyes were pleading, and the taut expression on her face was morphing into relief because someone now believed her.

"Nadine, have you told Mitchell?" I asked this in a soothing tone but I was so hyped up at this point that my voice sounded high and cracked. "Have you contacted the police and told them about this theory?"

"It's not a theory." She shook her head like a little girl. "It is not a theory, Bret. Those boys were not abducted. There've been no ransom demands. There've been no bodies." She was rummaging through her purse and pulled out a tissue. "They have a plan. The boys have a plan. I think they have this plan. But why? Why do they have a plan? I mean, there's no other explanation. The police have nothing. Do you know that, Bret? They have nothing. They—"

I was talking over her. "Where are the boys, Nadine?"

"No one knows." She breathed in and shivered. "That's the point. No one knows."

"Well, maybe if we talked to them, to Ashton and—"

"They lie. They will lie to you—"

"But if—"

"Don't you think the boys have been acting strange?" she asked, cutting me off. She wanted me to validate something for her that, admittedly, I had not been paying attention to.

"In . . . what ways?"

"I don't know . . ." Now that she had admitted the worst, I thought she might relax and become less furtive, but her twisted hands kept bunching up the Kleenex. "Secretive . . . and . . . and . . . not available?" She phrased this as a question so I would have to answer and then become trapped in her own dream.

"Nadine, they're eleven-year-old boys. They're not comedians. Fifth-grade boys are hardly the most outgoing group. I was the same way at that age." I just wanted to keep on talking. I just wanted to say anything that might drown her out.

"No, no, no—" She had closed her eyes and was shaking her head violently. "This is different. They have a plan. They—"

"Nadine, come on, stand up."

"Don't you understand? Don't you get it?" Her voice was rising. "If we don't do something we're going to lose them. Do you understand that?"

"Nadine, come on, we're going to find Mitch—"

She grabbed my arm again, her hands tearing at the sleeve of my jacket. She was breathing heavily.

"We're going to lose them if we don't do some—"

The dream was rushing in the opposite direction, rewriting itself. I was trying to lift Nadine off the granite bench but she kept forcing her weight back onto it. And suddenly she shouted, "Let go of me!" and wrenched herself away. I stood there, also breathing heavily, not knowing where to go. I kept straining to piece this information together.

And then: an interruption.

"Is everything okay down there?" a voice above us called.

I looked up. The armed guard I had asked for a cigarette was standing against a railing and staring down into the courtyard before sweeping the beam from a small flashlight over my face. Covering my eyes with a hand, I said, "Yes, yes, we're fine," as courteously as possible. From my point of view the griffin's massive head floated directly below him.

"Madam?" the guard asked, training the ray of light on her.

Nadine composed herself, blowing her nose. She cleared her throat and squinted up at the guard and called back, smiling, in a restrained and faux cheerful voice, "We're fine, we're fine, thank you very much." The light was absorbed by Nadine's mask before the guard, peering down at us uncertainly, finally moved on. The guard's interruption had brought an air of reality to the proceedings and it caused Nadine to stand up and, without looking at me, walk quickly toward the steps as if she was now ashamed by what she had admitted. I had rejected her on some level and the embarrassment was too big to deal with. The stab at a tryst had failed. It was a gamble that hadn't paid off. It was time to go home. She would never mention any of this to me again.

"Nadine," I called out. I was staggering after her.

I followed her up the stairs and tried to reach out for her but she was moving too quickly, bounding up the steps leading out of the courtyard until she reached the top, where Jayne was standing, waiting.

Nadine glanced at my wife and smiled, then moved swiftly toward the library.

Jayne nodded back amiably. There was nothing accusatory in Jayne's stance—she was simply stifling a yawn, and she furrowed her brow only briefly when Nadine ignored her. At the sight of Jayne, my dream began returning, and as I stumbled over the top step I reached out and, letting the dream flow back over me, wrapped my arms around her, not caring when she refused to return the embrace.

And on the drive back to the house on Elsinore Lane, above the dashboard and out the windshield, visible in the wide horizon of darkness, I was seeing newly planted citrus trees that were appearing along the interstate, and the citrus trees kept flashing by, along with the occasional wild palm, their fronds barely visible in the blue mist, and the scent of the Pacific Ocean had somehow entered the Range Rover along with Elton John singing "Someone Saved My Life Tonight" even though the radio wasn't on, and then there was an exit ramp and the sign above it read SHERMAN OAKS in shimmering letters, and I thought about the city I had abandoned on the West Coast and realized there was no need to point this out to my wife, who was driving, because the windshield suddenly was splintered by rain, obscuring the palm trees now lining the highway everywhere and, above them, the geometry of a constellation from a distant time zone, and I also realized that there was no need to point this out to Jayne because, in the end, I was only the passenger.

14. the kids

As I moved slowly up the stairs toward Robby's room I could hear the muffled sounds of bullets ripping into zombies emanating from what I thought was his computer. At the top of the stairs I paused, confused, because his door was open, which it never was, and then I realized that since Jayne and I had walked into the house without speaking to each other (she just slipped silently away from me, carrying the complimentary stress basket into Marta's office) Robby hadn't heard us come in. Moving closer to the open door, I hesitated again, because I didn't want to surprise him. I peered cautiously into the room and the first thing I noticed was Sarah lying on his bed gazing dully at something while cradling the Terby. Robby sat cross-legged on the floor in front of the TV, his back to me, maneuvering a joystick as he caromed down another darkened corridor in another medieval castle. As I stared into the room my immediate thought: the furniture was aligned as it had been in my boyhood room in Sherman Oaks. The formation was identical—the bed placed next to the wall adjacent to the closet, the desk beneath the window that overlooked the street, the television on a low table next to a shelf containing stereo equipment and books. My room had been much smaller and less elaborate (I didn't have my own refrigerator) but the beige earth tones of the color scheme were exact, and even the lamps resting on the nightstands on both sides of the bed were distinct replicas of the ones I had, though the kitsch factor of Robby's was now considered cool, whereas my lamps from the midseventies were the epitome of a now distant and tacky chic. I let go of the decades separating Robby's room from mine and returned to the present when my gaze fell on his computer. On the screen, surrounded by text, was the face of a boy, and the boy looked familiar (in a few seconds I realize it's Maer Cohen), and the face caused me to quietly enter the room unobserved until Sarah looked away from the TV and said, "Daddy, you're home."

Robby froze and then stood up quickly, dropping the joystick carelessly to the floor. Without looking at me he walked over to the computer and tapped a key, erasing the face of (I was now certain) Maer Cohen. And when Robby turned around his eyes were bright and alert, and I was so disarmed by his smile that I almost backed out of the room. I started to smile back but then realized: he was putting on a performance. He wanted to distract me from what was on that screen and he was now putting on a performance. Any hint of last night's cry of "I hate you" had vanished, and it was hard not to stare at him with suspicion—but how much of that belonged to me, and how much of it belonged to Robby? There was an expectant silence.

"Hi," Robby said. "How was it?"

I didn't know what to say. I was now my father. Robby was now me. I saw my own features mirrored in his—my world was mirrored there: the brownish auburn hair, the high and frowning forehead, the thick lips pursed together always in thought and anticipation, the hazel eyes swirling with barely contained bewilderment. Why hadn't I noticed him until he was lost to me? I lowered my head. It took a moment to process what he was referring to. I just shrugged and said, "It was . . . fine." Another pause during which I realized I was still staring at the computer he was now blocking. Robby looked over his shoulder, a pointed gesture that was a reminder for me to end this interruption and leave.

I shrugged again. "Um, I just wanted to check if you guys had, y'know, brushed your teeth yet." This inquiry was so lame, so unlike me, that I blushed at the inappropriateness of it.

Robby nodded, standing in front of the computer, and said, "Bret, I was watching something about the war tonight, and I need to know something."

"Yeah?" I wanted him to be genuinely interested in whatever he "needed" to know, but I knew he wasn't. There was something off about his curiosity, something vengeful. Yet I wanted to make contact so badly that I let myself believe he wasn't distracting me from something he didn't want me to know. "What is it, Rob?" I tried to sound concerned but my voice was flat.

"Will I be drafted?" he asked, cocking his head, as if he sincerely wanted an answer from me.

"Um, I really don't think so, Robby," I said, moving in slow motion to the bed Sarah was lying on. "I'm not even sure if the draft exists anymore."

"But they're talking about bringing it back," he said. "And what if the war's still going on when I turn eighteen?"

My mind fumbled around until it reached: "The war won't last that long."

"But what if it does?"

He was now the teacher, and I was the student being manipulated, so I had to sit down on the edge of the bed in order to concentrate more fully on how this scene was playing out. This was the first time since I moved in that Robby was engaging me in a conversation of any kind, and when I tried to find a reason my stomach dropped: What if Ashton Allen had gotten in touch with him? What if Ashton had warned him about Nadine finding the alleged e-mails? My eyes were darting around the room looking for clues. I saw the two boxes half-filled with clothes marked SALVATION ARMY and swallowed hard, fighting off the small and rising panic I was becoming used to. I realized that this had been a scene so rehearsed that I could predict the last lines. I looked back at Robby and couldn't help feeling that behind the indifference was disgust, and beyond the disgust, rage.

He seemed to notice my suspicions when I found myself staring at the boxes, and he asked, more urgently, "But what if it does, Dad?"

My gaze jumped back at him. The "Dad" did not sound right. He was playing a game, and my instinct was to play along, since that was the only way I was going to find any answers. I wanted to crush the phony specifics and get at some larger truth—whatever it was. I didn't want to accept anything from him under a false pretense; I wanted him to be genuine with me. But even if he was just going through the motions, he had still initiated a conversation and I wanted to keep it moving.

"Well, you don't want to . . . die for your country," I said slowly, thoughtfully.

At the word "die" Sarah stopped playing with the doll and looked over at me worriedly.

"Well, then what should I do?" he asked casually, unconcerned. "If I'm drafted into the army?"

A long pause while I formulated my answer. I tried to come up with simple, practical advice, but when I glanced back at the Salvation Army boxes I suddenly hardened and decided not to play the game anymore. I cleared my throat and, staring straight at him, I said, "I'd run away."

At the moment I said this whatever false light was animating Robby went out in an instant, and before I could reframe my answer he had already shut down.

He knew I was daring him. He kept standing in front of the computer and I wanted to tell him he could step away, that the face of the missing boy was gone and he didn't need to block what wasn't there anymore. Helplessly, I looked at Sarah—who was whispering to the doll—and then back at Robby.

"Why is your sister in here?" I asked quietly.

Robby shrugged. He had already lapsed into his usual silence, and his eyes had become speculative and cold.

"I'm scared." Sarah tightly hugged the Terby.

"Of what, honey?" I asked, about to move closer to her, even though the presence of the Terby kept me at a distance.

"Are there monsters in our house, Daddy?"

This was Robby's cue to move away from the computer—the moonscape was now pulsing from the screen—and his confidence that I would become locked in a conversation with his sister relaxed him enough that he sat back down on the floor and recrossed his legs and resumed playing the video game.

"No, no . . ." I shivered as my mind flashed on the rush of images I had dreamt since Halloween. "Why do you ask that, honey?"

"I think there are monsters in the house." She said this in a thick, drugged voice while hugging the doll.

I wasn't aware I had said "Well, maybe sometimes, honey, but—" until her face crumpled and suddenly she burst into tears.

"Honey, no, no, no, but they're not real, honey. They're make-believe. They can't hurt you." I said this even as my eyes took in the black doll in her arms and all the things I knew it was capable of, and then I noticed that the doll didn't have claws anymore. They had grown, and warped; they were talons now, and they were stained brown. I began formulating plans to get rid of the thing as soon as possible.

Sarah somehow knew that there were monsters in the house—because she now lived in the same house that I did—and she knew that there was nothing I could do about it. She understood that I couldn't protect her. And at that point I realized the grim fact that as hard as you try, you can hide the truth from children for only an indefinite period, and even if you do tell them the truth, and lay out the facts for them honestly and completely, they will still resent you for it. Sarah's spasm of crying ended as quickly as it began when the Terby suddenly gurgled and rotated its head toward me, almost as if it didn't want this particular conversation to continue. I knew Sarah had somehow activated the doll but I had to clench my fist to keep from crying out and moving away, because it seemed so intently to be listening to us. Sarah smiled miserably and held the doll's grotesque beak (the beak that nibbled flowers at midnight and gutted the squirrels that had been found strewn across the deck—but it was just a matrix of sensors and chips, right?) to her ear as if it had asked her to. She cradled the thing tenderly, with such uncommon gentleness that with any other toy it would have moved me, but at the sight of this thing my stomach dropped yet again. And then Sarah looked up and whispered hoarsely, "He says his real name is Martin."

(*"Grandpa talked to me . . ."*)

"Oh . . . yeah?" I whispered back, my throat constricted.

"He told me to name him that." She kept whispering.

I could do nothing but stare at the thing. From outside, as if on cue, we could hear Victor barking, and then he stopped.

"Is Terby alive, Daddy?"

(*Go ahead, look at the scab on your palm. It had gone for the wrong hand, Bret. It was aiming for the hand with the gun in it, but it bit the wrong hand.*)

"Why?" I asked hesitantly. "Do you think he is?" My voice was quavering.

She held the doll up to her ear and listened carefully to it and then she looked back up at me.

"He says he knows who you are."

This forced me to speak up quickly. "Terby's not real, honey. It's not a real pet. It's not alive." I was intensely aware that I was still glaring at the thing, shaking my head slowly back and forth as if consoling myself.

Sarah held the doll up to her ear once again as if it asked her to.

I restrained myself from grabbing it away from her (I could smell its rotten scent) as she sat up to listen more carefully to what the doll was telling her. And then she nodded and looked back up at me.

"Terby says not in a human way but"—and now she giggled—"in a Terby way."

She clutched the thing, rocking back and forth, delighted.

I said nothing and looked to Robby for help, but he was lost in the video game or pretending to be, and over the sounds of gunfire and groans I could hear Marta's car pulling out of the driveway.

"Terby knows things," Sarah whispered.

I kept swallowing. "What . . . things?"

"Everything he wants to know," she said simply.

"Honey, it's time for you to go to sleep," I said, and then, looking over at Robby, "And I want you to turn that off and go to bed too, Robby. It's late."

"You don't need to worry about me getting enough sleep," he muttered.

"But it's my job to worry," I said.

He turned away from the television and glared at me. "About who?"

"Well," I said in a tender voice. "About you, bud."

He muttered something else and turned back to the TV screen.

I had heard what he said. And even though I did not want him to repeat it, I couldn't help myself.

"What did you say, Rob?"

And then he repeated it without difficulty or shame.

"You're not my father so don't boss me around."

"What are you . . . talking about?"

"I said"—and now he spoke very clearly, his back still to me—"you're not my father, Bret."

I was so weakened by this admission—something resentful that had been building up for a long time—and the entire day leading up to it that I was rendered silent. I was exhausted. I carefully stood up from the bed when Jayne entered the room and Sarah shouted out "Mommy!" and instead of saying, *I am your father, Robby, and I always have been and I always will be* I simply floated out of his realm, letting their mother replace me.

I walked down the hallway, the wall sconces flickering as I passed, and went into the master bedroom, closing the door behind me, and then I leaned against it, and for one brief, awful moment I had no idea who I was or where I was living or how I had ended up on Elsinore Lane, and I checked my jacket pocket for the Xanax that was always there and swallowed two, and then, very carefully and with great purpose, began undressing. I pulled a robe over the boxer shorts and T-shirt I was wearing and then I stepped into my bathroom and closed the door and started to weep about what Robby had said to me. After about thirty minutes passed and I came out of the bathroom, I simply said to Jayne, who was standing in front of a full-length mirror inspecting her thighs (cellulite paranoia), "I'm sleeping in here tonight." She made no response. Rosa had already folded down the sheets and Jayne, wearing a T-shirt and white panties, slipped into bed and hid herself under the covers. I stood in the middle of the vast room, letting the Xanax wash through my system until I felt calm enough to say, "I want Sarah to get rid of that thing."

Jayne reached for a script that lay on the nightstand and ignored me.

"I want her to get rid of that doll."

"What?" she asked irritably. "What are you talking about now?"

"There's something . . . unwholesome about that thing," I said.

"What are you overreacting to now?" She flipped the script open and stared at it intently. It occurred to me that I couldn't remember what day she was leaving for Toronto this week.

"She thinks it's real or something." My slacks were lying on my side of the bed, and I moved toward them and picked them up and draped them delicately on a wooden hanger—wanting Jayne to notice how careful and deliberate my movements were.

"Sarah's fine" was all Jayne said when I walked out of the closet.

"But we were told that she doesn't hold hands with the other kids at school."

Her jaw tightened.

"I think she needs to be . . . tested again." I paused. "I think we need to accept that."

"Why? Just because she has good taste? Because she's not the kind of kid who cares about winning Miss Popularity? Because judging by what a mistake it was sending the kids to that horrible school—well, good for her, and by the way . . ."—and now Jayne looked up from the script (its title was *Fatal Rush*)—"why are you suddenly so concerned?"

I realized that what the teachers had told Jayne that night had offended her deeply, beyond what I had even imagined. Either Jayne did not want to believe the truth about her children—that there were problems not even the meds could alter—or she could not accept that they were damaged in some way related to her behavior and the stress in the household. I wanted to connect with Jayne, but really, all I could think about were the awful drawings Sarah had made of the black doll swooping down on the house, and the things that I knew it was capable of.

"Well, it's a peer culture, Jayne," I said as gently as possible. "And that's—"

"She's just at an awkward age," Jayne said, her eyes refocused on the script. And then: "She *was* tested again, and she attended group therapy for three months and the new meds seem to be working and the speech disability has minimized itself—in case you haven't noticed." Jayne turned a page in the script, but I could tell she wasn't reading it.

"But you heard what the teachers were telling us." I finally sat down on the bed. "They said she doesn't know where her personal space ends and someone else's begins and she can't read facial expressions, and she's nonresponsive when people are talking directly to her—"

"The ADD was ruled out, Bret," Jayne said with barely contained fury.

"—and I mean, my God, didn't you hear all that shit tonight?"

"You're not her parent," Jayne said. "I don't care if she calls you 'Daddy,' but you're not her parent."

"But I did hear a teacher tonight tell you that your daughter stands too close to people and talks too loudly and she's unable to put her thoughts into actions and—"

"What are you doing?" Jayne asked. "What in the hell are you doing right now?"

"I'm concerned about her, Jayne—"

"No, no, no, there's something else."

"She thinks her doll is alive," I blurted out.

"She's six years old, Bret. She's six. Wrap your head around that. She's six." Jayne's face was flushed, and she practically spat this out at me.

"And let's not even get into Robby," I said. My hands were in the air, signifying something. "We were told he walks around like an amnesiac. That was the word they used tonight, Jayne. *Amnesiac.*"

"I'm taking them out of that school," Jayne said, placing the script on the nightstand. "And let's just stick to your ranting about Sarah. You have thirty seconds, and then I'm turning out the lights. You can either stay or go." The corners of her mouth were turned down, as they so often had been since I arrived last July.

"I'm not ranting," I said. "I just don't think she's able to tell the difference between fantasy and reality. Calm down—that's all this is about."

"Let's just talk about this tomorrow night, okay?"

"Why can't we have a private conversation?" I asked. "Jayne, whatever our problems are—"

"I don't want you here in this room tonight."

"Jayne, your daughter thinks that doll is alive—"

(*And I do too.*)

"I don't want you in here, Bret."

"Jayne, please."

"Everything you say and everything you do is so small and predictable—"

"What about new beginnings?" I reached out for her leg. She kicked my hand away.

"You screwed that up sometime last night between your second gallon of sangria and the pot you smoked and then racing around this house with a gun." A desperate sadness passed over her face before she turned off the lights. "You screwed that up with your big Jack Torrance routine."

I sat on the bed a little longer and then stood up and looked down at her in the faint darkness of the room. She had turned away from me, on her side, and I could hear her quietly crying. I stepped softly out of the bedroom and closed the door behind me.

The sconces flickered again as I walked down the hallway past Sarah's closed door and the door Robby always locked, and downstairs in my office I tried reaching Aimee Light on my cell phone but only got her message. On my computer screen was an e-mail from Binky asking if I could meet with Harrison Ford's people sometime this week, and I was looking at the screen about to type back an answer when another e-mail appeared from the Bank of America in Sherman Oaks. This one arrived earlier than usual, and I clicked on it to see if the "message" had changed, but there was only the same blank page. I started to call the bank but then realized that no one would pick up because they were closed by now, and I sighed and just stood up from the computer without turning it off, and then I was moving toward the bed I had become so used to when I suddenly heard sounds coming from the media room. I was too tired to be afraid at that point and I listlessly made my way toward the noise.

The giant plasma TV was on. The movie 1941 was playing yet again— John Belushi flying a plane high over Hollywood Boulevard, a cigar clenched between his teeth, a mad gleam in his eye. As I pressed Mute, I assumed this was a DVD we had bought and that maybe the automatic timer had switched it on. Robby had been watching it last night before Jayne and I left for the Allens' and he probably hadn't taken the disc out. But when I opened the DVD player, there was no disc in it. I stared at the TV again, puzzled. I picked up the remote and pressed Info and saw that the movie was playing on Channel 64, a local station. But when I looked through the cable guide for that week the movie wasn't listed, on that channel or any other; and since Robby had watched it last night I checked the schedule to see if it had been listed for that date. According to the listings it had not been on last night either. And then I remembered passing by Robby's room on the night of the Halloween party, when Ashton Allen had been sleeping while 1941 blared from Robby's TV. I checked the cable guide for the thirtieth, and again there was no listing for 1941 anywhere. As I sat in front of the TV, desperately searching for any information about why this particular movie continued playing, I suddenly noticed scratching noises.

They were coming from outside the bay window of the media room.

I immediately turned the TV off and sat there, listening.

And then the scratching noises stopped. After a moment they resumed.

I stood up and started toward the kitchen, the ceiling lights in the living room dimming and flaring on again as I walked beneath them (trying—successfully—to ignore the green carpeting and the realigned furniture). This happened again in the hallway leading to the kitchen, which was dark until the moment I stepped inside, when the lights flickered on. When I stepped back out, the lights dimmed.

When I moved back into the kitchen—they flickered on.

I did this twice, with the same result—an experiment that woke me up slightly.

It was as if my presence was activating the lights.

(*Or maybe something is following you*—a second thought I did not want to consider at that point.)

From the sliding glass door in the kitchen I stared outside. It was drizzling, but Victor was sleeping on the deck, shivering, lost in a dream, baring his teeth at some unknown enemy, and he didn't wake up when I unlocked the sliding glass door and walked silently toward the side of the house where the scratching sounds were coming from. But I stopped suddenly when the pool lights flickered on, radiating the water a bright aqua blue, and then just as quickly dimmed, easing the water into blackness. I heard the faint hum of jets coming from the Jacuzzi, and when I looked over it was bubbling, and as if I knew they were going to be there, my eyes scanned to a railing where a pair of the same bathing trunks I had found on Halloween—the ones patterned with large red flowers, the ones from Hawaii that my father had owned—were draped. Steam was rising off them into the cool, damp air as if someone had just taken them off after a dip. I was about to retrieve them (to wring them out, to carry them with me back into the house, to touch them and make sure they were real) when the scratching noises shifted in another direction, farther away but amplified. I ignored the trunks and the wet footprints fading on the concrete surrounding the pool and moved with greater purpose toward the side of the house.

I just stared up helplessly at the great mirage of the peeling wall. The entire wall, from the ground to the roof, was now the color of pink stucco, dwarfing me. The scratching sounds weren't coming from that wall anymore. That wall had completed itself, I realized, and the peeling was now occurring elsewhere, around front. When I moved past the corner of the house and stood on the lawn, the scratching noises stopped, but only for a moment. They resumed the second I located the patch of paint above my office window that was starting to peel off. In the glare of the street lamps I could see the house actually scarring on its own accord. Nothing was helping it. The paint was simply peeling off in a fine white shower, revealing more of the pink stucco underneath. It was doing this without any assistance. I became entranced by the flecks of paint sifting down onto the lawn and I moved closer to the house, in awe of the widening patch of salmon-hued paint that was revealing itself. There was another house beneath this one. And my memory flashed to a summer day from 1975: I was in the pool, and I was looking up at our house in Sherman Oaks while lying on a raft, and the flash got stronger as I reached my hand to the corner above my office window, stretching my arm as high as it would go, and when I touched the wall of the house on Elsinore Lane I finally made the connection, and it was so simple. Why hadn't I realized this before?

The paint that was revealing itself to me was the same color as the house I grew up in.

It was the same color as the house on Valley Vista in Sherman Oaks.

This realization left me blind for a moment, and then the belief returned.

I moved quickly back inside, where I walked to the living room.

The lights didn't flicker this time. They remained steady and glowing.

I now realized what had been bothering me about the furniture and the carpet: the chairs and tables and sofas and lamps were arranged just as they had been in the living room of the house on Valley Vista.

And the carpet was now the same forest green shag.

I also knew that footprints had embedded ash into the carpet, but it was now so dark that they were no longer visible.

I stared up at the ceiling and realized that the entire layout of the house was exactly the same.

This was why the house had felt so sharply familiar to me.

I had lived in it before.

And then this was interrupted by another flash.

I walked back into the media room and turned on the plasma TV.

1941 was still on Channel 64 with the sound off.

I had seen this movie with my father in December of 1979 at the Cinerama Dome in Hollywood.

1941 was the year my father was born.

And in a matter of seconds—at the dawning of this realization—I heard the familiar sound of the AOL voice repeating itself, over and over, from the computer in my office: "You've got mail, you've got mail, you've got mail . . ."

As I entered the office I saw that I was receiving an endless scroll of e-mails from the Bank of America in Sherman Oaks.

When I stepped in front of the computer the e-mails abruptly stopped flowing.

Through that long night I just sat in my office, numb, waiting for something, while my family slept upstairs. Everything around me was faintly vibrating, and I kept picturing a gray river made of ash flowing backwards. At first I was filled with a sort of wonderment, but when I realized it wasn't tied to anything in particular, the wonderment crumbled into fear. And this was followed by grief and the piercing echoes from a past I didn't want to remember, so I concentrated instead on the predictions rippling through me that, because of their dark nature, I then had to ignore. The denial of everything would pull me gently away from reality, but only for a moment, because lines started connecting with other lines, and gradually an entire grid was forming and it became coherent, with a specific meaning, and finally emerging from the void was an image of my father: his face was white, and his eyes were closed in repose, and his mouth was just a line that soon opened up, screaming. My mind kept whispering to itself, and in my memories it all was there—the pink stucco house, the green shag carpeting, the bathing suits from the Mauna Kea, our neighbors Susan and Bill Allen—and I could see my father's cream-colored 450 SL as it crossed the lanes of an interstate lined with citrus trees, racing toward an off-ramp, not far from here, called Sherman Oaks, and sometimes on the night and early morning of November fourth I laughed with disbelief at the noises roaring in my head and I kept talking to myself, but I was a man trying to have a rational conversation with someone who was losing it, and I cried *let it go, let it go,* but I could no longer avoid recognizing the fact that I had to accept what was happening: that my father wanted to give me something. And as I kept repeating his name I realized what it was.

A warning.

15. the attachments

As consciousness returned I felt hungover even though I wasn't. I wanted a cigarette but it passed. The hours blurred as I sat outside in a chair on the deck. I had wrapped a blanket around myself and walked out of the house and sat in a chair on the deck. When the sky became a huge white screen I finally faced the house with my insomniac glare as its inhabitants began waking up. The blandness of its exterior contradicted what lay within the house and there was no reason to go back inside, even though I felt something pulling me toward it, some kind of force urging me to reenter. The reassuring smile was now useless. I was plastic. Everything was veiled. Objectivity, facts, hard information—these were things only in the outline stage. There was nothing tying anything together yet, so the mind built up a defense, and the evidence was restructured, and that was what I tried to do on that morning—to restructure the evidence so it made sense—and that is what I failed at. There was a crow hidden somewhere in the barren trees behind me and I could hear the flapping of wings and when I saw it circle above me tirelessly I stared at it since there was nothing else to look at in the blank air and there were things I didn't want to think about

(*and on this deck tonight another squirrel will be turned inside out by a doll you bought for a little girl*)

but this was what happened when you didn't want to visit and confront the past: the past starts visiting and confronting you. My father was following me

(*but he has been following you forever*)

and he wanted to tell me something and it was urgent and this need was now manifesting itself. It was in the peeling of the house and the lights that flickered and dimmed and it was in the rearrangement of the furniture and the wet bathing trunks and the sightings of the cream-colored Mercedes. But why? I strained but my memories weren't of him: a lit swimming pool, an empty beach at Zuma, an old New Wave song, a deserted stretch of Ventura Boulevard at midnight, palm fronds floating against the dark purple streaks of a late-afternoon sky, the words "I'm not afraid" said as a rebuke to someone. He had been erased from everything. But now he was back, and I understood that there was another world underneath the one we lived in. There *was* something beneath the surface of things. The leaves in the yard needed raking. A faint and secret argument was coming from next door in the Allens' house. Suddenly I thought, It will be Christmas soon.

From the chair on the deck I could see into our kitchen, which erupted in bright light at exactly seven o'clock. I was watching a film in a foreign language: Jayne dressed in sweats, already on her cell. Rosa slicing pears (imagine slicing a pear at this moment—I couldn't). And then Marta brought Sarah downstairs and Sarah was holding a bouquet of violets and Victor weaved slowly in and out of the crowded room and Robby soon appeared in his Buckley uniform (gray slacks, white Polo shirt, red tie, blue blazer with the griffin insignia on the front pocket) and he moved weightlessly, as if submerged in space, through the kitchen. It was all so calm and purposeful. He handed Jayne a piece of paper and she glanced at it and then gave it to Marta for proofreading. Robby's hair was brushed straight back without a part—was this the first time I noticed? Attention was being paid to a day's worth of packed schedules. The standard negotiations were being agreed upon. Plans were formed and accepted. The quick early-morning decisions were being made. Who was in charge of the first shift? Who would oversee the second? Certain things needed to be sacrificed so there would be a few complaints, some minor whining, but everyone was flexible. The pace quickened slightly as Robby let Marta reknot his tie, and then Jayne, hand on hip, encouraged Sarah to eat from a plate lined with pear slices. The new day was about to begin, and reluctance was not allowed. I wanted to be welcomed into the kitchen. I wanted to be part of that family, and I wanted my voice to sound neutral for them, but I was out of breath and a cold hand pressed lightly against my heart. I imagined Sarah asking how flowers got their names, and I remembered Robby, stone-faced, pointing out a star to Sarah in the night sky and telling us both that the light was coming from a star that was already dead, and his tone of voice suggested to me that the house on Elsinore Lane used to be *his* house before I arrived, and I needed to remember that.

(That I had this son was astonishing to me on the morning of November fourth, but I had to figure out how I got to this point—and why I was here— in order to take any pleasure in the astonishment.)

Robby frowned at something Jayne said and then looked up at her with a sly grin, but as she walked out of the kitchen the grin faded and I sat up a little (because it was a reproduction of a grin and not the real thing) and his face simplified itself. He stared at the floor for a long time, then efficiently rationalized something—it clicked right away—and he moved on. There was no place for me in his world or in that house. I knew this. Why was I holding on to something that would never be mine?

(*But isn't that what people do?*)

If anyone had seen me out on the deck wrapped in a blanket, they pretended not to.

The idea of returning to a bachelor's life, and the condo I still kept on East 13th Street in Manhattan, was sliding toward me with an acid hiss. But a bachelor's life was a hard maze. Everyone knew bachelors lost their minds, grew old alone, became hungry specters who could never be sated. Bachelors paid maids to do their laundry. Another Glenfiddich ordered in a nightclub you were far too old for, chatting up ponderous young girls who made you bristle and wince about all the things they didn't know. But in that chair on that deck I thought: Get out of Midland County, grow a goatee, smoke cigarettes again, seduce women half your age (but successfully), arrange a nice workspace in a sunny corner of the condo, become less maniacal about form, confide all your secret failures to friends. Free Bret. Start over. Get younger. Absorb yourself back into the world of teenage flameout and the curving murals of scorched corpses—the things that had made you a youthful success. Continue your refusal to embrace the mechanics of East Coast lit conventionality. Streamline yourself. Stop shrugging. Eliminate chic. Avoid all fey irony. Erase the jacket cover with the fuchsia lettering you had once desired. Get the full body wax and the spray-on tan and the tattoo in serif scarring your biceps. Act like you've just blown in from nowhere. Push the gangsta attitude with a very straight face. Force them to take the cover story seriously, even though you knew how awful and fake it all was.

Because 307 Elsinore Lane was haunted, and this was the only alternative I could come up with on that Tuesday morning. I needed something—the distraction of another life—to alleviate the fear.

But I didn't want to travel back to that world. I wanted the idyllic glossiness of our life (more accurately, the fulfilled *promise* of that life) returned to me. I wanted another chance. But I could express this wish only to myself. What I needed to do was put it into action and prove that I hadn't dropped out, that I hadn't killed the buzz, that I could rejuvenate. I needed to prove that somehow I could shift out of the slow lane. I was still young. I was still smart. I was still convinced of things. I hadn't lost it entirely. I could move through the hassle. I could erase Jayne's resentment

(*What had happened to the way she used to come as soon as I entered her and the nights I watched her face as she slept?*)

and I could make Robby love me.

I had dreamed of something so different from what reality was now offering up, but that dream had been a blind man's vision. That dream was a miracle. The morning was fading. And I remembered yet again that I was a tourist here.

(Though I didn't know this on November fourth, that morning would be the last time I ever saw my family together again.)

And then—as if it was preordained—all of these thoughts triggered something. An invisible force pushed me toward a destination.

I could actually feel this happening to me physically.

A small implosion occurred.

I was staring at the crow circling above me and in that instant I suddenly realized something.

There were attachments.

Where?

There were attachments on the e-mails coming from the Bank of America in Sherman Oaks.

My chest started aching and I could barely sit still but I waited in that chair on the deck until my family disappeared from the kitchen and I heard the Range Rover pull out of the driveway, and the moment the automated timers activated the sprinklers on the front lawn I hurried into the house.

I nodded to Rosa, who was cleaning the kitchen as I rushed past her, and then I bumped into Marta outside my office—the specifics of the conversation I can't remember; the only important information was Jayne's departure for Toronto the next day—and I just nodded at everything Marta said, wrapping the blanket tighter around myself, and then I was in my office, locking the door, dropping the blanket, fumbling with the computer, propping myself in the swivel chair. I could see my reflection in the computer's black screen. Then I turned it on and my image was erased. I logged on to AOL.

"You've got mail," the metallic voice warned me.

There were seventy-four e-mails.

On each of the seventy-four e-mails that had arrived the night before—the flurry of them materializing the moment I'd been making my connections—there was an attachment.

When I backtracked to the first e-mail—which had arrived on October third, my father's birthday—there was an attachment on that one as well.

I had never noticed these before, paying attention only to the blank pages that arrived nightly at 2:40 a.m., but now there was something to download.

I started with the first one that arrived on October third.

On the screen: 03/10. My e-mail address. And the subject: (none).

My right hand was shaking when I clicked on Read. I grabbed my wrist with the left hand to control it.

A blank page.

But a video document was attached, labeled "no subject."

I pressed Download.

A window appeared and asked, "Do you wish to download this file?"

(*Wish*—what a strange verb choice, I thought idly.)

I pressed Yes.

File name: "no subject."

I pressed Save.

"The file has been downloaded," the metallic voice promised.

And then I clicked on Open File.

I breathed in.

The screen went black.

And then a picture slowly emerged onto the screen, revealing itself as a video.

The video focused on a house. It was night and fog had rolled in and was curling around the house but its rooms were brightly lit—in fact the lights seemed too bright; it was as if the lights were meant to ward off loneliness. The house was a modern two-story structure in what looked like an upscale neighborhood. The houses on either side of this one were identical, and the image seemed both familiar and anonymous. The camera was filming this from across the street. My eyes locked on the silver Ferrari parked crookedly in front of the garage, its front wheels resting on the dark lawn that sloped down from the house. And I realized, with a sick amazement, that this was the house my father had moved to in Newport Beach after my parents divorced. I cried out and then clamped a hand over my mouth when I saw him through the large bay window, sitting in his living room, wearing a white T-shirt and the red, flower-patterned shorts he'd bought at the Mauna Kea Hotel in Hawaii.

A car drove by silently on Claudius Street, its headlights breaking through the fog, and after it passed, the camera started gliding up the granite pathway toward my father's house, agile yet unhurried, its movement cold and inscrutable.

I could hear the waves of the Pacific crashing and foaming against the shore, and from somewhere else the yapping of a small dog.

The camera carefully honed in through the large pane of glass to where my father sat hunched over in an armchair, surrounded by the polished wood and mirrors of the living room. And there was music—a song I recognized, "The Sunny Side of the Street," playing inside the house. It had been my grandmother's favorite song and the fact that the song meant anything to my father surprised and touched me, and this pushed away the terror for a moment. But the terror returned instantly when I realized that my father had no idea this video was being shot.

My father stood up abruptly when the song ended, gripping the chair as if for support, uncertain of where to go next. He had been a swaggering and theatrical man, tall and bulky, but in his solitude he looked tired (and where was Monica? Twenty-two, boots, a pink coat, blond—she had been living with him up until a month before he died, and she was the one who had found his body, though there was no sign in this video that she lived in the house anymore). My father looked exhausted. Gray stubble covered his neck and gaunt cheeks. He was holding an empty glass. He staggered out of the living room. But the camera lingered in front of the window, taking inventory: the lime green carpeting, the lame impressionist paintings (my father being the sole client of a rural French artist represented by the Wally Findlay gallery in Beverly Hills), a massive white sectional couch, the glass coffee table on which he displayed his collection of Steuben bears.

I enlarged the screen in order to see specifics.

His bookshelves were lined with an array of photographs that had not been there the last time I was in that house: a very brief lunch on Christmas Day, 1991.

There were so many photographs that my eyes started dancing around.

Most of them were of me, and I couldn't help thinking that they served as some kind of reminder that I had abandoned him.

In a silver frame, the faded Polaroid of a worried little boy wearing suspenders and a red plastic toy fireman's helmet, innocently holding out an orange to whoever was taking the picture.

Bret, twelve, wearing a *Star Wars* T-shirt, on a beach in Monterey, behind a house my parents owned in Pajaro Dunes.

My father standing beside me outside the auditorium at my high school graduation. I'm wearing a red cap and gown and am secretly stoned. There is a noticeable space between us. I remember that my girlfriend had taken the picture at my father's urging. (I flashed on the celebratory dinner at Trumps later that night, when he drunkenly came on to her.)

Another photo of the two of us. I am seventeen—sunglasses, unsmiling, tan. My father is sunburned. We're standing outside a white church, its plaster cracking, its fountain dry, in Cabo San Lucas. The sun is very bright. On one side is the blue and glimmering enamel of the sea, and on the other are the ruins of a small village. I became almost exhausted by grief. How many times had we fought on that trip? How drunk had he been that week? How many times did I break down during those grueling days? The trip proved so hard to bear that my heart had turned to ice. I had erased everything about it except for the feel of cold sand on my feet and a particular ceiling fan that whirred above me in a hotel room—all else forgotten until now.

And then my eyes drifted to a wall where my father had hung the magazine covers, framed, that I had been on. And another wall featured (even more sadly) photographs of me that he had cut from various newspapers. At that point I surrendered with a moan and had to look away.

My father had become a hermit, someone who either didn't know his son was lost to him or refused to believe it.

But then the camera—almost as if it realized how drained I was becoming—plunged forward and raced around the side of the house. The camera was bold and covert at the same time.

The camera maneuvered toward a window that looked into a large modern kitchen, where my father reappeared.

Horror kept sweeping over me. Because anything could happen now.

My father opened the stainless steel door of the freezer and pulled out a half-empty bottle of Stolichnaya and clumsily poured a large amount into a highball glass. His gaunt face contemplated the vodka. Then he drank it and began weeping. He took off his T-shirt and drunkenly wiped his face with it. And as he was pouring himself the rest of the vodka, he heard something.

He jerked his head up. He stood motionless in the middle of the kitchen. He turned and faced the window.

The camera dared him. It didn't move or try to hide itself.

But my father couldn't see anything. He gave up. He turned away.

The camera steadily rounded the corner of the house and now offered a view of the small, elegantly landscaped backyard.

The camera followed my father as he walked outside to where the Jacuzzi was churning with steam that the wind swirled around the yard. The moon hung over everything and it was so white that it cut through clouds and illuminated the vines of bougainvillea that covered the walls enclosing this space. My father staggered toward the Jacuzzi, still holding his drink, and tried to slip into it gracefully but instead stumbled, splashing water all over the surrounding Spanish tiles while managing to keep his drink raised high above his head, protecting it. My father submerged himself in the water with only his hand holding the glass of vodka visible above the roiling bubbles.

My eyes kept clinging to the screen. Please, I thought. Please let someone save him.

Once my father downed the vodka he heaved himself out of the Jacuzzi and lurched toward a towel lying on a chaise longue. After drying off he removed the bathing suit and draped it over the chaise. He wrapped the towel around himself and then moved unsteadily into the house, leaving a trail of wet, fading footprints on the concrete patio.

The camera paused and then raced around the corner and did something I was praying it would not.

It went into the house.

It moved through the kitchen. And then down a hallway.

It stopped suddenly when it caught sight of my father dragging himself up the stairs to the second floor.

And when my father turned and kept climbing, his back to the camera, the camera started creeping up the stairs behind him.

My hands were clamped over my ears, and I kept kicking the floor of my office involuntarily.

The camera stopped when it reached the second-story landing. It watched as my father entered the bathroom, a large marble space steeped in light.

I was now crying wildly, pounding my knee as I watched, helplessly transfixed. "What is happening?" I kept moaning.

The camera then crossed the hallway and stopped again. It had a vague and maddening patience.

My father stared at his frail visage in a giant mirror.

And then the camera slowly began moving toward him.

I was aware that it was about to reveal itself to him, and my entire body shuddered with dread.

It was now closer to him than it had ever been. It was directly outside the bathroom door.

And then I noticed something that had been nagging gently at whatever part of myself wasn't preoccupied with the shock of the video.

At the bottom of the screen, on the right, in digital numbers: 2:38 a.m.

My eyes instinctively darted to the other side of the screen. 08/10/92.

This was the night my father died.

Only the sounds of his sobbing brought me out of the stunned darkness that had instantly covered everything. This was a new dimension now.

Shaking, I refocused on the screen, unable to turn away.

My father gripped the bathroom counter, still sobbing. I wanted to avert my eyes when I saw an empty vodka bottle lying next to the sink.

From somewhere in the house, "The Sunny Side of the Street" began playing again.

The camera kept floating closer. It was now in the bathroom.

It was closing in on my father indifferently.

I stifled a scream when I saw that there was no reflection of the camera or who was behind it in any of the mirrors that walled the bathroom.

And then my father stopped sobbing.

He looked over his shoulder.

And then he straightened up and turned around to fully face the camera. He stared into its lens.

The camera was an invitation to die.

My father was now looking directly at me.

He smiled sadly. There was no fear.

He said one word.

"Robby."

And as the camera rushed toward him, he said it again.

The video collapsed into darkness.

The anticlimax of not seeing what happened to my father at the moment of his death forced me to rewind the video to a crucial point that I believed could help me understand what I had just seen and suddenly my movements were calm and purposeful and I was able to concentrate solely on what I needed to do.

Because I did not think there was a camera.

Even now I can't explain the logic of this, but I did not believe there was a camera in my father's house that night in August of 1992.

(There had been "certain irregularities," according to the coroner's report.)

I found the image of my father standing in the kitchen, with the camera watching him through the window.

And I located immediately what I thought was the answer.

A small, flesh-colored image in the corner of the video, in the lower right-hand quadrant of the screen. It was the reflection of a face in window glass.

It moved in and out of focus even though the image of my father remained steady.

There was no camera videotaping this.

I was seeing something through the eyes of a person.

I enlarged the image.

I pressed Pause and enlarged the image again.

The face became clearer without the overall image being distorted.

I enlarged the image once more and then stopped because I didn't have to anymore.

At first I thought the face reflected in the window was mine.

For one moment the video showed me that I had been there that night.

But the face wasn't mine.

His eyes were black, and the face belonged to Clayton.

Years had passed since that night. Almost a decade had passed.

But Clayton's face wasn't any younger than the face I had looked into in my office at the college on Halloween, when he held out a book for me to sign.

Clayton couldn't have been older than nine or ten in 1992.

The face reflected in the windowpane was that of an adult.

I checked the other attachments, and after viewing the next two—

October 4 and October 5—I realized it was pointless. They were all the same, except that Clayton's image became clearer in each one.

Without realizing it I had already reached for my cell phone and was dialing Donald Kimball's office. He didn't pick up. I left a message.

An hour passed.

I decided to leave the house and drive to the college and find a boy.

16. the wind

Clayton who?" the secretary asked. "Is that the last name or the first?"
It was almost three, and after driving aimlessly through town replaying the video in my head, I called Kimball again and left another message asking him to meet me in my office at the college, where I would be "hanging out" for the rest of the afternoon. My plan wasn't to tell him the specifics of what I had seen—I just wanted to place Clayton in his mind, as someone to watch, the possible suspect, the fictional character, the boy who was rewriting my book. And I kept my tone even and natural, reiterating "hanging out" twice so he wouldn't think I was losing it. Then I called Alvin Mendolsohn's extension and was surprised when he answered. He spoke coldly to me as we uselessly defined our territory in a very brief discussion that confirmed Aimee Light had not shown up for either of her two scheduled tutorials and also had failed to notify him of her "absentia," to which he added, "She's a very impractical young woman," and then I countered with, "Why—because she's not doing her thesis on Chaucer?" to which he replied, "Don't take yourself so seriously," and then I said, "That's not an answer, Mendolsohn," before we both hung up on each other. Needing to be bolder than I felt, I summoned up the nerve to stand in the admissions office, in front of the desk of a blandly good-humored young secretary perched next to a computer, and asked her to look up a student's name and any contact information regarding how I could reach him since, I admitted regretfully, I had to cancel an appointment. But even in my distracted state I realized, once I'd croaked the word

(if there isn't a person, how can there be a name?)

"Clayton," that I didn't have anything else. He had not supplied a last name. But the campus was small, and I assumed that "Clayton" might be rare enough that he would be easy to track down regardless. The secretary thought it was odd that I didn't know the last name of one of my students, so I blithely waved a hand around when she inquired about this lapse, the gesture explaining away my absentmindedness, my busy and special life, how unreliable the famous writer was. For some reason, we shared a wooden laugh that momentarily relaxed me. She seemed used to this—the faculty of the college apparently made up of other frantic misfits who forgot the names of their own students. I dazed out, and realized that I was nearing a period in my life when I was seeking assistance from people half my age. I watched the secretary swing toward the computer, her hands sweeping over the keypad.

"Well, I'll enter the name and we'll do a search."

(*"I'm a big fan, Mr. Ellis."*)

I spelled the name, correcting her (for some reason, she thought it began with a *K*, and who knew if it didn't?), and she typed it in and then tapped a key and sat back.

I could tell from the expression on her face that the screen might as well have been blank.

I was about to lean over and scan the screen with her when she tapped a few more keys.

I realized things were becoming complicated when I noticed her sighing repeatedly.

(You should have never come to Midland County. You should have stayed in New York. Forever.)

"I'm not finding anything with 'Clayton' in it," she said, scrunching her face up.

(*"I'm a freshman here."*)

"He said he was a freshman," I added unhelpfully. "Could you check again?"

"I mean, look, even if you had a last name, Mr. Ellis, nothing would come up in the student directory because there's no Clayton listed anywhere."

"This is extremely important."

"I understand that but there's no Clayton listed anywhere," she repeated.

"Please just check one more time."

The secretary smiled wryly at me—it was actually a sympathetic expression.

"Mr. Ellis . . ."—(and it was maddening that desirable young women were now calling me this)—"the school directory—do you know what that is?—has confirmed that there is no one with the name Clayton—either as a first name or a last name or a middle name—attending this college."

It wasn't just the information but her tone that shocked me into silence: I should have known the moment I walked into the admissions office that finding Clayton was a remote and unlikely thing. The secretary's search had answered something, but another false beginning was opening up. I slowly stepped away from the desk as the secretary continued studying me as if I were dwindling into another world. Since I was not offering any explanation for this waste of time, her face became taut with impatience and then she simply regarded me quizzically and said, "Mr. Ellis, do you feel okay?" But her concern was utterly superficial, even if she genuinely tried to make it seem unintended.

I couldn't let this challenge diminish me. I had to take this information and do something with it. I now knew—for fact—something about this boy who had called himself Clayton and had appeared in my office and in the front seat of Aimee Light's car and in my own home and I now knew that he had lied to me, and even worse—I felt with a premonitory shiver—that whatever intentions he had were not fulfilled yet. I was light-headed and my muscles ached from lack of sleep and I hadn't eaten anything except a cracker smeared with cheese in the Buckley library the night before, and as I walked out of the admissions office I stared at the Commons—the flat center of campus. It had been warm that morning and the air dead and still, but now a breeze caught the rust-colored leaves carpeting the field, revealing the green lawn hidden beneath them. The questions were too myriad (and outlandish) to systematically and rationally contemplate. It was a Tuesday—that was the only fact. I couldn't stand on the steps of the admissions building—lost and spacing out on a lone, scrawny dog sniffing around the perimeters of Booth House, a kerchief tied around its neck—any longer. I took off in the direction of the student parking lot to see if I could locate either the cream-colored 450 SL or Aimee Light's BMW. It was the only plan at the moment that could move me out of my stupor. In the distance, the sun glanced off the white dome of the art building and then the sky started darkening. Indian summer vanished rapidly that afternoon.

The student parking lot was situated behind the Barn, and as I walked under the entrance arc of the black ironwood gates a wave of panic-infused nausea flowed through me, then subsided. I recovered and then started scanning the rows of haphazardly parked cars, and the frantic worry returned when I could smell the sea and knew this was the scent of the Pacific thousands of miles away, and clouds were moving swiftly backwards, and crows flew high over the unpaved, dusty parking lot. It seemed as if the temperature was dropping in degrees by the second, and while looking over the roughly two hundred cars that occupied the lot I realized I was suddenly breathing steam. When I thought I saw a flash of white three rows over from where I was standing I started stumbling toward it, my shoes crunching the gravel beneath me.

As I passed a student waxing a Volvo—in that instant—a wind machine was activated.

Freezing air scorched the campus, piercing it.

Piles of dead leaves blanketing everything exploded upward and suddenly formed cones that raced across the ground. My coat flapped wildly behind me as I struggled through the lot. The air rushing forward felt like a knife. The crows were now reeling above me, black and cursing, their shrill cries drowned out by the roar of the wind, and the wind whipped the flag so hard that *thwack*ing sounds echoed out from the pole it was attached to. The wind subsided briefly but then another huge sheet was literally pushing me out of the parking lot, and when I saw students, startled and grimacing, running for cover into buildings, I lowered my head and staggered against the wind, heading for shelter in the campus pub, The Café, and stood beneath the awning, where I grabbed a wooden column to support myself, but then gave up, letting the force of the wind slam me against a wall. The wind lashed out with such force that a vending machine I was standing beside toppled over. When I looked up, squinting, I could see the hands on the clock tower swinging like pendulums. You could actually hear the wind snarling.

(I shut my eyes tightly and wrapped my arms protectively around myself and asked mindlessly: what was the wind? And, just as mindlessly, something answered: the dead screaming.)

And in the moment I decided to stop searching for the cars and retreat to The Barn and the safety of the office located there, the wind paused and silence ringed the campus.

My jumbled thoughts:

(*The wind forced you out of the parking lot*)

(*Because it didn't want you to find a car*)

(*You learn to move on without the people you love*)

(*My father hadn't*)

(*But the wind stopped: time for a drink*)

Shivering, I climbed the creaking staircase leading to my office, adjusting to the warm emptiness of the Barn. I unlocked my office and the moment I stepped over the stories that had been pushed under the door, I realized that the last time I had been here was on Halloween: the day Clayton introduced himself to me, and then I moved to my desk and slumped into a chair by the window overlooking the Commons and almost started crying because on that same day Aimee Light had pretended not to know him. Outside, the dark clouds that had been guarding Midland County were dissipating, the view growing so bright that I could see past the Commons and into the valley below the campus. Horses were grazing in a pasture near a canvas tent, and a yellow tractor was maneuvering through the huge oaks and maples that made up a forest leading into town, and then I saw my father, the crows turning in the sky above him, and he was standing at the end of the Commons lawn, and his face was white and his stare was fixed on me and he was holding out his hand and I knew that if I took that hand it would be as cold as mine and his mouth moved and from where I sat I could hear the name he kept repeating, insistently escaping his lips. *Robby. Robby. Robby.*

Someone knocked on the door of the office and my father disappeared.

Donald Kimball looked tired and his inquisitive manner had changed since last Saturday; he was now defeated. After I let him in he regarded me casually and gestured at a chair, which he fell into as I nodded. He sighed and sat back, his bloodshot eyes scanning the room. I wanted him to make a comment about the wind—I needed someone to verify it for me so we could share a laugh—but he didn't. When he spoke his voice was dry.

"I've never been up here," he sighed. "To the college, I mean. Nice place."

I moved over to my desk and sat behind it. "It's a nice college."

"Doesn't working here interfere with your writing schedule?"

"Well, I only teach here once a week, and I'm canceling tomorrow's class and—" I realized how careless that made me sound and so I began to make a case for myself. "I mean, I take my job seriously even though it's not very demanding . . . I mean, it's fairly routine." I was just making noise. I just wanted to prolong everything. "It's pretty easy." I couldn't sit still—I was too nervous—and I paced the office instead, pretending to look for something. I bent down to retrieve the stories when I suddenly froze: footprints stamped in ash trailed along the wooden floor.

The same footprints that had once been visible in the darkening carpet on Elsinore Lane.

I swallowed hard.

"Why?" Kimball was asking.

"Why . . . what?" I tore my eyes away from the footprints and stood up and placed the stories on a table that sat off to the side of the window overlooking the Commons.

"Why is it easy?"

"Because they're impressed by me." I shrugged. "They sit in a room and try to describe reality and they mostly fail and then I leave." I paused. "I'm good at professional detachment." I paused again. "Plus I don't have tenure to worry about."

Kimball kept staring at me, waiting for the lame interlude I imposed on us to reach its end.

I kept forcing myself to look away from the footprints.

Finally Kimball cleared his throat. "I got your messages and I'm sorry it took me so long to get back to you, but you didn't sound too upset and—"

"But I think I may have some news," I said, sitting down again.

(*but you don't*)

"Yes, that's what you said." Kimball nodded slowly. "But, um . . ." He trailed off, distracted by something.

"Do you want something to drink?" I asked suddenly. "I mean, I think I've got a bottle of scotch around here somewhere."

"No, no—that's okay." He stopped. "I've got to head back over to Stoneboat."

"What happened in Stoneboat?" I asked. "Wait, that's not where Paul Owen is?"

Kimball sighed heavily again. He seemed withdrawn, regretful.

"No, it isn't where Paul Owen is."

I paused. "But is Paul Owen . . . okay?"

"Yeah, he is, um . . ." Kimball finally breathed in and stared directly at me. "Look, Mr. Ellis, something happened in Stoneboat last night." He sighed, deciding whether to continue. "And I think it changed the direction of the investigation that I talked to you about on Saturday."

I asked, "What happened?"

Kimball looked at me flatly. "There was another murder."

I took this in and nodded and then forced myself to ask, "Who . . . was it?"

"We don't know."

"I don't . . . understand."

"There were only body parts." He unclasped his hands, opening them, revealing his palms. My eyes were drawn to Kimball's fingernails. He bit them. "It was a woman." He kept sighing. "I've been busy all day with this, and I didn't want to bother you about it because the crime deviated from the theory we had."

"Meaning . . ."

"It wasn't in the book," he said. "The homicides we investigated in Midland County starting this past summer—we thought—were ultimately connected to the book and, well, this one . . . wasn't." He looked over my shoulder and out the window. "This was a serious deviation."

Immediately: I was cut off. I was on my own. Telling Kimball about Clayton wouldn't mean anything. It didn't matter now. It already seemed as if Kimball was dismissing me. It was obvious from the expression on his face that he didn't trust the story line anymore.

The crime scene—the murder that shattered the pattern—at the Orsic Motel, just off the interstate in Stoneboat, was insanely elaborate. There were ropes and body parts positioned in front of mirrors; the head and the hands were missing, and the walls were splashed with blood; there was evidence that a blowtorch had been used at one point, and the bones in both arms had been broken before the skin had been peeled off, and a woman's torso was found in the shower stall, and a huge drawing—in the victim's blood—of a face adorned the wall above the gutted bed with the words— I'M BACK —also dripping in blood, scrawled below it. There were, again, no prints. "No one even knows how the room became occupied . . . The maid . . . she . . ." Kimball's voice was fading.

It was getting dark in the office and I reached over and switched on the lamp with the green glass shade sitting on my desk, but it failed to illuminate the room.

As I listened to Kimball my heart was whirring erratically.

Though the crime scene had not been contaminated, the print man could not even come up with smudges or smears, and technicians found no signs of footprints or fibers, and serologists inspecting the spatter trajectories and the defensive wounds had found no blood samples other than the victim's, which was exceedingly rare considering the brutality of the murder. The neighborhood had already been canvassed, and a psychic was now being consulted. And crushing everything was the fact that this crime did not exist in my book.

My armpits were damp with sweat.

I wasn't relieved

(*Aimee Light is missing*)

because even though no crime like this was featured in the Vintage edition of *American Psycho,* there was still a detail that bothered me. There was a suggestion in Kimball's description of something I had once come across. Immediately my eyes refocused on the footprints as Kimball's voice drifted in and out.

". . . won't have a positive ID for at least a week . . . maybe longer . . . maybe never . . . basically a wait-and-see situation . . ."

His stoicism was supposed to be comforting, and I realized he thought he was taking away something that was ruining my life and that I should be relieved. The more he spoke—in the soft voice meant to rid me of guilt and stress—the deeper my fear increased. Because what could I tell him at this point? Kimball waited patiently after he asked what it was I had called about, and he was unrewarded by my silence. My face actually reddened when I realized I had nothing to offer him—no proof, not even a name, just a young man who resembled me. And when he saw that I had nothing to give him—that I was hiding—he retreated back into trying to process what had hit him at the Orsic Motel earlier that day. He had no questions to ask me. I had no answers to give him. A train of futile incidence had led us here—that was all. Nothing was connected anymore. And while we both fell into our respective silences my mind started widening with possibilities I couldn't share with the detective.

A boy was making a book come true. But I did not have the name of this boy.

He had been in my house. (He denied this.)

He had been in Aimee Light's car. (But had you really seen him?)

He was involved with a girl I was involved with.

(Bring this up. Admit the affair. Let Jayne know. Lose everything.)

And he had been in a video that was made the night my father died twelve years ago.

(But don't forget: in the video he is the same age as he is now. That's the crowning detail. That's the admission that will really make this case fly. That's the thing that would be used against you.)

In the end it was the fear that Kimball might view me as insane that was the most legitimate reason I had for not saying anything.

(*The wind? What do you mean, the wind stopped you from searching a parking lot? What were you looking for? The car of a nonexistent student?*

A phantom? Someone who had the same exact car that you had driven as a teenager and was—)

Another horrible feeling: I was gradually being comforted by the unreality of the situation. It made me tense, but it also disembodied me. The last day and night were so far out of the realm of anything I had experienced before that the fear was now laced with a low and tangible excitement. I could no longer deny becoming addicted to the adrenaline. The sweeps of nausea were subsiding and a terrible giddiness was taking their place. When I thought of "order" and "facts" I simply began laughing. I was living in a movie, in a novel, an idiot's dream that someone else was writing, and I was becoming amazed—dazzled—by my dissolution. If there had been explanations for all the dangling strands in this reversible world, I would have acted on them

(but there could never be any explanations because explanations are boring, right?)

though at this point I just wanted it all to hang in the limbo of uncertainty.

Someone has been trying to make a novel you wrote come true.

Yet isn't that what *you* did when you wrote the book?

(But you hadn't written that book)

(Something else wrote that book)

(And your father now wanted you to notice things)

(But something else did not)

(You dream a book, and sometimes the dream comes true)

(When you give up life for fiction you become a character)

(A writer would always be cut off from actual experience because *he was the writer)*

"Mr. Ellis?"

Kimball was calling to me from someplace far away, and I faded back into the room we were both in. He was already standing and his eyes interlocked with mine as I got to my feet, but there was a distance. And then, after a few promises to keep each other posted in case anything "came up" (a term that was left so deliciously vague), I walked him to the door and then Kimball was gone.

Once I closed the door, I noticed the manila envelope next to the footprints stamped in ash, resting on the floor, an object I hadn't noticed before.

(Because it hadn't been there before, right?)

My mind shrugged: anything was possible now.

I stared at it for a long time, breathing hard.

I approached it not with the casual wariness I usually felt when a student was handing me a story, but with a specific trepidation that spasmed throughout my body.

I had to force myself to swallow before picking it up.

I opened the envelope.

It was a manuscript.

It was called "Minus Numbers."

The name "Clayton" was scratched in the corner of the title page.

I don't know how long I stood there, but suddenly I needed to talk to Kimball.

When I rushed to the window I saw the taillights of Kimball's sedan rolling down College Drive and in the distance, farther into the valley, the searchlights of an army helicopter sweeping over the deserted forest.

By now it was completely dark out.

But what was I going to tell Kimball? The paralysis returned when I realized I wanted to ask him something.

You will drive to Aimee Light's studio, which is located a half mile from the college in a series of perfunctory brick bungalows that house off-campus students and brackets a parking lot surrounded by pines. Her car will not be there. You will cruise through the parking lot, searching for it, but you will never find it (*because it was driven from the Orsic Motel and dumped somewhere*) and your palms will actually be sweating, which will cause your grip to slide off the steering wheel. The moon will be a mirror reflecting everything it looms over, and the smell of burning leaves will permeate the night air as you briefly reflect on a day that has passed too quickly. You will park in her empty space and get out of the Porsche and you will notice her lights are off, and the only noise will be the hooting of owls and the cries of coyotes lost in the hills of Sherman Oaks, emerging from their caves and answering one another as they lunge toward lit pools of water, and always with you everywhere will be the constant scent of the Pacific. You will walk to the door and then stop because you don't really want to open it, but after pushing uselessly against it you will give up and move to a side window and you will peer through it

(*because you need to be so much bolder than you feel*)

and the computer on her desk will be the only light in the room, illuminating a stack of papers, the Marlboros she smokes, the hurricane lamp next to the mattress on the floor, the Indian rug and the worn leather chair and the CDs scattered next to an ancient boom box and the framed Diane Arbus print and the Chippendale table (the only concession to her upbringing) and piles of books stacked so high they act as a kind of wallpaper, and as you scan the empty room suddenly something will jump up on the windowsill and scowl at you and you will scream and leap back until you realize it's only her cat, pawing hungrily at the pane of glass separating you from it, and you will rush back to your car when you notice the dried blood staining its jaws, and as the cat keeps clawing at the window you will pull out of the parking lot, wanting to drive to the Orsic Motel in Stoneboat, but that's forty minutes from here and will make you late to meet Jayne for couples counseling, though, of course, by this point, that isn't the real reason. You are afraid again because it isn't time to wake up from the nightmare yet. And even if you could, you know that there are so many new ones about to begin.

What I wanted to ask Kimball was: Did you find a navel ring on the torso in that shower stall in the Orsic Motel?

17. couples counseling

When I arrived back home Jayne was in the middle of packing. The studio's Gulfstream would fly her out of Midland Airport tomorrow morning and land in Toronto sometime after ten. Marta reminded me of this while Jayne busied herself in the master bedroom, fitting clothes into various Tumi bags spread across the bed, checking each item off a list. She was saving everything she needed to say for Dr. Faheida's office. (Couples counseling always reminded me what a terrible thing optimism was.) I took a shower and dressed and was so exhausted I doubted my ability to sit through a session—I shuddered at the energy it would take. Since these dreadful hours usually ended in tears on Jayne's part and a raging helplessness on mine, I steeled myself and didn't mention the phone call from Harrison Ford's office that I received in the parking lot in front of Aimee Light's studio, warning me that it would be in "everyone's best interests" (I noted the ominous new Hollywood-speak) if I could be there on Friday afternoon. In a zombie monotone I said I would call them back tomorrow to confirm while I stared through the windshield at the swaying pine trees looming up into the darkness above where I sat in the Porsche. Another failure on my part—though any excuse to get out of the house was now acceptable to me. Was, in fact, becoming a priority. While waiting downstairs I avoided the living room and my office and didn't glance at the house as Jayne and I walked to the Range Rover parked in the driveway because I didn't want to see how much more of its exterior had peeled off.

(*But maybe it had stopped. Maybe it knew that I understood already what it wanted from me.*)

And there was none of the casual bitching in the car that usually preceded these evenings. No argument ensued because I kept focusing on my silence. Jayne knew nothing about what was going on inside the house, or that a video clip existed of my father moments before his death, or that 307 Elsinore Lane was turning itself into a house that used to exist on Valley Vista in a suburb of the San Fernando Valley called Sherman Oaks, or that a vast wind had kept me from looking for a car I'd driven as a teenager, or that a murderer was roaming Midland County because of a book I'd written or—most urgently—that a girl I desired had disappeared into the Orsic Motel in Stoneboat sometime late last night. And I suddenly thought to myself: If you wrote something and it happened, could you also write something and make it disappear?

I concentrated on the flat asphalt ribbon of the interstate so I wouldn't have to see the wind-bent palm and citrus trees that suddenly lined the roads (I imagined their trunks pushing out of the dark, hard ground for my benefit only), and the windows were rolled up so the scent of the Pacific didn't seep into the car, and the radio was off so "Someone Saved My Life Tonight" or "Rocket Man" wasn't pouring from an oldies station in another state. Jayne was leaning away from me in the passenger seat, arms crossed, tugging her seat belt every so often as a reminder for me to strap myself in. She made a clicking noise with her mouth when she noticed my conscientiousness. It was taking every cell I possessed to destroy (for just this evening) all the things that had been whirling through my mind, but in the end, I was just too tired and distracted to freak out. It was time to concentrate on tonight. And because I started paying attention something eased as we walked through the parking lot. I made a joke that caused her to smile and then we shared another joke. She took my hand as we moved toward the building, and I felt hopeful as the two of us entered Dr. Faheida's office, where Jayne and I sat in black leather armchairs facing each other while Dr. Faheida (who seemed at once stirred and humbled by Jayne's stardom) perched on a wooden stool off to the side, a referee with a yellow legal pad that she would mark up and casually refer back to throughout the session. We were supposed to talk to each other, but often forgot and during the first ten minutes we usually aimed our complaints at the shrink, forgetting to not use specific pronouns, and I always zoned out while Jayne always started (because she had so much more to contend with) and then I would hear something that would snap me out of my lassitude.

Tonight it was "He hasn't connected with Robby."

A pause, and then Dr. Faheida asked, "Bret?"

This was the crux of the matter, the slashing detour from the numbing sameness that enveloped each hour. Very quickly I began formulating a defense with "That's not true" but was interrupted by an exasperated sound from Jayne.

"Okay . . . I *want* to say that's not true because it's not *totally* true . . . I think we get along a little better now and . . ."

Dr. Faheida held up a hand to silence Jayne, who was writhing in her chair. "Let Bret speak, Jayne."

"And, I mean, Jesus, it's only been four months. It can't happen overnight." My voice was rigid with calm.

A pause. "Are you finished?" Dr. Faheida asked.

"I mean, I could say *he* hasn't connected with *me*." I turned to Dr. Faheida. "I can say that, right? Is that okay? That Robby hasn't tried connecting with *me*?"

Dr. Faheida stroked her thin neck and nodded benevolently.

"He wasn't here when Robby was growing up," Jayne said. And I could already tell by her voice—just minutes into the session—that her rage was going to end up being defeated by sadness.

"Address Bret, Jayne."

She turned toward me, and when our eyes met I looked away.

"That's why he's just this boy to you," she said. "That's why you have no feelings for him."

"He's still growing up, Jayne," Dr. Faheida reminded her gently.

And then I had to stop my eyes from watering by saying: "But were you really there for him, Jayne? I mean, all these years, with you traveling everywhere, were you really there for him—"

"Oh God, not this shit again," Jayne groaned, sinking into the armchair.

"No, really. How many times have you left him when you went on location? With Marta? Or your parents? Or whoever? I mean, honey, a lot of the time he was raised by a series of faceless nannies—"

"This is exactly why I don't think counseling is helping," Jayne said to Dr. Faheida. "This is it exactly. It's all a joke. This is why it's a waste of time."

"Is this all a joke to you, Bret?" Dr. Faheida asked.

"He's never changed a diaper," Jayne said, going through her hysterical litany of how the damage we were trudging through was caused by my absence during Robby's infancy. She was actually in the middle of pointing out that I'd "never been thrown up on" when I had to cut her off. I couldn't stop myself. I wanted her guilt and anger to really start kicking in.

"I *have* been vomited on, honey," I protested. "Quite often I have been vomited on. In fact there was a year sometime back there when I was vomited on continuously."

"Vomiting on *yourself* doesn't count!" she shouted, and then said, less desperately, to Dr. Faheida, "See—it's all a joke to him."

"Bret, why do you attempt to mask real problems with irony and sarcasm?" Dr. Faheida asked.

"Because I don't know how seriously I can take all this if we're only blaming me," I said.

"No one is 'blaming' anyone," Dr. Faheida said. "I thought we all agreed that this is a term we don't use here."

"I think Jayne needs to take responsibility as well." I shrugged. "Did we or did we not finish last week's session talking about Jayne's problem? The little teensy-weensy one"—I held up two fingers, pressing them together tightly, to illustrate—"about how she doesn't think she's worthy of respect and how *that* messes up everything? Did we or did we not discuss this, Dr. Fajita?"

"It's Faheida," she corrected me quietly.

"Dr. Fajita, doesn't anyone see here that I didn't want—"

"Oh, this is ridiculous," Jayne shouted. "He's a drug addict. He's been using again."

"None of this has anything to do with being a drug addict," I shouted back. "It has to do with the fact that I didn't want a kid!"

Everything tensed up. The room went silent. Jayne stared at me.

I breathed in, then started talking slowly.

"I didn't want a kid. It's true. I didn't. But . . . now . . ." I had to stop. A circle was narrowing around me, and my chest felt so tight that I was momentarily lost in blackness.

"Now . . . what, Bret?" This was Dr. Faheida.

"But now I do . . ." I was so tired, I couldn't help myself and started crying.

Jayne stared at me with disgust.

"Is there anything more pathetic than a monster who keeps asking *please? please? please?*—"

"I mean . . . what more do you want from me?" I asked, recovering slightly.

"Are you kidding? You're actually asking that?"

"I'm going to try, Jayne. I'm going to really try. I'm . . ." I wiped my face. "I'm gonna look after the kids while you go off tomorrow and—"

Jayne started talking over me in a tired voice. "We have a maid, we have Marta, the kids are gone all day—"

"But I can look after them too, when, I mean, when they're at the house and—"

Jayne suddenly stood up.

"But I don't want you to look after them because you're an addict and an alcoholic, and that's why we need people at the house, and that's why I don't like you driving the kids anywhere, and that's why you should probably just—"

"Jayne, I think you should sit down." Dr. Faheida gestured at the armchair.

Jayne breathed in.

Realizing I had no other options (and that I didn't want any other options), I said, "I know I haven't exactly proven myself, but I am going to try . . . I am really gonna try and make this work." I hoped the more I said this, the more it would register with her.

I reached for her hand. She knocked it away.

"Jayne," Dr. Faheida warned.

"Why are you going to try, Bret?" Jayne asked, standing over me. "You're gonna try because your life is so much worse by yourself? Because you're too afraid to live it alone? Don't tell me you're gonna try because you love Robby. Or because you love me. Or Sarah. You are far too selfish to get away with fucking lying like that. You're just afraid to be by yourself. It's just easier for you to stick around."

"Then kick me out!" I suddenly roared back.

Jayne collapsed into the armchair and started sobbing again.

This caused me to regain my composure.

"It is a process, Jayne," I said, my voice lowered. "It's not intuitive. It's something you learn—"

"No, Bret, it's something you *feel*. You don't *learn* how to connect with your own son from a fucking manual."

"Two people have to try," I said, leaning forward. "And Robby is not trying."

"He's a child—"

"He's a lot smarter than you give him credit for, Jayne."

"That's not fair."

"Yeah, right, it's all me," I said, giving up. "I've betrayed everyone."

"You're so sentimental," she said, grimacing.

"Jayne, you took me back for your own selfish reasons. You didn't take me back because of Robby."

Her mouth dropped open in shock.

I was shaking my head, glaring at her.

"You took me back for yourself. Because *you* wanted me back. You *always* wanted me back. And you can't stand that that's how you feel. I came back to you because you wanted me back and this choice had very little to do with Robby. It was what Jayne wanted."

"How can you say that?" Jayne sobbed, her voice high and questioning.

"Because I don't think Robby wants me here. I don't think Robby ever wanted me back." I became so tired when I admitted this to the room that my voice became a whisper. "I don't think the father ever needs to be there." My eyes were watery again. "People are better off without them."

Jayne stopped crying and regarded me with a cold and genuine interest. "Really? You think people are better off without a father?"

"Yes." The room could barely hear me. "I do."

"I think we can disprove that theory right now."

"How? How, Jayne?"

Quietly, and with no effort, she simply said, "Look how you turned out."

I knew she was right, but I couldn't stand the silence that would have punctuated that sentence, the silence that would give it dimension and depth and weight, transforming it into the sentence that would connect with an audience.

"What does that mean?"

"That you're wrong. That a boy needs his father. It means that you were wrong, Bret."

"No, Jayne, *you* were wrong. It was wrong of *you* to have that child in the first place," I said, meeting her gaze. "And you knew it was wrong. It wasn't planned, and when you supposedly consulted me I told you that I didn't want a child and then you went ahead and had him even though you knew it was wrong. We did not make that decision together. If anyone is wrong here, Jayne, it's you—"

"You're a walking pharmacy—you don't even know what you're talking about." Jayne was sobbing again. "How can anyone listen to this?"

I thought I had reached a threshold of caring, but exhaustion kept me pushing forward in a rational tone.

"You did a very selfish thing by having Robby, and now you're understanding just how selfish it was and so you blame *me* for that selfishness."

"You fucking asshole," she sobbed, wrecked. "You are such an asshole."

"Jayne," Dr. Faheida interrupted. "We talked about how you should ignore Bret when he says something you disagree with or know to be patently false."

"Hey!" I exclaimed, sitting up.

"Oh, I try," Jayne said, breathing in, her face twisted with regret. "But he won't let me ignore him. Because Mr. Rock Star needs all the attention and he can't give it to anyone else." She choked back another sob, and then she directed her fury at me again. "You can't step back from any situation and see it from any perspective but your own. You are the one, Bret, who is completely selfish and self-absorbed and—"

"Whenever I try to give you or the kids the attention you all say you need, all you guys do is back away from me, Jayne. Why should I even try anymore?"

"Stop whining!" she screamed.

"Jayne—" Dr. Faheida jumped in.

"Robby was fucked up before I got here, Jayne," I said quietly. "And it wasn't because of me."

"He's not fucked up, Bret." She started coughing. She reached for a Kleenex. "Is this really all you've learned?"

"Whatever I've learned in the last four months is that the hostility directed toward me in that house has alienated me from connecting with *anybody*. That is what I have learned, Jayne, and . . ."

I stopped. Suddenly I couldn't keep it up. I involuntarily softened. I began weeping. How had I ended up so alone? I wanted everything to be rewound. Immediately I got up from the armchair and knelt in front of Jayne, my head bowed down. She tried pushing me away but I held her arms firmly. And I started to make promises. I spoke uninterrupted, my voice raw. I told her that I was going to be there for him and that things were changing and that I'd realized over the last week that I *have* to be there for him and that it was time for me to be the father. I had never spoken these words with such force and in that moment I made a decision to let the tide of narrative take me where it wanted to, which I believed at the time was toward Robby, and I kept talking while I wept. I was going to concentrate only on our family now. It was the only thing that meant anything to me. And when I was finished and finally looked up into Jayne's face it was fractured, distorted, and then something passed between us that was distinct and clear, and in the most dreamlike way, her head slowly tilted, and in that movement I felt something ascend and then her face composed itself as she stared back at me and her tears stopped along with mine, and this new expression was in such a contrast to the harshness that had scattered it before that a stillness overtook the room, transporting it to someplace else. She had been paralyzed, transfixed, by my admission. I remained kneeling, our hands still curled together. We were drawing each other inward. It was a faint movement toward countervision, toward comfort. It felt as if I had crossed a world to arrive at this point. Something unclenched in me, and her remorseful gaze suggested a future. But—and I tried to block this thought—were we really looking at each other, or were we looking at who we wanted to be?

18. spago

Spago had appeared off Main Street last April, almost twenty years to the day after the original had opened above Sunset Boulevard in L.A., and where I first took Blair in the cream-colored 450 SL after an Elvis Costello concert at the Greek Theatre, and at a window table overlooking the city I told her that I'd been accepted by Camden and that I was leaving for New Hampshire at the end of August and she fell silent for the rest of dinner. (Blair, a girl from Laurel Canyon, had actually quoted Fleetwood Mac's "Landslide" on her senior page in the Buckley yearbook, which made me silently cringe at the time, but now, twenty years later, the couplet she chose moved me to tears.) When Jayne and I entered the restaurant it was already half-empty. We were seated at a window table and our waiter had shiny hair and was midway through reciting the specials when he recognized Jayne, at which point his drone became falsely chipper, his timidity activated by her presence. I noticed this. Jayne did not, because she was staring at me sadly, and her expression didn't change when I ordered a Stoli and grapefruit juice. She accepted this and ordered a glass of the house Viognier. We touched hands across the table. Her eyes wandered away and out the window; it was cold and Main Street's storefronts were darkened and a traffic light swung above an empty intersection, flashing a yellow light. We were both less stern. We'd become simplified, anchored, nothing was shifting or panicked here between the two of us, and we wanted to be tender with each other.

"First the man takes a drink, then the drink takes a drink, and then the drink takes the man," she was murmuring.

I smiled apologetically. Ordering a cocktail had been so natural an act that I hadn't even thought about it. It had been involuntary. "I'm sorry . . ."

"Why are you having a drink?" she asked.

"It'll be my reward vodka?"

"How did I know you'd say something shitty like that?" But there was no rancor in her voice, and we were still holding hands in the dimness of the restaurant.

"Do you really want to be here this week?" Jayne asked.

It was as if the intensity of the heartfelt plea — on my knees, with my head bowed — in Dr. Faheida's office had vanished from memory. But then I thought, During that impassioned speech, were you thinking only of your-self? "What do you mean? Where else would I want to be?"

"Well, I thought maybe you'd want to take a week off." She shrugged. "Marta will be there. And Rosa."

"Jayne—"

"Or you could come to Toronto with me."

"Hey," I said, leaning forward. "You know that would definitely not work out."

"You're right, you're right." She shook her head. "That was a dumb idea."

"It wasn't a dumb idea."

"I just thought maybe you'd like to go someplace. Have a vacation."

"I've got nowhere else to go." I was doing my Richard Gere in *An Officer and a Gentleman* impersonation. "I've got nowhere else to go . . ."

She laughed lightly, and it didn't seem faked, and we squeezed hands again.

Then I decided to tell her. "Well, I'm up for this Harrison Ford thing and they might want to meet this week." I paused. "In L.A."

"I think that's great," Jayne said.

Though I wasn't surprised by her enthusiasm, I said, "Really?"

"Yeah. You should definitely think about it."

"It would only be for a day or two," I said.

"Good. I hope you do it."

Suddenly I asked, "Why do you stay with me?"

"Because . . ." She sighed. "Because . . . I get you, I guess."

"Yet all I do is disappoint you," I muttered guiltily. "All I do is disappoint everybody."

"You have potential." She stopped. The unspecific comment was trans-formed into something else by her tenderness. "There was a time when you made me laugh and you were . . . kind . . ." She paused again. "And I believe that will happen again." She lowered her head and didn't look up for a long time.

"You're acting like this is the end of the world," I said softly.

The waiter came with our drinks. He pretended to recognize Jayne only now and grinned widely at her. She acknowledged this and offered a sad smile. He warned us that the kitchen would be closing soon, but this didn't really register. I noticed people slipping away from the bar. There was a whirlpool in the center of the dining room. After Jayne sipped her wine she let go of my hand and asked, "Why didn't we work on this more?" Pause. "I mean in the beginning . . ." Another pause. "Before we broke up."

"I don't know." It was the only answer I could come up with. "We were too young?" I guessed. "Could that have been it?"

"You never trusted my feelings," she murmured to herself. "I don't think you ever really believed I liked you."

"That's not true at all," I said. "I did. I did know that. I just . . . wasn't ready."

"And you are now? After one particularly volatile session?"

"On the volatility scale I would say that was only about a seven."

And then after we both tried to smile, I said, "Maybe you never really understood me." I said this in the same soft voice I had been using since we entered the restaurant. "You say that you did. But maybe you didn't. Not really." I thought about this. "Maybe not enough to resolve anything? But that was probably my fault. I was just this . . . hidden person and—"

"Who made it so impossible to resolve anything." She finished the sentence.

"I want to now. I want to make things work out . . . and . . ." My foot found hers beneath the table. And then I had a flash: Jayne standing alone over a grave in a charred field at dusk, and this image forced me to admit, "You're right about something."

"What?"

"I am afraid of being alone."

You stumble into a nightmare—you grasp for salvation.

"I'm afraid of losing you . . . and Robby . . . and Sarah . . ."

If something is written, can it be unwritten?

I tensed when I said, "Don't go," even though this wasn't meant literally.

"I'll only be gone a week."

I thought about the week that had just passed. "That's a long time."

" 'There's always summer,' " she said wistfully, a famous line from a movie she had made—the elusive love interest who strands the fiancé at the altar.

"Don't go," I said again.

She was unfolding a napkin. She was quietly crying.

"What?" I reached for her. I felt the corners of my mouth sag.

"That's the first time you've ever said that to me."

This would be the last dinner I ever had with Jayne.

19. the cat

I woke up staring at our darkened ceiling in the master bedroom. The writer was imagining an intricate moment: Jayne saying goodbye to the children, kneeling on the cold granite of the driveway, a sedan and its driver idling behind her, and the kids were dressed for school and she'd left them so many times before that Sarah and Robby were used to this—they didn't sulk, they barely paid attention, because this was just business: Mom going nowhere again. (If Robby was slightly more emotional that day in November, he did not reveal it to Jayne.) Why was Jayne lingering when she said goodbye to Robby? Why was she searching his eyes? Why did Jayne stroke his face until Robby pulled back and flinched, Sarah's fingers still restlessly entwined with her mother's? She crushed them in a hug, their foreheads touching, the front of the house looming over them with the wall that was a map sprawling across its surface. She would only be gone a week. She would call them that night from her hotel room in Toronto. (Later, at Buckley, Sarah would point at the wrong plane cruising the sky, passing in and out of clouds, and tell a teacher, "My mommy's up there," and by then Jayne's pain would have faded.) Why did Jayne weep on the ride to the Midland Airport? Before Jayne left the darkness of our bedroom, why had I said the words *I promise*? My pillow was wet. I had cried in my sleep again. Sun was now filtering into the room and the ceiling was lighting itself indifferently in an enlarging diamond, and the umbrellas were still spinning and iridescent halos revolved around me—the remnants of a dream I couldn't remember—and mid-yawn my immediate thought was *Jayne's gone*. What the writer wanted to know was: why was Jayne so frightened the morning of November fifth? Or, more accurately, how did Jayne intuit what was going to happen to us during her absence?

Ignoring everything is very easy to do. Paying attention is much harder, but this is what was demanded of me since I was now the momentary guardian.

It was time to condense things, and because of this everything started moving faster. I now had a list that needed to be checked on the morning of November fifth. The newspaper needed to be scanned for any information about the missing boys. (Nothing.)

It also needed to be scanned for any information pertaining to a murder at the Orsic Motel. (Nothing.)

The last time I dialed Aimee Light's number was on the morning of November fifth. Her cell phone wasn't even on anymore.

I checked my e-mail. There were no longer any messages coming from the Bank of America in Sherman Oaks at 2:40 a.m.

I couldn't tell if the carpeting in the living room was darker. The writer told me it was. But he also said it didn't matter anymore.

The furniture was still in the same formation I'd known as a child. The writer confirmed this as well, then wanted to inspect the exterior of the house.

When we walked around to the side of the house facing the Allens', we saw that the wall was still in the process of changing. The salmon pink had darkened and the stucco was pronouncing itself more forcefully in wheeling patterns that were suddenly appearing everywhere. The writer whispered to me: the house is turning into the one you grew up in.

I moved on to the front of the house, where the peeling continued to spread its warning.

The sweet, rank smell of something dead was noticeable immediately.

There was a hedge that aisled the lower half of the northern side of the house and I scanned it until I saw the cat.

It was lying on its side, spine arched, its small yellow teeth locked in a frozen grimace, and its intestines leeched the ground, clinging to the dirt they had poured onto. Its eyes were squeezed tight with what I first thought was pain.

But when the writer forced me to look more closely, I realized that something had pecked them out.

The ground was soaked with blood, and viscera that the Terby had slashed from the cat's belly were sprayed across the daisied hedge, now hovering with flies.

I imagined that something was witnessing my discovery of the cat, and I whirled around as a sudden flash of black rounded the corner of the house.

The writer promised me this was not something I had dreamt.

But I could not imagine how the Terby had captured the cat.

I could not imagine the doll doing this.

The Terby was simply a prop from a horror movie.

But there was a part of the writer that wanted the Terby to have killed the cat.

The writer could imagine that scene: the doll keeping watch—a sentinel—from its perch on Sarah's window ledge, the doll spotting the cat, the doll swooping down, the doll grappling with the cat beneath the tightly trimmed hedge, a talon raised, and then what? Did it play with the cat before eventually slashing it in half? Did the thing feed on the cat? Was the last thing the cat saw the contorted face of the bird and above it an empty gray sky? The writer pondered the various scenarios until I stepped in and forced the writer to hope this was not true. Because if I believed that the doll was responsible, the ground I stood on would shift into a world made of quicksand.

But it was too late.

It was at this point that I recognized the cat.

I had seen it the night before.

When its mouth was stained red, and blood from a paw smeared a windowpane.

The mangled thing at my feet belonged to Aimee Light.

I did not tell this to the writer because the scenario he would have come up with—the obstacles he would solve and the world he would make me believe in—was more than I could bear on the morning of November fifth.

So just as quickly as I recognized the cat as Aimee Light's I immediately forced the thought from my mind before the writer could notice this detail and leap on it, expanding it with a horrible logic until everything surrounding us turned black.

Regardless of whether the Terby had killed the cat, I was determined to get rid of it that day.

I went back into the house to find it.

Marta had taken Robby and Sarah to school. Rosa was cleaning the kitchen.

I assumed that if the Terby was in the house it would be upstairs lying innocently in Sarah's bedroom.

But the Terby was not in Sarah's bedroom. This was a discovery I made after a cursory inspection of the room.

The writer told me it was hiding. The writer told me I needed to entice it from the hiding place.

I asked the writer how does something that's not alive hide itself?

I asked the writer how do you entice something that's not alive out of its hiding place?

This silenced the writer momentarily. The silence eventually worried me.

The writer was reactivated when I moved to Sarah's window and gazed down at the hedge and the mutilated cat.

The writer suggested we go to Robby's room.

I hesitated in the hallway outside Robby's room and stared at the grooves carved in the bottom of the door, then turned the knob and entered.

The room was pristine.

It was in the neatest condition I had ever seen. Nothing was out of place.

The bed was tightly made. There were no clothes strewn across the floor. The video-game cartridges and DVDs and magazines were stacked in even piles. The Martian landscape of the carpet had been recently vacuumed. There were no empty Starbucks cups lining the top of the minifridge. His desk was immaculate. The pillows on the leather sofa had no indentations on them. Every surface was clean. The room smelled of varnish and lemon.

It was a showroom.

Everything was exact.

And it felt empty.

It was supposed to feel peaceful.

But there had been a concentrated effort to also make it feel benign.

No one had ever lived in it.

There was something horribly wrong about this.

This wrongness drew me toward the computer.

The moon was pulsing on its screen.

Again: hesitation. And then: the need for things to speed up.

Nadine Allen's anguished theory whirled into the barren room.

The word *neverland* pushed the writer to reach out and tap the mouse.

The desktop appeared on the screen.

I knew no one was upstairs but I looked over my shoulder anyway.

After tapping "My Documents," I walked over and shut the door.

When I returned to the desk, on the Gateway's screen was a list of roughly one hundred WordPerfect documents.

I started perspiring.

As I scrolled to the bottom of the screen I saw there were ten documents that had been downloaded from somewhere.

These files had initials for titles.

The writer was immediately able to attach names to them.

MC could have been Maer Cohen.

Was TS Tom Salter?

EB was Eddie Burgess.

JW: Josh Wolitzer.

CM equaled Cleary Miller.

As I tapped the document for MC suddenly a box flashed on the screen, asking me for a password.

Why would a password be needed to open a document?

Because it doesn't want to be read by you, the writer whispered.

I scanned the room while the writer wondered what Robby's password might be.

The writer wondered if there was a way we might find out.

The writer wondered if Marta knew.

I looked up from the computer and caught my image in a full-length mirror.

I was wearing khakis, a red Polo sweater over a white T-shirt and Vans, and I was hunched over my son's computer, sweating heavily. I took off the sweater. I still looked ridiculous.

I turned my attention back to the computer.

I began typing in words that I thought might mean something to Robby.

The names of moons: Titan. Miranda. Io. Atlas. Hyperion.

Each word was denied access.

The writer had expected this and scolded the father for being surprised.

I was not aware as I bent over the computer that the door behind me was slowly opening.

The writer assumed that I had closed the door.

The writer even went so far as to suggest that I had locked it.

I held on to the possibility that I had left it ajar.

As I kept uselessly typing in passwords, the door opened itself fully, and something entered Robby's room.

And just as the writer decided to type in *neverland* I realized that Nadine Allen had gotten it wrong.

The word wasn't *neverland.*

The word was *neverneverland.*

Neverneverland was where the missing boys were going.

Not *neverland* but *neverneverland.*

The writer told me to type it in immediately.

It broke open the password.

And as the screen filled itself with a digital photo of Cleary Miller accompanied by a long letter dated November 3 that began with the words "Hey RD," another chasm opened in Robby's room.

(Robert Dennis was RD.)

I froze when I heard clicking noises behind me.

Before I could turn around there was a high-pitched screech.

The Terby was standing in the doorway, its wings outstretched.

It wasn't a doll anymore. It was now something else.

It stood perfectly still, but something was stirring beneath its feathers.

The presence of the Terby—and all the things it had done—loosened me from my fear, and I rushed toward it.

When I grabbed it with my sweater I expected it to react in some way.

The animatronic lips below its beak parted to reveal a wide, uneven set of fangs that I didn't know it had.

The black face seized up—its eyes brightly wet—and its feathers started bristling as I threw the sweater over it.

But when I lifted the doll there was no struggle.

Okay, I told myself, *Sarah had left it on. It could move around on its own accord. So it walked down a hallway. It entered a room. I hadn't shut the door. Sarah simply hadn't turned the thing off before school.*

I slowly pulled the sweater off the Terby—it was reeking and felt soft and pliable, and it was vibrating slightly in my hands.

I turned the doll over to switch off the red light in the back of its neck in order to deactivate it.

But when I turned the doll over the red light wasn't on.

This fact moved me immediately out of the room.

Whatever fear this caused was transformed into energy.

I rushed to my office for my car keys.

I threw the doll into the trunk of the Porsche.

I purposefully started driving to the outskirts of town.

The writer, beside me, was thinking things through, forming his own theories.

The doll wasn't activated because no one had turned the doll on.

The doll, Bret, had picked up on your scent.

The doll knew you were in Robby's room and did not want you to find the files.

Just as it had not wanted you to see what was in Robby's room on Sunday night.

The night it bit you, it had been aiming for the hand the gun was clenched in.

The thing was protecting something.

It didn't want you to know things.

Something had wanted the doll placed in your house.

You were simply the go-between.

I needed to call Kentucky Pete and find out where he got the doll from.

I told the writer that this would begin to answer all the questions.

Okay: I had bought the thing last August, and August was the month my father died and—

Stop it, the writer interrupted. There is an empire of questions and you will never be able to answer them—there are too many, and they are all cancerous.

Instead, the writer was urging me to head up to the college. The writer wanted me to pick up the copy of "Minus Numbers"—the manuscript Clayton had left in my office. This would provide an answer, the writer assured me. But the answer would only lead ultimately to more questions and those were the questions I did not want answered.

It was too early to get ahold of Pete, but I dialed his cell and left a message.

At some point I simply pulled the Porsche over next to a field on a deserted stretch of the interstate.

Outside the sky was divided in half: part of it was an intense arctic blue slowly being erased by a sheet of black clouds. Trees were becoming leafless now. The field was glazed with dew.

I opened the trunk.

The writer told me to take note of the sweater I had wrapped the doll in.

The red Polo sweater had been torn apart during the twenty-minute drive from Elsinore Lane to the field off the interstate.

As I lifted the Terby out of the trunk by a wing, I averted my eyes as the doll began urinating a thin stream of yellow that arced from its black body and splashed onto the highway's pavement.

The writer urged me to notice the crows lining the telephone wires above me as I hurled the doll into the field where it landed, immobile.

Leaves began lifting themselves off the field.

I could hear the sound of a river, or was it waves crashing against the coastline?

The Terby was almost immediately enveloped in a cloud of flies.

In the distance a horse was grazing—maybe a hundred feet from where I stood—and the moment the flies converged upon the doll, the horse jerked its head up and galloped even farther into the field as if offended by the presence of the thing.

Kill it, the writer whispered. *Kill the thing now.*

You no longer need to convince me, I told the writer.

The writer disliked me because I was trying to follow a chart.

I was following an outline. I was calculating the weather. I was predicting events. I wanted answers. I needed clarity. I had to control the world.

The writer yearned for chaos, mystery, death. These were his inspirations. This was the impulse he leaned toward. The writer wanted bombs exploding. The writer wanted the Olympian defeat. The writer craved myth and legend and coincidence and flames. The writer wanted Patrick Bateman back in our lives. The writer was hoping the horror of it all would galvanize me.

I was at a point where all of what the writer wanted filled me with simple remorse.

(I innocently believed in metaphor, which at this point the writer actively discouraged.)

There were now two opposing strategies for dealing with the current situation.

But the writer was winning, because as I ducked back into the Porsche I could smell a sea wind drifting toward me.

20. kentucky pete

kept my gaze fixed on the horizon. The sky was turning black, and the clouds roiling in it kept changing shapes. They resembled waves, crests, the foaming surf of a thousand beaches. My eyes kept checking the rearview mirror to see if anything was following us. I did not give a shit how Sarah would react once she noticed her doll was gone. She was going to have to deal with it, rock 'n' roll. The writer noticed we were not heading toward the college, and he brought up "Minus Numbers" again. I patiently told the writer that we were not going to the college. I told the writer we were heading back to 307 Elsinore Lane. I told the writer that we needed to get back to Robby's room. There was information on Robby's computer. We needed to see what that information consisted of. The information would clarify things. This was why we were heading toward the house and not the college.

What is in the computer is simply a warning, the writer argued.

The answer is in that manuscript and not in those files, the writer argued.

I was drifting off, thinking of my own manuscript. I was thinking of how I knew at that point in time that I was never going to finish it. I dealt with this fact stoically.

When the writer started laughing at me I felt transparent.

The writer laughed: *Pull over.*

The writer laughed: *Drop me off.*

The cell phone rang. I grabbed it from the dashboard. It was Pete.

"Where did you get that doll?" I asked the moment I clicked on.

"Hey, Bret Ellis," Pete drawled, hacking up something. "It's a little early in the day—we have ourselves an all-nighter?"

"No, no," I said, flinching. "It's not that. I just wanted to ask you about that doll—"

"What doll, man?"

"That bird thing that I asked you to get for my little girl?" I said, trying to sound like a concerned parent and not one of Pete's favorite drug fiends. "I needed one of those Terbys for her birthday? And they were sold out everywhere? Do you remember that?"

"Oh, right, yeah, that ugly freakin' thing you wanted so bad."

"Yes, exactly," I said, relieved that Pete actually remembered. We were on course. "Who did you get it from?"

I could hear him shrugging. "Just some contact."

"Who was it?"

"Why?"

"I need specifics, Pete. Who was it?"

"You sure you're not high, man?"

Realizing my voice sounded hoarse and labored, I tried to push it into a neutral tone.

"This is important, okay? You don't need to name names or anything. Did your contact get this through a toy store or someone else or what?"

"I didn't ask him where he got it." I could see the glazed expression on Pete's face in the way he said this. "He just brought it to me."

Okay. I breathed in. We were heading toward something. The contact was a man.

"What did the guy look like?" I was gripping the steering wheel tightly in anticipation of Pete's answer.

"What did he *look* like?" Pete asked. "What the fuck?"

"Was it a young guy? Was it an old guy?"

"Why do you wanna know this shit?"

"Pete, just give me some kind of description." I lowered my voice. "Please, I think it's important."

"It was a younger guy." Pete said this mystified.

"What did he look like?"

"Look like? He looked like a college kid. In fact he *was* a college kid. He was a student at that place you teach at, man."

The writer began grinning.

The writer was writhing ecstatically in his seat.

The writer wanted to applaud.

My silence encouraged Pete to continue.

"I was meeting up with some kids the first week of classes, and I gotta admit I tried everywhere, even a guy I knew down in Cabo—that thing was just not available—and I knew how much cash you were laying out, so I was getting kinda desperate and so I was just asking pretty much everybody and one night when I was . . . visiting . . . the college, making a little run, I asked this group of kids if anyone could get me one of those things and this kid said he could get me one the next day. No problem."

I was driving down the interstate.

I was ignoring the unswaying palm trees that had turned the interstate into a corridor.

I had aligned the car with the lane we were in.

The writer could no longer contain his glee.

Kentucky Pete kept talking, though what he said no longer mattered.

"And so I stopped by the parking lot of the Fortinbras and we met up and he had it and that's all she wrote." Pete inhaled on something, and his voice deepened. "I gave him half the cash and I kept the rest as a finder's fee and it was a done deal."

"What did he look like, Pete?"

"Jeez, man, you keep asking that like it means something."

"It does. Tell me what he looked like."

Pete paused and inhaled again. "Well, you're probably gonna think I'm taking the easy way out of this one, but he looked a little like you."

I found it in myself to ask: "What do you mean?"

"Well, he looked like you if you were a little younger."

I found it in myself to ask: "Was his name Clayton?"

"I don't keep records, dude."

Outside this car everything was a blur. "Was his name Clayton?"

"All I know was that I met him up at the college and he drove this little white Mercedes." Pete coughed. "I remember the car. I remember thinking damn, the kid is loaded. I remember thinking that this was going to be a very lucrative term." Static. "But I never saw the kid again."

The Porsche swerved slightly. Another wave of fear delivered.

"Was his name Clayton?" I stuttered and tried to sit up straight. I might as well have been talking to myself.

There was a long pause crackling with static. And then there was silence. I was about to click off.

"You know what?" Pete finally returned. "I think that *was* his name. Yeah, Clayton. Sounds right." A concerned pause during which Pete figured something out. "Wait a minute—so you know the guy? Then what the hell are you calling me for—"

I clicked off.

I concentrated on the blinding emptiness of the interstate.

What you just heard will not answer anything, Bret. This is what the writer said.

Look how black the sky is, the writer said. *I made it that way.*

21. the actor

The Porsche dived into the garage.

The writer's laughter had subsided. The writer was a blind guide who was slowly disappearing. I was now alone.

Everything I did had an intent that was solely mine.

The stairs seemed steeper as I climbed them.

I opened Robby's door.

The computer was off.

(It was on when I had been interrupted.)

After I restarted it I sat in front of its screen for three hours.

The moment I typed in the password to open the MC file the computer screen flashed back to the desktop.

The screen started blinking, its edges shallowing out, and then it burned green and was stubbled with static.

I kept trying to wade through the glitches. I kept telling myself that if I could read those files everything would become untroubled and weightless.

I unplugged the Gateway. I restarted it.

I was on hold with the company's emergency hotline for an hour before I hung up, realizing there was nothing they would be able to do.

My eyes were aching as I kept tapping keys with one hand while moving the mouse around in useless circles on its pad with the other, my face flushed with concentration.

The computer was now a toy made from stone that just stared back at me. The computer was not going to lose this game.

Each keystroke took me further from where I wanted to be.

I was receding from the information.

Within the random flashing and static I could occasionally make out the hills of Sherman Oaks rising up out of the San Fernando Valley, or I glimpsed the shoreline of a hotel in Mexico, my father standing on a pier and he was lifting his hand, and the sound of the ocean was coming from the computer's speakers.

Briefly there was a shadow of the Bank of America on Ventura Boulevard.

Another familiar apparition: Clayton's face.

And then the computer was dying.

Before the sound faded out completely there was the faint and muffled verse from "The Sunny Side of the Street."

And then the computer whirred itself into silence and died.

The only answers were going to come from Robby, I told myself as I pushed away from the desk.

The writer immediately materialized.

The writer asked in his thin voice: *Do you really believe that, Bret? Do you really believe your son will supply the answers?*

When I responded affirmatively, the writer said: *That is sad.*

I told Marta I would be picking Robby up from Buckley. I didn't let her say anything. I just walked out of her office as I announced this.

I could hear her reluctantly agreeing as I moved down the hall to the garage.

Outside, the wind kept altering its direction.

On the interstate I saw my father standing motionless on the walkway of an overpass.

After I unrolled the window and flashed my driver's license to a security guard, I pulled into a line of cars waiting in the parking lot in front of the library. The spires of gnarled pines rose up around us, encircling the school.

I glanced at the scar in the palm of my hand.

This was either going to be an ending

(*endings were always so easy for you*)

or something would get healed, and the healing would forestall a tragedy.

The writer, in his own way, vehemently disagreed.

Privileged children mumbled warnings to one another as they headed toward the fleet of SUVs waiting for them. Security cameras followed the boys. Sons would always be in peril. Fathers would always be condemned.

Robby's backpack was flung over his shoulder and his shirt was untucked and the gray and red striped tie loosened, hanging slackly from around his neck: the parody of a tired businessman.

Robby was staring at the Porsche and at the man in the driver's seat. Robby looked at the man questioningly, as if I were someone who had never known his name.

My questions were going to merge with his answers.

I could feel his doubt as he stood rigidly in front of the car.

I was begging him to move forward. You have to surrender, I was begging. You have to give me another chance.

The writer was about to hiss something, and I silenced him.

And then, as if he had heard me, Robby shuffled toward the car, forcing a smile.

He took his backpack off before opening the passenger door.

"What's up?" He was grinning as he placed the backpack on the floor.

As he sat down he closed the passenger door. "Where's Marta?"

"Okay, look," I started, "I know you're not happy to see me, so you don't have to smile like that."

Robby didn't even pause. He immediately turned away and was about to open the door when I locked it. His hand clutched the handle.

"I want to talk to you," I said, now that we were both encased within the car.

"About what?" He let go of the handle and stared straight ahead.

The division in the car asserted itself, as I had expected it to.

"Look, I want all the bullshit dropped, okay?"

He turned to me, incredulous. "What bullshit, Dad?"

The "Dad" was the giveaway.

"Oh, shit, Robby, stop it. I know how miserable you've been." I breathed in and tried to soften my voice but failed. "Because I've been miserable in that house as well." I breathed in again. "I've made everyone miserable in that house. You don't have to pretend anymore."

I watched his smooth jaw clench and then unclench as he stared out the windshield.

"I want you to tell me what's going on." I had turned in my seat so that I was facing him. My arms were crossed.

"About what?" he asked worriedly.

"About the missing boys." There was no way to control the urgency of my voice. "What do you know about them?"

His silence emphasized something. Around us, kids were piling into cars. The cars were maneuvered out of the circular drive while the Porsche sat stationary against the curb. I was waiting.

"I don't know what you're talking about," he said softly.

"I talked to Ashton's mom. I talked to Nadine. Do you know what she found on his computer?"

"She's crazy." Robby turned to face me, panicked. "She's crazy, Dad."

"She said she found correspondence between the missing boys and Ashton. She said the correspondence was dated after these boys disappeared."

Robby's face flushed and he swallowed. In rapid succession: contempt, speculation, acceptance. So: Ashton had sold them out. So: Ashton was the traitor. Robby imagined a streaming comet. Robby imagined traveling to distant cities where—

Wrong, Bret. Robby imagined escape.

"What does this have to do with me?" he asked.

"It has a hell of a lot to do with you when Ashton's sending you files to download and Cleary Miller is sending you a letter and—"

"Dad, that's not—"

"And I heard you in the mall on Saturday. When you were standing with your friends and someone brought up Maer Cohen's name. And then you all stopped talking, because you didn't want me to hear the conversation. What in the hell was that about, Robby?" I paused and kept trying to control the volume of my voice. "Do you want to talk about this? Do you want to tell me something?"

"I don't know what there is to talk about." His voice was calm and rational, but the lie was turning its black head toward me.

"Stop it, Robby."

"Why are you getting mad at me?"

"I'm not getting mad at you. I'm just worried. I'm very worried about you."

"Why are you worried?" he asked, his eyes pleading. "I'm fine, Dad."

There it was again. The word "Dad." It was a seduction. I momentarily left earth.

"I want you to stop that."

"Stop what?"

"I don't want you to feel that you have to lie to me anymore."

"What am I lying about?"

"Goddamnit, Robby," I shouted. "I saw what was on your computer. I saw that page with Maer Cohen. Why in the hell are you lying?"

He whirled toward me in horror. "You went into my computer?"

"Yeah, I did. I saw the files, Robby."

"Dad—"

He momentarily forgot his lines. He began improvising.

(*Or better yet*, the writer suggested, *he sent in the understudy.*)

Suddenly Robby started smiling. Robby slumped forward with exaggerated relief.

And then he started laughing to himself.

"Dad, I don't know what you thought you saw—"

"It was a letter—"

"Dad—"

"It was from Cleary Miller—"

"Dad, I don't even know Cleary Miller. Why would he send me a letter?"

I asked the writer: Are you writing his dialogue?

When the writer didn't answer, I started hoping that Robby was being genuine.

"What's happening with the missing boys? Do you know something we should all know? Do you or your friends know anything that would help people—"

"Dad, it's not what you think." He rolled his eyes. "Is this what you're all upset about?"

"What do you mean it's not what I think, Robby?"

Robby turned to me again and, with a grin tilting his lips, he said, "It's just a game, Dad. It's just a stupid game."

It took me a long time to judge if this was the truth or the black lie returning.

"What's a game?" I asked.

"The missing guys." He shook his head. He seemed both relieved and slightly embarrassed. Was this an intriguing combination—one I wasn't sure I trusted—or simply an attitude he rented?

"What do you mean—a game?"

"We kind of keep track of them." He paused. "We have these bets."

"What?" I asked. "You have bets on what?"

Now it was Robby's turn to breathe in. "On who's going to be found first."

I said nothing.

"Sometimes we send each other e-mails pretending to be the guys and it's really stupid, but we're just trying to freak each other out." He smiled to himself again. "That's what Ashton's mom saw . . ."

I kept staring at him.

Robby realized he had to climb onto my level.

"Dad, do you think those guys . . . are, like, dead?"

The writer emerged and pointed out that the question had no fear in it.

The question wanted a response from me that Robby could gauge. He was going to learn something about me from that response. He would then act on what he gleaned.

Things were slowing down.

"I don't know what to believe, Robby. I don't know if you're telling me the truth."

"Dad," he said softly in an attempt to calm me down, "I'll show you when I get home."

(*This*, the writer told me, *will never happen.*

Why not? I asked.

Because the computer died this afternoon.

How?

A virus was sent to infect the computer.

But what about the files?

Robby won't need the computer from now on.

What are you telling me?

You'll find out tonight.)

I grabbed Robby's hand and pulled him toward me.

It all came out in a rush. "Robby, I want you to tell me the truth. I'm here now. You can tell me whatever you want. I know that's something maybe you don't wanna do, but I'm here now and you have to believe me. I'll do whatever you want. What do you want me to do? I'll do it. Just don't pretend anymore. Just stop lying."

I was hoping this admission of vulnerability would make Robby feel stronger, but its nakedness actually made him so uncomfortable that he struggled away from me.

"Dad, stop it. I don't want you to do anything—"

"Robby, if you know anything about the boys please tell me." I grabbed his hand again.

"Dad . . ." He sighed. A new tactic was emerging.

I was so filled with hope I believed it. "Yeah?"

Robby's lower lip started trembling, and he bit it to make it stop.

"It's just that . . . I'm so scared sometimes and I just think maybe . . . we play this game to . . . make a joke out of what's happening . . . because if we really thought about it . . . we'd be too scared . . . I mean maybe one of us is next . . . Maybe it's just a way to deal with it . . ."

He glanced at me fearfully, again gauging my reaction.

I was studying the performance, and I couldn't tell if an actor was sitting in the passenger seat or if it was my son.

But there was no other way to respond to his admission: I had to believe him.

"Nothing's going to happen to you, Robby."

"How do you know?" he asked, his voice moving up an octave.

"I just do . . ."

"But how do you really know?"

"Because I'm not gonna let anything happen to you."

"But aren't you scared too?" His voice cracked.

I stared at him. "I am. Everybody is scared. But if we stick together—if we all try to be there for each other—we won't be scared anymore."

He didn't say anything.

"I don't want you to go anywhere, Robby."

He was breathing raggedly and staring at the dashboard.

"Don't you want us to be a family?" I asked in a whisper. "Don't you want that?"

"I want us to be a family but . . ."

"But what?"

"You never acted like you wanted it."

My chest started thudding with pain and it spread everywhere. "I'm sorry. I'm sorry for fucking everything up. I'm sorry for not being there for you and your mom and your sister, and I don't know how to make it up to you." My voice had tightened with so much sadness that I could barely speak. "I need to make the bigger effort but I need you to meet me a little bit of the way . . . I need you to trust me . . ."

"Everything changed when you came into the house." He was mumbling now. He was trying to keep his lips from quivering.

"I know, I know."

"I didn't like it."

"I know."

"And you scare me. You're so angry all the time. I hate it."

"That's all gonna change. I'm gonna change, okay?"

"How? Why? For what?"

"Because . . ." And then I realized why. "It won't work unless I do."

I caught the sob, but my eyes had already welled up and when Robby's face crumpled I leaned over and hugged him so fiercely I could feel his ribs through the layers of his school uniform, and when I was about to let go, he held on to me, sobbing. He was crying so hard that he was choking. We were heaving against each other, our eyes shut tightly.

Something was melting between us—the division was eroding. There was now, I believed, a tentative forgiveness on his part.

Robby kept choking out sobs until the crying subsided and then he pulled away, red-faced, exhausted. But the crying returned, forcing him to lean forward, his face in his hands, cursing his tears, as I reached over to hold him again. He removed his hands from his face once he stopped crying and looked at me with something approaching tenderness, and I believed he wasn't keeping a secret.

The world opened up to me in that moment.

I was no longer the wrong person.

Happiness was now a possibility because—finally—Robby had a father now and it was no longer his burden to make me one.

Of course, I was thinking, we had always loved each other.

Why did you feel this way on that Wednesday afternoon in November? the writer later asked me.

Because there was no betrayal in the smile that overtook my son's face.

But weren't your eyes blurred with tears? Were you really certain that this was an accurate assessment? Or was it something you just wanted so badly to believe?

Didn't you realize that even though you felt healed you were still blind?

It was true: the image of Robby's face became multiplied through my tears, and each face held a different expression.

But when we drove home without saying anything and it seemed like the first time we were ever comfortable with each other's silence, nothing else mattered.

22. interlude

one of us really knew each other because we were not a family yet. We were simply a group of survivors in a nameless world. But the past was being erased, and a new beginning was replacing it. There was another world waiting for us to inhabit. The tension had broken and the light in the house felt clean. There was a new language being taught to us. Robby took me upstairs to reveal the innocent files I had mistaken for something sinister and I refrained from telling him the computer had broken down; but when confronted with this, Robby took it in stride with a simple shrug, and when Marta brought Sarah back from ballet practice there was no complaint about the missing doll after Sarah had gone to her room and changed into pajamas. Neither Robby nor I mentioned the scene that had played out in the car at Buckley to anyone, but it seemed as if they knew because the people in the house were happier. (An example: Sarah had brought home drawings of starfish on a pearly white beach beneath a night sky filled with glowing asterisks.) Rosa made vegetarian lasagna and joined us at the table, and since I hadn't eaten all day I was ravenous. The conversation was soothing and Marta knew where to direct it, and just as plates were being cleared Jayne called from Toronto. She spoke to Sarah ("Mommy, Caitlin's daddy got divorced") and to Robby ("It's going okay") and to Marta, and once the kids had left the kitchen I took the phone and told her about the talk with my son (without explaining the reason I felt the talk was so necessary) and Jayne seemed heartened ("How did it feel?" "I feel my age." "That's good, Bret." "I miss you"). As Marta tucked Sarah into bed, Jayne's daughter waved at me from beneath her comforter and I waved back, cured of something (" 'Night" was her only word), and Marta was smiling curiously as I walked her outside and told her we would be "reunited tomorrow," bowing theatrically as I said it. (The only one at 307 Elsinore Lane on edge was Victor, who prowled the backyard, stopping every so often to bark at the woods beyond the fog-shrouded field because something had left tracks.) A new wind swept around the house, which felt so much emptier without Jayne in it, but she would be back, I thought to myself as I took a long bath. Everything previous to this was part of the dream, I sighed, contented, lying in the marble tub as it quickly filled with warm water. The dream was over for now. (*You're correct*, the writer agreed. *It is.*) Before I turned in I made sure the kids were safe—a new and involuntary urge. Sarah was already asleep, and I moved through her room and walked into the bathroom that connected her room to her brother's and told Robby he could stay up as late as he wanted, but only if he needed to get homework done. There was no rage, no misunderstandings, no double-speak—just a nod. Again Robby blurred because of my tears. His appreciative, clear-eyed glance was enough to cause them. I stepped out into the hallway and gently closed his door and I waited for the lock to click in place, but the sound never came. I found a bottle of red wine while rummaging through the kitchen and opened it, pouring myself a large glass. The wine would act as a gentle sleep aid. I would drink the wine while watching a rerun of *Friends* and fall asleep, and tomorrow everything would be different. At 11:15 the writer wanted me to turn the channel so we could watch the local news, because a horse had been found mutilated in a field near Pearce, which was where we had discarded the doll. And it all came back: on the screen was the divided sky and crows were descending from the telephone wires and dancing in patterns above a patrol car parked on the interstate where onlookers craned their necks and the camera zoomed in on the pile of remains, discreetly skimming the carnage, and a local farmer, his eyes watering, was answering a reporter's question with a sort of shrug and the horse was first thought to have "given birth" because it was so badly "ruptured" and then there was the uncertain talk of a sacrifice, and as I began responding to this a phone started ringing from my office.

23. the phone call

t was my cell phone ringing. It was lying on my desk, waiting for me to pick it up.

My mind was still picturing the field out by the interstate, and I answered the phone in a daze.

"Hello?"

I could hear someone breathing.

"Hello?"

"Bret?" I heard a voice say faintly.

"Yes. Who is this?"

Another pause.

"Hello?"

The sound of wind and static interspersed.

I pulled the phone away from my face and checked the incoming number.

The call was being made from Aimee Light's cell phone.

"Who is this?" I didn't even realize I had fallen into my chair. My heart was beating too fast. I thought clenching my fist would control it. "Aimee?"

"No."

Pause, static, wind.

I leaned forward and said a name.

"Clayton?"

The voice was ice. "That's one of my names."

I stood up. "What do you mean? Is this Clayton or not?"

"I'm everything. I'm everyone." A static-filled pause. "I'm even you."

This comment forced the fear to adopt a casual, friendly tone. I did not want to antagonize whoever this was. I would play dumb. I would pretend to be having a conversation with someone else. I had started shaking so hard that it was almost impossible to keep my voice steady. "Where are you?" I moved to the window. "I never got to see you again after you stopped by my office."

"Yes you did." The voice was now oddly intimate.

I paused. "No . . . I mean, where would that have been?"

"Did you get the manuscript?"

"Yes. Yes, I did. Where are you?" For some reason I reached for a pen, but it dropped from my trembling hand.

"Everywhere."

The way he said this was so ghastly that I had to compose myself before returning to my fake clueless demeanor. The voice had scales and was horned. The voice was something that had emerged from a bonfire. The fear it caused was unraveling me.

"Wait a minute," I said. "Yeah, I think I did see you again. Were you in our house on Sunday night?"

" 'Our' house?" The voice feigned bewilderment. "That's an interesting phrase. One highly open to interpretation."

I closed the blinds. I sat in the chair again and then stood up just as quickly. I suddenly couldn't help it. I decided to play along, my voice thick with urgency.

"Is this . . . Patrick?"

"We're a lot of people."

"So . . . what were you doing in our house the other night?" I asked casually. "What were you doing in my son's room?"

"That night it wasn't me, Bret. That night it was something else."

"What . . . was it then?"

"Something that is not an ally to our cause."

"Your cause? What cause? I don't understand."

"Did you read the manuscript, Bret?"

"Are any of you responsible for the boys?" I shut my eyes tightly.

"The boys?" I had interrupted his question with another question. The voice was on the verge of not behaving anymore.

"The missing boys. Are you—"

It was as if the voice hadn't anticipated this question. It was as if the voice assumed I knew where the particular truth of that situation led. "No, Bret. Again, you're looking in the wrong place on that one."

"Where should I be looking?"

"Open your eyes. Stop groping for things that aren't there."

"Where are the boys?" I asked. "Do you know?"

"Ask your son. He knows."

The fear curled into quick anger. "I don't believe that."

"This will be your downfall."

The writer had left. The writer was scared and had run away and was now hiding somewhere, screaming.

"What do you mean by that? My downfall? Are you threatening me?"

"I see that a Detective Donald Kimball visited you," the voice said airily. "Did he tell you about me?"

"What happened to Aimee Light?"

"Now we're getting somewhere."

"Where is she?"

"In a better world than this one."

"What did you do to her?"

"No, Bret. It's what *you* did to her."

"I didn't do anything to her."

"Well, a part of that is true: you didn't save her."

"What did you do to her?"

"I'd check the text of that dirty little book you wrote again."

"I'm not involved with anything that happened to Aimee Light. I'm going to hang up."

"Though of course I could make things happen." The voice lowered itself, yet became clearer. "I could get you involved."

Wounds kept opening.

"What do you mean? How could you do that?"

"Well, you were a mentor to her. She was the young and obliging student. Quite attractive, by the way." The voice paused, and considered something. "Maybe Aimee Light wanted more from the big famous teacher she was doing her dissertation on." The voice paused again. "Maybe you let her down in some way. Maybe there are even e-mails to back this up. Maybe Aimee Light left behind a trail that included a note or two. And let's just say these notes hinted at the possibility she was expecting you to fulfill a promise. Let's just say that maybe there was the possibility she was going to tell your very famous wife—"

"Who in the fuck is this?"

"—about the two of you." The voice sighed, then spoke quickly. "Though when I asked about your 'affair' it seemed like she was saying that nothing had happened between the two of you. Of course I had taped her mouth shut and by that point she was losing so much blood, but it was pretty clear that the two of you had never fucked. Maybe you were angry at Aimee Light for not putting out. That's another scenario we could pursue. The rejection was just too much for the writer who always got what he wanted and you snapped." The voice paused. "I see you haven't informed the authorities about your relationship with the deceased."

"Because I'm not connected to anything crimin—"

"Oh, but you are."

"How?" This was sending me out so much further than I had ever expected: a place beyond strength.

"You were seen outside her house by three witnesses the night her dismembered body was discovered in that very messy room at the Orsic Motel. Now, what were you doing there, Bret?"

"I have an alibi for—"

"Actually, you don't."

"There's no way—"

"You mean the night you wandered around 'your' house making some realizations about the past? Everyone was asleep. You were all alone. No one saw you after you got back from Buckley until the next morning when Marta saw you racing to your office because of those attachments. That gives you a lot of time, Bret. By the way, did you like the video? It took you an awfully long time to find it. I've been wanting to show it to you for years."

I leapt back to Aimee. "They don't even know that body is hers."

"I could send them the head. I still have it."

"This is a joke. You're not even real. You don't exist."

"If you think so, then why are you still on the line?"

I had nothing to say except "What do you want?"

"I want you to realize some things about yourself. I want you to reflect on your life. I want you to be aware of all the terrible things you have done. I want you to face the disaster that is Bret Easton Ellis."

"You're murdering people and you're telling me—"

"How can I murder people if I'm not real, Bret?" The voice was grinning. It was presenting a mystery. "Again, you are lost," the voice sighed. "Again, Bret doesn't get it."

"If you ever come near my family I'll kill you."

"I'm not particularly interested in your family. Besides, I don't think you've figured out a way to get rid of me, not yet."

"If you're not real, how am I going to accomplish that?"

"Did you read the manuscript?" the voice asked again.

I was on the verge of tears. I shoved a fist into my mouth and I was biting on it.

"Let's play a game, Bret."

"I'm not—"

"The game is called 'Guess Who's Next?' "

"You're not alive."

And then, suddenly and very sweetly, the voice began humming a song I recognized—"The Sunny Side of the Street"—before a roar overtook the humming and the line clicked dead.

When I laid the phone back on the desk I noticed a bottle of vodka that had not been there when I walked into the room.

The writer did not need to tell me to drink it.

24. the darkness

There is really no other way of describing the events that took place in 307 Elsinore Lane during the early morning of November 6 other than simply relating the facts. The writer wanted this job, but I dissuaded him. The following account doesn't require the embellishments the writer would have insisted on.

Sometime around 2:15 Robby had a nightmare from which he awoke.

At 2:25 Robby heard "the sounds" of something in the house.

Robby assumed it was me until he heard the scratching at his door, and then he assumed it was Victor. (Later Robby would admit he had "hoped" it was Victor because he somehow knew "it wasn't.")

Robby decided to move through the bathroom into his sister's room (according to his account, she was seemingly involved in her own nightmare) where he opened Sarah's door and looked out into the hallway so he could see what was causing the scratching noises and leaving the deep grooves in the lower right-hand corner of his door. (At one point, Robby said, he feared he was dreaming all this.)

Robby didn't see anything when he peered from his sister's door and down the hallway.

(Note: The sconces in the hallway were flickering, and according to Robby this was something he had noticed before, as I had, though neither Jayne nor Sarah—nor Rosa nor Marta, for that matter—had seen it.)

Robby did, however, hear something as he stepped from his sister's room and into the flickering hallway. There was a "rustling" sound farther down the corridor.

At this point, Robby realized something was coming up the stairs.

"It" was "breathing raggedly" and, according to Robby, "it" was also "mewling"—a word I had never heard before. (Dictionary definition: "to cry, as a baby, young child, or the like; whimper.")

The "thing" noticed Robby's presence and, because of this, suddenly stopped advancing up the staircase.

Robby turned away—panicking—and walked quietly in the opposite direction, toward the master bedroom at the end of the hall.

What happened when he opened the door and stepped into the room?

The room was dark. I was lying on my back in bed. I believed I was dreaming. I had passed out after drinking half the bottle of vodka that had appeared on my desk while I was talking to whom I thought was Clayton, the boy who wanted to be Patrick Bateman. When I slowly became aware that I was no longer sleeping, my eyes remained closed and I felt a pressure on my chest. I was still swirling up from a dream in which crows were turning into seagulls.

"Dad?" This was an echo.

I couldn't open my eyes. (If I had, I would have seen Robby silhouetted in the doorway, backlit by the flickering hallway behind him.) "What is it?" my voice rasped out.

"Dad, I think there's someone in the house."

Robby was trying not to whine, but even drunk I could detect the fear in his voice.

I cleared my throat, my eyes still closed. "What do you mean?"

"There's I think there's something coming up the stairs," he said. "There was something scratching at my door."

According to Robby, I actually said the following: "I'm sure it's nothing. Just go back to sleep."

Robby countered with "I can't, Dad. I'm scared."

My first reaction: *Well, so am I. Welcome to the club. Get used to it. It never leaves.*

I could hear Robby moving closer, stepping through the darkness of the master bedroom. I could hear him nearing me as he made his way toward my black and shapeless form.

The weight shifted on my chest again.

Robby was speaking into the darkness: "Dad, I think there's somebody in the house."

Robby was reaching for the bedside lamp.

Robby turned on the lamp.

Behind my closed eyelids an orange light burned.

Robby was silenced by something.

He was contemplating what he was looking at.

The image he was contemplating momentarily knocked the fear away and was replaced by an awful curiosity.

His silence was rousing me from my inebriation.

The weight shifted on my chest again.

"Dad," Robby said quietly.

"Robby," I sighed.

"Dad, there's something on you."

I opened my eyes but couldn't focus.

What I saw next happened very quickly.

The Terby was on my chest, looming above me, its face seizing, its open mouth a rictus that now took up half the doll's head, and the fangs I had only noticed earlier that day were stained brown

(*of course they were because it "mutilated" a horse in a field off the interstate near Pearce*).

Its talons were locked into the robe I'd passed out in and its wings were fanning themselves and it wasn't the length of the wingspan that shocked me at that moment (it had grown—I accepted that within a second) but it was the wings webbed with black veins bulging tightly beneath the doll's skin (*the doll's skin, yes, tell this to a sane person and see their reaction*) and pulsing with blood that amazed me.

According to Robby, when he turned on the lamp the thing was motionless. And then it quickly rotated its head toward him—the wings were already outstretched, the mouth was already opening itself—and, when he spoke, the doll returned its focus on me.

I shouted out and knocked the thing off my chest as I bolted up.

The Terby fell to the floor and quickly clawed itself under the bed.

I stood up, panting, frantically brushing something nonexistent from my torn robe.

Except for the sounds I was making it was silent in the house.

But then I heard it too. The mewling.

"Dad?" Robby asked.

My nonanswer was interrupted when we heard something rushing up the stairs.

From where Robby and I stood looking out from the doorway of the master bedroom a shadow—maybe three feet high—was coming toward us in the dim, flickering light; it was shambling sideways along the wall and as it got closer to us the mewling turned into hissing.

"Victor?" I asked, disbelieving. "It's Victor, Robby. It's only Victor."

"It's not Victor, Dad."

According to Robby, I said, "Then what the hell is it?"

The thing paused as if it was contemplating something.

It was 2:30 when the electricity went out.

The entire house was plunged into blackness.

I uselessly reached for a light switch. I was weaving on my feet.

"Mom keeps a flashlight in her drawer," Robby said quickly.

"Just stand still. Just stay where you are." I attempted a normal voice.

I jumped onto the bed and reached for Jayne's nightstand drawer. I opened it. My hand found the flashlight. I grabbed it. I immediately turned it on, aiming the beam at the floor, scanning for the Terby.

"Let's get out of here," I said.

Robby followed behind me as I aimed the flashlight at whatever was in the hallway. (But I had done this inadvertently—because in those brief moments spent looking for the flashlight in the blackened room I had forgotten that something was waiting for us there.)

This is when we briefly glimpsed it.

Robby was never sure what he actually saw in the glare of the flashlight. He was "hiding" behind me, his eyes squeezed shut, and the thing moved away from the beam of light as if offended by it—as if darkness was all it knew and what it thrived on.

The vodka was straining my senses. "Victor?" I whispered again, trying to convince myself. Robby was shivering against me. "Robby, it's okay. It's just the dog."

But when I said this we both heard Victor barking from outside.

According to Robby this was when he began crying—when he realized that the thing in the hallway was not his dog.

I persisted. "Victor, come here. Come on, Vic." This was the alcohol making concessions.

According to Robby this was when he heard me mutter: "No fucking way."

It was three feet high and covered in hair streaked black and blond, and it moved on feet that weren't visible. When the beam of light caught it, there was another hissing sound. It shambled quickly to the other side of the hallway. But with each movement it was advancing toward us.

The thing stiffened when the beam from the flashlight caught it again. I couldn't tell where the hissing came from. Once it stopped hissing its entire body began to shudder.

According to Robby I was saying, "Oh shit oh shit oh shit."

It turned toward me, this time defiantly. It was waist high and shapeless—a mound. It was covered with hair entangled with twigs and dead leaves and feathers. It had no features. A cloud of gnats were buzzing above the thing, following it to where it had pushed itself up against the wall. The beam was locked on it.

Within the hair, a bright red hole ringed with teeth appeared.

The mouth opening, the baring of its teeth, I realized—with a sickening clarity that immediately sobered me up—was a warning.

And then it rushed toward us, blindly.

I was frozen in place. Robby was holding on to me, his arms wrapped around my lower chest. He was shaking.

I kept the flashlight trained on the thing and as it approached us I smelled dampness, rot, the dead.

Its mouth was locked open as it shambled forward.

I slammed Robby and myself against the wall in order to avoid it.

It rushed past us.

(Because it was sightless and depended on scent—I already knew this.)

I whirled around. Robby was holding on, gripping me fiercely. I started backing away in the opposite direction of where the thing now stood.

It was shuddering again.

The worst thing I noticed was a large eye, haphazardly placed on top and rolling around in its flat, disc-shaped socket involuntarily.

Robby: "Dad what is it what is it what is it?"

The thing stopped in the doorway of the master bedroom—we had traded places—and it began making its mewling sounds again.

I tried hard to stop panicking but I was hyperventilating and my hand holding the flashlight was shaking so badly that I had to use the other hand to steady it and locate the thing in the beam of light.

I steadied my hand and found it.

It was standing still. But something inside it was causing the thing to pulsate. It opened its mouth, which was now coated with froth, and rushed toward us again.

When I turned around I dropped the flashlight, causing Robby to shout out in dismay.

I picked up the flashlight and trained the beam on the thing, which had stopped moving—seemingly confused.

Outside, Victor's barking became hysterical.

The thing resumed rushing us.

And that's when I dropped the flashlight again. The bulb cracked, drowning us in darkness as the thing continued rushing toward us.

I grabbed Robby's sweaty hand and ran to his room and opened the door.

I tripped as I fell into the room, hitting my face against the floor. I felt wetness on my lip.

Robby slammed the door shut and I heard the lock click.

I stood up, wavering in the darkness, and wiped the blood from my mouth. I shouted out when Robby steadied me with a frightened hug.

I listened closely. It was so dark in the room that we were forced to concentrate on the scratching sounds.

Suddenly the scratching subsided.

Robby's grip on me loosened. I exhaled.

But the relief couldn't be sustained because there was a cracking noise. It was pushing itself against the door.

I moved to the door. Robby was still holding on to me.

"Robby," I whispered. "Do you have a flashlight in here? Anything?"

I felt Robby immediately let go of me and heard him move in the direction of his closet.

In the darkness of the room a green light saber appeared. It floated toward me and I took the toy from him. The glow was faint. I aimed the light saber at the door, illuminating it.

"Dad," Robby whispered, his voice shaky. "What is it?"

"I don't know." (But even as I said this, I knew what it was.)

The scratching resumed.

I was asking myself: What is it scratching with?

And then I realized it wasn't scratching. (I remembered something.)

It had never been scratching.

It was gnawing at the door. It was using its mouth. It was using its teeth.

And then the gnawing stopped.

Robby and I stared at the door, which was now bathed in green.

And we watched in horror as the doorknob began to twist back and forth.

In a sickening flash I understood that it was using its mouth to accomplish this.

I had to remind myself to breathe again when the doorknob rattled violently.

There was a snarling sound. It was the noise of frustration. It was the noise of hunger.

And then it stopped. We could hear the thing dragging itself away.

"What is it? What does it want? I don't understand. How did it get in?" This was Robby.

"I don't know what the hell it is," I was saying absurdly.

"What is it, Dad?"

"I don't know I don't know I don't—"

(Note: This was not technically true.)

Our moaning was cut off by the sound of Sarah screaming. "Mommy! Mommy! It's getting me!"

I rushed through the bathroom and into Sarah's room. In the instant before I grabbed her off the bed I waved the light saber over the scene.

Sarah was backed up against the headboard as the thing attempted to pull itself onto her bed. It had fastened its mouth over one of the bedposts and it was moving frantically and squealing.

"What's happening?" Robby was screaming this from inside the bathroom.

I shouted out in disgust and grabbed Sarah off the bed. As I carried her toward the bathroom, the thing froze and then leapt onto the floor and I could hear it rushing toward us.

I slammed the bathroom door shut, and Robby locked it. I was still holding Sarah and the light saber. We were waiting while staring at the door.

Calmly, I asked: "Where's your cell phone, Robby?"

"It's in my room." He gestured over his shoulder.

I was contemplating something. I would unlock the door that led into Robby's room and find the phone and run back into the bathroom and call 911. This was the idea that formed inside my mind.

Victor continued his freakout in the backyard.

Then something slammed into the door to Sarah's room with such force that it bulged inward.

Robby and Sarah screamed.

"It's gonna be okay. Robby, unlock your door. We're gonna get out through your room."

"Daddy, I can't." He was weeping.

"It's gonna be okay."

The thing slammed into the door again.

The door cracked down the middle. When the thing hit it again, the door was falling off its hinges.

This moved Robby to immediately unlock his door and run out of the bathroom.

I followed, still holding Sarah and the light saber.

We ran through Robby's room and Robby unlocked the door and without hesitating we started moving down the staircase. The moon was streaming through the window and now we could see more clearly.

Halfway down the staircase I could see the thing rushing across the landing above us.

It began to chase us down the stairs. I could hear its mouth opening and closing, making wet snapping sounds.

Sarah turned her head and shrieked when she saw it lurching toward us.

My office seemed closest. The door was open. The front door was not.

My office had the gun in the safe.

In my office we closed and locked the door. I put Sarah down on the couch. Both of the kids were crying. I uselessly told them it would be "okay."

Holding the light saber toward the dial, I unlocked the safe and pulled out the gun.

I scanned my desk with the saber until I located my cell phone.

I asked Robby to hold the light saber while I dialed 911.

Robby was just staring at the gun I was holding. This caused him to close his eyes tightly and cover both ears with his hands.

The thing began slamming itself into the door.

"Jesus Christ," I shouted out.

The slamming was becoming more frequent. The door was bulging forward in its frame. I looked frantically around the room. I rushed to the window and opened it.

(Note: The paint was peeling off the house so rapidly that it looked as if snow flurries had drifted onto Elsinore Lane.)

But then the door cracked and fell to the side, hanging off the top hinge.

The thing stood in the doorway.

Even with the faint glow of the saber I was swinging at it, I could see the froth wreathing its mouth.

"Shoot it! Shoot it!" Robby was screaming.

I pointed the gun at the thing as it began shambling toward us.

I pulled the trigger.

Nothing.

The gun was not loaded.

(Note: Jayne had removed all the bullets from the gun after the night she thought I "imagined" an intruder had broken into the house.)

We could barely see the thing as it advanced toward us. It was making sucking sounds.

The electricity came on so quickly that we were blinded by the lights. The smoke alarm was beeping incessantly. Everything that had been turned off before bed was now on. Every light in the house was burning. The television was blasting. From the stereo blared a Muzak version of "The Way We Were." My computer flashed on.

The house was sunstruck with light.

The light kept us from witnessing the thing's disappearance.

"Daddy, you're bleeding." This from Sarah.

I touched my lips. My fingers came back red.

As I stood there I noticed the time on the battery-powered clock on my desk.

The electricity had come on at exactly 2:40 a.m.

25. the thing in the hall

our minutes after a 911 call was made, the flashing blue lights of a patrol car pulled up to 307 Elsinore Lane.

I had told the 911 operator that there had been a break-in but no one had been injured and the "perpetrator" had escaped.

I was asked if I would like to stay on the line until the officers arrived.

I declined because I had to think things through.

I had to make a few key decisions.

Would the threat I was about to relate entail something that had found its way into our house? Or would I try to push the lie (the more plausible scenario) that it was—what?—your basic home invasion? Would I refrain from using the word "creature" as I gestured toward the woods? Would I make an attempt to describe the thing in the hallway? Would I act "concerned" while downplaying the true extent of my fears since there was nothing anyone could do to help us?

The police would arrive.

Yes . . . and?

The police would inspect the house.

And they would find nothing.

All the police could do was escort us to our rooms, where we would collect our belongings, since there was no way we were spending another night in the house.

But how could I, much less the kids, explain to them what had happened to us?

We were dealing with something so far beyond their realm that it was senseless.

I realized dimly that no police report would be filed.

I had not figured out the Terby yet. All I knew was that somehow I had brought it into the house—and that it had wanted me to—but what had appeared in the flickering hallway was a secret I had to keep to myself. In this, the house and I were in collusion.

I called Marta. I chose my words carefully and explained that "something" had gotten into the house and assured her that everyone was fine and I had called the police and we were going to spend the night at the Four Seasons downtown and would she please make arrangements. I said all this in as calm a voice as I could create and I said it quickly—in a run-on sentence—mentioning the intruder in the lead so that the only thing that would register was the need to book a room in a hotel. But Marta was a professional and she was wide awake the moment her phone started ringing and she told me that she would be over to Elsinore Lane in fifteen minutes and before I could say anything she had clicked off.

Sarah was still in my arms and Robby was sitting on the lawn when the two officers—guys in their late twenties—walked up to us and introduced themselves as Officer O'Nan and Officer Boyle.

They noticed the blood on my lip and the bruise forming on the side of my face and asked if I required medical attention.

I told them I was fine and that it happened when I fell in my son's room, gesturing at Robby, who nodded faithlessly, confirming this.

They asked if "Ms. Dennis was at home," which I took in stride and explained that, no, my wife was on a film set in Toronto, and that it was just myself and the children in the house.

While another patrol car pulled up carrying two more officers, I explained to O'Nan and Boyle that an intruder had broken in, but because the electricity had "gone out" we were unable to "get a good look at it."

This is when everything changed.

The word "it" was what clinched the night.

The word "it" was what labeled me the "not credible witness."

O'Nan and Boyle conferred with the two other officers.

I cleared my throat and clarified that the intruder "might" have been a "wild animal."

There was a not very convincing discussion about whether to contact the local ASPCA, an idea that was soon left abandoned. If anything was found—meaning "it"—then they would reconsider.

Boyle stayed with me and Robby and Sarah as the three other officers entered the house, which was radiating a light so intense that it seemed as if it were day for night on our lawn, and the decibel level of noise ("The Way We Were" sung over and over)

(*but you don't even own that CD*)

had awakened the Allens.

I felt a pinprick of fear as the men entered the house. I didn't want them to enter the house. I didn't want anything to happen to them in that house. I wanted to cry out, "Be careful."

I sensed it then (though it didn't prove to be true): I was the only one in the family who would ever enter the house again.

And I also knew that our family—even outside the house—was not free from danger.

I suddenly looked behind me to see if the cat I had found yesterday was still decaying beneath the hedge.

When Officer Boyle saw Mitchell and Nadine Allen standing on their black granite driveway in matching robes, gesturing to him, Boyle asked us to "stay put."

The light from the house became muted. Someone found the sound system and the singing stopped abruptly.

The silence was momentarily startling.

I asked the writer: What is Officer Boyle telling the Allens?

(Yes, the writer was back. He did not want to be left out of this scene and was already whispering things to me.)

As Boyle walked toward the Allens, I didn't notice Robby taking the cell phone from my hand.

Officer Boyle is telling them that you are insane, and they are not disagreeing with him. Officer Boyle is telling them about your ridiculous wild animal scenario. Look at the Allens—they are not nodding at what Officer Boyle is telling them. He is telling them that a giant hairball forced its way into your house. And, of course, the Allens do not believe this, not after the freakout they witnessed Sunday night—remember that, Bret? And they are going to ask Officer Boyle, "Does he appear to be drunk?"

I looked away from Mitchell and Nadine and up to the second story of their house, where I could see Ashton silhouetted against the curtains of his room, and he was talking on a phone, and when my eyes moved back to our lawn I saw Robby holding my cell to his ear, his head turned slightly away from me, nodding.

That's so you can't hear what he's saying.

I looked back up to Ashton's window, but he had moved away from it.

How could Robby make a phone call when he had been weeping with fear only ten minutes ago? He had been urging me to kill the thing only ten minutes ago—how was he able to manage a phone call when I could barely move? What was he hiding from me? Why was the actor back? Hadn't we tearfully reconciled only hours ago?

I was staring at Robby when suddenly Officer Boyle appeared in my line of vision.

He was leaning into Robby and asking him something.

Robby immediately looked over at me and then nodded.

Robby stood up and clicked off the cell as Officer Boyle kept talking to him, their conversation dotted occasionally by Robby's nods and the glances he kept giving me.

Marta had arrived, and Sarah asked me to put her down.

I was unaware I had been holding her all this time until I handed her to Marta.

Marta was arguing that there was no need to file a police report since it would ultimately end up in the press. But her attitude was the same as mine: if everyone was okay, let's just get the kids to the hotel.

Two of the officers walked out of the house.

Predictably, they'd found nothing.

Yes, doors were scratched. Yes, force had been applied to each. Yes, two doors were unhinged. But no windows were broken or open and all the doors leading into the house were locked.

Whatever I had seen must have gotten into the house earlier that day.

This was the consensus view.

I asked Officer O'Nan, "Did you check under the bed in the master bedroom?"

O'Nan turned to an Officer Clarke and asked him if he had looked under the bed in the master bedroom.

Officer Clarke walked up to us and said, "Yes, we did, sir. There was nothing there."

"So the thing's still in the house? Is that what you're telling me?" I was not supposed to say this—I just couldn't help myself at that point. The question came out in a croak.

"Sir . . . I don't understand."

"Wasn't there a doll—a bird—under the bed in the master bedroom?" I had turned away from Marta and Sarah, and lowered my voice when I asked this.

"Why would this doll be under your bed, sir?"

"So it's still in the house?" I asked myself, murmuring.

"Sir, what is still in the house?" O'Nan asked me this with a clenched patience.

Clarke stared at me as if I was wasting his time. But what is he going to do? I thought angrily. What were any of them going to do? I was married to Jayne Dennis. I was a famous writer. They had to put up with this. They had to do whatever I felt was required of them. Marta was identifying herself. They regarded her seriously.

And then a scene began arranging itself on the front lawn.

"If there are no broken windows and all the doors are locked, then that thing is still inside." I was answering my own questions.

"Mr. Ellis, we found nothing in the house."

Another officer appeared and asked, with barely disguised skepticism, "Mr. Ellis, could you give us a description of this intruder?"

I shuddered. Later, the writer reminded me of what I said. He had the transcripts.

"We were sleeping and . . . a noise woke my son up . . . it was . . . I don't know what it was . . . it was maybe a couple of feet tall and . . . it had a blond coat of hair and . . . it was growling at us—actually, no, it was making hissing noises . . . and it chased us . . . it chased us through the house . . . it broke the doors . . . it wanted something . . ."

Someone commented on the fact that I was out of breath.

It was at this point that one of the officers walked out of the house with Victor.

The officer was holding the dog by its collar as he led the animal to the group assembled on the lawn.

Victor was panting and had a glassy expression.

There was a knowing and conspiratorial silence.

I recognized it and something flared up within me.

I wheeled around.

Flashlights scanned the tired dog, who kept squinting up at us.

Victor sat down on the lawn. He noted our stares and was oblivious to them.

And then it seemed as if I was the only human he was directing his attention at.

I projected shame emanating from him.

I could hear the dog saying: "You are fucked up. You are fucking absurd."

I realized that everyone was looking at me, expecting something.

The presence of the dog seemed to be a question answered, and this was followed by—I could feel it—collective relief.

"Look, this thing was not a golden retriever, okay? The golden retriever was outside barking its ass off. The golden retriever wasn't even in the house. And that dog is not capable of knocking those doors off their hinges."

Silence again.

And then Officer Clarke said, "Mr. Ellis, the dog was in the house—we found him in the kitchen."

The officers were asking the children what they had seen.

When Sarah shyly turned away from them, I said, "Honey, you don't have to say anything."

Sarah told them she had seen "a lion."

Robby shrugged, uncertain. When asked by Officer Boyle if it could have been the dog, Robby kept shrugging. Robby did not look at me when he made this gesture. Robby did not look at me when he confirmed that what had invaded the house was not human but an animal and that it could have been the dog. But, Robby stressed, it was dark and he had kept his eyes shut during most of "what happened."

I realized I was the only witness at this point.

Officer Boyle asked me, "Have you had anything to drink tonight, sir?"

Push the trapdoor open. The gulls are squalling. The wind gusts toward you. Your father is standing on the walkway of an interstate overpass.

"Pardon me?"

You heard him, the writer hissed.

Boyle moved closer and, lowering his voice, asked, "Have you been drinking tonight, sir?"

"I don't have to answer that question. I'm not operating a motor vehicle."

(I realized I had never used the term "motor vehicle" in any sentence I had spoken or written during my entire life.)

Marta was still holding Sarah as she listened carefully to this exchange.

I was also highly aware of Robby's presence at this point.

Look at how dignified and sexy you are, the writer said. *Quite the dad you turned out to be. Drunk and spazzing out over some kind of monster in the hall. What a guy.*

The officers were becoming less concerned and more remote.

"Listen to me, whatever this was came in from the woods," I pressed. "And it was not our dog." Helplessly, I turned to my son. "Robby, tell them what you saw."

"Dad, I don't know what I saw," he said, anguished. "I don't know what I saw. Stop asking me that."

"There was a half-empty bottle of vodka on your nightstand, Mr. Ellis."

I didn't know who said this.

"And you think this is evidence of—what?" I managed.

"Mr. Ellis, are you on any medication?"

"Yes. I am. Actually, I am." This was answered in the defensive manner of the guilty addict.

"What is it that you're taking?"

"It's really none of your business, Officer, but I'm taking very low dosages of Klonopin for an anxiety disorder."

(The irony: I had never felt more sober in my entire life than at that moment.)

The four officers looked sharply at one another.

"And you were drinking while taking this medication?" one of them asked.

"Look, I can see where you're going with this."

Officer Boyle was looking at me with a very basic and casual disapproval.

"Mr. Ellis, I think maybe you should call the doctor who is prescribing this—"

"Funny. That's really funny. In front of my kids. Great, guys. Really nice."

"Why should Daddy call a doctor?" Sarah was asking Marta.

"Mr. Ellis, all I'm suggesting is that if this thing comes back, you should call your doctor—"

"I did not hallucinate anything tonight. Something—and it was not our dog—in fact it was something very *un*doglike—was in this house."

"Mr. Ellis, calm down—"

"Listen, um, thank you, Officer O'Nan and Officer Boyle and Officer Clarke and"—I gestured at the fourth—"whoever you are and you've all been a fabulous help and I'm—"

"Mr. Ellis—"

"Look, something invaded my home tonight and attacked me and my kids and scared the living shit out of us and you think I hallucinated this thing? You've been a big help. You can all go now."

(This was all for show, I realized. This was me playing the concerned parent. This was acting for the kids and for Marta, who would relay my performance as the concerned parent to Jayne. The cops were not to blame. Considering what was actually happening there was nothing they could do.

I should have never called 911. It had been a tactical error. I should have bundled the kids up and just driven to a hotel myself.)

But you needed an alibi to get out of the house, the writer was reminding me. *How else were you going to explain your "escape" from 307 Elsinore Lane? The thing in the hall gave you a very convenient reason.*

"We think it was probably your dog, Mr. Ellis."

"We're checking into a hotel," I said curtly. I turned to Marta. "Right?"

She nodded her head, staring at me wide-eyed.

So this was their theory: Drunk out of my mind on a combination of vodka and Klonopin, I had woken up my children because I believed we were being attacked by our pet. That was so lame-ass I could not even dignify it with a response.

But even the writer thought this was plausible.

The writer told me that the policemen thought I was taking advantage of them.

The writer told me that one of the officers had laughed when they came upon the green light saber on the floor of my office.

The writer told me that two of the officers had masturbated to sex scenes in *American Psycho*.

Boyle stayed with Robby and Sarah as O'Nan escorted Marta and me into the house. Marta would go to the kids' rooms to gather their things (uniforms, backpacks, schoolbooks) while I grabbed whatever I needed.

But first I followed Marta into Sarah's room and stood by the bathroom door.

Marta glanced at the door and paused.

O'Nan noted the pause and made a gesture—just a shrug, just a sympathetic glance—that indicated we would wait and see.

I wanted to shout, "Wait and see for what?"

The door had burst off its hinges, and slime glistened horridly from its doorknob.

The worst thing: the door had been gouged because the thing had splintered it with its mouth.

There were clumps of fur dotting the hallway—hair the thing had shed.

From the window in the master bedroom I watched as two of the officers scanned the field behind the house, looking for nonexistent clues. They were not going to find any trails. Nothing led up to any of the "unbroken windows" and "locked doors" of the house. They were gossiping about Jayne Dennis and her crazy husband. O'Nan made a sound that suggested I start packing my things. I blindly filled a large duffel bag with a suit, my wallet, my laptop. I packed toiletries and medication. I glimpsed myself in the mirror as I changed into a pair of sweats, a T-shirt and a leather jacket. The side of my face was a crescent of burgeoning purple. My lower lip was split in the middle by a thin black line. My eyes were fluttering.

After leaving the bathroom, I looked one last time at the bed the Terby had crawled under.

The writer was with me in the room.

Tell them you have information about the horse mutilation in Pearce.

Tell them about Patrick Bateman calling you earlier tonight, the writer suggested.

Tell them about the girl in Room 101 of the Orsic Motel.

Go ahead. Make the leap. Maybe you'll save yourself.

I piled the kids into the Range Rover, along with Victor, who would be staying in a kennel located in the basement of the Four Seasons. Marta left her car in the driveway and drove. This decision was made after the officers threatened to give me a Breathalyzer test. They also insisted on escorting us to the hotel, where the night manager would be waiting for us.

The Range Rover and the two patrol cars pulled away from the darkened house.

Look, it's still peeling. Did you look in the living room again? I think you'd—

As we drove through the barren town I leaned my head against the passenger window. The coolness of the glass felt soothing against the bruised cheek.

So, the writer said. *The thing in the hall.*

What about it?

It's memory lane time, isn't it, Bret?

I know what I saw.

What did you see? Or, more precisely, when did you first see it?

I actually saw it on Halloween night. It had been in the woods. I saw it scrambling in and out of the woods. Like a spider.

How old were you when you wrote the story?

I was twelve. Just about Robby's age. It was written in the hand of a child.

What was the story called?

It didn't have a title.

Actually, that's not true.

You're right. It was called "The Tomb."

What was the story about, Bret?

It was about a thing. This monster. It lived in the woods. It was afraid of light.

Why did you write this story?

Because I was so scared all the time.

What were you so scared of?

My father.

What did the monster in the story look like, Bret?

It looked like what was in our house tonight. It was identical to what I had imagined at twelve. I had written the story and illustrated it. And the thing in the hallway was what I had drawn.

Had you ever seen it before?

No.

What did this monster you created do?

It broke into the homes of families. In the middle of the night.

Why did it do this?

I don't want to answer that.

But I want an answer.

Why don't you tell me?

It broke into the homes of families because it wanted to eat the children.

The empty streets were sliding by, and no one in the car said a word. Robby was regarding the moon and it was whispering to him while Sarah hummed softly to herself, almost as if in consolation. At the corner of Fort and Sycamore I noticed that a massive eucalyptus tree had burst up out of the sidewalk.

I asked the writer: Why is it appearing—manifesting itself—on Elsinore Lane?

I'll answer that question with another question: Why is Patrick Bateman roaming Midland County?

What else is out there? How can a fictional thing become real?

Were you remorseful when you created the monster in the hall?

No. I was frightened. I was trying to find my way in the world.

A brief period of consciousness: checking into the hotel in the grand, deserted lobby.

The respite: the dullness of the exchange—all monotone and trance—between Marta and the night manager. My voice was too hoarse for me to talk to anyone.

A bellboy showed us to a two-bedroom suite. The kids would occupy one room with two queen-sized beds. A spacious, ornately decorated sitting room separated them from where I would be sleeping.

As Marta helped the kids to bed I remembered discussing "The Tomb" once with a psychologist my parents had sent me to when I was a teenager (I had parodied him in *Less Than Zero*), and he had been amused by the Freudian elements—the sexual imagery—present in the story that I couldn't have grasped at twelve. What was the mound of hair? Why did the orifice have teeth? Why was a light saber nearing the mound of hair? Why was the little boy screaming *Shoot it!*?

But something knocked me out of my memories of a story I had nearly forgotten and that played itself out in the early morning of November sixth.

And this was: the kids seemed okay.

I stood in the doorway and watched as they settled into their respective beds, Marta tucking them in.

I had imagined that the fear they had experienced during those roughly ten minutes of horror would be permanently sewn into their future. But this did not seem to be the case. It appeared that life was going to move on in its usual fashion. The bounce-back time amazed me. Their recovery would be complete by the time they woke up the next morning. What had been a frightening experience was now going to become a game, an emblem of pride, a story that would impress and enthrall friends. The nightmare was now an adventure. They were shook up but they were also tough and resilient. (This was the only relief I felt about anything that night.) Sarah and Robby had been bored and tired in the ride over to the hotel, and they kept yawning in the elevator, and soon they would be sleeping and then they would wake up and they would order room service for breakfast before being driven to school by Marta (though it would be up to the kids if they wanted to go) and Robby might even take a math test in the afternoon and then they would return to the Four Seasons and they would do their home-work in front of the television and we would keep waiting for Mommy to come home.

The kids fell asleep almost immediately.

Marta said she would give me a call around eight, just to check in.

It was now 3:40. From the moment the lights blinded us until now, every-thing had happened within the space of an hour.

I walked Marta to the foyer of the suite and feebly whispered, "Thank you" as I let her out.

Leaning against the door I had just closed, I was hit by the thought: Writing will cost you a son and a wife, and this is why *Lunar Park* will be your last novel.

I immediately opened the minibar and drank a bottle of red wine.

During the next four hours something happened that I don't remember. The writer filled in the blanks.

I plugged in my laptop and logged on to the Internet.

This is where I typed in the following words: "ghost," "haunting," "exorcist."

Surprise and dread: there were thousands of Web sites related to these matters.

Apparently I specified by typing in "Midland County."

This narrowed the list considerably.

Supposedly I checked out a few Web sites, but I don't remember doing so.

Supposedly I "decided" on Robert Miller's Northeastern Paranormal Society.

I sent a drunken e-mail. I left my cell number as well as the number at the Four Seasons.

According to the writer: Jayne called from Toronto at 5:45 after speaking to Marta, who told her what happened at the house. I have no recollection of this.

Also according to the writer: Jayne was sipping coffee while having her makeup done.

My wife thought I was overreacting and she appreciated it.

Your wife is a fool, the writer murmured.

You said, trying to control your slurring, "We'll be here until you get back—I just want to make sure the kids are safe."

You did not have an answer for Jayne when she asked you, "Safe from what?"

Hadn't you once wanted to "see the worst"? the writer asked me. *Didn't you once write that somewhere?*

I might have. But I don't want to anymore.

It's too late, the writer said.

26. the meeting

R obert Miller called the cell phone I held in my hand as I slept. The ringing was so muffled that it was the vibration that woke me. I automatically flipped the phone open and said "Yes" without checking to see who it was. The conversation was brief. I was barely paying attention because I was lying in a bed in a strange hotel room and it was nine o'clock in the morning and from where I was squinting through my open door I could see Marta dressing Sarah for school while Robby sat in front of a TV with his uniform already on, both of them seemingly unfazed—an image that had the gauzy quality of a clichéd dream. Someone was telling me over the phone that he had received an e-mail and had typed in my name on Google (the writer reminded me that this suggestion was his idea, and I had sent it along in order to legitimize myself) and that he believed I was, in fact, the man I claimed to be. He told me my "case" was intriguing to him. The voice suggested we meet at the Dorseah Diner in Pearce. The voice gave me an address that I scribbled down. And then last night came back. This happened when Robert Miller asked me to bring a diagram of 307 Elsinore Lane so I could point out where the "major haunting sites" were located within the house. We agreed to meet at ten o'clock.

I had grabbed about three hours of dreamless sleep, and as I hobbled into the sitting room wearing only boxer shorts and a white T-shirt stained with droplets of red wine I tried smiling for the kids but the smile and the concerned, subsequent "Hey, how's everything this morning?" were nonsense: Robby seemed relaxed and Sarah was blank-faced—until they both saw my bruise. Marta noticed the questions the bruise was raising—the memories of last night began trembling around the children—and immediately Marta made small talk about how she had called a cab from the lobby of the hotel last night that took her back to Elsinore Lane so she could pick up her car (and I panicked and had to restrain myself from asking if she went into the house and what color was it now?) so I could use the Range Rover today, and I thanked her. (She had also contacted Rosa to explain that her services would not be needed until Ms. Dennis got back from Toronto.) I asked the kids how they were again. Robby shrugged and tried to smile sincerely as he pulled his eyes away from my face. "Okay, I guess." Sarah was, luckily, lost in her meds and had trouble pulling on a sweater. Marta would take the kids to school—regardless of last night, they needed the return of routine—and bring them back to the hotel late that afternoon. Marta said this firmly, as if she expected disagreement, but since Jayne had made this demand there was nothing I could do to alter it. Both Sarah and Robby wanted to visit Victor in the kennel before heading to Buckley, and Marta assured them they could. I wanted Marta to deal with the kids since I was clearly in no shape to do so. My assumption was that the longer they stayed away from me, the better off they were. After everyone left I got up the nerve to look at my face in a mirror. I gasped.

The Dorseah Diner in Pearce sat off a bleak section of the interstate where the surrounding land was dead and flat—except for the huge eucalyptus trees that had burst up from the ground—trees that I was positive hadn't existed the day before. (I estimated the diner was about five miles from the field where the doll had been discarded and killed the horse.) The diner was small and had a gravel parking lot consisting of maybe twelve spaces that were empty at ten o'clock on the sixth of November. Only six booths lined the plate-glass windows, with twelve blue and white stools rimming the counter, where the only customer sat: an old man in a raincoat, reading the local paper. I fell into a booth that seemed the farthest away from everything and ordered a cup of coffee, ignoring the frayed menu the waitress placed in front of me. I was wearing sunglasses and a baseball cap I had picked up at the gift shop in the hotel lobby, and sweatpants and the stained T-shirt under a Kenneth Cole leather jacket. The side of my face ached from the bruise, and I had to be careful about my lip since it felt like it was on the verge of splitting. I was hungover, and my body was sore and battered, and I kept chewing Klonopin in the hope it would take effect. I glanced back at the field because it was watching me, and in the distance I noticed haystacks and beyond the haystacks a line of palm trees swayed.

A beige van swung into the deserted lot and parked next to the Range

Rover. Robert Miller appeared, belly first, dressed in faded jeans and a matching jacket and a turquoise shirt: a large man in his midfifties with a mustache and long graying hair tied back in a ponytail. Tired and drawn, he glanced at his watch, which moved me instinctively to clutch my wrist (it was numb). He walked into the diner holding a notepad, and at first I had no idea who this was. The man seemed to recognize me, though, as he hitched his pants up and hauled his way over to the booth I sat shivering in. When I looked up I saw a grizzled, wounded face that had experienced a lot.

"Are you Mr. Ellis?"

"Yes."

"I'm Robert Miller."

I just stared at him.

He wasn't sure that his introduction had received the desired response.

"You contacted me early this morning? We spoke on the phone?"

"Yes, of course." I stood shakily and offered my hand.

He took it in a businesslike fashion—he had a hard, callused grip, unlike the damp, soft, smooth hand of a writer—and after letting go of it he slid into the booth across from me. He calmly motioned to the lone waitress and ordered a cup of coffee and a glass of water and then he placed the notepad on the table. There was information about me on the notepad: the date of my birth, the titles of my books, the address of the house on Elsinore Lane.

I took a moment to arrange my thoughts. I had somewhat prepared myself in the fifteen minutes it took to drive to Pearce, and I thought the writer and I had constructed a fairly coherent story that would move Miller to help me. But now that I was actually here in front of him, I was embarrassed and I started stammering as soon as I opened my mouth. I began explaining what was happening in the house in a calm and linear fashion, but soon I was grabbing at everything I had witnessed and then the entire week rushed back to me all at once and I just kept haphazardly piling on the details—the Terby, the gravestone, the black hole in the field, the flickering lights, the intruder, the furniture that rearranged itself, the footprints stamped in ash, the dead animals, the video attachment, the wind, my father, how the house on Elsinore Lane was shifting into the house on Valley Vista—and, with my face straining, offered a muddled story that only I could make sense of. But Miller seemed to be taking me seriously. He kept jotting notes when a particular detail alerted him to, and he didn't appear to be bothered by even the most outlandish claim. His expression wasn't readable—he could have been drugged. He was taking the jagged, nonsensical plotline in stride. Where was the amazement? Where was the surprise? But then it hit me that, considering what Miller was here for, this was a common morning for him. I understood that his stance was routine, as was the gibbering of the frightened client. It did not relieve me to recount these events to someone.

I did not mention the missing boys or Aimee Light and the Orsic Motel, but I did tell him about the phone call from Patrick Bateman. At that point Miller interrupted me, looking up from the notepad.

"Who's that?" Miller asked.

"Patrick Bateman? He's a, um, fictional character . . . of mine."

"Oh yes, that's right. Yes, I remember."

"I mean, he doesn't actually exist. I made him up. I think someone is just, y'know, just impersonating him."

"You think someone is impersonating him?" he asked.

"Yeah." I tried to keep my voice steady. "Yeah, I mean, y'know, what other explanation is there? I don't know what other explanation there is."

Miller offered a thoughtful nod but then asked me, "Do you think someone was impersonating that thing you saw in the hallway last night?"

I started walking off the path.

"Um . . . no . . . no . . . that was something I had created . . . also."

I realized that lurking somewhere in Miller's question there was a theory being built and in an oddly soothing way I also realized that I was finally sitting with someone who was a believer.

Miller kept studying me. I had not taken off my sunglasses.

"I'm not sure . . ." I started haltingly. "I'm . . . how the house and these physical manifestations of these . . . um . . . fictional creations . . . are tied together but . . . I think that maybe they are . . ." I said this with a whispered desperation that physically pained me. Saying this out loud into the empty air of the diner, I grasped at whatever dignity remained. I sat up.

The silence lengthened while Miller took me in. He had removed his mirrored sunglasses—his eyes were a plain and milky blue—in a gesture that implied I ought to do the same, but I couldn't; my eyes had sunk too deeply into their sockets.

"It's hard for me . . . to admit all of this and . . . it's hard for me to believe that any of this is happening, I guess, and it just escalated into this . . . event last night and . . . I'm here—I mean, we're here—because . . . because I want these events to stop."

"Otherwise known as the unexplained events."

"Yeah," I murmured, staring out at the flat and desolate land beyond the highway. "The unexplained events," I murmured.

Sensing I was finished with my story, Miller shifted his girth around in the booth and said flatly, "Technically, Mr. Ellis, I'm a demonologist."

I was nodding even though I didn't want to. "Which is?"

"Someone who is an expert on the study and handling of demons."

I stared at Miller for a long time before I asked, "Demons?"

This is not a good sign, the writer warned me.

Miller sighed. He had noted the disbelief in my grimace. "I also communicate with what you would call ghosts—if that works better for you, Mr. Ellis. In laymen's terms, you could call me a ghost hunter as well as a psychic researcher."

"So you basically study . . . anything that's supernatural?" The words came out just as I had expected they would because the writer was telling me, *You are in so over your head.*

He nodded. I looked at him hard while trying to recall phrases I had drunkenly encountered on the Web sites last night.

"Can you . . . clean an infested house?" I finally removed my sunglasses.

Miller flinched and drew in a wince when he saw the side of my face and the extent of its bruising fully revealed. This jangled something in him. This was another blow that would convince.

"You don't think I'm crazy, do you?" I asked quickly.

"I'm making that decision as we speak," he said, recovering. "That's what this initial meeting is all about: trying to figure out if I believe you."

I had closed my eyes and was talking over him. "I mean, I'm not an unstable individual. I mean, maybe I am but I'm not, like, um, trouble or anything."

"I'm not so sure about that yet." Miller sighed, sitting back in the booth and crossing his arms. "Is there anything else you want to tell me?"

"I don't know any more." I helplessly raised my hands.

"Have you ever had a psychotic episode, Mr. Ellis?" Miller asked. "Have you ever been in any kind of delusional state?"

"I . . . I think I'm in one right now."

"No. This is just fear," Miller said. He marked something down on the notepad.

Pretend this is an interview, the writer whispered. *You've done thousands. Just pretend this is another interview. Smile at the journalist. Tell him how nice his shirt is.*

I suddenly guessed at what Miller was getting at.

"I had a drinking problem and . . . a problem with drugs and . . . but I don't think that's related . . . and . . ."

In that second everything fell apart.

"You know what? Maybe I've made a mistake. Maybe it was just some kids who were pulling a prank and I don't know anymore and I'm a famous man and I've had stalkers and maybe someone is actually impersonating this fictional character of mine and maybe all of this—"

Miller interrupted what was becoming a rant by asking, "Are you the only target of these unexplained events?"

"I . . . guess I am . . . I guess I was . . . until last night happened."

"Is there anything you've done to anger these spirits?" He asked this as if he casually wanted the opinion of a book I had recently read, but it implied something sinister to me.

"What are you saying? Do you think this is my fault or something?"

"Mr. Ellis, there's no fault here," Miller said with wary patience. "I'm just asking if you have perhaps antagonized—inadvertently in some way—the house itself." He paused so this could sink in. "Do you think that your presence in this house—which according to you was not infested when you first arrived—has somehow caused the spirits to become angry—"

"Hey, listen, this thing last night, whatever the fuck it was, went after my kids, okay?"

"Mr. Ellis, I'm just saying you cannot antagonize the spirit world and expect them not to react."

"I'm not antagonizing anyone—*they're* antagonizing *us*." This admission prodded a newfound nerve. "And the house wasn't built on an ancient Indian burial ground either, okay? Jesus Christ." This flash of anger—a release—calmed me down momentarily.

Miller noticed my hand trembling as I lifted the coffee cup to my mouth and then, remembering my lip, I placed it back on its saucer. I was about to start weeping at the pointlessness of this meeting.

"You seem very defensive. You seem angry." Miller said this without any emotion. "I feel your fear, but I also sense anger and an antagonizing personality."

"Jesus, you sound like my fucking shrink."

"Mr. Ellis"—and now Miller leaned in and shattered everything by saying, "I have seen a person turn to ash because of their antagonism."

My heart stopped, and then resumed beating faster than it had previously when Miller said this. I started crying softly. I put my sunglasses back on. I kept trying to stay calm, but if I believed what he just said I would get sick. The crying was magnified by the silence in the diner. Shame suddenly caused the crying to stop.

"Ash? You've seen this?" I grabbed a napkin from a dispenser and blew my nose. "What are you talking about?"

"One was a farmer. One was a lawyer." Miller paused. "Did you read the journal on the site where I recounted these two incidents?"

"No." I swallowed. "I'm sorry. I didn't."

I had to get out of the diner. I had to force myself to stand up and steadily make my way toward the Range Rover. I would drive back to the Four Seasons. I would climb under the covers of the bed. I would wait for whatever it was that wanted me and let it take hold. I would become unafraid of madness and death.

I could not understand why the Klonopin was not working this morning.

Every few seconds a semi would rumble past; the only hint that there was a reality outside of where I was sitting.

"These people just burst into flames." Miller was not lowering his voice, and I glanced worriedly at the lone waitress sharing a conversation with the cook. Sometime during this conversation, the old man had disappeared from the counter and I thought that maybe he was a ghost too.

"How long have you been doing this?" I was asking him. "I mean, I don't understand what you're telling me. I mean, you say something like that and I think I'm cracking up and—"

"This information is all available on my Web site, Mr. Ellis—"

But I was lost in the anxiety of the moment. "I mean do you have a résumé or, like, recommendations because when you tell me that you've seen people burst into flame I feel like I'm going crazy—"

"Mr. Ellis, I was not handed a diploma. I did not go to 'ghost college.' I have only my experience. I have investigated over six thousand supernatural phenomena."

I lost it again. I was crying and trying not to breathe too loudly. "What am I going to do?" I kept asking.

Miller began to console me. "If you want to hire me my job is to come to your home and invoke the physical manifestations of whatever is haunting your residence."

"How . . . bad does that get? I mean, do I have to be there?" I forced myself to stop crying and was surprised that I had the power to accomplish this and I wiped my eyes and blew my nose with another napkin. I realized there were nearly a dozen of them crumpled and strewn in front of me.

"How bad does it get?" Miller actually said the following: "I once dealt with an accountant who said he was possessed. On the afternoon of the exorcism in his condominium, he began speaking backwards in Latin and then bled from his eyes and his head started to split open."

The only way my shock dealt with this was to mumble, "Hey, I've been audited. I've been through worse."

Such a tough guy, the writer muttered. *So cool.*

Miller didn't understand that this was the normal response.

There was a stony silence during which Miller glared at me.

"I'm just kidding," I whispered. "It was just a little joke. I was —"

"That incident, Mr. Ellis, gave me a heart attack. I was hospitalized. It was not a joke. I have this incident on tape."

My exhaustion suddenly was forcing me to concentrate intently on Miller, and I was curious enough to ask, "What . . . do you do with that tape?"

"I show it at lectures."

I was reflecting on the information. "What . . . was this person possessed by?"

"It was the spirit of what he told me was an animal that had scratched him."

I wanted Miller to repeat this.

"He had been attacked by this animal, and after the attack he believed he was now the thing that had attacked him."

"How does that happen?" I was almost wailing. "How does that happen? What are you talking about? Jesus Christ —"

"Mr. Ellis, you would not be making fun of me if someone possessed by a demonic spirit had thrown you twenty-five feet across a room and then tried to slash you into a bloody pulp."

Again it took me a long time to start breathing regularly.

I was reduced to: "You're right. I'm sorry. I'm just very tired. I don't know. I'm not making fun of you."

Miller kept staring at me, as if deciding something. He asked if I had the diagram of the house. I had quickly drafted a crude one on Four Seasons stationery, and when I pulled it out of my jacket pocket my hand was shaking so badly that I dropped it on the table as I was handing it to him. I apologized. He glanced at the sketch and placed it next to his notepad.

"I need to ask you some things," he said quietly.

I clasped my hands together to make them stop shaking.

"When do these manifestations take place, Mr. Ellis?"

"At night," I whispered. "They take place in the middle of the night. It's always around the time of my father's death."

"When is that? Specifically."

"I don't know. Between two and three in the morning. My father died at two-forty a.m. and this seems to be the time when . . . things happen."

A long pause that I couldn't stand and had to question. "What does that mean?"

"And do you know the time of your birth?"

Miller was scrawling notes along the pad. He didn't look at me when he asked this.

"Yes." I swallowed hard. "It was at two-forty in the afternoon."

Miller was studying something he had written down.

"What does any of that mean?" I asked. "Beyond a coincidence?"

"It means this is something to take seriously."

"Why is that?" I asked in the voice of a believer, in the voice of a student seeking answers from the teacher.

"Because spirits who show themselves between night and dawn want something."

"I don't know what that means. I don't get it."

"It means they want to frighten you," he said. "It means they want you to realize something."

I wanted to cry again but I was able to control it.

None of this is very comforting, is it? I heard the writer ask me.

"You mentioned in one of the interviews I glanced at that you based this fictional character, this Patrick Bateman, on your father—"

"Yes, I had, yes—"

"—and you say this Patrick Bateman has been contacting you?"

"Yes, yes, this is true."

"Were you and your father close?"

"No. No. We weren't."

Miller was studying something on the notepad. It was bothering him.

"And there are children in the house? Whose are they?"

"Yes, I have two," I said. "Well, actually, only one of them is mine."

Miller looked up suddenly. He didn't respond but was staring at me, clearly troubled.

"What?" I asked. "What is it?"

"That's strange," Miller said. "I don't feel from you that you do."

"You don't feel what?"

"That you have a child."

My chest ached. I flashed on Robby holding me in the car after school, and how tightly he gripped me last night because he thought I would protect him. Because he thought that I was now his father. I didn't know what to say.

Miller moved on. "Is there a fireplace in the house?" he asked suddenly.

Shamefully, I had to think about this. I had been in the house for five months and I had to think about whether there was a fireplace in the house. If there was one it had never been used. This forced me to realize that there were two of them.

"Yes, yes, we do. Why?"

Miller paused, studying the notepad, and murmured offhand, "It's just an entrance point. That's all."

"Can I ask you something?"

Miller said yes while flipping a page in the notepad.

"What if . . . what if this unexplained presence . . . doesn't want to leave?" I swallowed. "What happens then?"

Miller looked up. "I have to let them know that I am helping them move on to a better place. They are actually quite grateful for any assistance." He paused. "These are souls in distress, Mr. Ellis."

"Why are they . . . distressed?"

"There are a couple of reasons. Some of them haven't realized yet that they are dead." He paused again. "And some of them want to impart information to the living."

It was my turn to pause. "And you resolve this problem . . . for them?"

"It depends." He shrugged.

"On what?"

"Well, on whether it's a demon, or whether it's a ghost or, in your case, whether the things you created—these tortured entities—have somehow manifested themselves into your reality."

"But I don't understand," I was saying. "What's the difference between a ghost and a demon?"

By the time this question was asked the diner had disappeared. It was only Miller and myself in a booth suspended outside of whatever the real world now meant to me.

"Demons are malicious and powerful. Ghosts are just confused—lost, vulnerable." Miller abruptly reached into his denim jacket and pulled out a cell phone that had been vibrating. He checked the incoming number and then clicked the phone shut. During this movement he continued talking as if he had given this information a million times before. "Ghosts draw their energy from any number of sources: light, fear, sadness, anguish—these are the things that make the spirit precedent. Ghosts are not violent."

You have demons, the writer whispered.

"Demons are a manifestation of evil, and they haunt people who have carelessly let them into their lives. Remember what I said about antagonism? A demon appears when it feels it has been antagonized, and what it wants to do, its purpose, is to return this antagonism. Demons are angry."

"You have to help me," I was saying. "You have to help us."

"You don't need to convince me that you're a frightened man anymore, Mr. Ellis," Miller said. "I know you are."

"Okay, okay, okay, now what?"

"I'll come to your house and determine the nature of the haunting."

"And then what?" I asked hopefully before saying, "Thank you."

"If a demonic presence is in your house—and it sounds like it—then you're in for a battle."

"Why?"

"Because whatever this is draws on your fear. They draw on the collective fear that is in the house. And depending on the amount of fear, the damage some of these spirits cause can be catastrophic."

"Why did this happen to me? Why is this happening to me?"

"It sounds as if you're being haunted by a messenger." Miller paused. "By your father and by Patrick Bateman and by something you created in your childhood."

"But what is the message? What does it want to tell me?"

"It could be any number of things."

The world no longer existed. I was just staring at him. I didn't feel anything anymore. Everything was gone except for Miller's voice.

"Sometimes these spirits become whoever *you* are."

Miller studied me for a reaction. There wasn't one.

"Do you understand that, Mr. Ellis? That these spirits might be projections from your inner self?"

"I think . . . that I'm being warned . . ."

"By what?"

"By . . . my father? I think my father wants to tell me something."

"From the information you've supplied, this might be very likely."

"But . . . something is . . . seems to be stopping him . . . like the . . ." I trailed off.

Miller paused. "Who brought the doll into the house, Mr. Ellis?"

"I did," I whispered. "It was me."

"And who created Patrick Bateman?"

In a whisper: "I did."

"And the thing you saw in the hall?"

Another whisper: "Me."

I was brought back when Miller pushed his pad across the table.

There was something on it he wanted me to see.

I noticed a word spelled in capital letters: T E R B Y.

Below this, the word spelled backward: Y B R E T.

Why, Bret?

I finally hitched a breath.

"What's your birthdate, Mr. Ellis?" I heard Miller asking.

"It's March the seventh."

Miller tapped the bottom of the notepad with his pen.

Miller had drawn a slash between two numbers.

In red ink: 3/07 Elsinore Lane.

"Could we just move to another house?"

I was panting.

"Can we just get out of the house?"

I couldn't control it.

"Can we just move somewhere else?"

Miller grabbed my hand to calm me.

"Mr. Ellis, in this case I don't think that's an option."

I couldn't breathe anymore.

"Why not? Why isn't it an option?"

"Because the house may not be the source of the haunting."

I had started weeping again.

"If, if, but, if, the, house, is, is, not the source—"

"Mr. Ellis—"

I could hear Miller but he wasn't visible.

"But if the house is not the source . . . what is the source of the haunting?"

Miller finally said it.

"You are."

27. the haunted

The world was now dimmed, a shallow island of light floating in a vast darkness, even though it was noon and we were heading toward the house on Elsinore Lane and I was sitting in the back of a converted van behind two assistants (from what I learned was a staff of twelve, and who could have passed as anonymous computer nerds, with requisite crew cuts, from the college). Dale, who had greeted me with "Wicked bruise," was driving while Sam rifled through a CD case, and they were carrying on a disagreement about a recent movie—just two dudes on their way to the "preliminary investigation" or the "ISR" (initial site reading) and the casualness of their conversation was supposed to be a calming reminder that this was no big deal, just another assignment. But Miller was overlapping them—the two of us side by side, our knees pressed against a generator—explaining to me where the last haunting had taken his team, a remote location where the ghosts and demons of the dead had congregated: an abandoned slaughterhouse. I didn't care. I wanted this all to be over as quickly as possible. As usual I pretended it was a dream. This made things easier.

"When should we do this?" I had asked Miller after recovering in the Dorseah Diner. "As soon as possible" was his answer. Outside, standing in the gravel-strewn parking lot (which was slowly becoming a carpet of beach sand), Miller made a series of calls as I watched a new line of palm trees rising in the distance. He followed me back to the Four Seasons, where a valet parked his van, and as we went up to the suite to pick up the keys to the house a fee was discussed. If the house was infested and I wanted to retain his services, a check would have to be written for $30,000, which to me seemed like a bargain. When he asked if I had access to that much money, I assured him, gravely, that I did. But I would have agreed to any amount since I was staring at the ashy footprints that had circled my bed in the hotel suite while I was cringing in a booth at the Dorseah Diner (they had come from nowhere) and then I saw the gray handprint on a pillow and almost broke down again and said that I wouldn't go back to the house, but Miller told me that because I was the focus of the infestation I needed to be there. When I was about to protest again, and offer him a larger fee so I could stay away from the house, Miller had already guided me outside, where a van much larger than Miller's was waiting for us, and as I stepped into that van my world—already drifting away from me—became inverted.

Miller was explaining what the various pieces of equipment were for, and I strained to pay attention but couldn't focus on anything except the fact that we were heading back to the house. There were infrared digital cameras and motion detectors and electromagnetic field meters (EMFs as the crew referred to them); there was something called a laser thermometer as well as an audio recorder that could be fed into a frequency analyzer and read off a laptop. I tried to steady myself by asking questions—but this was just a way to pretend that we weren't rolling toward a situation the writer had already witnessed and was calling, with chilling ambiguity, *complicated*. I heard samples of Miller's dialogue skipping through my mind. Vaguely gesturing at something, I asked, "What does that do?"

"An EMF," I heard. "It filters out normal electromagnetic frequencies."

"What do you mean?" I inquired dreamily.

"Like from a computer or a TV or a phone or even a human body—all of which can give a false reading." Miller's voice had a rubbery quality and it was bouncing around inside the van, moving away from me, echoing.

"And what's that?" I found myself pointing at a large, bulky machine that resembled an oversized air-conditioning unit.

"A galvanometer. It registers unexplained energy flow."

Of course. Of course that's what it is. You knew that, Bret.

I was now hunched over and about to lose it again as the van was gliding around the corner of Bedford and onto Elsinore.

The house sat innocently in daylight, but even in daylight the house seemed menacing.

I was scowling with fear because I couldn't help studying it as the van pulled into the driveway.

"Here goes," one of the guys said. They both eagerly exited the van. They had been filled in on the various particulars of "the situation" and they were ready to party. They moved to the doors at the back of the van and started unloading equipment with frat-boy expectancy.

I wasn't aware I had left the van and was floating toward the house until I was standing so close to it that I could have touched the thing.

The front of the house was now the same color as the side of the house.

The writer forced me to notice this since I was blind.

Look, the writer said. *Touch it.*

The wood had turned to stucco.

Because of this, I couldn't go back into the house.

I walked away.

Miller followed me out into the field behind the house, and then I was pacing, and then I was standing still again. I couldn't control my breathing. My mouth was dry and chalky from chewing the Klonopin tablets.

"You'll be protected," Miller promised.

"This was not a case of possession," he assured me.

"You need to be in the house" was his gentle order.

"Why?" I pleaded. "Why?"

"Because you are its focus. Because we need to find out what the source of the haunting is."

They needed to invoke the spirits.

And you're being used as bait. Do you get it now, Bret?

I didn't even crave a drink at this point—I would have thrown up if I swallowed alcohol.

Pass that sage advice along: Want to stay sober? Move into a haunted place.

Miller impatiently redirected me to the house, because there was nowhere I would be safe if this was not dealt with.

(The writer prodded me along with a reminder of the ashy handprint on the pillow.)

My response: "If there's anything inside the house, I don't think I can take it."

I hesitated then shuffled quickly toward the front door.

I slipped the key into the lock.

I opened the front door.

I stepped into the foyer.

The house was silent.

Miller stood beside me.

"Where have the main occurrences taken place?" I was asked.

The three men were waiting for me to guide them to the hallway of flickering lights, the master bedroom that had been invaded, the living room that was now the living room of Valley Vista—just a brief intake of breath as I glimpsed the dark green shag that was still growing, and then I had to turn away.

Miller was studying the office door, unhinged, gnawed on.

"Yeah," I said. "It happened."

While Dale and Sam began setting up equipment throughout the house, I showed Miller the video attachment I had received.

I couldn't look at it so I wandered. Upstairs I peered into Robby's and Sarah's rooms and then (delicately—I did not go in) the master bedroom.

The unmade beds in all three rooms relieved me.

There was no sign of the Terby anywhere, but that didn't mean anything.

Back in my office the video was ending.

My father was staring out at us.

"Robby . . . Robby . . ."

Miller turned to me wordlessly, unimpressed.

"All electrical appliances need to be unplugged" was all he said.

"Why don't we just turn off the fuse box?" I asked.

"We'll do that as well."

The equipment would be plugged into the generator that had been dragged into the foyer and was sitting at the bottom of the staircase.

While we began the process of unplugging anything connected to a power outlet, everyone began feeling it.

(I pretended not to.)

There was a new pressure in the house.

It was weighing down on us.

I tried to ignore the moment our ears started popping.

But when Sam and Dale laughed I had to accept it.

Once everything was disconnected, Sam and Dale began plugging various cords into the generator.

The infrared video cameras and sound-activated microcassettes were mounted on tripods.

Sam would oversee the one placed in the upstairs hallway.

Dale would oversee the one placed in the master bedroom.

And Miller would oversee the one placed in the living room with the widest field of vision, including the foyer and the staircase.

Each of them held an electromagnetic field meter—an EMF.

All the curtains and blinds in the house were drawn shut—I did not ask why—and the interior of the house darkened considerably, but with enough light still scratching through from outside.

Once Sam and Dale were in position upstairs, Miller asked me to turn off the fuse box.

It was located in the hallway that led to the garage.

I opened it.

I breathed in as I shut off the power.

Walking quickly back to Miller's side, I realized that this was the quietest the house had ever been.

During this thought all three EMF meters started beeping—instantly, in unison.

According to the flashing red digital numbers I saw a reading jump from 0 to 100 in what seemed like less than a second.

Immediately the cameras sensed something and started whirring, moving in a continuous circular motion atop the tripods.

"We have liftoff," I heard one of the guys whoop from upstairs.

The beeping suddenly became more insistent.

The cameras kept flashing as they turned.

The locks on the French windows in the living room made a cracking sound.

Another cracking sound and the windows swung outward, causing the green curtains to start billowing even though it was a cold, still November afternoon.

But then they stopped billowing.

The curtains weren't there last night, the writer said. *Don't you recognize them?* the writer asked. *Think back.*

Air gusted over us, and the faint sound of something being pounded echoed throughout the house.

The pounding continued.

It was moving through the walls and then into the ceiling above us.

The pounding was competing with the sounds from the EMFs but the pounding soon overtook it.

I shut my eyes, but the writer told me that the pounding culminated when a huge puncture appeared in the wall above the couch in the living room.

(Later, the writer told me that I had screamed while standing perfectly still.)

And then: silence.

The EMF monitors stopped beeping.

"Hoo-ah!" This from one of the guys upstairs.

The other whooped gleefully again.

They had been on this ride before.

Miller and I were breathing hard.

I didn't care if I appeared afraid.

"I'm sensing a male presence," I heard Miller murmur, scanning the room.

"The lights are flickering, Bob," Sam called down from the upstairs hallway.

From where Miller and I stood we looked up and could see the flickering lights of the sconces reflected in the massive window near the top of the stairs.

It seemed as if something knew we had noticed this and the flickering stopped abruptly.

Miller was now standing in front of the freshly punctured wall.

He stared at it, humbly.

"An angry man . . . someone very lost and angry . . ."

I was so afraid I could not feel myself. I was just a voice asking: "What does that mean? What's going on? What does it want? Why is it stopping?"

Miller scanned the ceiling with his EMF.

"Why did it stop?" I kept asking.

Miller answered quietly.

"Because it knows we're here."

This was part of his performance. He was trying to project self-assurance, confidence, a sense of command, but there was one lucid fraction within me peering through the fear that knew whatever resided in the house was going to defeat us all in the end.

(I flashed on: You *resided in this house, Bret.*)

"Because it knows we're here," Miller murmured again.

Miller turned to me.

"Because it's curious."

We waited for what felt like eternity.

The house seemed to grow darker as time passed.

Finally, Miller called up. "Dale—anything?"

"It's quiet now," Dale called back down.

"Sam—anything?"

Sam's answer was interrupted when the EMFs resumed beeping again. This was followed by the cameras whirring.

And then a sound announced itself that unnerved me more than the pounding or the noise emanating from the meters.

A voice was singing.

Music began playing throughout the house.

A song from the past, flowing from an eight track on the long drive up the California coastline to a place called Pajaro Dunes.

. . . memories light the corners of my mind . . .

"Did we unplug the stereo?" I asked, wheeling around in the semidarkness.

. . . misty water color memories . . .

"Yes, we did, Mr. Ellis." This was Miller, holding his EMF as if it was guiding him toward something.

. . . of the way we were . . .

The living room instantaneously became hot. It was a greenhouse, and the smell of the Pacific slowly traced itself in the muggy air.

. . . scattered pictures of the smiles we left behind . . .

Suddenly, from upstairs: "There's something here," Sam called. "It just materialized." Pause. "Bob, did you hear me?"

. . . smiles we gave to one another . . .

"What is it?" Miller called up.

Sam's voice, less enthusiastic: "It's, um . . . it's a human form . . . skeletal . . . it just exited the little girl's room . . ."

Actually, the writer informed me, *Sam was wrong. It came from Robby's room, since Robby is, in fact, the focal point of the haunting.*

Not you, Bret.

Did you grasp that yet?

Not everything's about you, even though you would like to think so.

From Dale: "I see it too, Bob."

"What's its location now?" Miller called up.

. . . the way we were . . .

"It's moving toward the staircase . . . it's gonna head downstairs . . ."

Their excited cries were suddenly replaced by what sounded like a choked awe.

"Holy Christ," one of them shouted. "What the fuck is it?"

"Bob." This was Sam, I think. "Bob, it's coming down the stairs."

The song stopped midlyric.

Miller and I were facing the grand staircase that flowed into the foyer and the adjacent living room.

There were clicking noises.

(I am not going to defend what I'm about to describe. I am not going to try to make you believe anything. You can choose to believe me, or you can turn away. The same goes for another incident that occurs later on.)

The only reason I witnessed this was because it happened so quickly, and the only reason I did not immediately turn away was because it seemed fake, like something I had seen in a movie—a prank to scare the children. The living room might as well have been a screen and the house a theater.

It was lurching down the staircase, pausing on various steps.

It was tall and had a vaguely human form, and though it was skeletal it had eyes.

Rapidly my father's face was illuminated in the skull.

And then another face replaced it.

Clayton's.

I was stunned into rigidity.

My panting could not be heard above the meters or the cameras.

The skeleton-thing was now standing at the bottom of the staircase.

It was making the clicking noises with its teeth.

Within the skull were eyeballs.

Suddenly, it launched itself toward us.

Miller and I quickly backed away and when we did, the thing stopped.

It began raising its arms, extending them upward.

The arms were so long that finger bones scraped the ceiling.

I was moaning.

What were we waiting for? I didn't understand what we were waiting for it to do.

My father's face flashed on again, followed by Clayton's.

As the faces rapidly interchanged, sharing the skull, the resemblance between the two men could not be questioned.

It was the face of a father being replaced by the face of a son.

It kept clicking its teeth, as if chewing something invisible.

Its fingers started trailing across the ceiling as it moved toward us.

When it started lowering its arms, both Miller and I noticed something.

It was carrying a scalpel.

As it lunged toward us I braced myself, my eyes locked open.

"*I hear you,*" I whispered. "*I hear you.*"

And then the lights in the house flickered for a moment.

When the house was suddenly reborn with light the thing stopped and tilted its head before swirling into a cyclone of ash.

Sam and Dale watched this from the top of the stairs.

The moment the house burst into light they raced toward us.

Miller was asking me, "Did you turn off the fuse box?"

"Yes, yes."

Miller breathed in. "There are two spirits at work here—"

At the moment Miller said this, the door to my office—visible from where we now stood—flew off its hinges with such force that it sailed across the room and dented a wall.

(I did not see this because I was staring at the ash that had sprayed across the generator. The writer described it to me later on the plane.)

The ceiling above us suddenly cracked open in a long, jagged strip, dusting our hair with plaster.

(I don't remember seeing this but the writer insisted I had. The writer said, *You were gaping.*)

Paint began to peel and curl in waves off the walls.

No one knew where to look.

And as I watched this in a dream, I saw that underneath the paint was the green-striped wallpaper that had covered the walls of the house in Sherman Oaks.

When I whispered to myself the words *"I hear you"* the house was again plunged into darkness.

Outside, I stood on the lawn, dazed, muttering to myself.

Outside, Dale and Sam were pacing the sidewalk excitedly, talking into cell phones, recounting what they had seen to the rest of Miller's staff.

Outside, Miller tried to explain a situation to me.

It involved a ghost who wanted to tell me something.

It involved a demon who did not want this information imparted to me.

There were actually two forces opposing each other within the house.

It was fairly simple. Yet what Miller defined as "simple" did not apply to anything in my life.

But I didn't believe in my life anymore, so I was forced to accept this as if it was standard.

Outside, on the lawn, Miller was chain-smoking.

Miller tried explaining things but you wouldn't listen.

You just said, "Get rid of it."

You were standing in one place.

You weren't aware of anything.

You didn't admit that the words you'd whispered made the thing dissolve into ash.

You were thinking that you would come back later in the afternoon.

You were thinking of burning the house down.

"The house will need to be fumigated," Miller was saying.

It would need to be fumigated because the spirits could enter any living thing in the house—and this included any animal or insect life—in order to continue their existence.

After the fumigation it would take twenty-four hours to set up the equipment required to cleanse the house. The entire process should take less than two days.

But what was happening after the fumigation? Had I missed something? Did any of us still exist? What world had I moved to? What was occupying my mind?

"What will happen after the fumigation," Miller said, lighting another Newport, "is an exorcism."

I had started making a plan.

"Mr. Ellis, I'm curious about something."

I did not know that my plan was coinciding with Miller's.

"Was your father cremated?"

I was going to travel, and I nodded my answer.

"Where are your father's ashes?"

I was going to fly across the country.

"Did you spread them according to his wishes?"

I was shaking my head silently, because I understood what Miller was saying.

"What were you supposed to do with them?"

I was going to reorganize myself.

"Mr. Ellis? Are you here with us?"

28. Los Angeles

security guard at the gate checked my name before I drove up the winding road that led to a house the size of a hotel and made entirely from glass at the top of Bel Air. After a valet took my rental car, I stepped into a party where an old girlfriend who was wearing fake eyelashes and had married a billionaire called out, "Hey, gorgeous!" when I entered the room, and we talked about old times and movie people and what she was doing with her life ("I rock" was all I could ascertain), and since guests seemed to be avoiding me because of my battered face I just moved on until I was standing in a library filled with leather-bound scripts and golden retriever puppies were stumbling around everywhere and I found an issue of next week's *National Enquirer* in a bathroom and there was a framed poster in the eldest son's room of two words in huge red block lettering (GET READY) and there was the actress who had costarred in the movie that Keanu Reeves and Jayne made back in 1992 and we had what I felt was an inappropriate, if innocuous, conversation since we had never met ("Jayne left the set for a couple of days to be with you. Someone in your family had died, right?" "Yeah, my dad") and then Sarah's father—the record executive—showed up and seemed shocked to see me (I wasn't shocked by anything since I wasn't reacting to anything) but then he asked about Sarah and listened haltingly as I told him how great she was doing and even though the record executive kept promising me that he wanted to see his daughter there would always be another "setback" to keep him away but he added not unhopefully that Sarah was always "free" to visit. Seated at the large dining table were wives from Pacific Palisades with a few key members of the Velvet Mafia and Silver Lake hipsters and couples from

Malibu and a good-looking chef with his own reality show. Conversations began as the food was served: the second house in Telluride, the new production company, the frequent trips to the plastic surgeon, the tantrum so violent that the police were called, all the exertion that led nowhere. I listened to it all, or imagined I did. There were too many words I didn't understand the meaning of anymore (*happy, cake, jingle, preen*), and I was so over this world that it made no impact on me: the number of explosions per scene, the movie that took place in a submarine, the script that lacked a sympathy portal, the S&M dalliance with an underaged hooker, fucking the prom queen recovering from implant surgery, the screaming rockets, the washboard abs, the sex on the air mattress, the Vicodin binge. And then the conversation took a more sober route when talk of a certain movie came up: if it didn't gross over a billion dollars, the certain movie would lose money for the three studios financing it. After that, the pointlessness of everyone's enterprise hung placidly over the dinner. And soon you were noticing that the facial surgery had rendered so many of the women and men at the party expressionless, and an actress kept wiping her mouth with a napkin to stem the drooling after too much fat had been injected into her lips. A giant cactus stood blocking a downstairs hallway with the words **"believe the skeptics"** scrawled in black across its green skin, and as storytelling resumed I wondered how you could ever get past the cactus. But then I realized I was concentrating on that only because I wondered who was going to listen to my story? Who was going to believe in the monsters I had encountered and the things I had seen? Who was going to buy the pitch I was making in order to save myself?

After the initial site reading indicated—no, confirmed—that the house was infested, I had been driven back to the Four Seasons, where I wired a transfer into Miller's account. I was told "the process" would take two days to complete and I did not want to know the specifics of how they planned on cleansing the house. Obviously, I told myself, this was something they knew how to do—they were professionals; they had proved this to me during the ISR—and I would stay out of their way for those two days by traveling to L.A., under the auspices of the Harrison Ford meeting, where I would retrieve my father's ashes from the Bank of America on Ventura Boulevard in Sherman Oaks. Carrying out this plan was my only focus (I was not going to be waylaid by anything) and so by two o'clock on that Thursday afternoon I had already booked a flight and—after meeting with

Marta at the hotel to explain that the house on Elsinore Lane was being fumigated and she would be staying with the children at the Four Seasons until I returned on Sunday—I was driving to the Midland Airport. While steering the Range Rover down the empty interstate, I called ICM and asked them to set up the meeting with Ford's people for the following day since I was flying in that night and was leaving Sunday morning. Everything went so efficiently that it was almost as if I had willed it. There was no traffic, I was whisked through airport security, the plane left on schedule, it was a smooth flight and we landed before the estimated arrival time at Long Beach (since so much of LAX was under reconstruction). When I spoke to Jayne while driving down the 405 toward Sunset she was "glad" (which I interpreted as "relieved") that I was doing this for myself. I had opted out on the Chateau Marmont since it was a haunt from the drug days and stayed at the Bel Air Hotel instead; it was close to the dinner party that the producer of the Harrison Ford project had invited me to when he heard I was coming to town, and also to my mother's house in the Valley. It wasn't until I was ensconced in my suite at the Bel Air, sorting through a stack of Harrison Ford DVDs the producer had messengered over—along with directions on how to get to his house—that I realized there was one thing I had left undone: saying goodbye to Robby.

On Friday afternoon the Harrison Ford meeting occurred without Harrison Ford. The project that Ford and the producer and the two studio executives were interested in me for concerned a father (a tough rancher) and a son (a lonely drug addict) overcoming the obstacles of loving each other in a small town in northeastern Nevada. I sold them whatever I could muster up, which was absolutely nothing since I had no interest in the project. I was told to think about it and promised numbly that I would, and then voices asked about Jayne, and the kids, and the new book, and what happened to my face ("I fell"), and since I was somewhere else during the entire meeting it seemed over in a matter of minutes.

Later that afternoon, I drove to the Bank of America on Ventura Boulevard to retrieve my father's ashes. I did not leave the bank with them.

· · ·

I had dinner with my mother and two sisters and their various husbands and boyfriends on Saturday night in the house on Valley Vista in Sherman Oaks (an exact, if much smaller, replica of the house on Elsinore Lane, with an identical layout). My mother and sisters understood (once the press reported I was the father of Jayne Dennis's son) that only when I had acquainted myself with Robby to the point at which he felt comfortable enough would my family meet their grandson and nephew. This was the understanding that Jayne and I, and our therapists, had reached—everyone except for Robby (who knew nothing about this arrangement and had never, to my knowledge, inquired about aunts or a grandmother). The saddest moment of the night came when I realized—once they asked—that I carried no photographs of my son. There were questions about Jayne, about life back East in the suburbs, about the damage to my face ("I fell"). My sisters marveled at how much I had begun resembling our father as I moved toward middle age. I just nodded and asked my sisters about their recent triumphs and dramas: one was an assistant to Diane Keaton; the other was just out of rehab. I helped my mother's boyfriend—a man from Argentina whom she had been living with for the past fifteen years—grill salmon. Dinner was calm, but afterward, out by the pool, while smoking cigarettes with my sisters, a tense debate ensued about what to do with Dad's ashes (I did not say anything about what I had found in the safe-deposit box earlier that afternoon) and then morphed into various old issues: the girl he was living with at the time of his death had a boyfriend—had I even known about this? I couldn't remember. Of course I couldn't remember, my sisters argued, since I had run away and refused to deal with anything. And then, in rapid succession: the invalid will, the lack of an autopsy, the conspiracy theories, the paranoia. I escaped this by heading upstairs to retrieve something from my old bedroom. (This was another reason that I was in L.A.) Plus the backyard was haunting me; the pool, the chaise longues, the deck—they were all identical to the backyard on Elsinore Lane. As I stood up to leave, my sisters commented on how guarded I seemed. I told them I was just tired. I didn't want to keep our father alive, which is what we did whenever we had these inevitable conversations. I did not tell them anything about what had been happening to me during the last week. There wasn't enough time. Inside the house I stopped at the top of the stairs and gazed down into the living room. My reaction was dulled.

. . .

Not only was my bedroom just as I had left it as a teenager but it was also Robby's room as well. I had stayed here often when I visited L.A., after I made the move to Camden and then to New York, and over the years part of this large space overlooking the San Fernando Valley had slowly transformed itself into an office, where I stored old manuscripts and files on shelves built into a walk-in closet. This was where I was heading. I immediately started rummaging carelessly through stacks of papers—drafts of novels, magazine essays, children's books—until the floor became littered with them. And then I finally located what I was looking for: the original manuscript copy of *American Psycho*, which had been typed on an electric Olivetti (four drafts in all, which continued to fill me with disbelief). I sat on the futon beneath the framed Elvis Costello poster that still hung on the wall and began flipping through its pages. Without even knowing what I was looking for, I felt a vague desire to touch the book and rid myself of something that Donald Kimball had said. There was a piece of information that had never fit into the pattern revealing itself to us. I wanted to make sure it did not exist. But as I kept turning pages I began knowing what it was.

It made itself apparent the moment I hit page 207 in the original manuscript.

On page 207 was the drawing of a face.

I had drawn a face onto the thin sheet of typing paper (leaving enough space between the chapter breaks to fit it in).

And beneath the face I drew the words, scrawled in red pen: " **I'm Back**."

This image of words scrawled in blood was used later on, but I had cut the scene that preceded this warning.

This chapter had been omitted.

And I had also removed the crude drawing of the face from any subsequent manuscripts.

Something became confirmed.

This was a copy of the manuscript I had shown no one.

This was the copy that had been rewritten before I handed the book to my agent.

This was the copy that no editor or publisher had ever seen.

This was the one chapter I had cut from the very first draft and that no one but me had ever read.

It included details of the murder of a woman called Amelia Light.

I flashed on the phone call I received on November 5.

"What did you do to her?"

"I'd check the text of that dirty little book you wrote again."

The fictional details—the missing arms and head, the ropes, the blow-torch—were identical to the details of the murder in the Orsic Motel in a place called Stoneboat, according to what Donald Kimball had imparted.

As I kept turning pages, I realized even before I arrived at the next chapter that it would be titled "Paul Owen."

The murder that followed Amelia Light's would be Paul Owen's.

Donald Kimball was wrong.

Someone was tracking the book.

And a man named Paul Owen in Clear Lake would be the next victim.

I reached for a phone to call Donald Kimball.

But something stopped me.

I reminded myself again, this time with more force, that no one except me had ever seen this copy of the manuscript.

This led to: What was I going to say to Kimball?

What was there to say? That I was going insane? That my book was now reality?

I had no reaction—emotional, physical—to any of this. Because I was now at a point at which I accepted anything that presented itself to me.

I had constructed a life, and this is what it now offered me in return.

I pushed the original manuscript away from myself.

I stood up. I was moving toward a wall of bookshelves.

I was flashing on something else now.

I pulled a copy of the Vintage edition of *American Psycho* from a shelf.

I flipped through it until, on page 266, I found a chapter titled "Detective."

I sat back on the bed and began to read.

May slides into June which slides into July which creeps towards August. Because of the heat I've had intense dreams the last four nights about vivisection and I'm doing nothing now, vegetating in my office with a sickening headache and a Walkman with a soothing Kenny G CD playing in it, but the bright midmorning sunlight floods the room, piercing my skull, causing my hangover to throb, and because of this, there's no workout this morning. Listening to the music I notice the second light on my phone blinking off and on, which means that Jean is buzzing me. I sigh and carefully remove the Walkman.

"What is it?" I ask in monotone.

"Um, Patrick?" she begins.

"Ye-es, Je-an?" I ask condescendingly, spacing the two words out.

"Patrick, a Mr. Donald Kimball is here to see you," she says nervously.

"Who?" I snap, distracted.

She emits a small sigh of worry, then, as if asking, lowers her voice. "*Detective* Donald Kimball."

Yes, the room turned sharply at that moment, and yes, my idea about the world changed when I saw the name Donald Kimball printed in a book. I forced myself not to be surprised, because it was only the narrative saving itself.

I did not bother rereading the rest of the scene.

I simply placed the book back on its shelf.

I had to think about this.

First thought: How did the person who said he was Donald Kimball ever see this original unread manuscript with the details of Amelia Light's murder in it? A murder that was identical to the one that occurred on November third in the Orsic Motel.

Second thought: Someone was impersonating a fictional character named Donald Kimball.

He had been in my home.

He had been in my office.

I suddenly realized—hopefully—that everything he had told me was a lie.

I suddenly hoped that there had been no murders.

I hoped that the book I had written about my father was not responsible for the deaths "Donald Kimball" had relayed to me.

(Will I find out later that this Donald Kimball's private number was, in fact, Aimee Light's cell phone number? Yes.)

But then I thought: If Donald Kimball was responsible for the murders in Midland County, then who was Clayton?

As I thought about this I glimpsed something by my shoe.

There was a drawing from a children's book I had made when I was a boy.

One of a number of pages that had scattered to the floor as I rifled through my closet.

These pages were from an illustrated book I had written when I was seven.

The book had a title.

The title was "The Toy Bret."

I slowly reached down to pick up the title page but stopped when I saw the tip of a black triangle.

I pulled the other pages away until the entire sheet was revealed.

And I was confronted with the wrecked stare of the Terby.

As I moved the pages around, I saw the Terby replicated a hundred times throughout a book I had written thirty years ago.

The Terby emerging from a coffin.

The Terby taking a bath.

The Terby nibbling the white petal of a bougainvillea flower.

The Terby drinking a glass of milk.

The Terby attacking a dog.

The Terby entering the dog and making it fly.

It was at this moment in L.A. on that Saturday night in November—when I saw the children's book about the Terby and knew that a person named Donald Kimball did not exist—that I made a decision.

If I had created Patrick Bateman I would now write a story in which he was uncreated and his world was erased.

I would write a story in which he was killed.

I left the house on Valley Vista.

Driving back to Bel Air, I began formulating a story.

I began making notes.

I needed to write the story hurriedly.

It would be short and Patrick Bateman would be killed.

The point of the story: Patrick Bateman was now dead.

I would never find explanations.

(*That's because explanations are boring,* the writer whispered as I drove through a canyon.)

Everything would remain disguised and remote.

I would struggle to piece things together, and the writer would ultimately deride me for attempting this task.

There were too many questions.

This would always happen. The further you go, the more there are.

And every answer is a threat, a new abyss that only sleep can close.

No one would ever say, *I will show you what happened and I will make everything perfect by taking you to the vacant places where you won't need to think of this anymore.*

B ack at the hotel in Bel Air I slipped *Dead Heat on a Merry-Go-Round* into the DVD player, simply because it was the first credit on Harrison Ford's résumé and I wanted background noise. It would wash out the distracting silence.

I sat down at the desk and opened my laptop and began writing as the movie played.

Formlessness quickly led to shape.

"Patrick Bateman stands on a burning pier . . ."

I sat motionless during the half hour it took to write the story.

The story was static and artificial and precise.

It wasn't a dream — which is what a novel should be.

But that was not the purpose of this story.

The purpose of the story was to let myself be carried into the past, advancing backwards and rearranging something.

The story was a denial.

Soon Patrick Bateman's voice was resonating faintly, whispering and scattered, until he flickered away and was void.

(*But he was curious, and he lusted*, the writer argued. *Was it his fault that he had abandoned his soul?*)

Even as he is consumed by flames he says, "I am everywhere."

At the exact moment I was completing that last sentence, voices from the TV forced me to acknowledge them.

I turned in my chair to face the screen, because coming from the TV, thirty-three minutes into the movie, were the words "Paging Mr. Ellis. Paging Mr. Ellis. Paging Mr. Ellis."

An impossibly young Harrison Ford in a bellboy's outfit wanders through the bar of a hotel. He is looking for a guest. He has a message.

James Coburn is sitting at a table in the bar checking out waitresses when he glances over and says, "Boy?"

Harrison Ford walks over to James Coburn's table.

"Bob Ellis?" James Coburn asks. "Robert Ellis? Room 72?"

I spun around to the computer and clicked Save.

"No sir," Harrison Ford replies. "Charles Ellis. Room 607."

"Are you sure?" Coburn asks.

"Yes, sir."

"Oh."

And then Harrison Ford wanders deeper into the bar, calling out, "Paging Mr. Ellis. Mr. Ellis. Paging Mr. Ellis. Mr. Ellis?" until his voice disappears from the soundtrack.

When I looked at the clock above the TV, it was 2:40 a.m.

29. the attack

obert Miller had begun the cleansing on Thursday, November sixth, starting with the exterminator he always used in such cases, tenting the house at six o'clock that evening. On the following night of November seventh Miller's team set up their equipment in 307 Elsinore Lane and left, returning on Saturday night—exactly twenty-four hours later—and once it was understood that the space had been cleaned removed their equipment from the house. This was all relayed to me by Robert Miller in a phone call after my plane landed at the Midland Airport at 2:15 on Sunday afternoon as I was driving the Range Rover back into town. Miller felt confident that the house was "safe." He mentioned "specific changes" that had occurred after his team returned on Saturday. He assured me that I would be pleased with these transformations. The damage that had occurred during the ISR was not "corrected" (the door that flew from its hinges; the hole punctured in the wall) but he insisted I would be gratified by the "physical differences" in the rest of the house. After this conversation, my need to see the house was overpowering. Instead of heading to the Four Seasons I drove to 307 Elsinore Lane.

The first thing I noticed—and I gasped at this as I pulled up to the house—was that the lily white paint had returned, replacing the pink stucco that had infected its exterior. I remember parking the Range Rover in the driveway and walking toward the house in awe, my hand clutching the keys, and the sheer relief washing through me caused my body to *feel* different. The regret that had been defining me lifted off, and I became someone else. I walked to the side of the house—now the same blank white that had been there in July—and I touched the wall and felt nothing except a sense of peace that, for once, I hadn't imposed upon myself. It was genuine.

Inside the house, I felt no fear; there was no trepidation anymore. I could sense the change; something had been freed. There was a new scent, a lack of pressure, a difference that was intangible but still able somehow to announce itself forcefully. I was surprised when Victor came loping out of the kitchen to greet me in the foyer. No longer in the basement kennel at the hotel, he was wagging his tail and seemed genuinely excited by my presence. There was none of the usual glowering reluctance emanating from him whenever I entered his line of vision. But I couldn't concentrate on the dog for long, since the living room had changed miraculously. The green shag had returned to a flat beige sheet, and the curtains from 1976 that were hanging from a window (only days ago) had disappeared, and the furniture was arranged as it had been when I moved in. I closed my eyes and thought: thank you. There was a future (though not in this particular home—I was already planning on moving elsewhere) and I could think about the future because after becoming so used to things not working out I now, for one moment, believed things could change. And the transformation of the house validated this.

Victor's licking of my hand caused me to reach for the cell phone in my pocket.

I dialed Marta.

(The following exchange was pieced together following a conversation I had with Marta Kauffman on Tuesday, November eighteenth.)

"Marta?"

"Hey—what's up?" she said. "Are you back?"

"Yeah, I'm actually here at the house. I drove in from the airport to check it out." I paused as I moved into the kitchen.

"Well, everything's been pretty good—"

"What's Victor doing here? I thought I told you not to—"

"Oh yeah," Marta said. "We just brought him back this morning."

"Why did you bring him back?"

"He was freaking out in the kennels, and the hotel told me we had to get him out of there. And since you told me the house would be finished by Sunday, we dropped him off a couple hours ago. Is he okay?"

"Yeah . . . he's okay . . ."

At this point I had moved out of the kitchen and into the foyer.

I was standing at the bottom of the stairs, and then, with no hesitation, I started climbing them.

"Well, he was completely unhinged over here," Marta said. "The cages were small, and he just wasn't happy and of course Robby and Sarah started getting upset. But once we dropped him off at the house he seemed fine. He totally relaxed and—"

"How are the kids?" I asked, cutting her off, realizing how unimportant Victor seemed to me.

"Well, Sarah's right here with me—"

"What about Robby?"

(Marta Kauffman later testified that I asked this with an "unnatural urgency.")

"Robby went to the mall with some friends to see a movie."

("Who came back to the house when you dropped Victor off?" I do not recall asking this but according to Marta Kauffman's deposition on November eighteenth, I had.)

"We all did." Marta paused. "Robby needed to pick up some stuff."

I do remember, however, that at this point I was heading toward Robby's door.

"Pick up some stuff for what?" I asked.

"He said he was going to spend the night at a friend's."

"What friend?"

"Ashton, I think." She paused. "Yeah, I'm pretty sure he said Ashton."

(Before walking into the room I murmured something that neither I nor Marta Kauffman could recall on November eighteenth but was, according to the writer: "Why would Robby have to pick up stuff if Ashton lives next door?")

"Bret, it's no big deal. It was just some clothes. He was in his room for ten minutes. Nadine Allen's picking them up from the mall, and he should be back at their place by four—"

"Can you give me his cell number?"

Marta sighed—which pissed me off, I recall that flicker of rage—and gave it to me.

"I'm coming right back to the hotel," I said. "I'll see you guys in about twenty minutes."

"Do you want to talk to Sarah—"

After hanging up on Marta, I dialed Robby's number.

I waited by his door. There was no answer.

But I wasn't worried and I didn't leave a message.

Why would I?

He was at the Fortinbras Mall with friends and they were watching a movie and he had diligently turned off the phone once it began (a scenario impossibly distant from what actually happened that day) and then I would see him back at the hotel, and even though we were not checking out of the Four Seasons and returning to the house (that was never going to be an option), Robby could still spend the night at the Allens' (even though at that moment I had a shivery premonition about this being a school night) and Jayne would come back on Wednesday and our lives would move on as they were supposed to ever since I had accepted Jayne's offer and moved to Midland County in July. I thought expectantly about the upcoming holidays even while I stared at the gnawed, cracked door in front of me.

(I don't remember actually opening the door to Robby's room but—for some reason—I do remember the first thing that came to my mind when I walked in. It was something Robby had told me when he was pointing out things in the night sky at that picnic in Horatio Park over the summer: *the stars you see in the night sky actually do not exist.*)

The room was still in the same state it was left in on Wednesday night when we fled the house. An unmade bed, the dead computer, an opened closet.

I moved slowly to the window and looked out onto Elsinore Lane.

Another quiet Sunday, and everything felt okay with the world.

(Is that a sentence you ever thought you would actually write?)

I stood in the room for a long time, taking inventory.

What I had not done: I had not turned around.

I had walked straight into the room. I had stood there. I had contemplated my son and his motives. I did not see what was behind me.

At first I didn't understand. It took a moment to grasp.

When I turned around I saw scrawled across the giant photomural of the deserted skate park, in massive red lettering:

D I ss a pE AR
HE r e

I breathed in but did not start panicking immediately.

I wasn't panicking because something on the floor caught my eye and momentarily replaced the panic with curiosity.

It was sitting next to the open door, off to the side.

As I neared it I thought I was looking at a large bowl made from chewed-up newspaper scraps (it was) that someone had placed two black rocks in.

I assumed it was an art project of some kind.

But the black stones were wet. They were glistening.

And as I stood above the bowl, looking down into it, I realized what it actually was.

It was a nest.

And in the nest the black oval objects were not stones.

I knew immediately what they were.

They were eggs.

There was another nest next to the closet door. (And another one was later found in the guest room.)

I flashed on something Miller had warned me about.

Miller had said that fumigation was necessary so nothing living would be left in the house once the cleansing began.

That was why the house had to be fumigated: the spirits, the demons, would try to find anything living to enter so they could "continue their existence."

A question: What if a doll had hidden itself and waited?

What if the Terby had hidden itself in the house?

What if it had survived the exterminators?

What if something else had entered it?

The connection between the doll and the nests was sane and immediate.

I remember rushing out of the room and tumbling down the staircase, gripping the railing so I wouldn't fall.

When I hit the foyer I started dialing Robby's number.

Again, I don't remember this exactly, but as I waited to leave a message, I think that was when I noticed Victor.

Because of Victor, again I didn't leave a message for Robby.

(But if I had called a third time—as any number of people did later—I would have been told that the cell phone had been deactivated.)

Victor was lying in a fetal position, shivering, on the marble floor of the foyer.

The grinning dog that had excitedly loped toward me minutes ago did not exist.

He was whimpering.

When he heard me approach he looked up with sad, glassy eyes and continued to shake.

"Victor?" I whispered.

The dog licked my hand as I crouched down to soothe him.

The sound of his tongue lapping the dry skin of my hand was suddenly overtaken by wet noises coming from behind the dog.

Victor vomited without lifting his head.

I slowly stood upright and walked around to his backside, where the wet noises were coming from.

When I lifted the dog's tail I tried leaping out of my mind.

The dog's anus was stretched into a diameter that was perhaps ten inches across.

The bottom half of the Terby was hanging out of the dog and slowly disappearing into the cavity, undulating itself so it could slide in with more ease.

I was frozen.

I remember instinctively reaching forward as the talons of the doll disappeared, causing the dog's body to bulge and then settle.

Victor quietly vomited again.

Everything stayed still for one brief moment.

And then the dog began convulsing.

I was already slowly backing away from the dog.

But as I did this, Victor—or something else—noticed.

His head suddenly jerked up.

Since the dog was blocking the front door and I did not want to step over it I had started moving back up the staircase.

I was moving deliberately.

I was pretending to be invisible.

Victor's whimpering had suddenly morphed into snarling.

I stopped moving, hoping this might calm Victor down.

I was taking deep breaths.

The dog, still curled on the marble floor of the foyer, began foaming at the mouth. Foam, in fact, was simply pouring out of his mouth in a continuous stream. It was yellow at first, the color of bile, and then the foam darkened into red, and there were feathers in it as the foam continued pouring out. And then the foam became black.

At that point I remember running up the stairs.

And in what seemed like an instant, something—it was Victor's jaw— had clamped itself around my upper thigh as I was midway up the curving staircase.

There was an immediate pressure, and a searing pain and then wetness.

I fell onto the stairs face-first, shouting out.

I turned over onto my side to kick the dog away, but he had already backed off.

The dog was standing, hunched, three steps below where I was writhing.

Then the dog started expanding.

The dog began mutating into something else.

His bones were growing and then began breaking out of his skin.

The noises Victor was making were shrill and high-pitched.

The dog looked surprised as his back suddenly bent up—and his body stretched another foot on its own accord.

The dog made another pained sound and then started gasping for breath.

For one moment everything was still, and as I wept I reached over mindlessly, foolishly, to comfort the dog, to let him know I was his friend and that he didn't need to attack since I wasn't a threat.

But then the dog's lips peeled back and he started shrieking.

His eyes began rolling in their sockets involuntarily until only the whites were visible.

I started screaming for help.

At the moment I began screaming the dog lurched forward, slamming itself against the wall as it kept enlarging.

I tried to stand up but my right leg was so damaged that I collapsed back onto the staircase, the steps slippery from all the blood pouring from the wound in my thigh.

The dog stopped moving again and started shuddering as its face elongated and became lupine.

Its front paws were manically scratching at one of the steps with such force that they were shredding the smooth, varnished wood.

I kept trying to push myself up the stairs.

The dog lowered its head, and when he slowly looked back up, approaching me, he was grinning.

I kicked at it with both feet, panting, backing myself up the staircase.

The dog stopped its approach.

The dog cocked its head and then it started shrieking again.

Its eyeballs bulged until they were pushed out of their sockets and hanging down his muzzle on their stalks.

Blood began pouring from the empty holes, drenching the dog's face, staining its bared teeth red.

It had what looked like wings now—they had sprouted out of both sides of the dog's chest.

They had snapped through the rib cage and were flapping themselves free of the blood and viscera that were keeping them weighed down.

It crept up toward me.

I kept kicking at it.

And, effortlessly, a mouthful of teeth sank into my right thigh again and bit down.

I reared up, screaming, and blood sprayed in an arc across the wall as the thing let go of my thigh.

It was suddenly freezing in the house but sweat was pouring down my face.

I began crawling up the stairs on my stomach when it bit me again, right below the place it had just ripped open.

I tried to shake the thing off.

I began sliding back down toward the dog because the stairs were so wet with blood.

It lashed out again.

The teeth were now the fangs of the Terby and they sank into my calf.

I realized with an awful finality: It wanted to keep me still.

It didn't want me to go anywhere.

It didn't want me to rush to the Fortinbras Mall.

It didn't want me to find Robby.

I became furious and I smashed my hand into the dog's face as it kept blindly snapping at me. Fresh blood burst from its snout. I smashed my hand again into its face.

The face kept spouting blood, and the dog continued shrieking.

I started screaming back at the dog.

I was sliding in place as I looked up to see how far I had to go before reaching the landing.

It was about eight steps.

I started pulling myself upward, dragging my mangled leg behind me.

And then I felt the thing leap on my back when it realized where I was going.

I whirled over, knocking the thing off me.

I thrashed around in all the blood, trying to kick it away.

I vomited helplessly onto my chest, and then whispered, "*I hear you I hear you I hear you.*"

But this promise did not work any longer.

The dog gathered strength and reared up like a horse on its hind legs, looming over me, its wings obscenely outstretched, flapping them, spraying us with more blood.

At that moment I lifted my left leg up and, without thinking, kicked it hard in the chest.

It toppled back, trying to beat its wings to keep in place, but they were still too heavy with blood and flesh and it fell backwards, sliding to the bottom of the staircase and landing on the floor, shrieking, while trying to scramble upright with insectile urgency.

On the landing, I began crawling madly toward Robby's room at the top of the stairs.

Below me, the thing righted itself and started scrambling up the staircase after me, snapping the horribly uneven rows of fangs that now made up its mouth as it neared.

I lunged forward and slid into Robby's room, slamming the door shut and locking it with a hand soaked in blood.

The thing threw itself against the door.

It had moved up the staircase that quickly.

I lifted myself up and clumsily hopped on one foot toward the window.

I collapsed in front of it and fumbled with the latch.

I looked behind me because it was suddenly so quiet.

Beyond my trail of blood the door was bulging forward.

And then the thing started shrieking again.

I opened the window, balancing on my left leg, and crawled onto the ledge, blood splattering everywhere.

I remember not caring as I let myself fall.

It wouldn't be a long drop. It would be escape. It would be peace.

I landed on the lawn. I didn't feel anything. All the pain was concentrated in my right leg.

I lifted myself up and I began limping toward the Range Rover.

I slid into the driver's seat and I started the ignition.

(When asked, I answered that I did not know—nor can I supply a reason now—why I hadn't gone to a neighbor after the attack.)

Moaning to myself, I put the car in reverse and pressed on the accelerator with my left foot.

Once I had backed out of the driveway and was stationary in the middle of Elsinore Lane, I saw the cream-colored 450 SL.

It had turned the corner of Bedford and was now a block away.

Watching it glide closer I saw someone in the driver's seat: grim-faced, determined, recognizable.

As if he had been sequenced into my dreams, it was Clayton who was driving the car.

When I saw Clayton's face I let go of the steering wheel and the Range Rover, still in reverse, spun backward and then halfway around so that it was blocking Elsinore.

I tried to regain control of the car as the 450 SL kept moving forward.

It was speeding up.

I braced myself as it slammed into the passenger side of the Range Rover.

The collision pushed the SUV over a curb and into the oak tree that stood in the middle of the Bishops' front yard, with such force that the windshield exploded.

Everything started falling away from me.

The 450 SL extracted itself from the wreckage and backed away into the middle of Elsinore Lane. The Mercedes was not damaged.

It was daylight, I noticed as I began losing consciousness.

Clayton stepped out of the car and started walking toward me.

His face was a red and indistinct moon.

He was wearing the same clothes he'd worn when I saw him that Halloween day in my office at the college, including the sweater with the eagle on it. The sweater I had once owned when I was his age.

Steam was curling from the Range Rover's crumpled hood.

I couldn't move. My entire body was throbbing with pain. My leg was soaked with blood. It kept gushing through the bite marks in my jeans.

"What do you want?" I started to scream.

The Range Rover kept shuddering because my foot was locked against the accelerator.

The boy was floating closer, moving steadily toward me, relaxed.

Through my tears I began to make out his features more clearly.

"Who are you?" I was screaming as I sobbed. "What do you want?"

Behind him I could see the house melting away.

He was now standing by my window.

He was staring at me so starkly it was as if he were sightless.

I tried positioning myself so I could open the door, but I was trapped.

"Who are you?" I kept screaming.

I stopped asking that question as his hands reached out to me.

That was when I realized there was someone else who was more important.

"Robby," I started moaning. "Robby . . ."

Because Clayton was—and had always been—someone I had known.

He was somebody who had always known me.

He was somebody who had always known *us*.

Because Clayton and I were always the same person.

The writer whispered, *Go to sleep.*

Clayton and the writer whispered, *Disappear here.*

30. the awakening

I regained consciousness in a hospital room at Midland Memorial the day after the first surgery to save my leg was completed. The operation had lasted five hours. I had been sleeping for more than twenty-four hours.

When I woke up Jayne was standing over me. Her face was swollen. My first thought: I am alive.

The relief was short-lived when I saw the two police officers in the room. My second thought: Robby.

I realized that they had been waiting for me to wake up.

I was asked, "Bret . . . do you know where Robby is?"

The room was cold and empty and I felt something humming beneath the fake calm. There was a horrible insistence to the question that was barely restrained.

I whispered something that caused a disturbance. What I whispered was not what they were hoping for.

Jayne's exhausted face died. I became blinded by it.

When we were told that Robby Dennis was now officially missing I could not describe the sounds Jayne began making, and neither could the writer.

31. the endings

Questions the writer asked me: *How long do you hold on to a child? You have to decide if the world is worth returning to, and in the end, what are your options? I know where Robby went, but do you?*

For the first few days after Robby's disappearance I was still recuperating and underwent four more operations—so substantial was the damage to my right leg—and during this time I was lost in the mercy flow of the morphine drip. Ultimately the leg would be saved, and doctors told me I should be grateful, but the only thing I could think about was Robby. There was nothing else to take the place of that. We were conscious of only that one thing. We could only wait and then, as time passed, we began waiting without hope. But Jayne kept coming out of the cave she would hide herself in and emerge newly determined, even after admitting it was all useless. Why? Because I had offered her something to grasp on to with the deposition I gave when I told the Midland authorities I believed our son was a runaway and that he had not been abducted. When asked why I believed this "theory," I realized very quickly that there was nothing to sell them. I had not seen the e-mails to—or from?—the other missing boys on the afternoon of November fifth because the computer had died (and when the police searched the house after the attack, the computer was no longer in Robby's room, even though I told them I was positive I had seen it) and the evidence of a conspiracy (a drunken Nadine Allen, the playful whispers of boys in the courtyard of a mall, the two Salvation Army boxes I'd glimpsed in Robby's room—no one could ascertain if any clothing was missing or not—and the twelve trips we eventually estimated he made to Mail Boxes Etc. in October alone, the point of which we still could not decipher) was too thin to hang anything on. But again: what did it matter if they ran away or if they had been kidnapped? The boys were gone. All that anyone knew was that Robby and Ashton had been dropped off at the Fortinbras Mall by Nadine Allen on the morning of November ninth (according to Nadine, Robby was wearing a backpack) and had bought tickets for a movie that began at noon. Robby, according to an oddly calm and eerily serene Ashton, had whispered that he needed to use the restroom and left the theater. He never returned. No one saw him wandering the mall. No one saw him anywhere else in Midland County. Only the writer saw him disappearing into his new world.

Jayne could not fathom my lack of fear or anger. She called my despair "rehearsed." Her resentment toward my acceptance caused us—almost immediately—to separate from each other. Our only consolation: nothing worse can come to us. I didn't want explanations, because in those, my failure would take shape (your love was a mask, the scale of your lies, the irresponsible adult at loose, all the things you hid, the mindless pull of sex, the father who never paid attention). The case received, at first, substantial media coverage, but because Jayne refused to participate in the parade of grief that was demanded of her, the press slowly lost interest. Plus there were so many fresh horrors—the dirty bomb in Florida, the hijackers who killed the air marshals—that the disappearance of a movie star's son took a back seat to what was becoming this country's future. Jayne hired a private investigator to stay on the case. (But what case? Boys leave. He was gone. He had orchestrated this absence himself, as had all the others.) Jayne went into seclusion while Sarah just kept asking, "When is Robby coming back?" until the question conspired against her and additional meds were prescribed so that Sarah became as catatonic as her mother. And even though I knew Robby was never coming back, and that Robby had left us and that he had wanted to leave, I still asked, "Why?" The writer whispered answers to me that I half heard before the Ambien took effect: *Because his spirit had been broken. Because you never existed for him. Because—in the end, Bret—you were the ghost.*

. . .

Regarding the details of the attack, I didn't tell anyone about them (how could I?) even though I remembered enough of what happened that I relive it daily. People seemed satisfied that the dog had attacked me, and there was too much evidence—my mauled leg, the blood on the staircase leading to Robby's room, the manager of the kennel at the Four Seasons verifying that Victor had been "unstable and uncomfortable" and "behaving so strangely" that the dog had to be removed—for my story not to make sense. (And it made sense because I never mentioned what the Terby did.) However, when I described what happened on the street concerning the accident with the Range Rover and the 450 SL, I was greeted with skepticism. At that point my recollection was deemed unreliable by everyone, and I was supposed to be comforted by the idea that I had lost too much blood to remember anything clearly. When Ann and Earl Bishop called 911 and ran out to the car smashed against their oak tree, they did not recall seeing another vehicle. The scenario that seemed most viable was that I had swerved out of the driveway, losing consciousness, and careened into the oak in the Bishops' yard. There was "minimal" evidence (very faint traces of a cream-colored paint) that another car "might" have been involved, but since no cream-colored 450 SL was registered in this or any bordering state, my account of the accident was written off; it was considered a memory lapse due to blood loss. In other words, I had hallucinated the car and the boy walking toward me. (All the writer would say: *The boy was you.*) Also, "Victor" was not found. Something that the authorities first thought was perhaps a "skinned deer" was located that Sunday afternoon in the woods behind the house. But there was no blood trail leading from the house to the woods where it died, which meant that whatever had attacked me had not dragged itself all the way from the second floor of the house and across the meadow to the bank of trees. (The writer mentioned that something had crawled up the chimney; the writer mentioned that something had "flown" across that field.) The veterinarian who examined the carcass determined it was most likely "a coyote" that somehow had been turned "inside out." (I never discovered exactly what it actually was, but according to the veterinarian it was not Victor.) The police who surveyed the scene at the house had confirmed the existence of the nests but in the end these were attributed to something "your son" had made, though Robby took no classes at Buckley in which any remotely similar project had been assigned, but did it really matter? What part did the nests play in the "unfortunate incident" with our dog? When I asked about the "objects" in the nests, I was told they were "cracked open" and "empty"—they were just the remnants of shells. "Why did you want to know this, Mr. Ellis?" I was asked with a grave concern bordering on hostility. (The writer whispered so no one could hear him: *Tell them they hatched.*) Added note: When I was found in the Range Rover, my hair had turned completely white.

I was "allowed" to resign from the college. When I cleaned out the office a week after my release from the hospital, I finally looked at the manuscript that "Clayton" had left on November fourth. Entitled "Minus Numbers," it seemed almost to the word the rough draft of the novel I had written my freshman term at Camden—the novel that became *Less Than Zero.* Only one copy existed before I rewrote it (and, like the others, it was on a shelf, in a closet, in the bedroom in Sherman Oaks). But by then I had stopped wondering how "Clayton" had gotten ahold of this. When I went back to L.A., I compared the manuscript to mine and it was a total duplicate—an exact replica. Even the misspellings and typos had been transcribed. The reason I let go of this was that there was no information suggesting that "Clayton" had ever existed. *This is the easiest route to take,* the writer assured me.

But Aimee Light had existed. And the body that was discovered in the Orsic Motel was, in fact, hers. The man responsible for her murder, Bernard Erlanger, had presented himself to me as Donald Kimball, a man who believed he was, in fact, Patrick Bateman. A man who had become so obsessed with a book and its main character that he fell over the edge. Bernard Erlanger, who had run an unsuccessful detective agency in Pearce (that never had any affiliation with the Midland County Sheriff's Department), confessed to the killings that "Donald Kimball" had told me about in my home on November first. These admissions were made after Bernard Erlanger was arrested outside a residence in Clear Lake, wearing an Armani linen suit, a cotton shirt and silk tie, leather wingtips from Cole Hahn and a raincoat. He was also carrying an ax. The residence belonged to Paul Owen, sixty-five, a widower who ran an independent bookstore in Stoneboat. At approximately 2:30 a.m. on the Sunday morning of November ninth, Paul Owen heard someone breaking into his home. He dialed 911. He locked himself in his bedroom. He waited. Someone tried to open the door. There was a pause before Bernard Erlanger began swinging the ax at the door repeatedly, until a patrol car arrived. He was arrested and without any questioning simply admitted to the killings of Robert Rabin, Sandy Wu, Victoria Bell and Aimee Light, as well as the attack on Albert Lawrence, the transient he had blinded the previous December. I did not want to know anything more about Bernard Erlanger. I did not want to believe that Bernard Erlanger had anything to do with the murders in Midland County because I wanted to believe the killer never existed. I never disputed the crimes—they actually happened and people had died brutally. But I still wanted to believe that the killer was fictional. That his name was Patrick Bateman (not Bernard Erlanger, or even Donald Kimball), and for a brief time over the course of a year he had become real, as so many fictional characters ultimately are for their creators—and for their readers as well. The reasons I wanted to believe this (and a part of me still does) not only lay in the Amelia Light murder in that unread draft of *American Psycho* but also because at the exact moment I finished the story at the Bel Air Hotel in which Patrick Bateman dies burning on a pier, the Clear Lake Patrol arrived at Paul Owen's residence.

Four weeks after Robby was officially declared missing, Ashton Allen disappeared.

Jayne left Midland County and moved to Manhattan, as did I. She wanted a divorce, and there was nothing to negotiate, but I learned a few things. I hadn't known there was a house in Amagansett that Jayne had recently purchased for the family, or that she had already planned an elaborate Christmas trip to London that was going to be a surprise (and now, of course, was canceled). When I had arrived in Midland County that summer I did not pay attention to the fact that Jayne wanted to build a long future with her husband. She really had wanted things to work out between us. But she should have known that you could look right through me. She should have known that the reason I was there had nothing to do with her, but that I was just trying to locate someplace where I might find the will to live again. The process of the divorce struck me as fairly meaningless since we had hardly seemed married in the first place. But her lawyer insisted. Jayne wanted a complete break and she did not want anything connecting us ever again. I would give her that: no contact whatsoever with her or Sarah. I was distressed but explained to my lawyer that our strategy was one of acceptance. So I met with our respective lawyers (men we were paying six hundred dollars an hour to help terminate everything) on a warm, rainy day the following April in an office in the Empire State Building. I apologized for being late. My reason: "I've never been to the Empire State Building before." An important pause seemed to fill the room after I admitted this. Hands were extended, smiles were forced. It was hard for me to stay awake because of the heroin I was now taking daily. As if in an echo chamber, I heard someone mention that since there had been no prenuptials, would this cause a "difficulty" with the proceedings? No. Our son was lost, so the word "custody" never came up. Jayne waived alimony. My lawyer tiredly went through the rest of the motions. Jayne was thinner and did not say anything to me, which made me flash back to a time when we were so close that we could finish each other's sentences. I wanted to tell her that I still loved her, but that was not what she wanted to hear. She kept tucking a strand of hair behind her ear, a gesture I had never seen her make before but which she constantly repeated during the forty-five minutes in her lawyer's office. We were so high above the city that I had to focus very hard on the wide oak desk in front of us in order not to drop free-falling into vertigo. What was framed within the window was an aerial photograph. I was considering Europe when I asked myself: Why are Jayne and I taking the easy way out? But then it was over. The papers had been signed. I was the first to leave the office. As I pushed the button for the elevator I had to clench my jaw tightly so I wouldn't start crying. For reassurance I reached in my raincoat and touched the gun lodged there that I now carried with me everywhere. On Fifth Avenue I could barely raise my arm to hail the cab that would take me back to the condo on 13th Street, the space I had first moved to in the spring of 1987 when I was a young and famous novelist and didn't know anything except that luck kept sighing over me, a place where it seemed as if I had all kinds of time, a place where fame seemed to be a good idea and the flash from a light meter had been my only source of guidance. By now I was living with a young sculptor named Mike Graves (who was about twelve years younger than I) and sometimes he was in the condo on 13th Street, and sometimes he was in his studio in Williamsburg. I fell into the relationship not knowing what I was doing or whom I needed, and I assumed he felt the same, or at least I hoped he did. He had a grimness, a resolve, that I mildly responded to, and I liked the way he folded himself against me, and how he would trace his fingers over the scars on my leg, and I needed him on the mornings when summer lightning would awake me from nightmares and twisting in bed I would grasp his hand and moan my son's name.

I actually had the cab drop me off on Third Avenue, half a block from the condo, and I floated into Kiehl's to buy Mike a particular type of shampoo I remembered he kept in my apartment. Over the store's speakers Elton John was singing "Someone Saved My Life Tonight," and the song followed me back out onto Third Avenue. It had been a song my father had liked, and one night while we were driving through Westwood during the summer of 1976 when I was twelve he had even asked me who sang it, and when I told him he turned the volume up, and the fact that he liked the song made me grateful. Outside Kiehl's I ran into a college classmate who had moved to Manhattan the same year I had and had just gone through his second divorce. (This wife had left him for someone on the Mets, and I vaguely remembered reading about it.) He was tan and had gray in his hair—which I immediately noticed, and I was suddenly ashamed of the coloring I'd had done to mine the day before in the Avon Center in Trump Tower. He had read about the disappearance of my son (actually taking hold of my hand as he told me how deeply sorry he was, a man I barely knew) and commented wryly about my breakup with Jayne ("Marriage is about love, and divorce is about money"), and when I answered certain questions he observed that I was speaking too slowly. I made vain gestures with my hands, trying to explain things. He had been through rehab recently, and as we compared notes I could tell—as he hurriedly walked away—that he knew I was high. His last words were "Well, maybe next time?" I walked across the street to a deli on the corner, where I bought a *Post* since I was now reading my (and Robby's) horoscope daily (follow the tea leaves, avoid tragedy, ignore pentagrams, guess the hint, reconcile the future, the possible blazing, sleeper awake). And as I shuffled slowly back to the condo, I stopped in the middle of the block and turned around. Someone had been singing softly behind me, but no one was there. The song was so familiar that I shuddered. It wasn't until I lay down in my empty space that I realized it was "The Sunny Side of the Street."

And then I floated into a very soft place, surrounded by all the framed photos of Robby I had clipped from newspapers and magazines concerning his disappearance. This grim shrine to his biography sat in an orderly row on a shelf above my bed ("Your dark throne," Mike called the sloping shelf, shivering). The heroin flowing through me, I thought about the last time I saw my father alive. He was drunk and overweight in a restaurant in Beverly Hills, and curling into myself on the bed I thought: What if I had done something that day? I had just sat passively in a booth at Maple Drive as the midday light filled the half-empty dining room, pondering a decision. The decision was: should you disarm him? That was the word I remember: *disarm*. Should you tell him something that might not be the truth but would get the desired reaction? And what was I going to convince him of, even though it was a lie? Did it matter? Whatever it was, it would constitute a new beginning. The immediate line: *You're my father and I love you.* I remember staring at the white tablecloth as I contemplated saying this. Could I actually do it? I didn't believe it, and it wasn't true, but I wanted it to be. For one moment, as my father ordered another vodka (it was two in the afternoon; this was his fourth) and started ranting about my mother and the slump in California real estate and how "your sisters" never called him, I realized it could actually happen, and that by saying this I would save him. I suddenly saw a future with my father. But the check came along with the drink and I was knocked out of my reverie by an argument he wanted to start and I simply stood up and walked away from the booth without looking back at him or saying goodbye and then I was standing in sunlight, loosening my tie as a parking valet pulled up to the curb in the cream-colored 450 SL. I half smiled at the memory, for thinking that I could just let go of the damage that a father can do to a son. I never spoke to him again. This was in March of 1992 and he died the following August at the house in Newport Beach. Lying in bed on 13th Street, I realized the one thing I was learning from my father now: how lonely people make a life. But I also realized what I hadn't learned from him: that a family—if you allow it—gives you joy, which in turn gives you hope. What we both failed to understand was that we shared the same heart.

. . .

Them was one last story to write.

I went back to Los Angeles in August and on the afternoon of the anniversary of my father's death I waited in the parking lot of the McDonald's on Ventura Boulevard in Sherman Oaks. It was 2:30. After composing myself sufficiently I left the car and limped into the restaurant (I was still using a cane). I ordered a hamburger, a small bag of fries, a child's Coke—I wasn't hungry—and I took my tray and sat at a table by the window. The 450 SL pulled into the parking lot at exactly 2:40. A boy—seventeen, maybe eighteen—who looked strikingly like Clayton—stepped out of the car. He was taller now, I noticed, and his hair was short and even though he had sunglasses on I recognized him immediately. I was holding my breath. I watched as he walked hesitantly toward the entrance. He had a shadow—this was evidence. Once inside, he spotted me and moved with confidence toward the table I was trembling at. The world became hushed. I pretended to be absorbed in the task of opening the paper the hamburger came wrapped in and then I lifted it to my mouth and took a small bite. Robby was sitting across from me but I couldn't look at him or say anything. He was silent as well. When I looked up, he had taken off the sunglasses and was staring at me sadly. I started crying while chewing on the hamburger and wiped my face while trying to swallow. All I could say before turning away was "I'm sorry."

"It's okay," he said softly. "I understand."

His voice had deepened—he was older now, and was no longer the shy boy I knew those months on Elsinore Lane—and there was something in him that suggested forgiveness. His secret life made him seem less brooding, less sullen. Something had been solved for him. The actor was gone.

I had to keep turning away from him because I was breaking down.

"Why did you leave?" I managed to ask in a hoarse voice. "Why did you leave us?"

"Dad," he sighed. The word sounded different from how he had said it in the past. He placed his hand on mine. It was real. I could feel it. "It's okay."

I reached over and touched his face with the palm of my other hand, and then his shyness returned and he looked down.

"Don't worry," the boy said. "I'm not lost."

He said it again, "I'm not lost anymore."

I wanted another chance but I was too ashamed to hear his answer. I asked anyway. "Robby," I choked, my face wet. "Please come back."

But all he eventually saw was the flowering smile of acceptance.

He was standing outside, staring through the window at me for one last time.

He was looking at this story with affection.

I noticed my son had left a drawing behind: a landscape of the moon. It was so detailed that I had to linger over it, wondering about the patience required of my son to draw this particular moonscape. Where did this burning, ceaseless intention come from?

I also saw that one word was written on it, and I touched the word with a finger.

I didn't know what brought him here. I didn't know what called him away.

He was returning to the land where every boy forced into bravery and quickness retreats: a new life. Wherever he was going, he was not afraid.

The cream-colored 450 SL pulled out of the lot and turned right onto Ventura Boulevard, merging with the traffic until it was lost from sight and then the story ended.

The meeting lasted only minutes but when I limped back to my car it was twilight.

Across the street from the McDonald's was the Bank of America where my father's ashes were stored. What I hadn't told anyone was what happened on the eighth of November when I had gone to retrieve the ashes. When I opened the safe-deposit box that day, its interior was grayed with ash. The box containing what remained of my father had burst apart and the ashes now lined the sides of the oblong safe. And in the ash someone had written, perhaps with a finger, the same word my son had written on the moonscape he had left for me.

In a fishing boat that took us out beyond the wave line of the Pacific we finally put my father to rest. As the ashes rose up into the salted air they opened themselves to the wind and began moving backwards, falling into the past and coating the faces that lingered there, dusting everything, and then the ashes ignited into a prism and began forming patterns and started reflecting the men and women who had created him and me and Robby. They drifted over a mother's smile and shaded a sister's outstretched hand and shifted past all the things you wanted to share with everyone. *I want to show you something*, the ashes whispered. You watched as the ashes kept rising and danced across a multitude of images from the past, dipping down and then flying back into the air, and the ashes rose over a young couple looking upward and then the woman was staring at the man and he was holding out a flower and their hearts were pounding as they slowly opened and the ashes fell across their first kiss and then over a young couple pushing a baby in a stroller at the Farmer's Market and finally the ashes wheeled across a yard and swept themselves toward the pink stucco of the first—and only—house they bought as a family, on a street called Valley Vista, and then the ashes swirled down a hallway and behind the doors were children, and the ashes flew across the balloons and gently extinguished the candles burning delicately on the store-bought cake on the kitchen table on your birthday, and they twirled around a Christmas tree that stood in the center of the living room and dimmed the colored lights stringing the tree, and the ashes followed the racing bike you pedaled along a sidewalk when you were five, and then drifted onto the wet yellow Slip 'n' Slide you and your sisters played on, and they floated in the air and landed in the palm fronds surrounding the house and a glass of milk you held as a child and your mother in a robe watching you swim in a clear, lit pool and a film of ash sprawled itself over the surface of the water, and your father was pitching you into the pool and you landed joyfully with a splash, and there was a song playing as a family drove out to the desert ("*Someone Saved My Life Tonight*," the writer says) and the ashes dotted the Polaroids of your mother and father as young parents and all the places we went as a family and the lit pool kept steaming behind them with the scent of gardenia flowers rising up into the night air, wavering in the heat, and there was a small golden retriever, a puppy, bounding around the sides of the pool, ecstatic, chasing a Frisbee, and the ashes dusted the Legos that were spilled in front of you and in the morning there was your mother waving goodbye and calling softly and the ashes kept spinning into space with children running after them, and they dusted the keys of the piano you played and the backgammon board your father and you battled over, and they landed on the shore in Hawaii in a photograph of mountains partially blocked by lens flare and darkened an orange sunset above the rippling dunes of Monterey and rained over the pink tents of a circus and a Ferris wheel in Topanga Canyon and blackened a white cross that stood on a hillside in Cabo San Lucas, and they hid themselves within the rooms of the house on Valley Vista and the row of family portraits, drifting over all the promises canceled and the connections missed, the desires left unfulfilled and the disappointments met and the fears confirmed and every slammed door and reconciliation never made, and soon they were covering all the mirrors in every room we lived in, hiding our imperfections from ourselves even as the ashes flew through our blood, and they followed the brooding boy who ran away, the son who discovered what you are, and everyone was too young to grasp that our life was folding in on itself—it was so foolish and touching to think at one point that somehow we would all be spared, but the ashes pushed forward and covered an entire city with a departing cloud that was driven by the wind and kept ascending and the images began getting smaller and I could see the town where he was born as the ashes flew over the Nevada mountains mingling with the snow that fell there and crossed a river, and then I saw my father walking toward me—he was a child again and smiling and he was offering me an orange he held out with both hands as my grandfather's hunting dogs were chasing the ashes across the train tracks, dousing their coats, and the ashes began bleeding into the images and drifted over his mother as she slept and dusted the face of my son who was dreaming about the moon and in his dream they darkened its surface as they flew across it but once they passed by the moon was brighter than it had ever been, and the ashes rained down earthward and swirling, glittering now, were soon overtaken by a vision of light in which the images began to crumble. The ashes were collapsing into everything and following echoes. They sifted over the graves of his parents and finally entered the cold, lit world of the dead where they wept across the children standing in the cemetery and then somewhere out at the end of the Pacific—after they rustled across the pages of this book, scattering themselves over words and creating new ones—they began exiting the text, losing themselves somewhere beyond my reach, and then vanished, and the sun shifted its position and the world swayed and then moved on, and though it was all over, something new was conceived. The sea reached to the land's edge where a family, in silhouette, stood watching us until the fog concealed them. From those of us who are left behind: you will be remembered, you were the one I needed, I loved you in my dreams.

So, if you should see my son, tell him I say hello, be good, that I am thinking of him and that I know he's watching over me somewhere, and not to worry: that he can always find me here, whenever he wants, right here, my arms held out and waiting, in the pages, behind the covers, at the end of *Lunar Park*.

A NOTE ON THE TYPE

The text of this book was set in Electra, a typeface

designed by W. A. Dwiggins (1880–1956). This face

cannot be classified as either modern or old style. It is

not based on any historical model, nor does it echo any

particular period or style. It avoids the extreme con-

trasts between thick and thin elements that mark

most modern faces, and it attempts to give a

feeling of fluidity, power, and speed.

COMPOSED BY

Creative Graphics, Allentown,

Pennsylvania

PRINTED AND BOUND BY

Berryville Graphics,

Berryville, Virginia

DESIGNED BY

Iris Weinstein